The
Toffee
Heiress

Rare Confectionery Book Two

SYDNEY JANE BAILY

cat whisker press
Massachusetts

First Paperback Edition
ISBN 978-1-938732-33-1

Published by **cat whisker press**
Imprint of JAMES-YORK PRESS

Cover: Wicked Smart Designs
In conjunction with Philip Ré
Book Design: Cat Whisker Studio
Editor: Martha Stites

DEDICATION

For Neelia

From third grade onward,
I have cherished our friendship.

OTHER WORKS
by
SYDNEY JANE BAILY

The RAKES ON THE RUN Series

Last Dance in London
Pursued in Paris
Banished to Brighton
Gretna Green by Sunset

The RARE CONFECTIONERY Series

The Duchess of Chocolate
The Toffee Heiress
My Lady Marzipan

The DEFIANT HEARTS Series

An Improper Situation
An Irresistible Temptation
An Inescapable Attraction
An Inconceivable Deception
An Intriguing Proposition
An Impassioned Redemption

The BEASTLY LORDS Series

Lord Despair
Lord Anguish
Lord Vile
Lord Darkness
Lord Misery
Lord Wrath
Eleanor

PRESENTING LADY GUS
A Georgian-Era Novella

ACKNOWLEDGMENTS

I am happy to acknowledge my father, James Baily, a Londoner, who passed along his love of toffee to me.

When I started this series and began researching confectionery, I was thrilled to find toffee was already a long-standing treat in the U.K. by the time of the Victorians and so I could make one of my Rare-Foure sisters a toffee-maker. My father enjoyed it plain, with nuts and raisins, or smothered in chocolate, and I have one of the little toffee hammers that many manufacturers included with the purchase. (Suffragettes purportedly used them to break windows during their protests!)

Big thanks to Toni Young (best big sister ever), and she knows why!

As usual, thanks to my beloved mom, Beryl Baily, also a Londoner, for her constant love and support.

CHAPTER ONE

London, 1878

The bell attached to the door of Rare Confectionery rang its pleasant tinkling sound, alerting Beatrice Rare-Foure to a customer's untimely entrance. Setting down her cup of tea with an indecorous clunk, she rose from the gaily painted, blue stool in the back room of her family's shop. It wasn't the first time she'd wished she could get away with turning the "open" sign over to declare they were "closed."

Glancing down at herself, she hesitated. A few treacle stains from her earlier toffee-making endeavors graced the front of her cream-colored day dress.

"Hm," she murmured. She'd neglected to put on an apron before starting her work hours earlier. Her mother, Felicity, would say that was her first mistake. As Beatrice was the only one of her family working at that moment, she ought to have been in the front of the shop after setting the last tray of treacle toffee to harden in the cold box. Her mother would point out that was her second mistake.

Moreover, Beatrice should not have been relaxing in the back, sipping tea while reading an article about the Egyptian obelisk, Cleopatra's Needle, which had recently arrived on British soil. By year's end, the sixty-nine-foot monolith of red granite would be raised to stand on the Victoria Embankment. Many thought its placement to be in "defiance of good taste," as it said in the paper, and Beatrice was eagerly reading how the feud over the location raged on. If her mother knew she'd been reading instead of minding the shop, Felicity would be raging, too.

The middle Rare-Foure sister was perfectly aware how unwelcoming it was when a customer entered a place of business and found it deserted. And Beatrice agreed in principle, but she had never quite mustered the dedication to such a belief to care one way or the other, or to alter her practices when alone.

Besides, she would rather face her mother's fury than stand behind the marble counter of the confectionery all day, waiting on tenterhooks for the next sweet-seeking clodhopper. Although everyone agreed she had a talent, if one could call it that, for making delectable toffee, not a soul considered her affable when dealing with the public.

Her younger sister, Charlotte, was the best with customers but was out with a bad case of the sniffles. No one wanted a shopgirl with a runny nose serving them their confections.

"Hello!" she heard a man's voice call from the front. "Salutations and all that. Is there anyone here?"

Snatching up an apron, Beatrice quickly pinned it in place over her stained dress and tied it around her waist. Then she pushed through the thick, blue curtain to the front of the shop and saw two large hands, not gloved, plastered against the front of one of their display cases. The hands belonged to a sandy-haired man, bowed down to look at the sweets.

What kind of oaf leaned against glass? She would definitely have to clean it again.

"May I help you?" she asked, not particularly caring if she sounded friendly despite Charlotte having told her how a smile and a little chatting often made the customers keep adding to their confectionery order.

The head raised, the whole body straightened, and a tall man with blue-gray eyes looked at her over the top of the case.

"I didn't see you there a moment ago," he said, scrutinizing her like another one of the sweet treats.

"I wasn't here a moment ago," Beatrice snappily told him. "I am now. May I help you?"

Not taking offense at her answer, he smiled. "I hope you may indeed, ma'am. I would like some boiled sweets, I believe they're called. Those hard, flavored candies everyone is sucking on these days. But I don't see any at all."

Perfect! She would be rid of him in an instant and back with her tea and her Egyptian obelisk article.

"You don't see any because we don't carry them. Good day to you."

His face registered surprise. "Isn't this a candy shop?" He glanced around as if to make sure he wasn't suddenly at the barber's or a cobbler's. "I see those little boiled balls everywhere. Why don't *you* sell them?"

Beatrice sighed with an exaggerated puff of air, hoping it aptly displayed her exasperation. *Questioning what they sold— how rude!* Even his use of the term *candy shop* irritated her. There was more than one reason she was usually relegated to the back room, but her ire at foolish people asking silly questions was the main one.

"First of all, this isn't a candy shop. It is a confectionery. And we don't sell them because those cheap sweets are, as you say, *everywhere*, and therefore, we do not need to have them *here*. Do we?"

He paused. "That seems short-sighted of you, from a business view, I mean."

"We'll be sure to take your well-informed, thoughtful comment under consideration," she said, still hoping to drive him away quickly. Her tea would be growing cold. "Meanwhile, if you turn around and take a few steps forward, you will find the door. On the other side of it, either to the left or to the right, somewhere in London, you will find your *little boiled balls*."

He started to chuckle, then he bent over and laughed so hard she feared he would do himself an injury. However, he didn't leave, her tartness having the opposite effect and giving him great amusement. When he got ahold of himself, he looked at her with a broad smile as if she were his long-lost friend.

What an annoying man! And he had a strange accent, to boot. Beatrice wanted to wipe the smile off his equally annoying face. She realized it was actually a handsome face, a little craggy, just as his hair was somewhat wild, but he was in possession of an attractively strong chin, nice eyes, and, quite clearly, a ready sense of humor.

The bell tinkled again, and two women came in. She hoped the sandy-haired man would take the opportunity to vacate the premises since she didn't have what he wanted. But he regarded her a moment longer, then looked back at the confectionery in the display case.

Shrugging, Beatrice moved along to where the customers browsed in front of the other display case, as the shop counter and cases were set up in an L-shape. The women were eyeing Charlotte's marzipan sculptures on the top shelf.

"May I help you?" she asked them.

One looked up, her smile dying when she saw Beatrice. "Where is Miss Rare-Foure?"

Inside, Beatrice gave a silent scream of irritation. It was no one's business outside the family. *What if Charlotte were on her deathbed or had eloped to Gretna Green, for goodness sake?*

"*I* am Miss Rare-Foure," she insisted.

In fact, there used to be three of them, but her older sister, Amity, had recently married and, amazingly, had become the Duchess of Pelham. If that weren't enough, her sister was off on a wedding trip to the Continent, touring chocolate factories and coffeehouses. Amity and her duke,

Henry Westbrook, the Duke of Pelham, were a perfectly matched pair.

Beatrice was happy for them without a doubt. At that moment, though, she wished Amity were in the shop dealing with these pesky people.

Both women in front of her frowned, and one said, "I meant the other Rare-Foure, dear."

"I'm sorry, she isn't here." Beatrice managed to stop herself from adding, "obviously." Instead, she repeated, "May *I* help you?" After all, it didn't take a great deal of skill to put some confectionery in a bag or tin.

"Yes, of course. It's only that Miss Rare-Foure, the other one, that is, always gives us samples and knows what we want to buy."

Again, Beatrice blew a great sigh with enough force to move the hair that had fallen onto her forehead. "If you know what you wish to buy, then why do you need a sample?"

At her impertinence, she heard the sandy-haired man chortle under his breath.

In any case, her question was met with momentary silence. "Sometimes, there is something new," the other woman pointed out.

"Well, there isn't anything new," Beatrice told her. "Not today." There couldn't be, not with Amity, their chocolatier, trotting through France all starry-eyed and in love, and Charlotte in bed with a towel over her head. She was probably bowed over a bowl of hot water and eucalyptus oil. *Lucky girl!*

"I see," said the first woman. "Do you know who I am?"

Beatrice always dreaded such a question. It usually meant she was dealing with an aristocrat and bungling it enough to get the lord or lady's dander raised.

"As it happens," she said with exaggerated solemnity, "I do not. I have no idea. What's more, it is of absolutely no consequence."

This statement was met with two great gasps of outrage.

Beatrice could practically hear her mother's voice in her head: *Do not chase away our customers.*

"What I mean," Beatrice clarified, "is even if I knew which ladies you were, such knowledge would not assist me in guessing the type of confection you are looking for. Why, even if you were Queen Victoria herself, I could not read your mind. Are either of you, in actual fact, the queen?"

Silence fell again as these two ladies stared at her, their faces severe as thunderclouds. Beatrice's tea would be stone cold, she had plainly not placated the customers, and she still had to get rid of the strange man.

"Is there something you wish to buy?" she tried again in her most polite tone.

"No," said the second woman. They left in a bustle of satin and silk, as well as unconcealed annoyance. They would probably never return to Rare Confectionery, and for that, Beatrice was ashamed. Slightly.

"Maybe they wanted boiled balls," the man quipped as soon as the door closed.

Beatrice closed her eyes. When she reopened them, sadly, he was still there.

"Luckily, they can get them just about anywhere," she reminded him.

"Not on this street. I already looked in a few other shops before coming in here, and they weren't there either."

"Naturally," she responded.

"What do you mean, *naturally?* Is there a moratorium on boiled candies on this street?"

She sighed. "I meant naturally, if you'd found them elsewhere, you wouldn't be here, bothering me."

"Bothering you?" His expression was incredulous but entirely unoffended. He was harder to get rid of than the plague.

"Indeed, you are. Unless you intend to buy something."

"Well, I might," he said. "Everything looks very good. I am simply curious about the hard sweets and their conspicuous absence."

He was like a dog with a bone. Beatrice sorely wished she had some to give him so she could send him on his way.

"You are on New Bond Street, sir. A shopping street for luxury items, including luggage, jewelry, antiques, works of art, and all manner of bibelots. And, of course, our fine confectionery." She indicated the display cases again with a wave of her hand, noticed toffee on her index finger and, before she even considered her actions, stuck it into her mouth to suck it clean.

That task accomplished under his amused glance, Beatrice continued, "Nevertheless, nearly anywhere else you go in London, be it a green grocer or even a bookstore, you can find jars of boiled sweets. If you go ten minutes due north, they sell them at every blasted shop on Oxford Street. If you reach the northeast entrance to Hyde Park, you've gone too far. If you go twenty minutes due east, they sell them from carts at Covent Garden. If you go farther afield, you can find old women selling them from their kitchen windows in nearly any town or village. I suggest you start looking. Good day!"

Turning heel, Beatrice pushed her way through the blue velvet curtain to the back room, and then she waited. The bell did not tinkle. After a few moments, there was nothing she could do but return to the front. He was in the same position, except farther down the case, hands once more pressed upon the glass.

"May I help you?" she tried again.

He raised his sandy-haired head and shot her his friendly smile. "I would like to try a chocolate. Since I have no idea what I wish to purchase, I will need a sample. What do you suggest?"

That you leave. She desperately wanted to say it out loud.

"I'm very busy," Beatrice said instead.

He stared at her, then pointedly looked around the otherwise empty shop.

"In the back. I make the treacle toffee," she mumbled, immediately wishing she hadn't explained herself to him.

Too late! He grasped onto this fact the way a monkey at the Zoological Gardens grabbed a piece of fruit thrown across the fence.

"*You* make the toffee? You are a Miss Rare-Foure, as you told the other customers before you drove them off, so your family owns this shop. And yet you make the candy yourself?"

"Candy?" she repeated his unusual use of the word, which made her think of candied fruit, not what she made. "I don't make all of the confectionery, only some." She would not explain to him the dynamics of her sisters' contributions. That would encourage him to stay longer and ask more questions.

"Then I would like to sample some toffee, if you please."

Grinding her teeth, Beatrice approached the shelf with trays of the buttery, sweet, golden confection. Deciding it best to get it over with, she snatched up one of the sample plates, the size of a saucer, and using the tongs, she placed upon it one piece each of the plain, the chocolate-smothered, and the toffee with almonds, then handed it over the counter to him.

He took it graciously, staring down, then brought the plate to his face and sniffed it.

"Smells heavenly, but then, the entire shop does."

As if a chocolate-scented shop could smell anything other than delicious! She grimaced at the inanity of his remark, then crossed her arms and waited.

He took the piece with nuts first and began to chew.

"Careful," she said, a little alarmed. "If you have any loose teeth, it's better to suck on it or let it soften on your tongue first."

He nodded, too late, with his teeth stuck together.

"Would you have simply chomped down on a boiled sweet?" she asked exasperatedly. "Or would you have sucked it slowly to savor it?"

He shrugged, still working his jaws until he swallowed. "It was delicious, even though nuts are not my favorite."

Beatrice rolled her eyes. "Then you shouldn't have eaten it. You could see it had nuts, couldn't you?"

He nodded again, and she knew she was chastising a customer, but she couldn't seem to help herself.

"Why don't you skip the plain one, or slip it in your pocket to eat later"—*for all I care*—"and try the chocolate-covered one next. Then I'll fill a bag of whichever one you like. Without nuts or covered in chocolate."

"What if I want both?" he asked, but he did as she suggested and sampled the piece with Amity's prized chocolate coating it on all sides.

His eyes widened, which was no surprise because everyone knew chocolate was a divine taste. It always outshone her toffee as far as Beatrice had experienced. She waited what seemed an eternity while the man enjoyed the confections.

"Well?" she prompted at last. "Do you wish to purchase some or not?" Not the dulcet tones Charlotte would have used when trying to make a sale, but the best she could summon.

"Yes, of course. I'll take half a pound."

Nodding, she reached for one of their bleached white bags with "Rare Confectionery" stamped upon it in sapphire blue ink. Picking up the tongs again, she went to the tray of chocolate-covered toffee.

"The other one, if you please, ma'am—the plain, no nuts, no chocolate," he requested, surprising her into hesitating.

It wasn't that many customers didn't, in fact, buy tray upon tray of her plain treacle toffee. Yet she'd always assumed they hadn't really tasted or considered the perfectly delicious combination of toffee and chocolate. In any case, she wasn't about to ask him if he were positive of his decision or debate the matter.

Guessing at the quantity, she placed the bag on the scale, added another piece, then folded the top over to close it. Her mother liked them to tie each sack with blue satin ribbon, but she didn't think this particular customer would care. Unless . . .

"Is this a gift? For a female perhaps?"

He raised an eyebrow at her question, and she could practically read his thoughts. He was wondering if she were trying to determine his availability. Again, she rolled her eyes.

"If so, I shall add a ribbon," Beatrice explained, her tone flat. Tying on the ribbons were a nuisance.

He grinned—crookedly, she noted. "No ribbon needed, ma'am."

She assumed that meant the toffee was for himself. Placing the bag on the counter, she told him the price. He reached into his coat pocket and pulled out a collection of coins.

"Gracious!" she exclaimed when she saw what he had. Not only ha'pennies, farthings, and groats, as expected, but a fair number of shillings and crowns, as well as—*hard to believe*—half-sovereigns and sovereigns!

She stared at the coins in the large palm of his hand. The man was decidedly well off.

"Have I got enough?" he asked, sounding innocent of the goodly sum he was carrying.

"Yes, unless you wish to buy everything in the shop and perhaps a few things in the store next door."

He chuckled. "Are these that much?" He jostled the coins in his hand.

For the first time, she smiled, too. "No, not really, but those are gold sovereigns," she pointed out.

"Like a dollar, I take it."

She shrugged. "I am not sure about that. I've only just realized you're an American."

He seemed to stand a little straighter as he nodded. "I am, indeed. From the great state of New York."

Unimpressed by such a declaration, she took a few of the small copper coins, her fingertips grazing his bare palm, and put them in the till, or the *cashbox* as her mother called it, to pay for the toffee. Next, she pointed her finger at one of the half-sovereigns before looking him in the eye.

"A couple can have a really bang-up meal with liquor and a pudding course, what you call dessert, for that one coin."

"Really?" He looked down at his hand. Picking out one of the gold coins, he placed it in front of her on the counter, precisely as the shop bell tinkled again. "There you go, then. I want you and your beau to have a—what did you call it?— a bang-up meal."

In the space of a heartbeat, blazing anger roared a trail through Beatrice's slender body, and she slammed her hand down upon the coin, ready to hurl it at the stranger's head.

How dare he!

CHAPTER TWO

Greer took a step back as the young woman before him grew red in the face, and he knew he'd made an error. He wasn't sure whether he'd caused her fury by giving her the gold coin or by presuming she had a gentleman friend, or even by his bold assumption she liked to eat. *Who could tell with this crabby miss?*

Whatever it was, she was mad as a wet cat, and her hyacinth-blue eyes glittered with flecks of fire—or perhaps that was simply the watery English sunlight bouncing around the white interior of the shop and reflecting in them. Either way, he knew he'd bungled it.

Miss Rare-Foure opened her mouth undoubtedly to give him a sharp dressing-down, he was certain of that, but she glanced past him to the new customers who'd entered the candy shop.

Glaring at him, she snatched up the coin. "Your change, sir." She held it out and quickly let it drop from her fingers.

If he hadn't caught the coin, it would have rolled onto the clean wood floor. As it happened, he did catch it and stuffed the offending gold coin back into his jacket pocket, wishing females—and British ones in particular—came with some kind of guide.

"Well, thank you," he said to her stiff back, as she walked away to help the newcomers. With no clear understanding of these British folks, he hoped to do better if he was to gain a titled lady, which was his foremost goal, along with a spiffy London townhouse.

"Goodbye," he added, although she ignored him, already boxing up some chocolates for the young couple who'd entered.

Greer had reached the door when he suddenly heard her call out to him, "You there! American!"

Turning with a half-smile starting to form on his lips, ready to receive an apology for her churlishness, instead he was hit by a half-pound of toffee, catching it and smashing the crinkly paper sack against his chest.

"Don't forget your confectionery," Miss Rare-Foure quipped, a smirk on her pretty face. The other customers had turned to watch the buffoonery.

He decided then and there he would return to speak with her again. The way she'd fearlessly handled the aristocratic ladies—and even put him in his place—gave Greer the idea she would be able to tell him all he needed to know to navigate the peculiar and foreign conventions of her country. Perhaps she could even help him infiltrate the ranks of the nobility.

In any case, while closing the shop door behind him and stepping into the stream of pedestrians, he realized he'd thoroughly enjoyed the unique and abrasive spunk of Rare Confectionery's toffee-maker.

BEATRICE WAS PLEASED AS Punchinello when Charlotte felt better a day later and returned to work, her usual cheerful, smiling self.

Her sister was counting the money in the till as they opened for the day. "It seems sales have been down a bit."

"That's right," Beatrice told her. "Ever since you deserted me, leaving me to wait on these wretched people."

They both laughed.

"Customers, wretched or not, must have come in as usual. Did you manage to drive most of them away before they could buy anything?"

"Some," Beatrice said with a sniff, as she wiped down the glass with vinegar and newsprint. Then she recalled the American. "However, one of them bought toffee even *after* I was rude, and I ended up hurling his sweets at him when he forgot them on the counter." She laughed some more, recalling his expression.

Charlotte was not joining in this time. In fact, she looked horrified. "You didn't!"

At hearing her younger sister's tone, Beatrice said, "You sound like Mother."

"With good cause. I told her she should come spend the day with you, but no, she had to play nursemaid to me. What if the gentleman had accused you of assault?"

"Silly girl."

"No, don't dismiss me. You always think you can say what you like and do whatever you want without consequence. Only recall what a mess you made of Amity's life last year, telling off an earl's daughter and nearly ruining our shop."

"It all worked out in the end," Beatrice protested, not wishing to recall one particularly rude young lady who had thoroughly infuriated her. "Besides Mother told off the same earl's daughter. Why, I think *you* did as well, didn't you, at the duke's party?"

"That's not the point," Charlotte said. "Luckily, I've forgotten what the point was. I'm turning the sign around, so get yourself in the back room where you belong. Treacle toffee, if you please."

Gathering the broom and her glass cleaning supplies, Beatrice went happily to the back room.

"Tea?" she called out to her sister. Although their older sister drank mostly hot chocolate, the rest of the family were solidly tea drinkers.

"Yes, please," Charlotte said, then gave her usual piercing whistle of happiness, guaranteed to make one jump.

"What now?" Beatrice asked, lighting the flame under the kettle on the stove, as well as another under the large pot to which she quickly added brown sugar, treacle, vinegar, butter, and milk. Her basic recipe for treacle toffee, she could practically create it in her sleep.

"Nothing, I'm simply happy to be back."

Thank goodness for her sisters! Amity had made their shop into a gold mine as a renowned chocolatier before marrying the Duke of Pelham a few weeks earlier. And Charlotte, an artist with her delicate marzipan creations, thoroughly enjoyed working in the front of the store while engaging with their customers.

Beatrice's toffee was very popular, but it lacked the skill of her sisters' creations, and she made for a poor shop girl indeed, abiding neither the snout-nosed aristocrats who came in with their silent servants to get free samples despite having more money than God, nor the foolish people who asked her question upon question, as if sweets weren't simply uncomplicated treats of enjoyment.

"Just taste it," she'd hissed at one curious fellow the day before.

Her family accepted she was a bit bookish, happy to spend her evenings reading, mostly because doing anything else involved other maddening people.

However, she didn't thrive upon the novels of sentiment generally considered acceptable for young women. Or at least, she didn't read them often. Beatrice preferred books of facts and history, biographies, scientific improvements, explorations.

To that end, her father paid for a subscription to the London Library on her behalf, and she'd also been known to frequent the British Museum Library during the hours women were admitted. Sometimes she attended what was loosely termed "a lecture" at the London University in the evening. However, these often turned out to be more entertainment than educational and, thus, somewhat disappointing. She didn't care for the meetings of the Literary Society for Women, as they were too esoteric. Instead, she had a subscription to the practical and idealistic *Women's Suffrage Journal,* right alongside her favorite magazine, *The Athenæum,* and she greatly admired women who were making advancements.

Truthfully, though, Beatrice was equally impressed by the accomplishments of men, and rather unsure what she would achieve by being allowed to vote upon things she usually had no interest in. As for herself, she wondered if a life of making treacle toffee was enough and suffered occasionally from the *doldrums,* as her father called it if he caught her moping at home.

Along with Amity, she had declined an official coming-out party at their home on Baker Street, while also knowing she could never be presented at the palace before the queen. That was not for the likes of a shopkeeper's daughter. Thus, she eschewed a wardrobe of useless ballgowns for more books of her very own and the chance to travel with her family to the Continent. They had done so thrice already.

The bell tinkled above the door as the copper kettle started to boil, and Beatrice was very glad she didn't have to attend the customers that day.

Pouring water over the loose leaves in the bottom of their ugly but efficient brown-Betty teapot, she considered her next tray of toffee. She was going to add sultanas for the enjoyment of added texture.

"Beatrice," came her sister's voice, summoning her.

Adjusting the knitted cozy onto the teapot, she parted the velvet curtain and went out front.

"This gentleman wishes to speak with you," Charlotte said.

To Beatrice's surprise, it was the American. Strangely, her spirits lifted. He was as good a remedy for tedium as any.

"THE PLAIN TOFFEE WAS the best." Greer decided to tell Miss Rare-Foure immediately. "Without nuts," he added, in case she'd forgotten. Although, by the look upon her face, she remembered their encounter only too well.

"Thank you," she replied, and he thought it might have pained her to be nice since her tone plainly did not match her words.

"I found assorted flavors of boiled candies right where you said they'd be, all along Oxford Street."

Her mouth drew into a thin line, and he was sorry to have mentioned them.

"Why do you despise them so much?" Greer couldn't help asking.

The sisters—for by their appearance, they were obviously related—turned to one another, and they exchanged a glance.

Then the toffee-maker said, "They need very little skill to produce, except to take care you neither burn the sugar, nor yourself. And any number of nasty things can be put in them to make them colorful and for *children*, no less." She emphasized the word in such a way as to let him know she disapproved of adults eating the hard sweets.

Greer considered the bag of brightly colored candy residing in his pocket. "Such as what type of nasty things exactly?"

"Ha!" she exclaimed. "You are from America and likely haven't heard of the Bradford humbug poisoning of more than two hundred people. Twenty died from eating the sweets containing arsenic from a market stall in Bradford, Yorkshire."

He swallowed the lump in his throat, thinking of the boiled candies he'd eaten since the day before. "Surely that was an aberration."

"Someone got greedy and didn't want to pay for pure sugar," her sister pointed out. Unlike the blue-eyed Miss Rare-Foure, she had warm, brown eyes and darker brown hair. Moreover, she looked . . . friendly—a distinct difference! "It could happen again," she added.

"It could," the toffee-maker agreed. "Adding cheap ingredients, or 'daft,' as it's called, is often harmless plaster powder or limestone. Terrible to put in your food but not deadly, until some idiot used arsenic by mistake. They used to put stuff into cocoa, too," she added, casting a glance over the chocolates on the shelves in the display, "before they figured out the best way to refine it. Although since it was usually starch to soak up the cocoa butter in a cup of hot chocolate, it didn't kill you."

"Would you care to sample something, sir?" asked the friendly sister, who seemed to realize it might not be the best idea to mention poisoning and death to a customer while trying to sell confectionery.

However, the crabbier Miss Rare-Foure continued undaunted. "It's only since they abolished the sugar tax a few years back that you can be fairly certain sugar is what you're getting in anything." She nodded at her own words. "But you still have to worry about boiled sweets made with lead, mercury, chalk, and copper for the red, yellow, white, and green colors."

Greer wasn't too certain about the health risks, but had a feeling he didn't want to eat copper or any of the other things she'd mentioned. He reached into his pocket and drew out the plain brown paper sack, looking extremely shabby compared to the bleached white bags Rare Confectionery used.

"I think I shall toss these in the trash heap," he admitted.

For some reason, this caused Miss Rare-Foure to start laughing. *At him!* She laughed until she snorted. Her sister, noting his discomfort, did not join in, but simply stared at her sibling with quiet disapproval.

After a moment, she said, "Beatrice usually stays in the back," as if by way of apology.

Beatrice? Beatrice Rare-Foure, a pretty name for a pretty female. She could probably get away with her tart tongue and rude comments, and even laughing at customers, because of her high cheekbones, brilliant blue eyes, and generous lips.

The aforementioned Beatrice eventually got hold of her rampant humor and asked him, "Are you back to buy more toffee already? If so, my sister will help you."

With that, she turned on her heel and started to leave. He sent a glance to her sister, who offered him a small shrug along with a congenial smile.

"I will," she said. "Help you, I mean."

Greer nodded. Unfortunately, he felt driven to prod the serpent, compelled to speak further with the sharp-tongued Beatrice. That was why he had returned, after all.

"Miss Rare-Foure," he said to her back, but she didn't turn around, apparently thinking he was addressing her sister.

"You," Greer tried again, "the toffee-maker one."

At this, she whirled around to face him as her sister muttered something that might have been a warning. Returning to the counter, the formidable young woman leaned over it, looking up at him with a direct glare.

"I am working," she said, biting out each word sharply. "What exactly do you wish?" Her words ended on a long hiss of annoyance. *Serpent, indeed!*

"I was hoping we could have a chat, perhaps over a cup of tea, if that's your drink of choice."

Her sister gasped. At the same time, the toffee-maker reared back, her eyes widened, and her mouth opened and closed. Finally, Miss Rare-Foure glanced over at her sister as if to ask her opinion. Neither spoke, then she turned back to him.

"I know you are from another country, so I must ask you this: Do *you* understand I am an honest shopkeeper's daughter?"

Greer wondered what she was getting at. "Yes, of course, *and* you make delicious toffee. It is quite superior to what I've eaten at home."

She nodded, her eyes narrowing slightly. "Do you also understand I do not provide any other services?"

Her sister gasped for the second time in under a minute.

Greer considered her words. *Other services? What on earth . . . !*

"I am asking," the young woman continued, "because first you tried to give me a half-sovereign."

"What?" exclaimed the other Miss Rare-Foure, and then she blinked her big brown eyes at him with interest.

"And because now you seem to think it proper to ask me to be alone with you. To chat. Over tea."

The way she said the words almost made them sound lascivious. Greer couldn't help himself. He started to laugh. Then he slapped the counter, right where she'd slapped it the day before over the infernal coin. Then he doubled over and continued to laugh. If she knew how far off the mark she was!

The two women were silent as he had his own fit of good humor. It felt good to laugh so hard. Obviously, he and the toffee-maker knew how to amuse one another. The notion he would be so brazen as to make a lascivious proposition over tea tickled him. If he were going to make any kind of untoward offer to a woman, it would be over a glass of wine!

Strangely, even though he'd been in London a mere few days, this was the second time someone assumed his thoughts were improper. A cabbie had told him where to find a strumpet if he needed one, and all he'd wanted to ask was where to get a good meal.

What was it with these Londoners? Was it because he was American and they thought him uncivilized?

When he straightened, he realized Miss Rare-Foure's face had reddened, perhaps with embarrassment. He had probably committed all sorts of offences by laughing at her and her outrageous assumption.

"Not that I don't think you are worth . . . *chatting* with . . . over tea," he said lamely, as his levity turned to chagrin. "You are pretty, and I'm certain any man would be lucky to . . . to . . . chat with you. However, I'm not interested in you in that way."

Her mortification seemed to be growing along with his, and he looked to her sister for help, but that one simply smiled and shrugged. Then the bell behind him tinkled gently, and he turned to see three well-dressed women entering with a gentleman, making the store shrink in size.

The friendly sister moved away from the scene of humiliation to help the customers, and when he turned back, he saw only the swishing of the blue curtain.

Now what? Dammit! He squared his shoulders. He was Greer Carson, son of an impoverished petroleum heiress and a dead war hero. He would make this right, even if he had to break a few more rules. Slipping between the counters, he parted the velvet curtain and strode into the unknown.

It wasn't a dark, seedy back room as he'd feared. A window to the alley behind the row of shops brought in the sun, shining daylight upon a cast iron stove with copper counters on either side of it, a marble countertop, gleaming pans, a spiffy cooling box, shelves of what he assumed were candy-making supplies, and one extremely irritated toffee-maker staring at a pot of something black and smoking.

"Miss Rare-Foure," he began.

"Out," she ordered, pointing back the way he had come, before she snatched up a large metal lid and slammed it on top of the bubbling mess. Then she grabbed for a thick cloth and used it to grab the pot handle.

"Allow me," he said, not thinking it right to stand idly by while she took care of this kitchen disaster by herself.

She started to protest, but this young lady was not going to heft a heavy, smoldering pot while he was there. Practically shoving her aside, he asked, "Where do you want me to set it?"

She hesitated, and Greer thought she might balk once again, and the handle was starting to heat through the cloth.

"Set it on the flagstone over there." Beatrice pointed to the far wall between the window and a slim door, where stones indicated a hearth for a fireplace that no longer existed.

Having set it down, he stood and turned. "Please, if I could explain."

"Out," she repeated as before. "And by the time I count to three, if you haven't left not only this room but the shop as well, then I shall be forced to flag down one of the Metropolitan police force."

"I've heard of your bobbies. I would very much like to see one in action."

"You may very soon get your wish. One," she said, tapping her foot.

He glanced down to see what kind of footwear she wore. His uncle always said you could tell a lot about a man by his choice of footwear. Greer wasn't sure that applied to women as well. The best he could tell, Miss Rare-Foure wore short boots, plain leather, dyed gray. Although, they might be shoes. He couldn't quite tell.

"What are you looking at?" she demanded.

"Your feet," he explained. "If I could just see your ankle—"

"Two," she said in a severe tone with her hands on her hips.

"It's no matter. Even if I knew whether you wore shoes or boots, I don't know what that would say about you. I guess boots are more the footwear of a woman who gets things done and has to be on her feet much of the day. I suppose regular shoes could also do that, but not those fancy slippers I've seen in the shop window up the street. They look as though they're thin as paper."

"Those are for dancing," the toffee-maker told him, "not for wearing on the street. Surely, you've been to a dance and seen them worn." Then she shook her head. "Do you really not know how improper it is to try to see a woman's ankles? Are you so uncivilized in America?"

"I had an inkling," Greer confessed. "Not that I've spent much time going to dances. None in fact. Nor, quite frankly, am I much in the company of genteel women."

"Why? What's wrong with you?" she asked him in her surly manner.

CHAPTER THREE

"Nothing is wrong with me," the American asserted.

Beatrice supposed the man could be telling the truth. After all, she and her sisters had been to very few dances by choice.

"Well," she mused, "you seem a little awkward and ill-mannered. I thought perhaps that was the reason New York's polite society kept you out of its ballrooms."

She was pleased to see him pause and his jaw tighten. Then he shook his head.

"*You* are calling *me* ill-mannered?" And he chuckled again, which annoyed her.

"You are not allowed to be back here." She was about to yell the word *three* when she realized she wanted to know his purpose. "What do you want anyway?"

He smiled. "May we first exchange names?"

"You already know mine," she reminded him. "You may call me Miss Rare-Foure. You may call my younger sister Miss Charlotte. That is, if you have any need to address either of us again."

"Would you care to know my name?" he asked frankly, tilting his handsome face slightly.

"Not particularly. I cannot imagine that I will ever see you again once you leave the shop."

"And if I return, or if you pass me on the street?"

In her mind, Beatrice would think of him as *the American.* "A polite greeting is a nod of the head. I would hardly shout your name by way of greeting. However, if it makes you happy, you may tell me your name." Because now, she was devilishly curious.

He stuck out his hand. "I am Greer Carson."

He wasn't wearing gloves for some incredible reason, and naturally, since she was working, neither was she. However, there was nothing for it but to take his outstretched hand.

He pumped her arm up and down a few times in a friendly, somewhat exuberant manner—and absolutely unnecessary, Beatrice felt, since they were standing right there addressing one another.

"Nice to meet you, Miss Rare-Foure."

She knew she should return the quaint sentiment, but it was nearly as false as the upper echelon's insistent declaration of being *enchanted* with one another whenever they met.

As he released her hand, she said, "We are properly introduced now, Mr. Carson. State your business, and then you must leave. Quite obviously, I have another tray of toffee to make."

"I am looking for a titled lady to be my wife."

She couldn't help the snicker of laughter that escaped her, nor the flush of irritation at such shallowness as his words invoked. "Well, you won't find one here at Rare Confectionery. Although it does sometimes work the other way around."

He stared at her, but she didn't elaborate. It wasn't his business to know how a duke had swept in and married her older sister.

Mr. Carson slipped his hands into his pockets, looking relaxed. "You probably know everyone who is anyone in London," he insisted.

Beatrice shook her head. The man was deranged. "Why would you think that?"

"The aristocrats come in here, don't they? I saw those two ladies the other day, the ones you chased off with your *courteous* shop-girl manner." He coughed as if laughing at her. "This is the best confectionery in Mayfair. I was told that by another shopkeeper. And this is the most exclusive shopping street. Where else would the upper class go for their sweets?"

"True, but the nobility usually send in their servants. And when they do come in, I'm not very nice to them because they're not very nice to me. Or to anybody."

"Those two ladies seemed pleasant enough," he said.

Beatrice tossed up her hands. He didn't understand how dismissive the nobility could be, how some wouldn't even speak to her but insisted she and her sisters speak to their servants. It was galling, and she, for one, pushed back against such class rudeness.

"Mr. Carson, even if I knew how to get you into the company of the nobility, you would be disappointed. Titled ladies want titled men—or at the very least, extraordinarily wealthy ones. I don't suppose you are one of those."

"I am, as it happens." He stated it plainly, without boasting or lifting his chin.

She ought to have known. He was probably the equivalent of a rich American heiress, except for being a rather attractive, devilish man.

"Hence the inappropriate tossing around of your gold half-sovereigns?"

"Precisely," he agreed.

"Then you are probably destined to succeed. I'm sure there are any number of titled young ladies whose parents do not have as much as they could wish, not enough for massive dowries, and thus, their prospects are hampered. It is quite expensive to keep a London townhouse as well as run a country home."

"I intend to do both," Mr. Carson said assuredly.

Beatrice considered the earnest man before her. "So you stepped off the boat a few days ago with one goal in mind, to marry an English lady?"

"Or Scottish," he added.

"May I ask why?" She was almost surprised at herself that she even asked, but she couldn't deny experiencing a mild interest. "I assume it's for the novelty of taking one home to New York, like going to Africa and returning with a tiger."

He smiled, and it made him even more handsome.

"Not exactly like that, and I don't intend to take her anywhere. I intend to live here in Britain."

"You still haven't told me why," Beatrice persisted.

"I had a peculiar great-grandfather, who owned a country estate near Canonbie, Scotland. As it turns out, I'm the direct descendant, although there is a cousin who could have laid claim. Stupidly, he made the mistake of marrying for love."

That got her attention. She blinked. "How was that a mistake?"

"His wife isn't titled, and the estate can only go to a nobleman or a noblewoman."

"That's absurd," she exclaimed. "What happens if neither of you marry a titled woman?"

He shrugged. "I don't know, nor does it matter since I will do so. Naturally, my great-grandfather on my father's side never dreamed the last of his sons would die with no living male issue. There was supposed to be a Baron Carson always. However, if I have a Lady Such-and-Such as my wife, apparently that will satisfy."

"Absurd," Beatrice couldn't help muttering again.

He heard her. "That may be true, and I may have to reach too high for my nut." Then he smiled. "Will you help me?"

"I cannot." *How could she?*

"Or *will* not? I have no friends here, Miss Rare-Foure. But perhaps we can make it a business arrangement. Perhaps I can help you in return."

"I don't see how."

"You are not married," he said, knowing her to be a miss.

The cheekiness of the man, pointing out such a thing! "No."

"Engaged?" he asked.

She felt her cheeks grow warm. "It would have been unseemly to do so *before* my older sister. And she has very recently married."

"You are a lovely young woman, who is stuck in this shop hour after hour, day after day. We have large dances in the city where young people from New York's high society can show themselves to one another. It's called a debutante ball. You should have one of those in London so the young ladies can meet the eligible men."

Beatrice burst out laughing. "Yes, we have that. In fact, I believe we invented it, as it has been going on since the seventeenth century when your newborn country was a wilderness. Have you ever read Balzac?"

"I confess I haven't," he said, not looking the least bothered by his own ignorance.

"There's a passage in it perfectly describing what goes on here. The character Madame de la Baudraye says, 'London is the capital of trade and speculation and the center of government. The aristocracy hold a *mote* there for sixty days only; it gives and takes the passwords of the day, looks in on the legislative cookery, reviews the girls to marry, the carriages to be sold, exchanges greetings, and is away again; and is so far from amusing, that it cannot bear itself for more than the few days known as 'the Season.'"

The American's mouth was open when she finished. "That's extraordinarily impressive. To quote like that."

Beatrice lifted a shoulder in a shrug, but inside, she was pleased at his praise.

"I read a lot," she confessed. "In any case, we call it *the Season*. It occurs, as Balzac said, so the men can examine the women who are hoping to catch a husband. But he was wrong about its duration. Instead of a few days, it lasts for months."

"Perfect. We shall go together," he offered. "I will escort you and, thus, by having a man seemingly to be already at your beck and call, you will look even more desirable. I know how a man's mind works, believe me."

It was her turn to look astonished. She was starting to recall all she'd heard of brash Americans. "If I were going to do it, I would have done it last year or the year before. I'm too old."

"Ridiculous!" His expression was all-over shocked. "You can't be more than seventeen, maybe eighteen." He started to peer more closely at her, making her skin prickle.

"It's not polite to wonder about a woman's age, but I'm twenty, too old for any of this nonsense. Besides having a Season is expensive. I have already told my parents I do not want them to bear the burden."

"Then I shall bear it for the both of us. When can we start?"

Beatrice was starting to think Mr. Carson to be a most determined individual or—and this was quite possible—a halfwit.

"It's not that simple. I would need new gowns for balls and dinner parties. You would need new suits. We have to purchase tickets for some events. For others, we must be lucky enough to receive invitations or know someone who is already invited. And still, it would do you no good."

"Why not?" he demanded, looking as if he were ready to go shopping for his new clothes immediately.

"Because only the titled young lords and ladies are presented to the queen at court, as well as daughters and sons of the clergy and military officers. Also, physicians and barristers' children, I believe." She had to dash his hopes. "But most definitely not daughters of merchants, nor sons from New York, not even those with Scottish great-grandfathers who were barons."

He looked unimpressed by this impediment. "Then we won't go to court. Can't we attend the Season without doing so?"

"We would not be at the same events as those who officially came out before the queen and are, therefore, considered acceptable to be on the marriage market in polite society. In other words, you would be in with the likes of me and not with the titled ladies you desire."

Beatrice couldn't believe she was still talking about this, but he intrigued her. Helping him was something to do with her free time besides reading. Moreover, in truth, as she'd told her sisters, she would like a husband of her own, as well as children. She was not a revolutionary who wanted to throw the order of society upon its head. If she had to remain a spinster, so be it. But if she didn't have to . . .

"On the other hand, my older sister is now a duchess," she mused.

His eyes widened with renewed interest, and then he smiled. "You are having me on. Pulling my leg and making fun of me because I am an American. I was born at night, but not last night. Even I know a duke doesn't walk into a sweet shop and marry a shopkeeper's daughter."

Beatrice would take offense if what he said wasn't normally the truth. *Who could believe it?*

"You are correct," she agreed, "Marrying a duke is nearly impossible. It is like catching a shooting star in your pickle jar. And to do so when not a member of the nobility is next to impossible."

"And yet your sister did it." His tone was suitably awestruck as he realized she was telling the truth. "How?"

"For one thing, the duke came to us looking for the best chocolate. For another, my sister is lovely and sweet-tempered. Nevertheless, seeing as he was the only duke in the country at the time under forty and looking for a wife, it was quite a feat."

"I can imagine London's elite are still talking about it."

"They are. Or, at least, my younger sister who reads the society pages tells me they are." Beatrice considered the man before her and her own situation. "My sister, the duchess, will be back from her wedding trip any day. Her new status certainly opens up new avenues of social engagement. While you and I still cannot be presented at court, we could attend the events of the titled if we do so with my sister and her husband, as their guests. No one would gainsay a duke and duchess."

Mr. Carson was grinning from ear to ear. "I knew I came to the right place. I had a feeling, Miss Rare-Foure, that you and I would be a good match."

"Indeed," came her mother's voice. "And who in blue blazes might you be?"

Felicity Rare-Foure had stepped through the curtain, wafting rose-scented toilet water with her, and stopped at the sight of her daughter and a man, secluded in the back room, chatting seriously.

Beatrice didn't mind her mother's bluster, but she could appear quite formidable if one didn't know her reasonable, unflappable, if somewhat forceful nature.

"Mother, this is Mr. Carson from America."

Felicity looked him up and down, then at her daughter, before glancing again at the American.

"Are you healthy?" she demanded.

"Yes, ma'am."

"Mother," Beatrice interrupted, knowing where this was going.

"*Hm*, and you are neither engaged nor married? With no abandoned wife back in the United States?"

"Mother!" Beatrice tried again.

"No, ma'am. I came to England to find a wife."

"I see." Felicity looked thoughtfully at her middle daughter.

Beatrice was about to explain the situation, but Mr. Carson dove in.

"I am pleased to meet you, Mrs. Rare-Foure," he said, sticking out his hand in his forthright manner. "I am sorry if my being here is inappropriate, but I assure you I did *not* see her ankle."

Beatrice snickered at his preposterous words while her mother gave him another long look. However, Felicity did shake his hand before turning to her.

"He's a handsome young man. Good manners, too, except for being alone with you, which is most assuredly unacceptable."

As if she'd ever given her mother cause to worry! "I was just telling Mr. Carson about the Season and—"

Felicity glanced at the American. "Well, you might as well resign yourself to marrying my daughter," she warned him. "That's what happened the last time a man came into the back room—where he should not be. It's probably inevitable."

"Oh no," Beatrice said, hearing Mr. Carson say the same words.

"We are not—that is—" she stopped talking. It was pointless. Her mother would learn soon enough that she was ineligible for this particular man.

"The last man to come back here was a duke," Felicity added with relish, "and now my eldest daughter is a duchess."

"I heard about that. And congratulations to them both," Mr. Carson said. "I myself am in need of a wife, and your daughter has agreed to help me."

"That's exactly what the duke said, too. Do you have means to support a wife?"

"Yes, ma'am. And more."

Beatrice let them continue. It was all *stuff and nonsense* anyway.

"Then good luck to you, Mr. Carson," Felicity concluded. "As long as you are kind and loyal, I am sure you will make me an excellent son-in-law."

"But ma'am, I'm afraid I'm not—"

"Good day to you. Beatrice, he must leave the back room at once, even if he is your betrothed." And with that, her mother strode out.

They looked at one another. Before either could speak, Felicity reappeared.

"You really should speak to her father next, Mr. Carson. Why don't you come to dinner tonight? Shall we say seven o'clock? My daughter will give you the address if she hasn't already." And she disappeared again.

The silence grew thicker. He offered her a grimace of a smile. "That went off the rails rather quickly."

"Do not worry, Mr. Carson. I will explain it to her later. In any case, there is little we can do until my sister returns and opens up the doors of the privileged to us."

"We can prepare our attire. Shall we start this afternoon?"

"Are we truly doing this?" Beatrice asked out loud, speaking more to herself than to the stranger in front of her. It would certainly alleviate the boredom she'd felt recently, not to mention her dissatisfaction with a life stretched out before her with nothing more exciting than making the next batch of treacle toffee.

A Season amidst the nobility would undoubtedly be exciting, even if she ended up with nothing more to show for it than tired feet from dancing. Mr. Carson was silently waiting for her decision. She hardly knew the man except for his obvious good humor, a distinct sense of earnestness, and a pocketful of sovereigns. If he could pay for her wardrobe, then he must be wealthy and, therefore, not a charlatan.

Perhaps seeing her wavering, he said, "I promise, I'm not here to wake snakes."

What was he on about now? At her puzzled expression, he said, "I won't cause any trouble."

That remained to be seen, but she'd made up her mind.

"I can give you the name of a reputable tailor always mentioned in the papers as clothing the finest gentlemen.

Obviously, there are some here on Bond Street, but you'll find equal quality and a better price on Savile Row."

"What about your wardrobe?"

Hardly able to believe she was going along with this, she said, "I'll ask my mother about a modiste and whether it is too late."

"Come out of there, Mr. Carson," came Felicity's voice at that moment. "No respectable fiancé would do such a thing."

"Fiancé!" she heard Charlotte exclaim, followed by her ear-piercing whistle of happiness.

"Please go. As soon as she learns we are not engaged, my mother will be pleased I am to attend a Season."

The American smiled again, and his gray-blue eyes seemed to deepen in intensity. "Then you are really going to help me?"

"If you are truly willing to pay for my wardrobe, and if my sister deems it acceptable to let us partake in the amusements of the nobility, then yes, why not?"

GREER HADN'T EXPECTED THE toffee-maker to acquiesce as easily as she had. However, discovering her sister was a duchess proved his luck was holding.

He left the shop, past the watchful eye of the girl's mother and the curious gaze of her sister, and headed directly to Savile Row and the recommended tailor. As it turned out, the same establishment had clothed the infamous Beau Brummel himself, and Greer knew Miss Rare-Foure had sent him to the best place.

Within a few hours, he had paid for a splendid new wardrobe, with the first suit being ready in a week. Upon returning to his hotel, the luxurious Langham at Portland Place, so pleased was he by the day's accomplishments, Greer didn't even mind taking Miss Sylvia for a walk. His mother's cat tried to bite him in the elevator on their way to the closest greenery, but he was used to that. In his cabin on the journey across the Atlantic, he'd found himself the object of her feline ire on more than one occasion. He supposed since their arrival in England, he had been neglecting the cat somewhat.

"Stop fussing," he ordered, dashing across Mortimer Street, and making sure her collar and leash were secure, before he set her down at the base of a tree in Cavendish Square. Strange to think she was the last connection to his deceased mother and his life in America. His next thought was how he would like to introduce Miss Rare-Foure to Miss Sylvia and hoped she liked cats.

CHAPTER FOUR

B eatrice hadn't thought she would enjoy this part of the Season so much, the fussy preparation part. However, following the seamstress into the dressing room of Madame Solit's shop while her mother and Mr. Carson waited close by, she felt very much like a real debutante—even if, at twenty, she was a few years beyond the dewy age of coming out.

Naturally, her mother had insisted on accompanying them. Felicity now understood the situation and the agreement Beatrice had made—to help the American in exchange for an escort and a wardrobe. Infuriatingly, however, her mother continued to speculate upon possible romantic feelings springing up.

"I would say this is very kind of you, Mr. Carson," Beatrice heard her mother from the other side of the dressing room curtain, "but I think it is money well spent on the woman who will inevitably become your wife. If you are wishing to move up in the social world, then having a well-dressed bride is a necessity."

At her mother's persistence, Beatrice heard Mr. Carson cough distractedly. Despite explaining to her mother and Charlotte, they'd agreed to tell no one else how they would use one another to find spouses. Although her mother wasn't entirely approving of the somewhat unsavory plan, she was thrilled her middle daughter had finally agreed to attend a Season of balls, dinner parties, boating events, concerts, and the like. Moreover, her excitement was contagious.

"If not for your inheritance issue, Mr. Carson, I would advise you against going after a lady of title. I haven't been impressed with those whom I've met."

"Mother!" Beatrice called out. "You cannot base your opinion on the few encounters we've had in the shop."

Besides, her mother would think nothing of pushing her or Charlotte into the arms of some young titled gentleman, as long as he professed to be wealthy enough to support a wife.

"That color is lovely on you," said the seamstress, turning Beatrice toward the full-length mirror so she could fasten the small satin-covered buttons down her back. "This gown was for a marquis's wife, but she changed her mind when she found out his mistress wore this exact shade of blue."

Taking in her reflection, she had to agree with the woman. She looked good in blue. And it wasn't the palest, namby-pamby blue of the youngest debutantes. It had a bit of depth to it without looking gaudy.

"Are you coming out to show us?" came her mother's voice.

Beatrice's gaze caught in the mirror with that of the seamstress.

"You should show your gentleman friend," the woman urged as she pinned along the side seam, taking the dress in by an inch. "Besides, Madame Solit will want to see you in it. She is a very good modiste. She will never sell you a gown that doesn't do you justice in style and color."

In another moment, Beatrice stepped through the curtain. Mr. Carson rose to his feet, a strange look upon his face. It might have been admiration, and a wave of self-consciousness shuddered through her. Unused to being the center either of attention or praise, she found herself staring at the floor rather than the rapt faces of her mother and Madame Solit.

"You have a beautiful daughter," said the modiste.

"I have three actually," Felicity said. "But my Beatrice is unique."

Startled, she wondered what her mother meant by that but couldn't ask while they were in mixed company. Mr. Carson still said nothing, and she dared for the briefest of moments to make eye contact.

Even though she didn't know him, nor should she value his opinion, his warm gaze gave her the greatest encouragement. After all, if one man thought she looked appealing, then possibly others would, too. Possibly a husband—titled or not—was within reach. And unlike Amity, Beatrice wouldn't go through the torturous handwringing, wondering whether she could continue to make toffee after marriage. While she liked her confectionery skill, it wasn't her passion as was her older sister's chocolate-making. Of course, she would continue to make toffee, but she wouldn't turn down a man she loved if there was a choice to be made.

"That blue suits her well, don't you think, Mr. Carson?" her mother asked.

The American nodded, seemingly tongue-tied for the first time, another good sign.

"Why ask a man?" scoffed Madame Solit, yanking fabric swatches off the low table. "No offense, monsieur, but if you like a woman, she could walk out here in a sackcloth and you would think her beautiful. Isn't that so?"

"Oh, well, I don't know," he said, and Beatrice nearly giggled at his confused tone.

"On the other hand, if she had come out in the wrong

shade of blue, maybe a turquoise green with too much yellow undertone, we women would have known immediately it didn't suit her."

Her mother nodded, and Beatrice caught Mr. Carson's gaze while the other ladies' backs were turned looking at the fabrics. He crossed his eyes and pursed his lips in jest, and any odd tension between them disappeared.

Beatrice laughed, until she felt one of the seamstress's pins jab her in the side. She gasped and vowed to comport herself with more decorum, at least until away from the pins.

"This gown is a must," said her mother to Madame Solit. "What other colors do you think compliment her brown hair and eyes?"

"How about red?" asked Mr. Carson unexpectedly.

Both her mother and Madame Solit gasped while the seamstress shook her head. Even the shopgirl charged with keeping their wine glasses filled giggled from her discreet place on the other side of the room.

"Red!" Madame Solit exclaimed. "Do you wish your lovely lady to be branded a lightskirt? After marriage, yes, you may dress her in a vivid hue, but not before."

Beatrice didn't bother to correct the modiste. The women were blinded by the notion of romance. Moreover, her mother would assume Mr. Carson had a personal interest in her middle daughter until such time as they each pledged their troth to another person.

"I was thinking how pretty her hair would look against red," he said, sounding not the least put off and fully ignoring the inference they would marry.

"In any case," Madame Solit said, "I know she would look splendid in a dusky pink, not too pale, not too pastel. Also, a cool green, not too vivid, nor too dark." To display her knowledge, she held a bolt of each up against Beatrice's face, one after the other.

"Yes," her mother agreed. "Both."

"Surely that's enough," Beatrice protested, not wanting to take advantage of Mr. Carson's generosity, only too aware he would, with any luck, have a wife to clothe in the not-too-distant future.

"You must have enough for an entire Season," Felicity insisted. "Neither of you can expect to find a suitable partner during the first ball, for goodness sake, if that is truly your aim."

"Besides," said Madame Solit, "I have something special. Fabric of fine satin, a little more expensive than the others for the rarity of its color. But we shall see if it suits." She was moving around the store as she spoke, rifling through baskets, looking under bolts of material.

"Ah ha!" she said at last, hurrying over to drape a shimmer of copper around Beatrice's shoulders.

"How expensive?" Beatrice asked, looking down at the unusual fabric whose color was warm and fiery. As she raised her arms to look, it seemed to change from golden orange to deep mahogany with her movements.

"Gracious," her mother said. "It's splendid."

"It doesn't matter how much," Mr. Carson said, his voice sounding strangely thick.

Beatrice's gaze locked with his, and a thrill of excitement sizzled through her at his expression.

"That is some pumpkins!" he exclaimed. "Miss Rare-Foure must have a gown made from it," he insisted. "I may be merely an ignorant man, but even I can see . . . ," he trailed off. Then he blinked, looked away from her, and drained his wine glass.

"I have to leave you now. Please carry on." Mr. Carson started toward the door. "We are up to four dresses, if I am counting correctly from the colors you've suggested and the one she's currently wearing. She'll need at least eight, won't she? Maybe ten. Send the bill to my hotel. The Langham. Mr. Greer Carson." His cheeks went a ruddy color.

"Of course, you know all that already." He reached for the door handle. "I'll stop into the shop again soon to discuss what comes next. Well done. Good day."

He hurried outside, avoiding eye contact.

Beatrice watched as her mother exchanged a smug look with the dressmaker. They thought he was well and truly ensnared by her. She didn't want to shock them by mentioning how this was practically a business deal. With Beatrice's connection to the Duke of Pelham, Mr. Carson would get his titled lady, and with the American's assistance, she would get herself a husband . . . or at the very least, she'd have fun trying for a Season.

"Some pumpkins," murmured the modiste, shaking her head. "These Americans!"

GREER WASN'T ONE TO mope or feel lonely. Usually satisfied with his own company if that was all he had, in this foreign land, he felt himself growing oddly attached to Miss Rare-Foure. Moreover, while dining alone at The Cock Tavern on Fleet Street, he did feel a little solitary. Around him, men were laughing loudly, engaged in discourse, downing drinks, smoking cigars, occasionally shouting out to the serving wench to bring more baked potatoes, ale, porter, or wine.

In the chophouse, he drank ale and recalled the moment when the toffee-maker had come out of the dressing room in a silky blue dress with lace and ribbons. She'd taken his breath away, and he was positive he'd never seen a prettier girl. And then, when the dress-maker had held the shimmery, copper material close to Miss Rare-Foure's caramel-colored hair, she'd looked like a goddess.

He'd had to escape the close confines of the dress shop in order to regain control of his senses and not appear to be a drooling, eager greenhorn. She didn't want a rough-hewn American to sweep her off her feet with passion and lust any more than he wanted a middle-class shopgirl. He needed a titled lady, and she probably wanted a refined, reserved Englishman such as she was used to encountering.

But she had certainly stirred his blood six ways from Sunday.

He tossed down some coins and started for the door when he bumped into a man standing up abruptly from a table.

"Here now!" the man exclaimed. "What are you trying to do?"

"Just trying to leave," Greer told him, hoping the questioner wasn't as drunk as a Virginia fence, as his uncle might have said, staggering this way and that. Nor did he fancy a bunch of fives swinging in his direction should the rest of the man's drinking companions decide they needed to anoint him in the ways of British pugilism.

"American?" came the next inquiry.

"Yes," he answered tightly. Either this would gain him instant rancor or favor, one never knew with these Englishmen.

By the hard but friendly slap on the back, it was the latter. "Let's have a drink and you can tell us all about yourself," was the man's invitation. "We're sick of our own tales."

If Greer hadn't been feeling all-overish and out of sorts—with no plan except to head back to his hotel room, give Miss Sylvia some attention, and go to bed—he might have shrugged the man off and continued on his way. However, there was nothing to prevent him from enjoying a little local camaraderie.

On the other hand, if he sensed they were trying to honey-fuggle him or engage in any chicanery, he would go.

"It seemed you were leaving," he pointed out to the big man who'd given him the hearty slap.

"Nah, just going to take a piss."

"Can't hold his ale," said one of the others.

"Or his women," said another, who looked at Greer over the top of a glass of brandy instead of a pint. This man with his salt-and-pepper hair drawn back in an old-fashioned queue had a shrewder look about him. They all laughed at the words, even the man who was now walking away, holding his hand up to give his friends a particularly rude salute.

"Take his seat while he relieves himself," another man said. "He'll find a new one upon his return, and he won't be angry, I assure you."

Greer paused for a second, but except for the brandy-drinker, the rest of the men all had open, interested expressions.

"Very well," he said. "Shall we introduce ourselves?"

In a very few minutes, he felt as if he'd known these fellows all his life. John Delorey, the man with the small bladder, was in textiles like Greer's Scottish grandfather. He had a wife and two children. The man who sipped brandy, Randall Molino, was a purveyor of antiques, owning a shop a fair distance from Rare Confectionery north of Hyde Park. There were also George and Jeremiah, both friendly sorts.

"We meet here most Wednesday nights," John Delorey said toward the end of the evening. "You're welcome to come again."

WHEN GREER ENTERED THE confectionery two days later, having given himself a little respite away from the powerful draw of Beatrice Rare-Foure, he felt renewed vigor. Hopefully, they could discuss the next step in their joint entrance into high society, and he had to admit, he felt better for doing it with the outspoken toffee-maker at his side. She might not be the most experienced of guides, but he knew she would be a dependable companion as they attempted to insinuate themselves into the unfamiliar arena of the British aristocracy.

Miss Charlotte was at her station behind the counter, shaping some type of dough between her nimble fingers.

"What are you working on there?" he asked.

"Marzipan," she offered with her ready smile. "From ground almonds. I make all the marzipan sweets we sell." She gestured to the shelf in the display case with artfully made small fruit, flower, and animal shapes. Some were painted, if that was the right word, while some were adorned with nuts and seeds.

"You are a true artist. Have you ever worked with clay?"

Her cheeks turned pink. "I like to work with something that pleases the tongue as much as the eyes. I'm not sure I would be satisfied with work that sat around, gathering dust. Not when I can see the pleasure on a customer's face as they eat one of my creations. Have you tasted one?"

A peal of laughter came from the back room, not that of Beatrice, either, if he could credit his own ears.

"My oldest sister has returned from her wedding trip," Miss Charlotte told him, before picking up a small, pear-shaped treat and handing it to him. "The green shade is pistachio."

Then, while Greer wondered whether he fancied eating a pistachio-colored pear that was made of almond paste, the young woman before him let loose a shrill whistle, which caused him to jump slightly and for silence to descend upon the back room.

Footsteps followed a moment later, and the toffee-maker appeared with another woman, obviously the other Rare-Foure sister by her hair coloring and resemblance.

"Oh, there you are," Beatrice said.

Greer was pleased to hear welcome in her voice, a far cry from their first few encounters when she wished him to leave the shop and never return. He hadn't seen her since she'd appeared as a vision of loveliness in a blue gown at the dressmaker's. And he was glad to see her in an unremarkable dress, which caused him less of a strong visceral reaction. It wouldn't do to let her uncommon loveliness and her witty nature draw him into an impossible romantic liaison.

"Amity," she added, "this is Mr. Carson. Mr. Carson, may I present the Duchess of Pelham."

Miss Charlotte laughed at Beatrice's words, and he glanced at her.

"My sisters and I are still getting used to the new title," the duchess said. "I am pleased to meet you, Mr. Carson."

He stuck out his hand, and then faltered. "Is there a special way to greet a duchess?"

"Of course," Beatrice said sternly. "You must drop to your knees at once and place your forehead on her left shoe."

He paused for a split second, then they all laughed.

"Honestly, Mr. Carson, in the confines of Rare Confectionery, I will always be Miss Rare-Foure, the chocolate-maker. I am happy to shake your hand." And they did so.

"More than that I'm pleased to meet someone who has managed to convince my sister to partake of a Season. She has been telling me of your plan to infiltrate the highest tier of society."

"With your help," he interrupted, "if you would be so inclined."

"I see no reason why not. And back to your question about greeting, when you are in a drawing room, even my husband's, surrounded by lords and ladies, you must address everyone properly or risk ostracism and humiliation. I know this from personal experience."

"Then I shall need some lessons. I am a quick study and have a good memory."

"Indeed, you both shall need lessons," the duchess said. "I hope you will come to my home tonight to begin. I will tell you the basics of what I have learned during the course of my engagement. And I shall ask my husband for his assistance, too."

"The duke is very nice," Miss Charlotte said.

"Indeed," the newlywed duchess agreed, her cheeks pinkening at discussion of her husband. Then she looked Greer over with a discerning eye. "He, too, once thought he needed a titled lady to be his wife."

Greer hoped they didn't think less of him for his goal. "I am glad you disabused him of that notion, my lady."

"No, no, no," Beatrice said. "That's your first error. She is not to be addressed as anything other than *Your Grace* or *my lady duchess.*"

"You can also call me simply 'Duchess.' For example, if I'm on one side of the room, and you want me to . . . I don't know . . . to bring you over a glass of wine, then you should say, 'Duchess, will you bring me a glass of wine?'"

"That's ridiculous!" Miss Charlotte exclaimed. "He would never ask *you* to bring him a glass of wine. You have oodles of servants now, don't you?"

They all laughed again.

"Your sister is quite right, Duchess," Greer agreed. "I fear if I yelled out 'Duchess,' and asked you to bring me anything at all, your husband would give me a blinker in short order."

Three lovely Rare-Foure sisters stared at him uncomprehendingly.

"A blinker," he repeated. "A black eye, yes?"

"Oh, my husband is not the type to resort to fisticuffs." The shop bell tinkled and customers entered, causing the youngest sister to turn away to serve them.

"We must get back to making sweets," the duchess declared. "Especially me. The shop is woefully low on chocolates. Now, don't forget. Come to my home for dinner, followed by lessons. Will you two come together?" She turned to Beatrice, who hesitated.

"I shall make my own way there," Greer insisted, not wanting any of them to get the wrong idea by him 'escorting' her.

"Very well. Seven o'clock, at number 35 St. James's Place, off St. James's Street. Good day, Mr. Carson."

With that dismissal, which seemed quite duchess-like, she turned and disappeared through the blue velvet curtain.

"I must get back to toffee-making, too," Beatrice said, even though she hesitated, and he thought she had something else to say. He waited a moment, but nothing more was forthcoming.

"I am so grateful for your help, Miss Rare-Foure," he told her. "I would still be wandering the streets—"

"Looking for boiled sweets," she added.

"And not getting any closer to my goal."

She gave him a genuine smile, which transformed her visage from pleasingly pretty to downright angelic before his eyes.

Careful, he warned himself. They were to be friends and nothing more.

"I, too, want to offer my gratitude," she said. "It always seemed a frivolous imposition upon my parents to invest in a Season's worth of gowns, not to mention any tickets we must purchase. You've made it possible while also providing me with an escort. We shall still need a chaperone, probably my mother, except when at my sister's home."

Suddenly, Greer's fingers itched to pick her up and twirl her around, he felt so pleased. "It seems hardly any time since I first wandered in here, and now, we're shinning around to your sister's tonight."

By the way she wrinkled her forehead, he knew he'd used a term she didn't understand.

"I mean," he added, "we're going along like a team of six horses, starting tonight."

Her frown cleared and she nodded. "Until tonight, then."

CHAPTER FIVE

Beatrice couldn't believe how easily and swiftly this was happening, like melting butter on the stove. Or as Mr. Carson had put it, "shinning around." She thought her parents or Charlotte might come to dinner as well, but her mother had one of her infamous gardening meetings, during which she and the other women would drink pot after pot of scandalous gossip-water in the guise of sherry. And her youngest sister had her painting class with her friend, Viola, and her brother, whom they all suspected Charlotte had an interest in.

Thus, her father accompanied her. As they entered Amity's new four-story, granite-and-brick townhouse, Armand Foure vowed he would stay only long enough to hug his eldest daughter, shake hands with his relatively new son-in-law, and meet the American.

They shook hands.

"You've added a dash of excitement, Mr. Carson, right as the last dash was wearing off," Beatrice's father said jovially, referring to the recent ducal marriage.

"I am pleased to have met all of you," Mr. Carson said. "You are a fine family, and your wife and daughters are the kindest people I've met in London."

"Beatrice? Kind?" her father said jokingly.

She didn't blush, nor did she bother to protest. It was pointless. Mr. Carson had already witnessed her lack of cordiality in the shop. She vowed she would do better when out in society.

"In what hotel are you residing?" the duke asked, as he signaled for glasses of wine to be distributed among the small gathering.

"The Langham," Mr. Carson stated.

"An excellent choice," her father said. "One of our most modern and well-appointed hotels."

"As well as expensive," added the duke.

"Is it?" the American asked. "I have nothing to which I can compare it. The hotel was recommended by the hackney driver who brought me from the train station."

"How much?" her father asked.

"Father!" Amity exclaimed.

"What? Can't a man ask?" Mr. Foure took a sip of wine, looking surprised that it was in his hand, since he'd intended to remain but a few minutes. "I'll never stay at the Langham although I wouldn't mind enjoying a meal there. I've heard the food is exquisite."

"The meals are delicious," Mr. Carson agreed. "And I don't mind telling you, if I have figured the money correctly, it costs fourteen shillings and six pence."

"Zounds!" said her father. "For a bed?"

"No," Mr. Carson explained. "That is the cost for a suite, breakfast with a hot beverage and cold meat, as well as a lavish dinner including soup and a joint of meat, along with a vegetable. And I have my own bathroom and WC, as you call the lavatory."

"Still!" Beatrice's father said, draining his glass in his amazement at the price.

"I have the convenience of a steam laundry. The

concierge can obtain tickets to any theater in London and even for railroad passage. There are Persian tapestries everywhere! The concierge said they're putting in electric lights throughout the hotel next year."

"They shall be able to afford to do so at those prices," her father said, shaking his head.

"I would like to treat you and your family to a meal there in the main dining room, the *salle à manger* as they call it," Mr. Carson insisted. "The place is something to see, I assure you, rows of perfectly symmetrical columns and sparkling chandeliers, beautiful white cloths, and the palms you are so fond of here in England, I've noticed. And there's a coffee room with a grand bowed front of at least seven massive windows."

"I've had the pleasure of the coffee room," the duke piped in. "They serve an excellent brew."

Mr. Carson nodded. "I hope it would show the extent of my gratitude for what you are all doing for me."

Her father appeared delighted and accepted the offer. After refusing to stay for dinner, he left them to their evening. While they awaited the cook's summons, Amity told stories about her wedding trip, visiting chocolate factories both in England and France.

"When we weren't eating or drinking chocolate, we were drinking coffee in some of my husband's favorite coffeehouses. As he mentioned earlier, he's had the pleasure of taking coffee nearly everywhere it is served. Do you like coffee, Mr. Carson?"

"Yes, my lady—" He interrupted himself and held up his hand before Beatrice could correct him. "I mean, yes, Duchess. We are quite fond of coffee in New York where I'm from. Also, I've traveled extensively across the United States, and people drink it almost exclusively, with practically no one drinking tea."

"No tea?" Amity wondered.

"Remember, my love," the duke said, "after the tea was tossed into the harbor of Boston because of high taxes, the

Americans decided tea was too English. Coffee is their patriotic drink of choice."

"What about chocolate?" Amity asked.

Beatrice watched Mr. Carson shake his head. "No, ma'am, I mean, Your Grace. I haven't seen a lot of people drinking chocolate."

"And you are giving up your home in America for Scotland?" asked the duke.

"There is nothing for me in the States anymore," Mr. Carson said. "Here, I seek a new life and an old legacy. As soon as I arrived, I went directly to southern Scotland to look at the estate. I decided I would let it be the deciding factor as to whether I attempted to gain a titled wife or let it go out of the family."

"I take it you liked it," Beatrice said. "Or we wouldn't be doing this charade."

He turned his gray-blue eyes to hers, and she nearly flinched at the intensity of his gaze. "I loved it, Miss Rare-Foure. It was like nothing I'd ever seen, maybe because I knew my grandfather had been born there. Just over the Scottish border, past the fork where the River Esk branches off as Liddel Water, it's located between Canonbie and Rowanburn. It's called Carsonbank." He laughed, perhaps self-conscious at the name. "I confess some of it is derelict, but you can discern its former beauty. It was built in the 1720s in the neoclassical style."

"Is there anyone living there now?"

"A very small staff paid by a trust set up by my great-grandfather, who died thirty years after my grandfather moved to America. His older brother, the only heir who remained in Scotland, died shortly after that. And it's been empty of Carsons ever since."

"You would think they would appreciate any member of the family wishing to return and renovate it," the duke pointed out.

"My great-grandfather was, by all accounts, an irascible coot. He was a baron, his father was a baron, and he wanted a titled heir living in the house. I don't think my grandfather thought his emigrating to America would cause such a problem. If I didn't believe the estate worth saving, I would walk away from it. But there was a painting in one of the rooms that looked like my father, even though I know it wasn't he. It reminded me that my blood is in those walls and on that land, something I never felt in New York."

"Does it turn a profit or go further into debt each year?" asked the duke, with the practicality of a landowner.

"I couldn't believe it, but it does turn a profit, from rents on the estate and from the sheep still being tended and a tremendous amount of wool sold to mills. But there's been no one to put the revenue back into the main house, not even to patch up the ceiling. It's all in a trust, waiting for a Carson to come along and take over."

"Dinner is ready, Your Grace," said a footman who had entered on silent feet.

Beatrice glanced at Amity, unable to keep from smiling, and knew they were thinking the same thing. How different was her sister's current dinner announcement from that at their home on Baker Street! Sometimes their father yelled to his girls, sometimes Charlotte was enlisted by him to use the awful skill he'd taught her, summoning her sisters with a whistle. Failing either of those, if their lackadaisical butler, Mr. Finley, didn't bother to find them, they might miss the start of dinner altogether.

Amity shrugged, looking so sweet Beatrice felt her heart squeeze with happiness for her sister's good fortune. And then their small group went into the magnificent dining room, still decorated as the Dowager Duchess of Pelham had left it before she'd moved out recently, giving the newlyweds privacy. The wallpaper was the brilliant green of a dragonfly, with accents of gold. Beatrice wondered if her sister would keep it that way. It seemed a bit last-century and gaudy, not that she would ever say anything.

Over dinner, Mr. Carson treated them to stories about riding the rails, as he called it.

"I was sent off by my mother's only brother to learn the business of railroads by observing the ashcat, the bug slinger, or the Brains, also known as the conductor. I became a railway boomer, doing whatever temporary job needed doing, and I got to see a lot of the towns that dot the American west."

Beatrice understood little of what he was saying, and thought, by the way her sister and her new brother-in-law nodded politely, the same was true for them.

"Your mother and father don't mind you taking an English bride?" Beatrice asked, having been curious for days about his parents.

He glanced at her, then shrugged. "They are both deceased. My mother died two months ago, and thus, here I am, having realized from documents that came to light after her death how I might benefit from the institute of marriage. My father perished in the War of the Rebellion, our Civil War, if you will, during the final months of it, in early 1865. I was young and kept hoping as the men came home, he would, too. But then we received word of his death."

If Beatrice knew him better, she would swear she heard a note of bitterness, but she might be mistaken. Strange to think his father, a first-generation American, had fought and died for that country, and yet Mr. Carson said he'd felt at home in Scotland. For her part, she couldn't imagine going to a new country and starting over, but then, she had her parents and her sisters. The American had no one, and she was more determined than ever to help him.

After offering condolences, the duke asked about the devastation of losing a generation of young men, even wondering if twenty years later, America was short of labor. Mr. Carson grew thoughtful.

"In many families, decisions were made how many brothers to send into battle. My mother's parents got rich from Pennsylvania petroleum and had but one son. Therefore, my uncle did not have to go to war, although he paid handsomely for the uniforms and upkeep of three men who went in his place. Ultimately, my mother's family had to move north to New York when the Confederate Army occupied their city of York. They lost everything. As for my father, as an only son with a wife and young child, not to mention having married into wealth, he could probably have bought his way out of the war, too. Nevertheless, he chose to go."

Again, Beatrice thought she heard an undertone of disapproval over his father's actions. Perhaps the young man he was at the time, hardly more than a boy, couldn't conceive of a father choosing war over his family if it were at all possible to avoid.

"He must have been very brave," she offered. "And your mother must have been proud."

Mr. Carson turned his gaze to her again. "Yes, she must have been proud," he agreed in a low voice. After a brief hesitation, he smiled. "Tell me, what is the first step in going out into London's grand social Season?"

She realized he didn't wish to speak about his personal life any further. Beatrice glanced at Amity. "I suppose we should ask you."

In turn, Amity looked at her husband. "Shall we start with a ball here or accompany them to an event elsewhere?"

The duke smiled. "You sound as if you're dreading it, my love."

Beatrice knew how her sister felt, like a fish out of water. Neither of them could have imagined they would be seated in a grand house with Amity as the mistress. And her sister had no more clue what to do than she did.

"Not dreading exactly, "Amity said. "I am glad I have you by my side and that Beatrice has Mr. Carson. I don't know how those young debutantes handle it alone."

With an expression of solemnity, the duke said, "Those debutantes have been tutored and trained with all the dedication and efficiency of Her Majesty's finest military. They are primped and prepared within an inch of their lives, and failure is not an option. Their mothers are usually a hairsbreadth behind, prodding them into the arms of each and every eligible man. They must dazzle while dancing, charm while chatting, and never, *ever* be found either dull or—far worse—*unusual.* Most of all, they must extract a commitment to marriage before letting the gentleman do so much as brush his lips against theirs."

He sipped his wine as Beatrice and the others remained silent, staring at him, the font of all aristocratic knowledge, as well as all things to do with the peculiarities of the London Season.

Then the duke looked at Mr. Carson. "As for the men, they must out-swagger, out-dance, and outflank every other man in the room. At the same time, they must appeal in a slightly wicked, swaggering way to the debutante, while seeming as unthreatening as a safe old slipper to the mother. Every female is trying to outshine her competition, and each man is attempting to be king of the Season. It is all-out war, I tell you."

Beatrice blinked at her sister, and even Mr. Carson appeared unsettled by this description.

Then the duke cracked a smile, dimples and all. He leaned back, closed his eyes and laughed. He laughed so hard, Beatrice thought his chair might tip over backward.

At first, none of them joined in, merely watching him. Slowly, however, they started to release the palpable tension his alarming words had engendered.

When her husband opened his eyes and looked at his guests, Amity asked, "So you were speaking in jest, Henry?"

He shook his head. "No, it's all true. Absolutely! I am only relieved—thrilled in fact!—not to have a fervid interest in any of it anymore. I have captured my prize." He glanced at Amity and their gazes locked. "I can dance with my lovely wife and not have to play a part in the machinations, except as I wish. It is bliss actually, and I shall enjoy myself immensely."

Beatrice waited, but he remained staring at her sister as

if no one else were there. After a moment, she tapped her wine glass with her fork to break the spell and regain the duke's attention. He turned his head slowly, and then his eyes refocused on her. He smiled.

"It's all true?" Beatrice repeated. "We don't simply go to dance and drink champagne? Mr. Carson and I have to partake of this ludicrous war between the sexes?"

"And take on the mothers?" the American added, looking a little shaken.

The duke shrugged, and Amity, with those rich brown eyes that had skipped Beatrice and gone to Charlotte, looked pityingly upon them both.

"And don't mention Scotland," the duke added, speaking again to Mr. Carson, "or the young ladies' mamas will think you're trying to get their daughters across the border for a quick, unlicensed and unsanctioned wedding."

Mr. Carson nodded at this advice, then he glanced at Beatrice. "Do not worry, Miss Rare-Foure. I doubt it can be as daunting as entering a saloon in Spring City that has just run out of whiskey."

She nodded. That did sound like a harsh reality. "Or as crushing as being told by a snout-nosed lady that she doesn't deign to speak with shopgirls, and I must speak only to her servant."

"Outrageous," the American agreed, which she appreciated tremendously. It had been a surprising set-down, not the first but the worst, and she'd lashed out with a particularly nasty retort. Another customer had been lost that day.

"Bea, I can see where your thoughts are going," Amity said, "but recall, you will be an invited guest, a duchess's sister and a duke's sister-in-law, and thus completely accepted, not a shopgirl disguised as a debutante."

Accepted perhaps, but still a shopgirl and definitely not a debutante!

"What's the classification for a female *after* she is no longer a debutante?" she asked.

The duke rapped the table with his knuckles. "Spinster, old maid, hag."

"Henry!" Amity reprimanded, but Mr. Carson laughed, irritating Beatrice to no end.

"And she remains on the shelf," the duke continued mercilessly, "probably because she is a shrew, a harpy, a—"

"Henry!" Amity exclaimed again, glaring at her new husband.

"A termagant!" the duke finished, then he laughed again. "Come along, my love, your sister knows I'm speaking in jest this time. She's younger than you are, and you know I don't think you to be any of those things, despite your having been on the shelf even longer than she has."

Beatrice decided they'd best get to the lessons before this line of conversation drove a wedge between the blissful newlyweds.

"What shall we do first to prepare for this delightful undertaking?"

CHAPTER SIX

After dinner, Greer followed his hosts and Miss Rare-Foure—*Beatrice*, as he already thought of her—into a ballroom. *Damn!* The Pelhams had a ballroom in their home. A decent size, too, although he supposed any size ballroom was impressive enough.

"Now," said the duke, "let's see about your dancing skills."

"What about music?" Beatrice asked from where she'd taken a seat by the double doors, changing into dancing slippers along with her sister. "Dancing is a challenge at the best of times, but to do so in silence—"

"I've taken care of that," the duchess promised, jumped up, and rang a bell discreetly tucked in one corner.

Greer could get used to this lifestyle, and a titled lady would give it to him. Although at present the family estate in Scotland was a drafty disaster, he would bring it back to its former glory. Moreover, he would keep a comfortable London townhouse and let his lady wife host parties and whatever else she wanted. And then high society would be the norm, and ballrooms would become commonplace.

An older lady entered, and the duke crossed to greet her. "Nanny Beryl, so good of you to join us."

"*Hmph,*" she said, and that was all, before going to the pianoforte that was located at one end of the room. "I need more light," she yelled when she reached the piano bench and took a seat.

While the duke went to turn on the two central pendant gas chandeliers, the duchess explained, "Nanny Beryl was the family nanny. She taught Lady Penelope, my husband's sister, to play the piano. She stayed on for all these years because . . . ."

Trailing off, Beatrice's sister looked to where the lady began to warm up, playing scales. "I have no idea why, to tell you the truth."

"Do you think she will be your children's nanny?" Beatrice asked.

Greer nearly laughed at the look of horror on the duchess's face. "Gracious, I hope not! She is ever so crotchety and ancient. I can't imagine letting her hold a baby for fear she'd drop it on its head. When I asked Henry about music, he mentioned her living somewhere in the house, the basement or the attic. For all I know, she resides in the mews out back."

The toffee-maker laughed delightfully, and Greer was again glad he'd persisted in making the young woman's acquaintance. She would make an excellent partner in this exciting endeavor.

The duke returned. "Are we ready? Nanny Beryl will start with a waltz. I know my wife can perform one quite well. What about you, Miss Beatrice?"

"About as well as my sister, I shall wager. And you, Mr. Carson?" she asked him in turn.

He had to confess. "I've never waltzed, not once."

Greer wished he hadn't seen a brief expression of disappointment flicker across Beatrice's face. "I've done the polka," he offered.

"The polka is a two-quarter dance," the duke said, "and the waltz is a three-quarter dance."

Greer shrugged. "How about if you and your wife start? Let me watch you for a minute, and with Miss Rare-Foure's help, we shall follow behind."

Which was precisely what they did. The duke bowed to the duchess, then took her hand. She gave a shallow curtsey, and they moved a few feet away. The music was already playing, and the man took his wife in his arms.

"One, two, three," the duke said aloud, and the rest was a series of steps and turns.

Greer couldn't figure out what the duchess was doing under her voluminous skirts, but he carefully watched the duke's steps—right, left, forward, left, right, back—yet at the same time they didn't stay in the same spot despite it appearing as if they formed a box. They moved as if they were one unit, turning, stepping, gliding.

Even Greer could appreciate the grace of the couple.

"Our turn," he said, after he thought he had the steps. He held out his hand to Beatrice, and she took it. Instantly, he felt a happy warmth at touching her, even better when they got into position, with his right hand pressed to her back and his left clasping her hand. They began.

Immediately, he trod on her foot. And again.

"Let me see what you're doing," the duke insisted. And they started again with the same result.

"Mr. Carson, the waltz is a close dance. When you step forward, your knee will inevitably be near Miss Rare-Foure's, despite hers being cloaked under an infernal amount of fabric. If you try to move your right foot farther right to avoid touching hers, or any woman's, you will collide with her left foot."

With that advice, they tried again to better results, at least for a few steps. When they turned and he was going backward, it happened again.

"My apology again, Miss Rare-Foure. I can't seem to get my feet to cooperate."

"The railroad," Beatrice muttered, probably with sore toes. "Think of our feet on parallel tracks that do not intersect. Just keep on your track, please."

He smiled. "That's brilliant. Let's be trains, Miss Rare-Foure."

Greer still struggled, but after half an hour he had the box step, as they called it, and then the duke taught him how to rock, transferring his weight from foot to foot before turning his partner. Eventually, they made it all around the ballroom.

"Bravo," said the duchess.

"Recall, of course, you will be with many other couples. Occasionally, someone will collide with you. Simply continue with the briefest nod of apology, even if it wasn't your fault, and no one will mind," the duke advised. "And don't ever cry out or bring attention to it."

Greer nodded. "As long as I'm not knocked off my feet, we shall soldier on."

Beatrice giggled. "How many dances must we learn?"

"Naturally, you must learn the proper way to do the opening Grand March and the quadrille. If you feel comfortable with the polka and the waltz, you should learn the mazurka, lancier, and—"

"Good God! I only intend to go to a few balls and snap up the first available lady who accepts," Greer insisted, "After that, I think I'll be done with the dancing."

"It's best you do as my husband says, Mr. Carson. At each ball, nearly every popular dance is performed at least once. What if you examine the lady's card to find the polka and waltz are already claimed?"

"I don't suppose I can cross out the other fellow's name and fill in my own?"

They all chuckled at such an insolent notion.

"Very well," Greer said. "Let's try one more lesson tonight, but if I do more than that, I'll probably muddle the steps up in my head. Would you mind allowing us to return for more instruction another time? Miss Rare-Foure says we have a few weeks before anything spectacular is expected of us."

"Indeed," the duchess said, "you must come again. I think it more enjoyable dancing here at home than at a ball. I vow the last time we were in a ballroom I heard whispers of 'chocolatier' at each rotation around the dance floor."

The duke draped an arm over his wife's shoulders. "You probably did, my love, but they were whisperings of either jealousy or admiration. I promise."

Beatrice put her hands on her hips. "Think how I shall feel when I hear murmurs of 'treacle toffee' as I circle the dance floor!"

The women laughed again, and Greer thought them the most cheerful two females he'd come across in years. It must be all the sweet treats.

"I believe you'll also need a little tutoring on greetings and title ranking," the duke said. "But I shall be there to introduce you, so you can follow my lead."

"Can't I introduce myself to the young ladies?"

Now, all three of the Brits laughed heartily at him.

"Oh, Mr. Carson," the duchess said, "that would mark you firmly as outside of polite society. In these situations, you must be introduced by someone who knows you and the lady. If my husband doesn't know the person, then one of us must find someone else to introduce you to her. However, since I am the hostess, I will be able to take you around and introduce you, as well."

"It sounds complicated," he complained.

"It is designed to keep dangerous people who don't belong away from the innocent and vulnerable," the duke explained.

Greer looked at Beatrice, and she widened her pretty blue eyes. Neither of them belonged where they were trying to go, but they weren't dangerous, either.

"Again, the only thing dangerous about me is how I might stand on a lady's toes."

"About that," the duke said, suddenly looking serious, "I

know Miss Beatrice will vouch for you, knowing you have already invested in the Season, but do you have any letters of recommendation?"

"Henry," his wife said quietly.

"Really, Duke," Beatrice added, "that sounds as though you don't trust Mr. Carson. I saw his gold sovereign for myself."

"And he likes your toffee, too," the duke agreed. "That's all very well, but still . . . ." The nobleman turned to Greer expectantly, one eyebrow raised. "I would be remiss in taking all you say on faith."

He thought about what he'd brought with him from home. "I have a letter from my uncle saying I am who I am, signed by him as head of his railroad company. Some people had travel documents, or *passports*, as we call them, during the war and for a few years after, but no one told me to get one to come to Britain, Your Grace."

"You have Scottish ancestry, and family still there?"

"Ancestry, yes. Family, hardly. We've practically died out. There is the trustee in Edinburgh, who manages our estate."

"Very well, perhaps it's time to send him a letter and receive one in reply. Also, you will need a solicitor who dares to take on the Chancery Division of the High Court to sort out your estate issues. You should count yourself most fortunate you no longer have to deal with the Court of Chancery, a quagmire of do-nothings that was finally abolished a couple years ago."

"I did secure a lawyer already, and I have recently written to the trustee."

"Good. I'm sure it won't be a problem, then. You understand, I would hate to be accused of introducing ladies to a scoundrel from New York City out for their fortunes."

"Henry!" the duchess exclaimed again, although the toffee-maker laughed.

"Personally," she said, "I think it would be greatly amusing if our Mr. Carson married some Lady Snout-Nose only for her later to discover he was a pauper from the United States."

Greer didn't take offense to any of this. "Without your help, I am as likely to find myself married to a female who pretended to be a lady and is really a common miss."

As soon as he said it, he knew it was wrong and wished he could call the words back. Beatrice stiffened.

"Indeed, how terrible that would be," she snapped. "To end up with a common miss." Turning to her sister, she said, "I am ready to learn the mazurka."

Greer was glad when they stopped talking and got back to dancing.

"Truthfully," the duke informed them, "while the count is the same as a waltz—one, two, three—you will find the accent, as I think of it, is on the opposite count. The waltz is highlighted on the one and three, and the mazurka on the second count."

"Oh, Duke," Beatrice moaned.

"And it can feel more . . . jumpy," the duchess added. "As if you're skipping along instead of gliding."

"Oh, Duchess," Greer echoed, but he was game to try.

When he held out his hand, he hoped Beatrice would take it as easily as she had before his ill-advised remark. After all, he hadn't meant her. She was not common in the least. Quite the opposite, she was special, open to speaking her mind and wonderfully sharp-witted. Despite her initial behavior, she wasn't mean, nor judgmental. She seemed to have encountered some unfairness that left a lasting mark upon her, making her quick to feel slighted. Other than that, she was damn near perfect.

Particularly her blue eyes, the color of hyacinths or delphiniums.

She did take his hand and even gave him a smile. Another one of her good traits—while she seemed quick to ignite, she was quicker to calm and regain her pleasant humor. They followed the regal couple onto the dance floor again.

"I NEVER THOUGHT I would be so happy to return to work," Beatrice told Charlotte the following morning as she cleaned the glass display cases. "Have you ever tried the mazurka?"

"Sadly, no," Charlotte said, her head resting on one hand as she leaned upon the counter.

"Well, it's difficult. I trod on Mr. Carson's toes, he stood on mine. I slipped once. I even backhanded him in the chin. And one time, he turned one way while I turned the other and he wrenched my wrist."

Charlotte sighed without sympathy. "At least you were in the arms of a handsome man and have many more dances to look forward to."

She could not deny Mr. Carson was handsome. He was also funny and witty, to boot. Moreover, she thoroughly enjoyed his company, so very glad she hadn't scared him off that first day when he'd wanted boiled sweets.

It had been easy to get swept up in the excitement of what was ahead of her, something she'd never thought she wanted until it was laid at her feet. *But Charlotte!* Beatrice looked at her. Of the three of them, her youngest sister was the only one who had really wanted a Season, and not to find a man but for the pageantry of it. *How much more fun it would be with Charlotte at her side!*

"Let's ask Mother if you can join us and partake of this wretched experience."

Charlotte sighed again. "People will think we've been hiding ourselves in order to spring double beauty upon the unsuspecting world."

Beatrice blinked. "Dear sister, I don't know what to say to that, but I don't think we have to follow the rules of those presented at court, who then make a grand debut or have a coming-out party at home and all that. We are slipping *in media res,* as it were, pretending as if we already are in society and our wonderful duchess of a sister is simply letting people know."

"But the gowns and the tickets," Charlotte protested, even as her smile returned.

"*Pish,*" Beatrice said, hoping she wasn't setting her sister up with false hope.

"Easy for you to say when you have Mr. Carson with his dash-fire and deep pockets, ready to outfit you and escort you."

Dash-fire? First remarking on his handsomeness and now this. *Was Charlotte beginning a* tendre *for the American?* If such was the case, Beatrice would nip it soundly in the bud since he was entirely off limits.

"Mr. Carson, as an escort, might as well be an old woman or a donkey."

"What?" Charlotte said with a laugh as the shop door opened. "Poor Mr. Carson."

"Poor Mr. Carson why?" asked Felicity Rare-Foure. "What has Beatrice done to him now?"

"Nothing, Mother. I was explaining how he is merely an escort and might as well be a donkey since I cannot have designs upon him for all his handsome face and thick hair."

Her mother looked at her sister, then back at her. "*Do* you have designs on him, dear girl?"

Beatrice threw her hands in the air. "Does anyone listen to me?"

Naturally she had noticed his unusually captivating eyes, his well-proportioned physique, and his sensual mouth. Of *course* she'd enjoyed being held by him in Amity's ballroom, but that was beside the point. He needed a titled lady, and there was no getting around it.

"Mother, you must let Charlotte have a Season. This Season! With me! Please say yes."

"Yes," said Felicity.

"Mother! That's not fair. Why shouldn't she? You saved oodles of money by Amity and I refusing our Seasons. And now Mr. Carson is paying for my Season and—" Beatrice interrupted herself when Charlotte clapped her hands with obvious glee.

"She said *yes*," Charlotte told her.

"Oh, you did, didn't you?" Beatrice said. "We must go back to the same modiste this very afternoon and get her started on gowns for Charlotte. She can't possibly wear any of my dresses without getting them all taken up, nor Amity's without getting the bodice loosened." Their youngest sister was the most well-endowed, and the most apt to capture attention in that area.

Charlotte let loose a loud whistle of happiness as her enthusiasm spilled over. Then she took a breath and said, "On my dresses, I would like lots of ribbons and lace and ruffles and bows and—"

"The garniture will be suitable, Charlotte," their mother said. "However, I order you not to make that sound again, or I shall change my mind."

"Yes, Mother." But Beatrice could tell her sister wasn't going to stop smiling for the rest of the day.

"You must come to the next dance practice at Amity's tomorrow."

"I'll need a partner."

"Maybe a footman can help out."

"Beatrice!" their mother exclaimed. "Charlotte is not going to dance with a footman. Besides, he wouldn't know the dances either."

"True. Then Amity shall have to share her duke. I'm sure she won't mind."

AS IT TURNED OUT, Amity didn't mind, but the duke looked surprised the following evening when Charlotte turned up with Beatrice. Mr. Carson arrived at the front door nearly at the same time, and they strolled in together about an hour after dinner.

She and Mr. Carson had agreed they didn't want to be such a burden they had to be provided dinner each time they showed up for a lesson. No matter that Amity had said it was no trouble, they'd insisted on lessons alone.

"Three of you now," the duke remarked.

Beatrice couldn't tell if he was feeling put upon. But Amity hugged them both happily, then let Mr. Carson bow over her hand.

They went directly upstairs to the ballroom, and once more, Nanny Beryl was sent for.

"So we're launching you, as well, Miss Charlotte," the duke intoned.

"Launching!" Charlotte said, then laughed. "What a delightful word!" She spun in a circle, as excited as a child with a new toy. "Yes, I shall be by my sister's side and perhaps I'll catch a husband of my own."

Beatrice had the briefest flash of worry. Charlotte had an effortless charm about her, not to mention bowed lips with a sweet smile and a couple of other assets that constantly drew men's notice.

"We don't have to be right beside each other at every minute," she said without thinking.

Charlotte, looking puzzled, cocked her head.

"I mean," Beatrice corrected, "you shall want to shine on your own and enjoy yourself with many dashing young men at your beck and call. If we stand talking together, thick as thieves, we might seem unapproachable."

Her younger sister's frown vanished. "Honestly, I'm far more interested in dancing and mingling, not to mention seeing all the spectacle, than in finding a husband, although I intend to help *you* find one, and to assist Mr. Carson if I can. But you may be right about our not standing together all the time."

Then Charlotte offered her warm smile. "We shall arrive and depart together, and during the middle time, we shall make the rounds, circle our prey from two fronts, and compare notes at night's end."

The American gave a startled bark of laughter. "Sounds most expeditious."

"Agreed," said the duke. "The young gentlemen will have no defenses against the Rare-Foure sisters. I should warn you, there may be a few unfavorable whispers from the other ladies."

"Why?" asked Amity, as her husband's ancient nanny arrived and went directly to the piano.

"It's considered polite to have only one girl from a family debuting in a year, unless they're twins. I'm not really sure the reasons, perhaps respect for an elder sister or the strains of financial burden in some cases. I don't know which of the sisters is looked at unfavorably because of two coming out, but I suspect the younger is thought impatient."

Charlotte shrugged, undaunted, already tapping her toe as the waltz began.

"Oh well," Beatrice said. "We are not truly debutantes anyway, and frankly, we don't care what the *ton* thinks about our private arrangement."

"If someone so much as looks sideways at Bea, she'll tell them where to go," Charlotte said before changing into her dancing slippers.

Amity shook her head. "I hope not."

"No," Mr. Carson said, "that won't do." And he looked Beatrice directly in the eye with his clear bluish-gray ones. "Even I know we must be courteous and not insult fellow party guests the way you do in the shop. These particular members of the nobility aren't going to be demanding service or free samples."

The duke laughed, and Amity joined in. They laughed too long, as far as Beatrice was concerned. *Her behavior wasn't so terrible, was it?*

When he caught his breath, the duke asked Mr. Carson, "You've witnessed that, have you?"

"Witnessed it?" he repeated. "I've experienced it! Miss Rare-Foure even threw toffee at me."

The duke started to laugh again.

"It was in a bag," Beatrice said by way of defense.

"Are you lot going to dance?" asked Nanny Beryl. "Elsewise, I'm going back to my room to put my feet up."

"You had best get started," Amity said, "before she departs."

The duke put his hand out to take Charlotte's, and Mr. Carson did the same with Beatrice. They showed Charlotte the mazurka, then learned the lancier and the redowa before the duke took his wife into his arms and waltzed her around the room to everyone's applause.

"I'm so happy for them," Beatrice said.

"I want that happiness, too," Charlotte whispered loudly on one side of her.

"I wouldn't mind a duchess of my own," Mr. Carson said on her other side.

"The duke didn't choose a duchess," Beatrice reminded him. "He chose a chocolatier." Nevertheless, she felt the same as Charlotte. *How wonderful it would be to have a man look at one with such love.* She sighed.

"That was a large sigh, Miss Rare-Foure."

"I cannot believe I am going to say this, Mr. Carson, but I cannot wait for the Season to begin."

CHAPTER SEVEN

Greer directed his hired hackney to the Rare-Foure
residence on Baker Street. Tonight was their first
foray into high society. Happily, it would be on familiar
territory, at the Duke and Duchess of Pelham's home. He
didn't feel nervous so much as anticipatory. He might meet
his future wife that very evening.

The Foure butler opened the door after a long pause, but
Greer was used to the man. This was his third visit in as
many weeks. He didn't know a lot about butlers, as his
mother and friends in New York City more often had
housekeepers or maids who answered their doors. But he
did know that the Foure butler was far more casual than the
Pelhams' butler and apt to go missing entirely.

The Foures didn't appear to mind, and almost seemed
to think it a favor the man ever answered the door at all.

That night, Greer didn't let the butler take his hat or coat
since they were due at St. James's Place within the half hour.

"If you'll please tell the Rare-Foure sisters that I've come
to collect them," he instructed the man, "that would be

appreciated. The butler nodded and wandered off down the hallway.

While waiting, Greer walked in circles on the polished floor of the foyer, thinking about the dance steps he'd memorized, until a herd of buffalo came charging down the staircase. The herd turned out to be merely Beatrice and Charlotte. They came to a sudden stop at the foot of the stairs, looking surprised to see him.

"You two could wake the dead," Greer told them, noticing their finery. The toffee-maker wore the blue gown with silver lace and ribbon he'd seen her in at the dressmaker's, and she was easily the most fetching woman he'd ever laid eyes upon. Her younger sister wore pale green with cream trim. Both had low necklines, not that he was staring, and the shortest of sleeves, displaying their graceful arms. And each had a spray of flowers tucked into her hair. The effect was enchanting.

He swallowed. "I hope I am dressed well enough to escort you two lovely ladies."

Beatrice gave him a long, measuring look, taking in his black suit, well-fitting trousers, his low white waistcoat, showing off his new shirt, and a black cravat.

However, Miss Charlotte spoke first. "Mr. Carson, you look handsome indeed. That suit fits you to perfection." Then she clapped her hands, already clad in short lacy gloves, as were her sister's. "Isn't this exciting?"

"It is," he admitted, wishing Beatrice had said something kind about his looks, as well. "Are you ladies ready?"

"Yes. I wonder where our man is," Miss Charlotte mused.

"Your man?" Greer asked. "Do you mean the butler?"

"Father thinks *butler* is too grand a term," Beatrice explained. "Anyway, Mr. Finley ought to have brought our mantles, or we could ask Delia."

"Didn't this Finley fellow tell you I was here?" Greer had assumed he'd gone up the back staircase to summon them.

"No," Beatrice said, "but I'm sure he was about to. Mr.

Finley is relaxed but usually reliable. Anyway, Delia makes up for any slack on his part. I'm sure she's put them right here."

Going to the closet under the stairs, she withdrew two cloaks. They didn't match their dresses but instead were neutral black. He supposed they were designed to go with anything.

"Was I remiss in not insisting you purchase a cloak specifically to go with each gown?"

The girls looked at one another, then they chuckled.

"Oh, Mr. Carson," Miss Charlotte said, "how sweet of you to think about such a thing. But that seems so wasteful since we shall leave them in the cloakroom anyway. Besides black goes with nearly everything, don't you think? We match your attire, at least, and that is as good as we can hope."

Another compliment from the younger sister. Greer could get used to her nice manners. He draped each one's cloak across her shoulders, noticing Beatrice's warm vanilla scent.

He wanted to tell her how delicious she smelled, but that seemed inappropriate. Even more so when it made him want to bury his nose in her hair.

"What about your dancing slippers?" he asked, recalling how they'd changed into them each time they'd met at the Pelhams' home to practice.

In response, Miss Charlotte grasped her gown and drew it up a few inches, sticking out a dainty foot.

"Already wearing them" she said, as he got over the shock of her raising her skirt, no matter how little.

"Charlotte!" Beatrice admonished her. "Whatever you do, don't do that at Amity's, and also no——"

"Whistling. I know," Miss Charlotte said, snatching up her reticule from the hallstand and handing a blue one to Beatrice.

Beatrice turned to him once more. "I know there are many times when ladies take a change of footwear, especially if it's wet out or bitterly cold, but with this being such an easy trip to our sister's, we decided to wear them. If mishap occurs to our slippers, Amity will have extra."

Miss Charlotte chuckled again. "Your foot would never fit into one of Amity's slippers, any more than I could fit into one of her slender bodices."

Beatrice sighed with exaggerated exasperation and shook her head. "And to think I was concerned that *I* might say something untoward."

"What did I say now?" Miss Charlotte asked, and Greer decided to get them moving along.

"Are your parents here to see you off?" he asked.

"Father and Mother went on ahead," Beatrice answered. "They decided seeing all three of their daughters out at a ball was too remarkable an event to miss, and they wanted to watch us make our grand entrance into society."

"I wish I had a man of my own and didn't have to share yours," Miss Charlotte said.

Instantly, Beatrice's cheeks reddened, and Greer hastily went to the door to open it since the butler had never returned.

"Really, Charlotte," Beatrice muttered going ahead down the single step and along the path. "Mr. Carson isn't mine. And after all, that's the whole point of tonight and the entire Season, isn't it? To find ourselves men of our own. Whatever you do, don't—"

"Whistle. I know. You already said that."

He helped them into the hackney, and they continued to talk as if he wasn't there.

"I didn't mean Mr. Carson is yours, as in *yours*." She waggled her eyebrows. "I meant as in *your escort*. Besides, I am *not* searching for a husband. I simply want to dance and to look at the other gowns. And don't *you* snap at anyone," Miss Charlotte added.

Beatrice stopped arranging her skirts and stared hard at her sister.

Greer wanted to laugh but averted his face, looking out

into the dark street as if he were in a different carriage altogether.

After a moment, out of the corner of his eye, he saw Beatrice relax, leaning back onto the seat.

"I suppose it is fair for you to say such. I shall try to hold my tongue, as long as no one says anything rude or cutting or positively stupid."

At this, Greer could keep silent no longer. "Miss Rare-Foure, in a gathering of any size, especially when privileged people are involved like we shall mingle with tonight, it is highly probable someone will do at least one of the things that causes you to snap. Perhaps we should develop a system by which we douse your fire before it explodes."

"Douse my fire?" she murmured, raising a lovely eyebrow, and he wondered what she was thinking. "I suppose it is a good idea, as my temper has been known to reach a boiling point faster than unwatched milk on a stove."

"Godey's *Lady's Book* says you must not give off the slightest indication of ill-temper. Perhaps one of us will poke you in the ribs if you start to seethe," Miss Charlotte offered.

"Ha!" Greer exclaimed before he could stop himself. "She'll be black and blue before the dinner break."

Beatrice crossed her arms until her sister reminded her she might wrinkle her bodice, and then she rested her hands gracefully in her lap.

"Speaking of dinner," Miss Charlotte said, "what shall we do at the eleventh dance if we're not all partnered? Will we go to dinner together?"

Greer looked at Beatrice and then back at Miss Charlotte. "Our aim is to be partnered with others. We'll cross that bridge when we come to it. Anything else we should be mindful of?"

Miss Charlotte nodded sagely. "As to you, Mr. Carson, do not speak with any lady to whom you haven't been introduced. And the proper way to ask her to dance is something like, 'Will you favor me with your hand for this or the next dance?'"

"Will you favor me?" he repeated.

Miss Charlotte continued. "For heaven's sake, do not sit next to a lady, even if you've danced with her, unless she expressly invites you."

Beatrice laughed, but the younger Rare-Foure wasn't finished yet. "Sister, dear, don't forget the other rules as expressed in the *Lady's Book*. In your speech, avoid affectation, and with your expression, you must not appear to be frowning or quizzing."

"Is that all?" Beatrice asked, appearing surly at the notion of such rules.

"No, it's not," Miss Charlotte said. "No loud laughter, loud talking, or staring."

"Can the staring be loud?" Greer asked.

They all chuckled, and then Beatrice said, "It hardly sounds like fun if we cannot laugh, nor barely look at one another."

Greer wasn't worried. That night was the beginning of all his hopes and dreams, and even if he didn't find his future wife, he did intend to have fun.

AMITY HAD TRANSFORMED HER luxuriously elegant home into a glittering palace of candles and flowers and sparkling champagne, at least in the ballroom, and Beatrice was reminded of the extreme wealth of a duke. The rest of the house was immaculate as usual, with staff taking ladies' cloaks and gentlemen's hats as soon as guests entered the foyer, before more staff escorted them upstairs to the party.

Deciding to do nothing by halves, the Pelhams' esteemed butler announced each guest who arrived in the double doorway of the ballroom.

"I cannot believe we were announced," Charlotte

murmured as they crossed the floor toward the windows where their parents were waiting. The musicians already played softly, not music for dancing but merely to keep the guests entertained.

"I hope not too many of the hoity-toities realize we're shopgirls at Rare Confectionery after hearing our name." Beatrice couldn't help but fret.

"I'm not embarrassed by our wonderful shop," Charlotte returned.

"That's hardly the point. If we seem inauthentic, we shall hurt our chances and possibly Mr. Carson's."

"There's hardly anyone here yet to have heard your names," the American pointed out. "I think that was your sister's plan in having us arrive when we did."

Beatrice thought him correct, seeing how only two of the many tables dotted around the room had been claimed, and one of those was by her parents. Besides, more guests were being announced every moment.

"But we are not going to lie, are we?" Beatrice asked Charlotte. "It wouldn't do to meet our future husbands and start with a falsehood."

"Of course not," Charlotte said. "I want my husband to fall in love with who I really am anyway, wherever I may meet him. Don't you?"

Beatrice nodded, but silently considered her sister's statement. She was a toffee-maker, an unremarkable middle sister, and considered cranky by many. None of that seemed particularly worth loving.

"Good evening," their father boomed. "You three look splendid. Dressed to the nines!"

"I am happy for you," their mother agreed. "This is the perfect treat for my hard-working girls. And you look dapper as well, Mr. Carson."

"Thank you, ma'am."

"We're going to mingle and make ourselves scarce," Armand Foure said, "so you can have our table."

"Whyever for?" Beatrice asked.

"If we're all together, it will be harder for your scheme to play out."

"Our scheme?" Charlotte asked, sounding delighted.

"Your father means if the whole family is standing around, it is less likely you two will be seen as mysterious heiresses," said their mother.

"But we're not mysterious heiresses," Beatrice pointed out, starting to feel a little panicky, again wondering what would happen if they were quickly discovered to be shopgirls amongst the *bon ton*. Even though it was Amity's house, she and Charlotte didn't belong. They should be at one of the regular dances for commoners, held at a hotel ballroom or a music hall.

"Tonight, in the safety of your sister's ducal mansion, you can be whomever you please," her mother said, reaching out to touch her hand. "Beatrice, look at me."

"Yes, Mother."

"You're a beautiful young woman with much to offer any lucky man. And don't forget Farrah's."

"Thank you." She would keep reminding herself of that. She wasn't simply someone who knew the best proportions of butter to treacle and sugar. On the other hand, she wished her mother hadn't spoken in front of Mr. Carson. Beatrice thought it made her sound slightly pathetic, with no vim and vigor of her own.

"And you, too, Charlotte," her mother added. "Any gentleman will consider himself lucky once you decide upon him." Then she took her husband's hand. "We'll see you at the dinner hour. Amity says it will be substantial, not mere soda biscuits and cheese." Then their parents wandered away through the growing throng.

"What or who is Farrah's?" Mr. Carson asked.

Distractedly, glancing around the room at those entering, Beatrice responded, "Mr. Farrah started making toffee in Harrogate in 1840, giving people something to take away the terrible, sulfuric taste of their renowned healing water."

Mr. Carson blinked. "They ate toffee because of bad water?"

Beatrice shrugged. "Farrah's is sold all over now. Mother reminds me of it now and again as proof that toffee isn't merely a frivolous sweet. But of course it is! It's a delicious confection, and using it to clean one's palate doesn't make it medicinal or elevate my abilities in any way. Such nonsense!" Then she took a long breath. "But I do love when Mother says it, anyway. It's like a soothing balm."

"The room is filling up," Charlotte remarked, "and the single gentlemen will start to make the rounds and ask us to dance. I hope you remembered a spare pencil."

Beatrice felt a flutter of nerves. Her sister, who was more a devotee of the society pages and the gossip rags, not to mention used to dealing with numerous strangers in the front of the shop, seemed much more composed.

"We all know how it works," Beatrice told her, turning to encompass Mr. Carson. "And yes, I have a pencil for any ill-mannered clout who didn't bring one. Do you have one?"

Mr. Carson grinned crookedly. "Even if I'd forgotten, I wouldn't tell you and risk being labelled an 'ill-mannered clout,' would I? Besides, I bet our hosts have plenty to spare."

"Then you don't have one," she guessed. "Here, take mine. I won't dance with a fog-pated jackdaw who has forgotten his."

Charlotte giggled.

Beatrice sighed. "Except for you, Mr. Carson," she said, retrieving the small pencil from her reticule and handing it to him.

"The best part of our arrangement," Charlotte continued, "is that our cards won't be pathetically empty. When other men take a look, we shall have a partner already written in, if Mr. Carson will allow and if you won't be such a cross-pot," she added, glaring briefly at Beatrice.

However, since Charlotte could never hold an ounce of anger or a grudge for more than a second, she smiled again almost instantly. "Quick, now, Mr. Carson, gentlemen will start to come over any minute."

Holding out her card, Charlotte seemed to be radiant with excitement, watching while the American scrawled his name next to the polka, fourth down on the list. Beatrice decided she might as well follow suit, for her sister's logic made sense.

"Shall we dance?" she asked Mr. Carson.

"We shall," he agreed. "And since we are new to this, why don't I sign up for the Grand March leading into the first quadrille."

That was perfect. Beatrice had been dreading the very first time she stepped out onto the floor with all the experienced lords and ladies, and being with her usual dance partner would make it far less nerve-wracking.

"Just remember," she said, repeating the duke's words of wisdom imparted during their lessons, "the lead couple, namely my sister and the duke, will have the fireplace on their left."

"Right," Charlotte said.

Beatrice frowned. "Are you agreeing, or are you saying I am incorrect?" she asked.

"Incorrect. The lead couple will have the fireplace on their *right*, taking the room lengthwise, of course. And the third couple will be on the right of the first. That's what the duke said."

"What about the second couple?" Beatrice asked with mounting panic.

The three of them looked at each other blankly.

Charlotte suddenly cocked her head. "Of course, it depends on whether it is a march in file or in column. Did Amity mention anything about it being a serpentine march or an arbor one? Did she say it might be a Grecian cross or—?"

"Oh, for pity's sake!" Beatrice was positive a bead of sweat was now trickling down her back under her shift, and her palms felt decidedly moist.

"I'm sure it will all come clear," Mr. Carson said. "We'll muddle through."

"What about me?" Charlotte asked, sounding equal parts anxious and thrilled.

"I doubt you'll have to worry. It's the gentleman's job to lead," Beatrice reminded her. To the American, she added, "You'd best get a move on, or the other ladies' cards will fill up before you get a chance." She glanced around. "Look, there's my sister, ready to take you under her wing and make introductions."

"I'll see you soon," he promised. With a nod to Charlotte and wink for Beatrice, he went over to Amity, and they disappeared into the burgeoning crowd.

Beatrice tried to take a relaxing breath, but then occurred the most terrifying moment so far—the duke approached with a handsome stranger.

CHAPTER EIGHT

"This young man asked me to make introductions," the duke said. "Ladies, this is The Viscount Beechum." He turned to the man. "Lord Beechum, these are my sisters-in-law, Miss Rare-Foure and her sister, Miss Charlotte."

The viscount bowed to them each in turn, asked if they would do him the honor of dancing, and dutifully filled in a single line on each of their cards before he nodded and wandered away.

"How can we even tell which one of us he was interested in?" Charlotte asked.

The Duke of Pelham grinned. "You can't, not yet. He probably has no idea himself. My duchess invited mostly debutantes and first-year gentlemen, so no cagey rogues will be roaming my ballroom. However, none of these guests know one another unless their families are aligned in some way. After a few balls and dinner dances, you will come to have a list of favorites safely tucked in your head as will these gentlemen."

"Like favorite sweets at our shop," Beatrice murmured.

"Precisely," the duke said. "I will continue to introduce you."

And he did. Every few minutes he came by with a new man, Lord Longden, Lord Burtley, and Lord Abendee, and then, as host, he had to take them around and introduce them to other female guests.

"This seems so strange," Beatrice said, having met more single men than she had over the course of her entire lifetime.

"And wonderful," Charlotte said. "I suppose it is the luck of the Season whether you find a mate in this crop of gentlemen or at a ball that has the previous year's harvest, maybe even some of those rogues our brother-in-law was talking about."

"Maybe," Beatrice wasn't really listening to her sister's words, something about agriculture. Studying her card, she hoped she could do all the dances without making a fool of herself.

When Amity showed up, she knew the first dance would begin soon.

"Where have you been?" Beatrice asked, belatedly realizing her tone had sounded a little sharp. "Sorry," she amended. "I guess I'm a little nervous."

"Don't be. You look beautiful," Amity said. "You both do, and your dancing has improved greatly. Don't forget, any missteps will be blamed upon the man."

"While it hardly seems fair," Beatrice said, "I confess I'm glad that's the case."

"In answer, I was introducing your Mr. Carson to eligible young ladies," Amity reminded her. "That was the primary aim of this endeavor, wasn't it? Also, I knew if Henry brought young men over to meet you and mentioned how you were his sisters-in-law, it would elevate you in the eyes of the nobility. It will serve you far better than if people start associating the three of us. This way, you can have your own identities and maybe even a little allure."

The three of them chuckled. However, Beatrice thought the real reason Amity had kept her distance was because she'd had a harsh introduction to high society, due to the simple error of calling the duke by the address of "my lord" instead of "Your Grace." It probably wouldn't have mattered to anyone if a spiteful earl's daughter who wanted the duke for herself hadn't decided to make a public scolding. What's more, it had happened right there in that very ballroom.

"In any case, no matter how terribly we may blunder," Charlotte said, "I intend to have a good evening. Besides, you said that day of your humiliation was also the day your husband knew he was in love with you."

Amity's cheeks turned a pretty shade of pink as the violinist drew his bow sharply across his instrument, signaling the start of the Grand March. The duke came an instant later to claim his blushing bride.

"Come along, my love, we have a dance to host." He held out his right hand, and Amity placed hers atop his, then he led her away.

As they walked to the middle of the polished floor, the other guests clapped, and those who were going to dance took up their places behind the Duke and Duchess of Pelham for the Grand March.

Mr. Carson reappeared and took Beatrice's hand, but she hesitated until a tall man with large sideburns showed up to claim Charlotte. They proceeded onto the dance floor as the *Radetzky March* began, and everyone promenaded down the middle and then split off side to side. Beatrice ended up strolling back along the length of the room on the opposite side to Charlotte.

"So far, so good, Miss Rare-Foure," Mr. Carson said.

"Indeed. My dance card is full, I believe. Did you manage to stake your claim to many titled ladies?"

"As to that, with your elder sister's assistance, I did. I shall be out here on the parquet treading on ladies' feet all night."

So, this would be their only dance. *Why should that bother her?* Undoubtedly, it was simply the familiarity of being with him versus every other strange man in the room, knowing he wasn't considering her for marital purposes and, thus, not passing judgment on any of her failings.

"I hope you find what you're looking for," she said.

"My sole thought at this moment is dancing with you, Miss Rare-Foure, and getting through the wretched quadrille."

That made Beatrice laugh, relaxing her, and she was ever so grateful the American had dragged her into this.

GREER FELT LIKE THE proverbial fox in a hen house. So many pretty ladies, and so many who were actually "my lady" ladies. He was minding his manners and his feet. He hadn't tripped himself or anyone else, or even bruised any dainty toes.

Strangely, he didn't enjoy dancing with any of these young women the way he had with Beatrice over the past couple of weeks. He supposed it was because these ladies behaved so formally. When he bowed and took a woman's hand, it wasn't really the time for frank discussion, jokes, or laughter. As it turned out, there was no time for any of that at all during the dance or after when he returned them to their table. Everything was curt and scripted.

He was becoming adept at carrying lemonade and champagne, also in escorting the ladies on and off the dance floor, handing them off to their next partner. Unfortunately, at that point, he promptly forgot their names. Each and every one seemed cut from the same bolt of cloth.

Even when he'd danced with Charlotte, it wasn't the same as with her sister. Partly because that young miss had her head on a swivel. Knowing he wasn't interested in her romantically, the youngest Rare-Foure girl spent her time spying out other men and even talking about who she thought cut a good figure.

It was a little galling. Beatrice hadn't behaved similarly. He thought that was because they had formed a friendship. At least, he felt they had.

And then it was time for the last dance before the dinner break. He went to the far end of the room to collect his next partner, Lady Emily St. George, not particularly recalling her until he approached her table, where she stood with her chaperone.

He bowed. "I believe our dance is coming up next," he said to the petite, dark-haired female. She nodded and took his arm. At the same moment, he heard laughter coming from the other side of the room. *Beatrice!* He was certain. Moreover, it was the dreaded loud laughter of which Charlotte had warned them to avoid.

Greer couldn't help wondering what had sparked the toffee-maker's good humor, wishing he'd been closer so he could have possibly shared in the jest.

Lady Emily shook her head. "Imagine!"

He wasn't sure what response to make or even if she wanted one, so he continued toward the dance floor. Already a little weary from trying so hard to recall steps, Greer was mortified when the music started and he couldn't recall what to do first, until he saw other gentleman take their partners and begin the steps.

"It's a lancier," his partner said softly, which he appreciated.

"I apologize," he murmured, but by then they were already keeping step with the rest. "I'm new at this."

"From America," she guessed. "I like your accent."

He smiled and really looked at her. She had a nice face, he decided.

"Thank you. I like your accent, too."

BOTH THE DINING ROOM and the drawing room had been set out with refreshments, with plenty of space for everyone so they could keep the ballroom clean of crumbs and grease.

Naturally, there was tea and coffee, if guests had grown tired of lemonade and champagne. And in each room was a massive spread of cold tongue, meat sandwiches, chicken, ham, roast beef, and bread. Everything chopped or sliced and put upon one's plate by a helpful footman if one but pointed toward it, and all of it easily edible with simply a fork in one's hand.

After finishing the savories, there was trifle and tipsy cake, all manner of sweet biscuits, and of course, trays of Rare Confectionery sweets.

Greer noted the platters with Beatrice's toffee nestled among the chocolates and small marzipan hearts with a smile. She must be in the other refreshment room for he'd seen neither her nor Miss Charlotte.

"May I suggest you have a piece of toffee or a chocolate?" he advised his companion.

Lady Emily nodded. "I was about to indulge," she agreed. "The Duke and Duchess of Pelham have made us all so welcome. What a grand start to the Season."

She seemed a thoughtful lady with whom he couldn't find fault. How lucky, and at his first ball, too. They each placed sweets upon small saucers and moved away from the table to make room for others.

At that moment, their hosts strolled in to make sure their guests were having a good time.

"How is everything, Mr. Carson, Lady Emily?" the duchess asked.

"Very fine," Lady Emily replied. "Thank you, Your Grace."

"Yes," Greer agreed. "It is the best fandango I've ever been to."

The duke laughed out loud, but his duchess looked perplexed, and Lady Emily might even have gasped.

"Not a word you normally use, I take it." Greer supposed it was a tad informal.

"No," the duke said, "not for a ball."

Greer felt certain Beatrice would have approved of the word. He shrugged as they moved off. Lady Emily still regarded him curiously.

"I suppose it's like calling a New York City cotillion a barn dance."

"I'm sure I wouldn't know," Lady Emily said, popping a chocolate in her mouth. After she'd chewed and swallowed, she added, "Having never been to America or danced in a barn. Will you escort me back to my mother? I believe she has returned to our table."

He was quite certain of it, since the woman in question had been watching them like a hawk from the moment Greer had collected Lady Emily from the St. George's table for their dance. And Lady St. George's eyes had continued to rest on him during the small meal. He'd seen her stand on tiptoe to view them better when they'd found two seats in the drawing room.

"I wish you had another empty place on your card," he told Lady Emily.

"Mr. Carson, although you might wish it and I might not mind it, one doesn't usually say such a preference out loud, at least, not upon first meeting."

"I see." *Should he apologize?* "May I hope if we meet again at another dance, you will look favorably upon my writing on your dance card?"

She smiled. "You may. Thank you for the dance, and the company."

Nodding to him, she took a seat next to her mother, and Greer knew he'd been dismissed although not set down. After all, Lady Emily had said she wouldn't mind dancing again, which was a good thing since, of all the eleven dance partners he'd had, he liked her the best. Apart from Beatrice, naturally.

With time to spare before the end of the intermission,

he went in search of the toffee-maker. He found her on the arm of a man leading her from the dining room.

"Now you don't need to take me back to the ballroom, my lord. This is my next partner," she said, fibbing outrageously.

"Very well, Miss Rare-Foure. I thank you for the dance and for the pleasant company while dining." He bowed, she nodded, and the man left.

"Thank goodness you showed up, Mr. Carson. That was the longest meal I've ever had. The only thing more interminable was the dance before it."

"I take it that young man was not to your liking."

She sighed, and her bosom rose delightfully. Greer made an effort to lock his gaze on her blue eyes and keep it there.

"He was extremely dry, to put it mildly. Stilted and proper and full of himself."

He smiled. "I think I met a few of his twin sisters tonight."

Suddenly, Miss Charlotte appeared with her parents.

"Everyone enjoying themselves?" Mr. Foure asked, holding a glass of brandy that looked beyond inviting.

"Yes," Beatrice said, not sounding entirely convincing. "However, I think Amity let the dinner intermission lag a little too long."

Charlotte laughed. "No, it was that pompous snout-nose you were with who lagged."

"Charlotte!" Mrs. Rare-Foure admonished. "We can use that term when alone, but not here."

"Why not?" the youngest Rare-Foure asked.

"Because there are so many of them lurking about."

Mr. Foure coughed. "I see you eyeing my drink, Mr. Carson. Sadly, it is not for guests. Only for fathers-in-law. Come along, wife." He led Mrs. Rare-Foure away.

"They seem very pleased with themselves tonight," Miss Charlotte observed.

"They weren't stuck with Lord Prig for the past three hours," Beatrice said.

"It was forty minutes, I think," Greer told her.

Beatrice rolled her eyes. "How have you fared, Mr. Carson?"

Her gaze seemed to pin him in place, a disconcerting sensation.

"I wish I had claimed another of your dances," he heard himself confess. "And yours, as well," he added belatedly to Miss Charlotte. When they both raised identical eyebrows, he explained, "It's nice to relax for a moment and speak freely."

"Agreed," said Beatrice.

"And me?" Miss Charlotte demanded her turn.

"Very well, how have *you* fared?" her sister asked her. "Any conquests yet?"

Miss Charlotte shook her head. "No one caught my particular interest, but I keep telling you, I am not on a husband hunt. In any case, I wouldn't go out of my way to dance with any one of them again."

"Don't be too quick to judge. It's not that easy to suss out someone's nature while dancing," Greer said. "I hardly even heard most of my partners speak, but I enjoyed the intermission with Lady Emily."

"The dark-haired lady in the cream gown?" Beatrice asked.

"The very one." Odd that Miss Rare-Foure had noticed with whom he'd danced and dined since they'd been in different rooms.

"I think I danced with her brother," Charlotte mused, "or maybe it was a cousin. He was perfectly able to speak on the dance floor. Too able!"

"What do you mean?" Beatrice asked, as they started walking together across the hall to the ballroom, carried along by the other guests.

"Asking questions."

He noticed Beatrice stiffen. "What kind of questions?" she asked.

"Nosy ones. About me and you," Miss Charlotte added.

"What did you say?" Beatrice asked, her voice filled with dread.

"I said I was the younger sister of a duchess and an heiress, happy to be out in—"

"An heiress!" Beatrice stopped in her tracks, and Greer stopped with her as did Miss Charlotte. They were nearly trampled by the guests behind until the flow of people rearranged itself and began to go around them. Greer felt like a stubborn mule stopped in a small stream.

"What can you mean?" Beatrice asked, keeping her voice hushed but sounding frazzled.

Miss Charlotte looked as cheerful as ever. "I told people who asked that you are a toffee heiress. I may have mentioned treacle, too."

Even Greer had no words for that, watching as Beatrice struggled not to shatter with fury on the spot. This could become a loud and inappropriately nasty discussion, disapproved strongly by that ladies' book Miss Charlotte had been quoting.

"I wouldn't worry, Miss Rare-Foure," he said, hoping to calm her. "Hardly anyone who is here has been in your shop. As you told me, most of the nobility send in their servants. And even if they have entered, you are usually in the back. Plus, your sister is a duchess. I doubt they know her origins either."

They'd gone over all this before, but she'd gone from red in the face to quite pale.

"You are insane," Beatrice said through gritted teeth. "Insane, I say. Both of you! Will people really believe my secret family has amassed a fortune from toffee? How would that even be possible?"

Miss Charlotte, bless her heart, started to giggle, seeming utterly unconcerned by her sister's distress.

"Well, they nearly have, haven't they?" Greer pointed out. "A fortune from confectionery."

"No, Mr. Carson, not a fortune. That term implies a great deal of money, such as the Duke of Pelham might lay claim to or a viscount with whom I was dancing earlier. It does not bespeak of my parents' modest livelihood. And what has that got to do with me? How would that make me an heiress in any case?"

"What if your family had some of those treacle wells I've heard about?" he asked.

At his question, both girls fell silent, looking at him with wide eyes, and then Charlotte burst out laughing, although Beatrice merely shook her head. He thought he heard her mutter something very unkind under her breath.

Then she looked him squarely in the eyes. "Those are a myth, a story, a tale told by drunkards and idiots," she hissed, "or by shifty spielers usually to unsuspecting green youths who haven't a clue what's o'clock, often in some swindle designed to separate them from their wealth. I can tell you precisely how treacle is made, and I assure you, it does not come from a well!"

"Then I was the victim of a shoddyocracy," he mused.

Miss Charlotte, who was wiping her eyes, paused at the word making him assume she was unfamiliar with it, but all she said was, "Treacle wells!"

Mr. Carson shrugged. "Then what are they?"

"The best I can determine," Beatrice said, "is the confusion comes from an etymological mistake between the Middle English word *treacle* and the Old French *triacle, which had to do with healing, and so any of the healing wells in England became treacle wells, like the famous one at St Margaret's church in Binsey.*"

Greer considered what she said. "So, the dormouse in Mr. Carroll's book about that Alice girl?"

Beatrice's expression became irate. "If you are going to take the word of a talking dormouse in a children's story over mine, then I cannot help you."

"What about the mines?" he persisted.

"The mines, Mr. Carson?" He'd hoped to soothe her, but as she said those words, she seemed nearly apoplectic.

"My first night here, I went to a pub," he told them both,

"and the bartender told me about treacle mines."

At this, the toffee-maker slapped a hand to her forehead. Miss Charlotte lifted a shoulder in a delicate shrug, tapping her toe as the music had begun again.

"Mr. Carson, treacle is boiled sugar syrup," Beatrice annunciated each word carefully, as if he were a dull-wit. "If you wish to persist in believing it comes out of the ground like coal, or from a well like water, so be it. But treacle mines are known to be an absolute hoax, a joke, and a treacle miner means simply a lazy, unemployed do-nothing. Why? Because no one mines treacle!"

She'd raised her voice along with her annoyance. "And none of this has helped me feel any better about being labelled a 'toffee heiress.'"

"Actually, a 'treacle toffee heiress,'" Charlotte corrected.

Beatrice clenched her fists, and he was sure her head would explode.

"Why are you so worried anyway?" Charlotte asked. "What's wrong with being known as the mysterious, blue-eyed toffee heiress?"

Beatrice moaned. "One can go to prison for impersonating nobility."

Charlotte shook her head. "Then it's a good thing you aren't doing any such thing. An heiress isn't noble, and you didn't make any claims. I did."

Suddenly, Amity was in their midst, and Mr. Carson could tell she was buzzing with bother, hopefully not about her sister being an heiress.

"All three of you are in terrible trouble. You've upset the entire gathering."

CHAPTER NINE

Beatrice felt the floor shift upon hearing those words. The look on her older sister's face was not one she'd ever seen before.

"What did we do?" she asked, slanting a glance at Charlotte who gaped back at her. "Was it the toffee heiress nonsense?"

Amity frowned. "Thankfully, I have no idea what nonsense you're talking about. But all of you," she included Mr. Carson in her censure, "left your partners standing on the edge of the dance floor awaiting you when the quadrille started."

Charlotte gasped, Beatrice's stomach sank, and Mr. Carson appeared shaken. With their first foray into high society, they'd committed one of the worst errors.

"Mr. Carson's partner took up with one of your gentlemen—Charlotte's, I believe—and they tried to slip in when the dance had already begun, causing a few moments' mayhem. The other gentleman stood out like a dog at a horse race. It was awful." The duchess shook her head in dismay. "He made an awkward bow to no one in particular and backed away from the dancers. I tried to reach him to partner him, but he'd already moved to the far end of the room and too much of the dance had transpired."

"Oh dear!" Charlotte said.

Beatrice snatched at her dance card, still on her wrist. There was the name, Lord Beechum. "Blast!" she exclaimed. "I will go at once and apologize, but we won't be able to dance tonight since the rest of my card is full."

"Sometimes hosts add dances," Amity said, "but it's always handled before intermission since it would cause more people to be left out if we tried to tack one on the end now." She wrung her hands. "Henry is a bit peeved, as well."

"Oh dear!" Charlotte said again.

"Stop saying that," Beatrice snapped. "It makes my insides twist each time you do."

"I'm going to the edge of the dance floor," Mr. Carson said, "to apologize to my partner as soon as I see her. If I could only remember what she looked like. I knew approximately which table she would be at, but . . . ," he trailed off uncertainly.

"She has pale brown hair, a pink dress, and is on the taller side, like Beatrice. Moreover, she's with Charlotte's partner, so you two can stand together in shame."

They hurried off, and then Amity looked at her again. "That was badly done, Bea."

"I know. We were talking about treacle and didn't hear the music begin. Or, at least, I didn't. I was too busy taking Mr. Carson to task, but it was really all Charlotte's fault. She—"

Amity held up her hand, and Bea could see the sparkling engagement ring and the thick band of gold on her ring finger. Somehow her shorter, milder sister had become more commanding and even formidable since becoming a duchess.

"It doesn't matter now. Before the dance ends and you are approached by your next partner, you must go make amends with Lord Beechum and beg his forgiveness."

"Beg?" Beatrice muttered.

"It's only an expression," Amity said, pushing her forward.

With assuredly little time left before she had to dance with—she looked at her card—*Lord Tuppence?* That couldn't be correct, but it was what the blighter's handwriting looked like. With probably a minute or two to spare, she would, indeed, ask Lord Beechum's forgiveness and hope he wasn't one of the gentlemen to whom Charlotte had fibbed.

"Ah, here she is, the wayward heiress, herself."

Drat! He had already danced with Charlotte. Maybe Beatrice should spread the rumor her little sister was the Marchioness of Marzipan. But that could land them both in trouble.

"My lord, please accept my sincerest apologies," she said, attempting a deep yet graceful curtsey, which she hoped was appropriate under the circumstances. "I would not have missed our dance for the world. I found myself"—*why hadn't she come up with an excuse?*—"stuck in . . . ." She could hardly say the ladies' retiring room as that brought up a vivid image she would rather not put into his lordship's mind.

"In toffee," he provided, a devilish gleam in his eye. "Were you stuck in toffee, perhaps?"

She laughed lightly, although she felt like being sick on his perfectly shiny boots.

"Would that were the case, my lord. I was stuck in a conversation with two rascals, as it turned out. Although my dance card is full this evening, I hope you will allow me to make it up to you at another dance."

"Very good of you to offer. Please, don't worry overmuch about it," he said, neither accepting nor declining. "The dance is ending, so we'd best find our next partners." With a shallow bow, he walked away.

His ego was probably a little bruised. She ought to have said she really had been stuck in toffee, because to learn she'd been gabbing away had insulted him further. She was a twitter-pated ninny, to be sure. Now, to find Lord Tuppence.

BEATRICE COULDN'T WAIT TO speak with Mr. Carson the following day, certain he would come to the shop. Sure enough, just after three o'clock, he arrived. With the shop momentarily empty, Charlotte whistled with infuriatingly loud sharpness, calling her from the back room.

"You used to do that solely to express happiness," she remarked to Charlotte as she parted the curtain, "not to summon people. I don't care for it, not one bit."

She eyed the American. There he was, handsome as ever, smiling and appearing more relaxed than at any time the previous evening.

"Maybe I am simply happy to see Mr. Carson," Charlotte protested. "But I will try to stop. It's simply so easy to be heard. If Amity had whistled in such a way last night to gain our attention, we wouldn't have missed the start of that dance."

"We did make a hash of it, didn't we?" Mr. Carson said with his good-natured ease. "I'm going to send over a bottle of brandy to the duke to thank him for the entire thing, if you think that's the right thing to do. Or is that too small a gesture? Should I send a horse or something?"

Beatrice chuckled. "I know my brother-in-law enjoys a good glass of French brandy. I'm sure that will be welcome."

"What about your sister? May I send the duchess something, too? Or is that considered too forward?"

"I'm certain she would appreciate any gesture." Beatrice had to admit to herself, she was impressed by Mr. Carson's thoughtfulness.

"I know she likes chocolate," he said, "but that seems inappropriate."

"True. Perhaps a bouquet of flowers," she suggested.

"Why don't you two deliver the tokens of *our* appreciation tonight," Charlotte interrupted, "and have dinner with them?"

Beatrice exchanged a look with Mr. Carson and knew he was thinking the same as she was.

"I believe, dear sister, we should leave Amity and the duke alone tonight. They've seen far too much of us lately as it is, what with all the dance and etiquette lessons. And still, we managed our egregious mistake."

"I agree with Miss Rare-Foure," Mr. Carson said to Charlotte. "Let me send flowers and brandy by way of courier, and leave the Pelhams in peace." He turned to her again. "How did you fare the rest of the evening?"

She and Charlotte had gone home with their parents, and Mr. Carson had gone back to his hotel in a hired hackney, giving them no chance to speak after their *faux pas*.

"Lord Beechum mentioned toffee," she confessed, sending a glare to Charlotte who looked unperturbed by any implied rebuke. "And he didn't warmly accept my apology or my request for a dance at another time. In fact, he seemed quite chilly."

"His loss," Mr. Carson said. "Any other prospects?"

"A few of the gentlemen were pleasant. None stepped upon my toes. I'm not sure I could put most of their names to their faces if my life depended upon it."

"I felt the same," Charlotte said. "But there will be new faces at every ball, especially the larger ones encompassing the previous Season's eligible gentlemen."

"*Hm,*" Mr. Carson said. "The men might be all right from last Season. However, for my part, I will wonder why the ladies were left on the shelf and not snatched up."

"That is a dreadful thing to say," Beatrice defended her sex. "'Snatched up,' indeed! Maybe a perfectly wonderful young lady, one who would make an ideal wife, didn't find any of the men to her liking last year, and therefore, she shelved herself."

"Maybe, Miss Rare-Foure. Don't get your dander up. We're not even speaking about people we know."

He was right, but she didn't like the sentiment all the same. It reminded her too closely of her own situation, shelved even without a Season. But that was in the past. Thanks to Amity, her future had opened once again. She supposed it was also thanks to Mr. Carson for convincing her.

"How did you get on last night?" she asked him. "Did you manage to make it right with the lady who had to dance with Charlotte's intended partner?"

"Not really. Apparently, the duchess was correct to be distressed at our behavior and how we'd disrupted the ball. The lady snubbed me spectacularly. And each of my next seven partners made mention of it, saying how glad they were I'd kept my promise to them. You would think I had reneged on a marriage proposal."

"The duke caught me between dances and gave me a very stern look," Charlotte said with a sigh.

"Is that all?" Beatrice asked. "Before we left, when you went to find Mother and Father, His Grace told me he would be hesitant to introduce any more gentlemen to me if that was how I was going to behave." She recalled the awful moment. "I tried to explain what a singular occurrence it was, but I think Amity will have to smooth things over with her husband if we are to hope for any further help from that quarter. We treat the duke as one of us, but these born-and-bred noblemen truly think differently than we do."

"Agreed," Mr. Carson said. "He also told me I would never catch myself a lady if I treated them so shabbily. He reckoned I could not get away with even one more misstep, and that had best be my first and my last."

They all sighed together. "Shall I put the kettle on?" Charlotte asked.

"I would prefer a glass of whiskey, frankly," Mr. Carson said.

"Sorry," Beatrice told him, wearing an exaggerated expression of woe, "we are all out of hard spirits."

"Just as well," Charlotte said. "It's time for me to leave. I've cleaned up. All you have to do is—"

"I know how to lock up," she snapped.

"She also knows how to chase away your customers," Mr. Carson said, not very chivalrously.

"Please, Bea, don't do that," Charlotte said, going to the back room to remove her apron and get her coat and hat.

"You look very smartly dressed today," Mr. Carson told her, and she did a twirl before him, blushing prettily, until Beatrice wondered why someone hadn't *snatched up* her sister the previous night.

Probably because most of the gentlemen at Amity's hadn't been able to see that far past their own upturned noses!

Perhaps this whole thing was a waste of time, putting middle-class shopgirls in with the nobility, except Mr. Carson still had every reason to expect success.

"I have my art class tonight," Charlotte said, explaining why she looked better than her usual everyday garb. "I probably won't see you until breakfast."

"Have fun." Beatrice watched her go.

"What are you thinking?" Mr. Carson asked.

"We all wonder if she has her cap set at her friend's brother who also attends art class. That would explain her lack of interest in finding a husband during the Season."

Instantly, Beatrice wished she could call back her words. She had no business gossiping about her own family. "I'm sorry. I shouldn't have disclosed such an intimacy about my own sister."

"Perhaps because we are extremely used to each other by now, Miss Rare-Foure. I feel as if I've known you a longer time than is truly the case, and I consider you my friend. I would never break your confidence by disclosing anything you tell me."

"Thank you. I understand how you feel, and I feel the same way."

Her statement engendered a silence that nearly belied their words of being friendly. Beatrice thought it not entirely comfortable, yet neither too awkward, either. And the strange interlude passed quickly.

"Have you finished making toffee for today?" he asked, breaking the odd tension between them.

"As it happens, I have."

"Good." He looked around the shop, and she wondered if she should give him something to taste. Her sisters were far more congenial in that regard, but she went around the counter and considered her options.

"I was filled with energetic productivity today, getting my toffee made. Probably due to our great *triumph* of last night," she added wryly, placing a flower-shaped marzipan sweet and a plain chocolate with fondant filling onto a small porcelain plate. She looked over the counter at him, and he smiled.

"Onward and upward, as they say, Miss Rare-Foure."

"I suppose." Wordlessly, she offered him the samples, and he ate them thoughtfully.

"In this case, however, sales have been down a little the past few weeks," she admitted, "so I didn't need to make as much as I have in the past."

"Not good," he said, handing her the plate.

"How can you say that? That's the finest marzipan and chocolate in London!" She was ready to give him a jab in the nose on behalf of her sisters.

"I meant the downturn in sales, *not* the confectionery. Truth be told, though, I prefer your toffee to either of those."

She felt her cheeks warm, immensely pleased and hoping he wasn't saying such only because she was standing in front of him. In any case, she went back to the display, put some plain toffee into a bag, and handed it to him.

"How much?" he asked.

"No charge, Mr. Carson," she said, and for the first time felt the joy in giving her craft away for the other person's pleasure.

"Thank you." He put a piece in his mouth, taking care to suck it while he tucked the bag in his coat pocket.

She watched his mouth as he enjoyed the hard confection, a very attractive mouth, to be sure. When he started to chew, she raised a hand.

"Best to suck, Mr. Carson."

"My teeth are strong, I assure you."

Nonetheless, she noticed he pushed the chunk of toffee into his cheek to melt and continued speaking. "May I ask whether your family advertises?"

"We do. Perhaps not enough, or maybe our ads need to change. My father handles all that. Do you know about such things?"

"A little." He didn't enlighten her further. "Have you used your sister's new connection?"

"*Used* it?" she asked, wondering if she was going to like where this was going. "If you are not in a hurry, you can tell me what you mean. I can't close up for another hour. Would you care for a cup of tea?"

He didn't hesitate. "Yes, I would," and without further discussion, he followed her into the back room.

Putting the kettle on, Beatrice tamped down the notion that there was something vaguely improper about the empty shop, the single man, their isolation, and the back room. However, she didn't feel threatened by him for an instant. On more than one occasion in the past, she'd experienced trepidation when a couple came in directly before she closed and seemed to linger too long. She was glad Charlotte kept the cash box under the counter out of sight. Mr. Carson, however, gave her no such alarming notions, neither for their profits, nor for her person.

Behind her she heard loud sucking sounds and smiled to herself.

"You were saying, Mr. Carson?"

He chomped a few moments and swallowed. "I wonder if your ads could say something along the lines of 'The Duke of Pelham's favorite confectionery.'"

Beatrice nodded. "That's certainly not a lie. I shall mention it to Father."

"I suppose you don't want to say 'Our chocolate is made by a duchess,' or something like that, in order to bring people in for the sheer novelty."

That made her laugh as she scooped tea into the teapot. "No, I don't think my sister would want that. She was worried from the start whether she might tarnish the duke's polished veneer, and turn all of London's *ton* topsy-turvy with the massive infraction of a nobleman marrying a shopkeeper's daughter. Amity was expecting the ladies to faint and the men to bear arms against her."

Mr. Carson didn't dismiss it out of hand. "I can see where she might have had concerns. Maybe if her husband had been a lesser aristocrat, her fears might have come true. But from what I understand, one can hardly shun a duke, or at least, one does so at one's peril. He is just about the biggest toad in the puddle."

She blinked at him. *The biggest toad?* It was as good a way as any, she supposed, to describe a duke.

"You're correct. Even the other noblemen must be careful not to offend him. That's why our angering the duke was such a dreadful thing to do. He truly could destroy your plans if he put a bad word in for you, as assuredly he can help us all with a good one."

After pouring the boiling water into the brown Betty, she tugged the knitted blue cozy over it, and left the tea to steep while she retrieved two mugs and set them on the copper counter beside the stove.

"No refined cups and saucers here, Mr. Carson," she told him. "And only one stool."

"Please, sit if you like," he offered. "I'm happy to stand."

Ignoring his offer—*she was a shopgirl but not a barbarian who would take the single stool*—she reached into the cold storage for the bottle of milk and poured some into the bottom of both cups.

"I definitely will speak with my father about our advertisements. Perhaps you would like to come to dinner some evening soon and tell him more of your ideas. I take it you have some knowledge, maybe even expertise."

He shrugged his broad shoulders, and she sighed inwardly. If he didn't need a titled lady, she might find herself attempting to catch his interest. He had surely caught hers.

"I helped my uncle with the advertising for his business."

"Railroad ads?" she asked.

He nodded. "Assuring customers of their safety and comfort on the line. That type of thing." Switching topics, he asked, "May I pour for such a gracious lady?"

"Thank you," she said, batting her eyelids with extra speed, hoping he was joking the way she was. However, his intense gaze looked utterly serious.

"That is exactly the offer you should make to a lady if you visit her at her home."

He coughed. "I know that. I remember your sister's lessons, Miss Rare-Foure. I am offering in earnest." With that, he picked up the teapot and poured into both cups without splashing a drop.

"Well done," she said.

"And sugar, my lady?"

She froze as did he.

"Sorry, I'm practicing." Without waiting for an answer, he scooped a teaspoonful into each of their cups and stirred.

"Better to wait for an answer, *my lord,*" she mocked him, lifting her mug in salute. "Some people take no sugar or a hundred spoonfuls. You might have ruined my tea."

"True." He lifted his cup and tapped it against hers. "And how many do you normally take?'

"Exactly one," she admitted.

"Ah ha!" he exclaimed, sending her a smug grin.

They sipped in silence, and she wished she could think of a funny story. Or better yet, Beatrice almost wished she could feel crabbed at him as she had in the past. Instead, her thoughts of him were all warm and happy. He was awfully nice, far too appealing for her to ignore his appearance, and on top of that, he smelled good. Pears soap, if she wasn't mistaken.

She cleared her throat. "Of course, this business of taking tea is all easier when seated and with a table between."

"It is nice *not* to have a table between us," he said.

Again, she froze. Looking up from her cup, she found his eyes trained upon her and experienced a strange twinge in her stomach. She'd hoped to feel the very same with some gentleman the previous evening but, alas, had not.

"A biscuit," she offered in order to have a reason for turning away.

"I will not say no. Although by the time I leave here, I believe I will have eaten all the sweet things I can handle for one day."

She found a tin of Amity's favorite Cadbury's chocolate-covered biscuits and offered him one. They munched happily, and he watched as she dunked hers in her tea.

"What are you doing? Is that something only females are allowed to do, or may I do that?"

"Of course," she said and laughed. "Don't dip it in too long or you'll have crumbs and grease floating atop your tea, but a little warmth makes the chocolate taste even better."

He did as she said, took a bite, and made a face. "And it gives you a soggy biscuit."

"I told you not to immerse it for too long."

"There are rules in England for everything," he said.

"Most probably true," she agreed.

"I'm sure there are rules against my being here this very instant, having tea with a beautiful woman."

She opened her mouth, then closed it. *He thought her a beautiful woman?*

"Yes, there are rules," she said finally, thinking she should tell him how, if discovered, he might damage his chances of securing a lady. And if her mother were the one discovering them again, he might get whacked heartily with the shop's broom.

"Sorry, I embarrassed you," he said, draining his cup. "I should let you get back to whatever you do when the toffee has been made."

She nodded. It would be best if he left. When they were alone, without the distraction of dance lessons, without Charlotte to interject every few moments, there was entirely too much time to simply contemplate the man himself.

He handed her the cup and their fingers touched. They both stared at their hands, and the next thing Beatrice knew, he'd set the mug down and pulled her into his arms.

In the blink of an eye, she was drawn against Mr. Carson's broad chest, and instinctively, she raised her hands up to his shoulders, feeling his strength beneath her fingers.

Looking up at him, Beatrice knew what would happen next. And if it didn't happen directly, then the moment would be lost. She would pull away, and he would probably mumble an apology.

The American claimed her mouth swiftly, his warm, firm lips covering hers. It was as if someone had stoked the embers of a banked fire. One moment she was placidly drinking tea, and the next, her body tingled with sizzling heat.

His arms went around her, and his hands rested low on her back, cinching her in against him.

She focused on tasting him, breathing him—*yes, the fresh woodsy smell of Pears soap*—and memorizing every second of her first real kiss. His head tilted, and, naturally, she tilted, too. In the wrong direction, as it turned out, for their noses bumped awkwardly.

Quickly, before he gave up, she slanted the opposite way, and their mouths seemed to fit perfectly. His lips moved against hers as if he were consuming her. Shocked to her toes but delighted, she did the same. It was wickedly exciting.

And then she heard the shop bell.

CHAPTER TEN

B reaking apart as if they were literally on fire, Beatrice put her finger to her lips, making sure Mr. Carson said not a word. She knew there was a reason she didn't like customers!

His lovely blue-gray eyes were wide, probably just like hers, and she could tell he realized the perilousness of their situation. They should never have gone in the back, not even to drink tea. She'd known that, and yet she'd willingly flirted with disaster.

Looking down at her dress, making sure her apron was still straight, she dashed out of the curtained back.

"GOOD DAY." GREER HEARD Beatrice greet the customer, sounding far cheerier than her usual self.

He didn't move an inch, didn't dare make even the smallest sound.

"What can I get you?" she said, sounding a little rushed.

"I'm not certain as yet," came a male reply, and Greer could imagine that response nettling the toffee-maker.

"I heard you make excellent confectionery, and thus, here I am, Lord Dunlop, at your service."

"No, my lord, I am at *your* service," she intoned, and he knew what that cost her. Any man who wandered into a sweet shop and had to promote his title was probably a stuffed shirt of great magnitude.

"Yes, naturally," the man replied.

"We have many fine chocolates, some flavored, some not. We have toffee with nuts and without, smothered in chocolate and plain. And we have marzipan in many shapes and sizes."

Greer could imagine her pointing out each shelf of confections to the lord.

"I can put a smaller quantity in a bag, or if you prefer a greater amount, then we have pretty tins."

"You are a helpful girl, aren't you?" he said.

This engendered no audible remark, so Beatrice must be simply staring at the man, hopefully smiling not scowling.

After another moment, the customer added, "You do have pretty tins, indeed."

Wait, what? Greer thought the man's voice had taken on a distinctly lascivious tone.

However, in a normal voice, Beatrice asked, "Would you care to sample something, my lord?"

The man chuckled. "Definitely. How much will it cost me?"

The hair on the back of Greer's neck stood up.

"Samples are complimentary, my lord. Perhaps a chocolate?"

The customer chuckled again. "Yes, let me start with a chocolate."

There was movement as Beatrice got one from the display case. Greer knew she would place it on one of their delicate plates and hand it over the counter.

Therefore, he was all the more shocked to hear the man ask, "Would you place it on my tongue?"

The rogue! Greer's hands had already balled into fists before he realized it.

"No, my lord. That would be unsanitary."

For the first time, she sounded annoyed.

"That's a clever new word, isn't it? I take your meaning, miss, and I can think of more unsanitary things we could do and enjoy far more than eating chocolate."

He heard Beatrice stomp her foot.

"Doubtful," came her insolent reply. "Do you wish to buy something, my lord, or not?"

Greer had to hand it to her. She kept her aplomb and even sounded bored by her lewd tormenter.

"What if I reach over this counter and fondle your bubbies? Merely to sample, of course. For free, as you promised."

"I must ask you to leave," came her tone, calm and firm.

"I'm a baron," he said.

"And I'm a duke's sister-in-law," she shot back, quick as a whip.

Greer wanted to cheer.

"Liar," said the man, not sounding at all pleased, perhaps from fear she was telling the truth. But then, undoubtedly thinking the odds of a nobleman's relation working in a store were slim, his syrupy, languid tone was back. "For that prevarication, I will ask for more than a small sample. It looks like you have a back room."

Greer took in a breath. Naturally, he would rescue Beatrice if the scoundrel tried to drag her into the back, but her reputation would be shredded by his presence already in hiding. And this seemed precisely the type of villain who would seek to use it against her, and perhaps come sniffing back at a more suitable moment to catch her alone.

"That is a workroom for employees," she bit out. "It seems you are not interested in our confectionery, so I must ask you again to leave. I'm closing up the shop now."

"Why don't you close it and lock the door, and I'll let you have a taste of me."

That was it! He couldn't believe any man—never mind a baron—would go into a shop in broad daylight and harass a shopgirl in such a fashion.

Quietly and as fast as possible, he removed his hat, slid out of his coat, and rolled up the sleeves of his white shirt. Then, remembering his ascot, he loosened it and tossed it aside. He wished he had something like a butcher's apron, but he would have to try his best.

"I've finished taking inventory, sister," Greer proclaimed loudly as he parted the curtain, attempting an English accent, "and I've swept the floor."

The so-called baron went white as a sheet.

"Oh, good, another customer," Greer said, as if only then noticing him. "You made it in the nick of time, good sir. We're about to close up."

He glanced at Beatrice who appeared red-cheeked, either with anger at the baron or embarrassment at Greer's sudden appearance, but she took a deep breath and returned to her normal, creamy complexion in seconds. Even her lovely blue eyes danced with merriment.

"Thank you, *brother*. I believe this gentleman was about to make a large purchase indeed. Fortunately, you haven't yet gone to Teavey's for your pugilistic workout. The baron, here, might need you to carry his order."

"I am looking forward to knocking someone into a cocked hat, for sure," Greer said, flexing his hands in front of him. "But I can wait a minute and carry out his lordship's purchases."

"No . . . no, that won't be necessary," the rogue said. "Give me a pound of toffee."

But Beatrice was shaking her head.

"No," the baron corrected. "A pound each of chocolates and toffee, and what did you say that was?"

"Marzipan," Beatrice said curtly.

"A pound of that, too."

"The tins are extra," she told him, "and we only accept ready money from new accounts. You cannot put it on credit."

"Naturally. Credit, indeed!" he said as if he would never do such a thing.

Beatrice named the enormous cost, enough for three dinners out if Greer recalled her first coin lesson correctly.

The baron hesitated.

"I am sorely looking forward to beating the tar out of someone at Teavey's," Greer said. "I can hardly wait to get started."

The man's coin purse came out at once, and he placed the amount on the counter. Beatrice drew it toward her and then proceeded to fill the order in silence. It felt like a long, tense time while she filled three pound-size tins, which she finally placed on the counter.

Snatching them up and without a word of farewell, the baron left, leaving the door open wide.

Greer went to close it, feeling certain that particular rascal wouldn't return to harass his toffee-maker. *His? Where had that inappropriate and inaccurate thought come from?*

In any case, he hoped she wasn't too upset. The thought of a tearful, frightened Beatrice made his stomach knot.

When he turned to her, however, she smiled and then began to laugh. He watched her beautiful face, relaxed and happy after what had just transpired, and couldn't imagine another female who would react in such a way.

After she caught her breath, she picked up the coins in front of her and bent down. He heard the cash box open and close. When she stood straight, she looked right at him.

"You were clever, Mr. Carson, even if I have no idea what a cocked hat has to do with it, or beating tar. Some American sayings, I suppose. When I saw you emerge, I thought you were adding to my woes, and then I realized you'd called me 'sister.' The rolled-up sleeves were an excellent touch. Pity we didn't have a proper apron for you."

"That's what I was thinking." He wanted to laugh off the

entire incident, but deep down, he was disturbed by it. "What if I hadn't been here?"

"I would have handled it as I have before."

Before? "Does this happen often?"

"No, but each of us has experienced some unwanted advances, even when there are two of us here. I must admit, I felt comforted and emboldened, knowing you were in the back room . . . taking inventory!" She smiled broadly.

"I couldn't think what else I might be doing," he admitted. "I confess to a feeling of worry over what might have occurred."

"As I said, it wasn't the first time." Beatrice bent down and retrieved something. "We use a bat when necessary, although that has happened very few times." Reaching up, she wielded a cricket bat, waving it over her head.

"Most of the lecherous men are popinjays and don't take kindly to being threatened. Sometimes, I honestly think the noblemen like the one today believe I will be honored to provide whatever service they demand, simply because they have a title. That idiot made sure to tell me he was a baron, and it seemed to go from bad to worse quickly after that."

"It did. I apologize on behalf of my kind." Greer felt a sense of outrage. She ought to be able to sell confectionery without fear of assault.

"Your kind?" she asked, sounding amused.

"Men, in general, particularly those who take advantage of—" he broke off recalling the kiss that now seemed a lifetime ago. With shame, he recalled taking hold of her and kissing her, the feel of her warm body pressed against him and her sweet lips under his.

Obviously, Beatrice could tell where his thoughts had gone, for she shook her head slightly and blushed. He hoped she didn't include him in the lecherous men who sought to take advantage of her—or in his case, succeeded in doing so.

He swallowed. "Now, I must apologize for my own behavior. It was not well done of me. You should probably slap my face." He took a few steps in her direction so she could do so if she wished.

"Probably," she agreed, looking solemn but not angry.

"I would prefer you didn't use the bat, however."

In answer, she put it away behind the counter.

"And we shouldn't be alone again if I am going to behave like an uncivilized animal," he added.

"Are you?" she asked. "Again, I mean?"

He groaned. She did think ill of him for kissing her. *And why shouldn't she?* He had a goal to marry a lady, and Beatrice knew it. *Had that changed?* It hadn't. Any relationship he had with her had to stop at friendship. Kissing her, no matter how compelled he'd felt earlier, was beyond the pale and couldn't happen again. He could only blame an overwhelming compunction once, and it had been truly overwhelming. One moment, he'd been sipping tea, and the next thing he knew, when their fingers brushed, desire for her sang through his body. He'd given in to it without thinking.

If their kiss gave her the wrong idea, it would be his own fault. Moreover, the last thing he wanted to do was lead her on. Since a second occurrence must be construed as deliberate, he would never let that happen.

What could he say? "I truly am sorry."

"You should have placed the mug back upon the countertop and that wouldn't have happened," she said. "In the future, avoid touching ladies' hands, especially when they are not wearing gloves."

He ran a hand through his hair. "As I suspected," he said. "There are rules for everything, even tea cups."

She sighed and shrugged slightly. "I may close early, Mr. Carson. I think my mother will understand. Getting home in the early hours of the morning isn't conducive to working in a shop all day."

"No, I imagine it isn't. I confess I slept in."

"I confess I did, too," she said. "Yet, I'm tired in any case."

"Very well." She was right. He should leave, mainly because he'd been so surprised by the strong desire to kiss her, he wasn't positive it wouldn't come upon him again. Therefore, it was prudent not to put either of them at risk.

"I'll get my coat."

With her silence as agreement, he passed through the opening between the counters and went into the back room. Grabbing up his coat, he shrugged into it quickly, hell-bent on returning to the front before anyone else came in. Snatching up his hat, he passed through the curtain, to see she hadn't moved.

"Two days until the next ball," he reminded her.

"Without the benefit of it being in the familiar territory of my sister's home."

"I'm sure we will muddle through," Greer promised, not sure at all. Patting his pocket, he added, "Thank you for the toffee." And bit his tongue before he also thanked her for the most splendid kiss he'd ever had.

AS SOON AS THE door closed behind Mr. Carson, Beatrice took in a large ragged breath and blinked back unexpected tears. Then she did, in fact, lock up and flip the sign hanging from a pretty blue ribbon to indicate they were no longer open for business. After all, she'd made more from that awful louse of a baron than they'd made in the previous two days. She could afford to close up shop early.

Even if she hadn't received the windfall, she would have had to close. She needed peaceful quiet to tame her ardent emotions. That kiss for which Mr. Carson so blithely apologized had been sublime and soul-shaking. Alone, she could relive it, the way he drew her toward his person, wrapped his strong arms around her, held her with ungloved hands.

When his warm, firm lips touched hers, the world had shrunk to the back room of Rare Confectionery, and nothing else had existed.

If that awful lord hadn't intruded, they might have been kissing still.

She giggled nervously at the ridiculous thought. Of course, they wouldn't have still been kissing. However, it might have gone on a little longer. Perhaps long enough for Mr. Carson to realize they suited one another perfectly, regardless of her untitled state.

After all, with his personal wealth, he could buy some other country house. He didn't need that old Scottish abandoned manor. *Did he?*

The tears pricked her eyes again. Their encounter and the knowledge it could never lead to anything saddened her. Having already cleaned up her workstation and everything else except their mugs being washed, she set them in the sink and poured the last of the soapy water from a pot on the stove into them. Charlotte would deal with it in the morning or leave it for her to do when Beatrice went in later the next day. No matter.

Pouring the remainder of the tea down the drain, she tossed the leaves into the stove to help bank the coals and then finished the job. Thankfully, she had a fifteen-minute walk before she reached her doorstep, time enough to settle her thoughts and realize nothing had changed.

Before she left the back room, she spied a white cloth on the floor by the stool. Picking it up, she realized it was Mr. Carson's ascot. Without thinking, she buried her face in the soft material, breathing in his familiar scent. Her body tingled again.

Blue blazes! The American had worked his way into her heart and mind. She couldn't deny it. Stuffing the ascot into the seam pocket of her day dress, she straightened. She would find a husband at one of those horrid dances. And even if she didn't, Mr. Carson would never be hers.

CHAPTER ELEVEN

Beatrice kept an eye out for Mr. Carson from a table close to the refreshments. This was a far larger ball than her sister's. The fact they needed to provide beverages at two places around the edge of the dance floor indicated the difference. There would be no hearty meal as Amity had laid out, although Beatrice could see on her dance card there would be an intermission for some light refreshments served in another room.

Charlotte in pale peach satin and Beatrice in a gray-blue that reminded her of the American's eyes, along with their mother, had arrived separately from Mr. Carson for the sole reason that Felicity Rare-Foure wanted to attend. That evening's dance was at Sandrall Hall, a place she'd heard of since she was a young woman but had never been inside, and she'd decided to take her girls in their own carriage.

"It used to be considered *the* place to dance," their mother said, having already expressed her disappointment at a somewhat shabby appearance to the venue. "I suppose like many things, except for our confectionery, reputations sometimes outlast the truth. I hear we have dry bread to look forward to later, and this champagne is watery and warm."

"So is the lemonade," Charlotte said, but she seemed less bothered than their mother. She was intent on making sure her dance card became filled by the young gentlemen still arriving.

Beatrice cared about that, too, but she would feel better when Mr. Carson arrived and added his name to her card. Just in case every other partner turned out to be a dreadful bore.

Then she spotted him. He looked more animated, more handsome, more attractive than all the other people entering around him. And when he looked across the room, her heart sped up. *Oh dear!*

He saw her almost immediately, smiled broadly, and lifted a hand. However, instead of racing over, he made his way slowly, signing other ladies' cards until he reached them.

"Greetings," he said, bowing to each in turn, starting with their mother. "This is a larger gathering than I could have imagined. And so many single females in one place."

"And to think," Charlotte chimed in, "some come here every Saturday until the Season is over."

"Excessive," Beatrice snapped, feeling irritated. Then she recalled one thing. "You must hunt more carefully tonight, Mr. Carson. Many females here are not titled. I believe it is the only one on our list that has this many people from both upper and middle-class levels of society."

"I do recall, Miss Rare-Foure, but I thank you for the warning. Tonight, I will have to simply enjoy myself dancing and meeting people, practicing my etiquette, and not worrying so much about finding a lady. Unless there is an easy way to determine such."

"I would assume the introduction would do that," she said, realizing neither her mood nor her tone had improved.

"There are floor managers here," her mother pointed out, speaking to Mr. Carson. "I've seen two already. They have the white carnations in their lapels. If someone balks at your approaching them without prior introduction, although that seems to be the normal mode at Sandrall Hall, then you must ask one of those men to properly introduce you."

"Thank you, Mrs. Rare-Foure. I shall seek one out at once."

He bowed to each of them and turned away before Beatrice could find her voice. He was already a couple feet away when she spoke.

"Mr. Carson, will you not dance with me and my sister?"

He halted, then turned, with his eyes not quite meeting hers. "I didn't want to take up space on your cards and stop either of you from finding more desirable partners."

You are the most desirable partner to me. Luckily, that impossible thought remained hidden in her own brain.

"That's very considerate of you," Charlotte said. "And I do believe our cards are almost full."

"True," Beatrice murmured.

"Then I hope to see you at the intermission," Mr. Carson said. After bowing again, he walked away.

She knew her mother was staring at her, and she pointedly looked elsewhere.

"He is a thoughtful young man," Felicity Rare-Foure said evenly, and Beatrice kept her eyes trained on the final stragglers entering the room.

"Mm," Beatrice agreed, as two more men came toward their table and filled up their cards.

While Charlotte was fizzing with excitement, hardly able to wait for the first dance, Beatrice was suddenly weary and wished the evening were over. She'd taken a look into the eyes of each man who'd signed her card. She'd taken their measure as best she could. None of them could hold a candle to Mr. Carson. And for the life of her, she couldn't figure out why.

Perhaps it was simply knowing she couldn't have him that made him head and shoulders above the rest. Or maybe it was that kiss! A thought struck her. She should kiss a few more men, as she'd advised Amity once, so she could make sure of the spectacular nature of one kiss over another.

With that in mind, she cheered up. A few notes on a French horn heralded the start of the dancing.

"Wish us luck, Mother," Charlotte exclaimed, and the next instant, they were met by their partners and heading to the floor.

THE EVENING PROGRESSED AS he had imagined it would. Greer wished he hadn't seen the hurt look in Beatrice's eyes. *Those gorgeous eyes!* He had wanted to spare them both the temptation of being close to one another or, God forbid, the excitement of a waltz. So he'd walked away.

Each dance had become a distraction as he hunted to see where she was, whom she was with, and whether she appeared to be happy. To his satisfaction—and strangely, to his disappointment, too—she seemed perfectly content, whirling around the old oak floor.

For his part, the women were a little more eager to ask about his background than at the Duke of Pelham's exclusive ball. He realized most were hunting for a fortune if they couldn't catch a lord, and he hadn't come across a single titled lady all night. Nonetheless, what he'd said to Beatrice was correct, each event was good practice. He didn't leave anyone hanging without a partner or commit any other terrible errors, as far as he could tell, and his dancing improved every time he stepped onto the dance floor.

However, he wouldn't want to attend a ball like this again, one that turned out to be lacking the quarry he sought. Also, he had learned something the Duke of Pelham had told him and he'd previously dismissed—one should not sign up for every dance. It became tedious.

By the intermission at midnight, Greer was tired of smiling politely and making even the smallest of conversation during the brief time he and his partner walked to and fro across the oak floor, as well as the even shorter period at the table when he returned a female to her chaperone. Each discourse was similar, starting with where he came from when the young woman first heard his accent: What was his family's business? Did he intend to stay in Britain? Did he have money to buy a home in London?

He considered himself a frank and open person, but the personal questions struck him as intrusive and mercenary. After he had something to eat, he might come up with a new group of answers to amuse himself. He was from Germany, a goat farmer, without a penny to his name.

"Mr. Carson," came Miss Charlotte's cheerful voice beside him.

He turned to find her alone, which left him momentarily disappointed as he tried to refrain from searching for her sister.

"How are you faring?" he asked her.

"Well, thank you. I've had some good dance partners."

"I'm glad you are enjoying yourself. Have you eaten already? And are your mother and Miss Rare-Foure in here, too?"

"It's not a very good banquet, I'm afraid. Just a few light nibbles. My family is over there." She gestured over her shoulder, gave a shallow curtsey, and walked toward a table of beverages.

He looked over the way she had pointed, and neither of the other Rare-Foures appeared to have noticed him. Spinning about, he went to the other end of the table, where he grabbed a plate from a tall stack and snagged a few crackers and some cheese pieces to stave off hunger until he returned to his hotel later that night. The concierge was starting to consider him a permanent resident and allowed him to keep some food in his room. He had a few apples and some leftover pork pie, and he still had his bag of toffee.

With the promise of all that later, he took his meager snack and walked farther away from Beatrice and her mother. It wasn't the desirable thing, but it was the right thing to do. He found another lone bachelor, and they discussed the news of the day and the price of coal, which Greer knew something about since his uncle's trains were hungry beasts in that regard. They purposefully did not discuss any of the females around them, as that would be not only ungentlemanly but dangerous, in case either of them had already formed an attachment to one whom the other also wanted.

Greer was ready to get back to the ballroom, finish up, and head home. He would do so sooner if he hadn't so enthusiastically written his name on dances right up until the last.

With eight to go after the intermission, he couldn't help counting them down. When they reached the sixteenth dance with two to go, he realized none of this was fun anymore and had been amusing *because* he'd been with Beatrice and Charlotte, or at least running into them every few dances.

After taking his latest dance partner back to her table, he hid a yawn and turned to see his toffee-maker standing uncertainly not too far away. He was struck by her appearance. Her gown, a becoming shade of gray—*or was it blue?*—fit her perfectly, hugging her bosom, nipping in at her waist, before widening over gently curving hips. With her grace and stature, a little taller than the average woman, she looked majestic.

All at once, he felt proud he had purchased the garment for her, as well as jealous that sixteen men had enjoyed dancing with her while she wore it.

And then her seventeenth partner made an appearance, said something to her, pointed behind him, and took off.

What the devil? He knew he had to find his next partner, but Beatrice was standing looking . . . alone. She was his friend. He crossed the few yards between them.

"What was that all about?" he asked without preamble.

"Were you spying on me, Mr. Carson?" she asked, humor flashing in her eyes.

"Of course. You are the loveliest lady here." He frowned at himself. He'd meant to say something outrageous to tease her, but he'd ended up speaking the truth. Her smile faltered.

"My next partner has had an emergency. His sister fainted, and his mother demands they leave at once."

"The cad!" he said without heat.

"Oh no, it's quite all right. He's a good brother, and at least he came to find me and didn't leave me standing at the edge of the dance floor as we did at Amity's ball."

"True. The cad is forgiven."

"I can understand the cad's sister fainting, too. It's become warmer and warmer in this room, and they ought to open some windows."

"If it weren't nearly the end, I would find one of those floor managers and demand he allow some thick, sooty London air in here at once."

They both laughed, and it was the best moment he'd had all evening.

"May I have this dance since you are without a partner?" Greer asked it before he considered, but more than anything, he wanted to take her in his arms and to breathe in her vanilla fragrance.

"I would not allow you to make the same error twice, Mr. Carson, not for all the world. Even though this is a decidedly different group of dancers, word will spread and you will get a reputation as a bad partner. Ladies will stop allowing you to put your name on their dance cards. Then you truly would be considered a cad."

"You are correct, as usual, but I hate to leave you here."

"I shall return to our table, but you'd best move quickly. The music has started."

Feeling like an oaf for turning away, he hurried to find his latest partner awaiting him near her table.

"Oh, you gave me a bad turn, sir. I thought you meant to abandon me."

Silently thanking Beatrice for her wisdom, he swept the young woman onto the dance floor and caught up with the others. When he looked back to where she'd been standing, she was gone.

At the next ball, he wouldn't be so foolish as to deny himself her company entirely. He would pencil his name in on her dance card. After all, there couldn't be any harm in a dance?

AT TWO IN THE morning as they rode home, Beatrice and Charlotte compared their dance cards and discussed with their mother the overall manners and quality of their partners. Each had danced with at least one man with whom they wouldn't mind doing so again, but not if they had to endure such a venue as Sandrall Hall. It had been overly warm and far too crowded.

"We were like fish in a barrel," Charlotte said.

"Such a pity," their mother said. "To think people used to vie for tickets to that assembly."

"Mr. Carson probably had very little luck," Beatrice added. "I think most of the young ladies were not titled any more than we were. But I did encounter one or two lords."

Her mother pursed her lips with disapproval.

"Why do you look like that? What's wrong?" Beatrice asked her.

"I think those men went precisely because you girls *were* like fish in a barrel, easily caught. In that place, a man need only mention himself the lowest level of aristocracy and the girls were falling over themselves to secure a dance."

"What's wrong with that, Mother?" Charlotte asked.

Beatrice and Felicity eyed one another. "Because, dear

daughter, those men might use their position to lead a gullible girl down the garden path."

"The garden path," Charlotte repeated softly. Then her rich brown eyes widened. "Oh, and with no good intention, I suppose. No promise of marriage."

"Exactly," their mother said. "At most of these events, there will be no mixing of the classes, which is as it should be."

"Mother!" she exclaimed, thinking it out of character for her own mother to believe in such a division.

"For the sake of the more vulnerable," Felicity clarified. "In a room with all nobility and daughters of such, unscrupulous lords would not be able to take advantage."

"If the girls weren't out to snag a title," Charlotte pointed out, "they would be in no danger of going into the garden with the wrong man."

They all pondered that, trying to decide if the bulk of the blame for a young woman's ruin could be placed at the feet of a man taking advantage or of a woman trying to use her feminine wiles to climb her way into the next class.

Beatrice grinned suddenly. "What about us? We're mixing where we don't belong. That was plainly the case at Amity's ball."

"*Pish,*" said their mother. "Of course you belong. Your grandfather was a French baron before your uncle got the title. Besides, I have nothing against classes mixing, as long as the power is fairly equal. If a lord truly loves a young woman, then let him marry her, and vice versa."

"And if Mr. Carson falls in love with a titled lady who doesn't mind that his pockets rattle with gold coins," Charlotte added, "then let him marry her, but *not* if he doesn't love her."

"Exactly," said their mother. "Hopefully, he will not marry simply to get his family estate."

"Hopefully," Beatrice agreed.

Her mother tried to fix her with a stare, but in the dimness of the carriage, Beatrice could easily look away.

"I'm glad tomorrow is Sunday," Charlotte said cheerfully. "I dread the next ball on Thursday."

"That one is all hoity-toities," Beatrice pointed out. "You and I will be the sole guests thinking about getting up for work the next day."

"It will be worth it," their mother insisted. "Only by the favor of your brother-in-law were you two and Mr. Carson invited to the Earl of Clarendon's party."

CHAPTER TWELVE

Naturally, Beatrice chose the new copper gown for the Earl of Clarendon's ball. It seemed her most impressive one, and this was their grandest event yet—a ball in Piccadilly, just west of Devonshire House, with a sit-down dinner. Not that Amity's ball hadn't been wonderful, but their sister's had been a new event, whereas Clarendon's was long-standing and, thus, prestigious, not to mention fully covered by all the daily papers the following morning.

"I feel all tingly," Charlotte said as they entered Clarendon House, turned in their coats and received numbered claim tickets. "Look, they've even given us pencils."

Beatrice slid the white ribbon holding her card onto her wrist and put the pencil and ticket in her reticule. Then she surveyed the earl's marvelous entrance hall—quite cavernous, expectedly ornate and gilded—with its grand staircase leading up to the public rooms. Beautifully dressed guests were streaming up, diverging at the landing halfway, going both to the left and the right up to the next level.

"Look," Charlotte said, craning her head as she gawked at the ceiling that truly seemed to stretch heavenward.

Beatrice, while not wanting to appear like a green country girl when she was a Londoner born and bred, couldn't help looking up as well. Mr. Carson promptly bumped into the back of her, nearly sending her flying. Luckily, Charlotte reached out and grabbed her arm saving her from a clumsy disgrace. They both turned on him.

"What on earth?" Beatrice hissed.

Since collecting them from their home, he'd been beyond affable, telling them how pleased he was to be joining them once again. Smiling at her—his crooked grin making her heart clench—he apologized.

"Sorry, I gave them my hat and thought you ladies were on the move, but you stopped before I noticed."

"I nearly made a spectacle of myself," she snapped, "and I haven't even made it into the ballroom yet."

He winced, then said, "Remember Farrah's, as your mother said. Does that help? Like a soothing balm?"

She lost her flash of temper at his excellent recollection. Besides, Charlotte's quick grab had saved her enduring a scene of ignominy. Otherwise, Beatrice would undoubtedly be head-over-heels with a tear in her new gown, or worse, her petticoats on display.

"Let's go upstairs, shall we?" she asked civilly. She'd been thrilled when Mr. Carson insisted he would pick them up, and when her mother said she had no interest in going— "only to be the old mare among the wide-eyed fillies"— Beatrice had accepted his offer.

"They gave me a pencil," she heard him exclaim behind them as they mounted the stairs.

"Left or right?" Charlotte asked as they reached the landing.

Beatrice didn't think there was a correct answer, nor that it mattered, but Mr. Carson said, "Right, of course."

"Why do you say 'of course'?" Charlotte asked, even as she cooperated and went up the right side.

"Because if you're right-handed, as most of us are, then you will want to grip the rail with your right hand."

"Very practical," Beatrice said, and they proceeded to climb the next staircase that put them at the front of the house again. Taking a left, they strolled along the gallery able to look down on all those still entering or up at the domed ceiling with a much closer view than they'd had previously.

"Why, I can see little moons and stars painted on the ceiling. Isn't that clever?"

"For goodness sake, Charlotte, don't dawdle," Beatrice teased, "or Mr. Carson will run you down."

The ballroom was much like Amity's except far larger, and across the hall, a secondary reception room was open with doors at either end.

"I think we can dance from one room directly into the next," Charlotte said with awe, her voice dropped to a low tone.

"Why are you whispering?" Beatrice asked.

"Because it's so opulent, so very grand. It seems like we're going to spend the evening at St. Paul's."

They entered the ballroom, and floor managers greeted them immediately. Despite there being no crush of people as at Sandrall Hall, even so, this ball would be better staffed than any public one.

When Mr. Carson asked one of the managers where the earl was, expecting him to be wandering about greeting his guests, the man gave a shallow bow.

"I have been informed his lordship will attend some part of this evening." Then he turned heel and walked away to see to another guest.

"I don't understand," Mr. Carson said . "It's the earl's ball, but he may or may not be here?"

Beatrice was as in the dark as he was. However, Charlotte, as usual, knew more about high society from reading the gossip rags.

"It's more a Clarendon House ball than it is this particular earl's event. He is continuing a tradition started by his father, but apart from him providing the venue and grounds and lending it his name, the ball is run by others, and the price we paid for admission will cover the cost of the musicians and the food. Look around you," Charlotte advised.

They did so, taking in the expansive room with an impressive line of chandeliers down its center and twelve curtained floor-to-ceiling windows along the length. A group of musicians nearly the size of an orchestra was set up at one end, and the ballroom still seemed spacious.

"One couldn't expect the Earl of Clarendon to host in the way Amity and the duke did for their more intimate affair," Charlotte concluded.

Beatrice stared at her sister. "You know so much more than I give you credit for, dear one."

Charlotte grinned, and it reminded Beatrice of a cat who'd eaten the canary. Her little sister might be insufferable for the rest of the evening. Right away, Charlotte said, "Let's get a table on the opposite side, away from the doors, so we can see more." And she strode across the parquet as if she owned the place.

"There shall be no living with her now," Beatrice mused.

Mr. Carson escorted them to a table and wrote his name on each of their cards before dashing off to secure his place with others.

"It is more fun when he's with us," Charlotte said, reading Beatrice's mind a little too closely.

"He's hardly *with* us, in any case," she protested. And then she could think no more of her American friend as the introductions and the new faces began to make the rounds.

Within twenty minutes, Beatrice's card was nearly full of unfamiliar names.

"Miss Rare-Foure," an unfamiliar gentleman greeted her. She glanced around for a floor manager, but none was to be seen. "Please, don't be alarmed. I apologize for my forwardness, but I missed dancing with you at the Duke of Pelham's ball, and I didn't want that to happen again."

She didn't recall seeing him at Amity and Henry's. He was a few years older than Mr. Carson, finer features, dancing brown eyes, and thick brown hair. She'd been extremely nervous at her first ball, and could scarcely remember the faces of those with whom she had actually danced.

"I am the Viscount Melton," he continued, bowing low to her and to Charlotte, but he addressed his next question only to Beatrice. "May I have the honor of a dance?"

"Yes," she said, holding out her wrist to him.

Raising the card, he examined it, then scrawled his name.

"I am most relieved to see you still had space, Miss Rare-Foure. I look forward to our dance."

With that, he disappeared into the growing throng.

"I guess he was chiefly interested in you," Charlotte mused.

"Why do you say that?" Beatrice asked.

"Because he didn't put his name on my card."

"Oh!" Beatrice was surprised. It was the first time, when she and Charlotte were standing together, that a gentleman hadn't wanted to dance with each of them.

"Do you fancy him?" her sister asked.

Lord Melton couldn't hold a candle to Mr. Carson. Beatrice dismissed that first thought. That was like saying Lord Melton couldn't hold a candle to Zeus, Caesar, or some ancient Pharaoh. *What was the point in comparing a man who was within reach to one who was an impossibility?*

"His appearance was pleasing, don't you think?" Beatrice returned carefully.

Charlotte agreed. "A good head of hair."

When the dancing began, Lord Melton claimed her for the fifth dance. They had very little time to speak, but after the dance, he said he hoped she might be agreeable to allowing him to call on her at her home.

So shocked by her first real arrangement with a man, and a viscount at that, Beatrice was silent for a moment.

"I've rendered the toffee heiress speechless," he said,

and she startled. *How on earth had he heard the silly story?* But he cocked his head, and she liked the spark of humor in his eyes. "I hope not from disdain."

"No, of course not." *Did he really think her an heiress?* If so, she should apprise him of the mistake at once. However, she didn't think he could possibly be serious.

"You are welcome to call on me, my lord. However, I am not often at home."

"Not during the common visiting hours?" He frowned slightly, perhaps unable to imagine what she could be doing.

She assumed he meant between eleven and three o'clock, as in every novel of manners she'd read in which the nobility's calling hours had been mentioned.

"No, especially not then. It would be best if you send me a note, and I shall reply as to my availability."

"I see."

Did he? He seemed disappointed, and she reconsidered.

"Or you may catch me at home until half past ten."

His expression brightened. "Very well then. I hope to see you at that frightfully early hour some day this week." Bowing over her hand, he strode away.

Before she could spend another instant thinking how a gentleman was going to call upon her at home, her next dance partner appeared, and dance number six began.

When Mr. Carson came to claim her an hour later, she had lost all track of time and been so distracted with new faces, she had entirely forgotten which dance he'd claimed.

"But this is directly before dinner," Beatrice protested, as he took her onto the floor for the start of a lancier.

"I know. I thought we would enjoy our roast beef far more without having to struggle though niceties and questions."

She felt the same way but couldn't help protesting. "Don't you wish to get to know some young lady better? Isn't that the point?"

He shrugged. "Right now, I'm content to dance and dine with you unless you prefer another dinner companion."

Absolutely, she did not. "I cannot believe we are to dine on roast beef instead of dry crackers!"

He laughed but didn't miss a step.

GREER HAD INTENTIONALLY PUT his name on Beatrice's card directly before the intermission. Even if they couldn't have a friendship outside of the ballroom, he could enjoy her company in the relative haven of a dining room over pottage and oysters.

Why not at least appreciate that? After all, he would have a lifetime of dining with whichever lady became Mrs. Carson, but she would probably not allow him to continue his association with Miss Rare-Foure.

Besides, Beatrice was easily the most desirable female in the place, and as they descended the great staircase to the downstairs dining room and the reception room, which had also been laid out for dining, he felt like the luckiest man at Clarendon House.

"There isn't another gown in the stunning copper color of yours."

She glanced up at him, her cheeks growing rosy and the blue of her eyes deepening. "I do believe it suits me."

She sounded so modest, he didn't think she had any idea of her beauty. Even if she were draped in a Rare Confectionery white bag, she would be fairer than any other woman at the ball. That evening, he'd found it hard to consider any of his partners as a potential wife when they all paled next to his vanilla-scented toffee-maker.

"I'm famished," she said suddenly, as the aromas of the supper awaiting them drifted up the staircase.

"I thought your sister—the duchess, I mean, not Miss Charlotte—said you had to eat ahead of time and then hardly eat at a ball in order to seem ladylike. Or was it birdlike?"

"Same thing, I believe," she quipped. "However, my understanding was I shouldn't eat too heavily so as not to feel ill for the remainder of the dancing."

"That, too," he agreed.

She smiled. "Perhaps if *you* were not my dining companion, Mr. Carson, I would make an effort to seem like a bird, happy with the slightest morsel off my plate. However, since it is you, I shall eat the roast when they offer it, as well as Yorkshire pudding if we are so lucky."

"I take it you won't play the lady for me." He found that immensely gratifying. The last thing he wanted was a false veneer between them.

She turned and looked up at him, not missing a step as he guided her into the dining room and found them two seats. The thoughts behind her eyes were a mystery.

Yet when he drew out a chair for her, she said, "Naturally, I won't pretend anything around you. You already know I'm no lady."

A couple passing behind her heard the words and exchanged a glance. A part of Greer wanted to laugh. The woman was dripping in jewels and obviously scandalized that possible riff-raff were among her kind. Another part of him wanted to punch the gentleman for daring to look over Beatrice's shoulder and down her décolletage.

Not realizing how her mildest words could cause a scandal, she craned her head around. "I wonder where Charlotte has got to. I hope she is with someone nice."

"We could ask her to warn us with her charming whistle if she is ever in distress."

"Good Lord, no! She must never be encouraged with that awful habit. It would ruin her."

Glancing at him, she realized he was speaking in jest.

"I wish I could pinch your shoulder," she said, "for teasing me."

I wish I could kiss you, he thought, and took time arranging his gloves in his lap so he didn't have to look at her lovely face and fall further under her spell.

BY THE BALL'S END at two in the morning, Greer recalled three high points, dancing with Beatrice, dining with her, and dancing with Lady Emily St. George, whom he'd been pleased to find among the mostly unfamiliar faces when he'd first arrived. Their dance came in the middle of the second set, and she seemed happy to see him, too.

She was graceful on the dance floor, murmured her responses, asked him a few polite questions, and didn't make him feel as if she were trying to find out how much was in his bank account. Also, she smelled nice. Not in the same way as Beatrice—more floral—but he liked it.

He knew they could continue like this all Season, having very little chance to get to know one another better unless he made a bold move.

"May I call on you at your home?"

He hoped he'd asked properly, thinking he ought to have worked in the words *honor* and *favor* as the British seemed often to do.

Lady Emily's cheeks went slightly pink. "Normally, one waits until one is off the dance floor," she said, although not unkindly.

He was about to ask why, when her steps in the quadrille took her away from him.

So that was why. One didn't like to be left hanging while one's partner twirled with another man.

When she returned to him, she still didn't answer, and he knew she would keep him waiting until the dance's end. As he escorted her back to her chaperone, in the brief space between where they'd danced and her table, she halted her steps.

"You may call on me," she said succinctly, looking up at him with her soft brown eyes.

"Thank you," he said stiffly, feeling a little unnerved. "Should I . . . that is, may I suggest a day and time, or . . . ?"

he trailed off, wishing he'd asked the duke for a little more guidance now that he'd come to the point when he wanted to start calling on ladies.

"You may ask someone else where my father's residence is," she told him. "And normally, good manners would dictate you come by with your personal card at visiting hours, hoping I am in, or send a nicely written request."

He knew his eyes were probably wide, and Greer made an effort to relax as if he knew all the civilities she mentioned.

"Of course," he said. "However, since we are here, speaking to one another," he trailed off.

Lady Emily smiled. "Since we are, indeed, here, then I will tell you that I am seeing visitors at eleven o'clock tomorrow. And now, I must return to my table so my next partner can claim his dance."

Soon, it was time to take the Rare-Foure sisters home to Baker Street for some much-needed rest. They were probably the only females at the ball who had to worry about getting up in a few hours. As for his part, he was looking forward to the following day when he would call upon Lady Emily St. George and perhaps begin the pursuit of a wife in earnest.

CHAPTER THIRTEEN

"Amity is very lucky," Charlotte said, yawning behind her gloved hand as they walked to work. Their mother had opened the shop so they could sleep longer, but they had no intention of shirking their duties after being blessed with such a wonderful ball. "She can sleep in whenever she wishes."

Beatrice nodded. "Yet still, she comes to make chocolate with us most every day."

"True!" Charlotte said it with a sense of wonder as if she hadn't considered it before.

"If you married an aristocrat or anyone well off for that matter, would you still work here?" Beatrice asked, pushing open the door and letting the delicious aroma fill her head. After she'd been in the shop for a few minutes, she hardly noticed the rich scent of chocolate and sugary sweets, but the first breath was always intoxicating.

Charlotte didn't answer immediately.

"There are my girls, belles of the ball," Felicity intoned, despite having two customers at the counter.

Both women turned, and Beatrice was glad to see by their clothing they weren't members of the aristocracy. She wasn't ashamed of being a confectioner, but she didn't want young ladies from the *haut ton* with whom she'd rubbed elbows the night before recognizing her. That would be an awkward moment indeed.

"My girls were at Clarendon House last night," her mother continued unabashedly, as she handed the women each a bag containing their purchases.

"How exciting," said one.

"Marvelous," said the other, and they gave Charlotte, already removing her hat, and Beatrice, still standing in the doorway, a second glance.

"You are fortunate girls! Imagine," the woman said to her friend, "working here during the day and then dancing the night away with wealthy gentlemen."

"Like Perrault's Cinderella," said the first.

"Not only do they work here," Felicity said, "my daughters make our delicious sweets."

"I make the marzipan," Charlotte volunteered.

"Very clever," said the second lady. "I bought two that look just like pears."

"Then you must make the chocolates we tasted," said the other. "I bought at least five different kinds."

Beatrice shook her head, hating to disappoint the women. Before she said anything, her mother responded, "No, our chocolatier is my eldest daughter, recently wedded to the Duke of Pelham."

"My word!" "Gracious!" both women exclaimed excitedly at once. "This is a special confectionery indeed," added the first. "We shall tell all our friends."

And they left chattering to themselves about noblemen and chocolate.

I make the toffee, Beatrice nearly called after them. Maybe they hadn't even bought any. Charlotte disappeared into the back room to remove her hat and coat, but Beatrice approached the counter.

"Do you think it's perfectly fine to tell people about our new connection to the upper class?" she asked.

"I think the publicity of our new duchess in the family, as well as of you girls rubbing elbows with London's finest will undoubtedly help our shop," her mother said.

"Where *is* our new duchess?" Beatrice asked, still thinking it would be humiliating to have a fine gentleman from the previous evening come in to buy sweets from her.

"She and the duke had some charity luncheon to go to, and Amity took our confectionery, of course. It will be very good for business."

Apparently, even Amity had changed her mind. Previously, she'd practically forbidden herself to fall in love with the duke for fear of the class difference and what it might mean. Yet now, her older sister seemed to be flaunting her shopgirl background. Beatrice intended to keep the two roles—that of confectioner and that of debutante—separate for as long as possible.

"When is the next event of the Season?" she asked, tugging off her gloves.

"Two days."

"Another ball," Beatrice murmured, not as thrilled as she ought to be. She was starting to understand how, despite the change in venue or music, they were all a similar experience. She supposed after a few more, she would even start to recognize the same faces.

"When the weather warms a little, the first boating outing shall take place at Richmond," her mother said. "And there will be a picnic soon, too."

"It seems odd," Charlotte said, having pinned on her apron and returned, "to picnic with strangers."

"There's often a ride through the park first or a stroll, perhaps even a tour of Kew Gardens," their mother said. "You won't simply arrive by the Thames and plop yourself down upon the grass to eat sandwiches."

They all laughed. "At least the river isn't so smelly at Richmond," Beatrice said. "Can you imagine boating by the

Palace of Westminster or down by Blackfriars? We would have to tie nosegays to our faces."

She started to remove her cloak when her mother stopped her. "I need you to take samples along to a swanky hotel."

Freezing, Beatrice guessed at once. "To the Langham?"

"Yes," her mother said, staring at her as if she'd become a necromancer. "How on earth did you know?"

"Is this to do with Mr. Carson?"

Her mother frowned. "I don't think so. Why do you ask?"

"The night Mr. Carson and I first went to Amity's, he said he was staying at the Langham. Naturally, when you said swanky, I assumed it was the same. I can't think of a nicer hotel in London."

"The Langham's manager placed an order for samples of practically everything, and we're billing the hotel, too."

"Billing for samples?" Charlotte asked, her tone awestruck. "That hardly seems fair."

"With the amount your father told me they charge their guests, being fair has nothing to do with it. They can afford to pay for every sweet their *maître d'hôtel* tastes. If they enjoy them, then our confectionery will be offered in their restaurant as well as for guests to take to their rooms."

"Why can't I go?" Charlotte protested.

"Because you are better with customers here in the shop. And Beatrice is better with," her mother paused, "with carrying samples."

Beatrice rolled her eyes. *What a thing for her mother to say!*

In any case, Felicity had a good-sized bag ready behind the counter. "Two types of toffee, a quarter pound each, twelve different chocolates, two of each, and six marzipan shapes. You may take a tramcar or a hackney cab if you like."

"No, thank you, Mother. I would prefer to walk. It's only ten minutes." She slipped her gloves back on and picked up the bag.

Stepping outside the shop, Beatrice thought how preferable it was to be out walking when she felt a little lazy, rather than sitting in the back room where she would undoubtedly fall asleep upon her stool within the hour. She didn't dally since she'd passed the same shops a hundred times and knew what was in every window.

Heading up New Bond Street, she turned right onto Maddox Street. After a quick left, she cut though Hanover Square and passed the magnificent edifice of the Earl of Harewood. She wondered if he would hold a ball that Season, as the earl was purported to have a fine collection of old China on display.

After traversing busy Oxford Street, in another minute, Beatrice was walking through Cavendish Square. She could already see the elegant Langham looming over Portland Place, past the square's northeast corner.

At the same time as she spied the six-story, yellow sandstone hotel, she recognized Mr. Carson approaching along the path between the shrubbery and the neatly manicured grass. The familiar pounding of her heart ensued at the sight of him, followed quickly by a burst of happiness.

A moment later, he saw her, and the very next instant, she realized he was walking a cat.

Unable to even consider not laughing, Beatrice let loose a peal of laughter at the sight of the tall man holding one end of a long, thin leash with a ball of grey fluff at the end of it. What's more, this fluff was prancing with its tail in the air, a tail nearly as big as the entire cat.

"What on earth?" she asked when they grew close.

While Mr. Carson stopped in front of her, the cat did not want to halt its promenade. It tugged at the leash, before turning to look up at him, whiskers quivering with disapproval.

"May I pet it?" she asked him.

"She's liable to scratch or bite you," he warned.

"Then I shall scratch or bite her back," Beatrice promised. Setting down her bag, she bent low and touched the top of the cat's head before giving it a little rub behind its ears. It leaned into her hand, enjoying the attention. She could even hear it beginning to purr.

"She seems to have taken an instant liking to you," Greer said, "perhaps sensing a kindred spirit."

"You mean a quick-tempered female."

"Precisely. Miss Rare-Foure, may I introduce you to Miss Sylvia, my mother's cat?"

"You brought her all the way from America?" Beatrice couldn't take her gaze off the sweet pussum's face. It had closed its eyes now and was purring loudly.

"I did. I didn't have the heart to leave her. All she's ever known is being pampered, spoiled, and utterly indulged. I believe the shock of a regular home with people who don't worship her might have killed her."

She stood again. "Why, Mr. Carson, I believe you have a tender heart and are deeply fond of her."

"Hardly, Miss Rare-Foure. If you must know, my mother's will demanded I look after her."

"I doubt your mother's last testament ordered you to bring her cat to Britain with you, in a first-class cabin, I'll warrant, and then put her in the most expensive Mayfair hotel and walk her through Cavendish Square on a leash." She glanced down at Miss Sylvia again, seeing what looked like rubies and diamonds, sapphires and emeralds encircling its neck, winking in the sunlight.

"Good God! Are those gemstones?"

"Of course not," he said, and her heart slowed from a hammering rate. "This is her outdoor collar, so those are merely glass."

"That makes sense," she said. *What person in his right mind would have a cat collar worth a fortune?* "How foolish of me!"

"Naturally, I leave her jeweled collar in my room in case she ever slips away from me."

She stared again at Miss Sylvia as the cat attempted to capture a small grasshopper in the grass beside her, and Greer took a step sideways to give her more leeway.

Pouncing, the cat had the bug under her paws in a flash.

Beatrice shook her head. "You mean she truly does have a collar with diamonds and rubies and whatnot?"

When he laughed, she realized he was joking.

"My mother spoiled this cat, but that would be over the top and beyond the pale even for her."

Beatrice nodded. "Besides, that type of spoiling is for the owner, not the animal."

"I cannot argue. Miss Sylvia would prefer to have sardines over sapphires." Greer looked at her bag. "What are you doing in our little square?" he asked, taking another few steps onto the grass as Miss Sylvia tugged him along.

Beatrice picked up her bag, left the path, and followed him. "I believe you are responsible for why I am here."

"Really?" he asked, but he had a twinkle in his eyes.

"Did you request the Langham Hotel carry our confectionery?"

"I am considered a long-term resident now. They want to keep me happy. They brought fresh fish for Miss Sylvia the other day," he added, looking fondly at the cat. " The least they can do is provide decent confectionery to their guests."

"Mother is making them pay for samples," she told him.

"Good. They can well afford it."

They both looked back at the cat, who was now at the base of a tree and, by her hunched manner and half-closed eyes, doing her private business. They made eye contact and grinned at the absurdity of taking a cat for a walk. She relished how much good humor they shared.

"Twice a day, I'm out here with her," he said. "Although if it's pouring rain, I put her face to the window, and you should feel the little beast recoil. Then she'll use torn newspapers in a box in my bathroom. She protests, but she'll use it."

"You seem quite the expert pet owner, Mr. Carson."

He shrugged. "Now that she has completed her task, we'll walk back with you."

"Very well." Beatrice watched as he pulled on the leash. At first, the cat seemed to plant her paws and refuse to move, making Beatrice chuckle again, but then Miss Sylvia began to walk in the proper direction. It was slow going and at times very fast going if the cat suddenly gave chase to a stray butterfly or a leaf.

"Why do they call this circular park a square?" Greer asked.

Beatrice opened her mouth to answer when a dog appeared at the entrance to the park. A moment later, she realized it, too, was on a leash.

Miss Sylvia, however, knew nothing of the sort and began to hiss and pull in the opposite direction. In the blink of an eye, Greer scooped up the cat and tucked her under his arm despite her struggling and her little legs scrabbling against his coat.

He does have a soft heart, she thought, *and cares for that cat.* It made her own heart glad. The dog and its owner passed without incident, and they crossed the street diagonally to enter the hotel by one of its back doors.

"I ought to meet with the *maître d'hôtel* by myself," she said. "Since you already told them you wanted our chocolate, I think it would be a bit suspicious if you were beside me when I deliver the samples. They might think you have a special interest in our success."

"As you wish," he said. "Also, while they tolerate Miss Sylvia, they don't want me roaming the halls with her in case she does anything nasty on their Persian rugs." He gave her a small bow, looking her directly in the eyes as he did. Something about him lately never failed to make her stomach do a little flip of excitement.

"Good luck," he said. "I'm certain they'll love everything you've brought and place many large orders."

"Thank you," she said, but neither of them moved. She reached out to stroke Miss Sylvia's head again. "If it happens as you say, my mother will be pleased to have a steady customer like the Langham."

"Not to mention all the guests who will want to take confectionery home with them. They'll taste it while staying in London and then dash over to New Bond Street to have Miss Charlotte pack them a tin."

She smiled at him. "They'll dash over, will they? They'll probably at the very least take a cab."

"Make sure the hotel manager agrees to your shop name being associated with every last sweet. I've met many Europeans in the dining room and even a few Americans, and I'm positive lots of important people stay here all the time, some dripping with wealth."

"Like you and Miss Sylvia?" she teased.

"Exactly so. Some probably have real jewels on their collars, too."

"The people or their animals?"

They snickered, but Miss Sylvia started to struggle, so it was time to part.

"We didn't come in through the grand entrance, but you need to go in that direction," Greer explained, "so that someone in the reception office can hail the general manager. Follow this corridor," he said, "past all those endless small sitting rooms on the left and the ladies' library on the right, though I bet you might want to look in there sometime. Take a right at the family staircase. You won't meet any strange single gentlemen on that side."

"Strange men such as yourself, holding cats?"

"Again, correct," he said. "You'll see the entrance foyer ahead of you. Go through it, past the doors to the central courtyard. Miss Sylvia has been known to do her business there in a pinch, but she was found disturbing the flowers one time and drinking from the fountain another, so we've been all but banned."

"Naturally," she said, imagining the horror of a guest paying dearly for an opulent room and looking from above over the exclusive hotel courtyard to see a cat defecating in the flower pots. She grinned at the thought.

"You'll find a reception room on your right, past the

courtyard doors. If the manager isn't nearby, they'll fetch him."

"I'm sure I shall manage quite well."

"I haven't a doubt," he said. "You have always seemed like a most capable woman."

"Thank you, Mr. Carson." He'd done them such a good turn, there was nothing more she could say.

"I will see you at the next ball," he added as she walked away.

CHAPTER FOURTEEN

Three evenings later, Beatrice alighted from the carriage to partake of yet another sparkling ball, although smaller than the previous massive affair at Clarendon House. She was flanked by Charlotte on one side and Mr. Carson on the other, looking ever more dapper as far as she was concerned. *Was that possible?*

"No cards," Charlotte said, her voice high with excitement.

When checking their mantles and Mr. Carson's hat, they'd paused to await the dispensing of dance cards, to realize belatedly that none were forthcoming.

Their hostess, the Dowager Duchess of Eastley, dressed as if she were still a few decades younger than she truly was, stood near the entrance to the ballroom, ushering guests inside like a butler. She heard Charlotte's exclamation.

"No cards tonight, dearies. So old fashioned, I think, and restrictive. Dance with your hearts," she added through lips with far too much false color plastered upon them. Her blond wig of ringlets and her ruddy cheeks reminded

Beatrice of a child's porcelain doll with perfectly coiled hair and craftily applied rouge. In the case of a flesh-and-blood older lady, however, the attempt at a façade of youth smacked of desperation.

"Thank you, Your Grace," Charlotte said first. Beatrice and Mr. Carson did the same and they crossed the parquet floor.

"What are the rules?" the American asked bluntly as soon as they found a place to stand in front of the curtains. Chairs were lined up along the walls, but it was too early to want to sit.

"We are each upon our honor expected to dance with many," Charlotte recited.

"Is that from the same preachy *Lady's Book* you mentioned before?"

Charlotte grinned. "Don't be a wallflower, Bea, but you must only dance with those to whom you've been properly introduced." Then she frowned. "Although I think they are allowed to introduce themselves in this instance."

They all considered that a moment, realized the absurdity, and started to chuckle.

"What I am gathering," Mr. Carson said, "is we shall do more talking in groups and less making the rounds and dashing off to secure partners? Each dance is a new opportunity for humiliation or triumph? It makes it a little more interesting."

"More nerve-wracking, you mean," Beatrice said with a huff. "What a silly idea, having us fend for ourselves and secure a partner for each dance as it comes. I shall be on tenterhooks all evening."

"I shall not let you be without a partner when you wish to dance," Mr. Carson said softly beside her, and she glanced at him. Their gazes locked, and she relaxed.

"*Pish,*" Charlotte said. "Beatrice won't let you sacrifice your own evening of wife-hunting to nanny her. Will you?"

Beatrice nearly snarled at her to mind her own business. However, Charlotte was right. "Of course not. Mr. Carson, if you are free and I am free, then I will enjoy dancing with you as always. However, you must endeavor to secure your own partners among the many titled ladies here tonight."

"Oh, I shall," he promised. "I may start with our hostess. She seems to be about my age, wouldn't you agree?"

They tried not to laugh. "Promise me," Charlotte said, "if I ever try to look thirty years younger than I am, you will stop me."

"I promise," Beatrice said. "I would never leave you open to such ridicule. I wonder she doesn't have a friend or loved one to suggest neither her make-up nor her low-cut décolletage do her any kindness."

"Then you don't approve of my trying to secure her as my bride?" Mr. Carson asked.

"She is certainly titled," Charlotte said, then lost interest as she spied a parade of servants entering with laden trays. "Oh, they are bringing in champagne at the start. This is a different kind of ball."

Yet Beatrice had a prickling of alarm, even as they each took a glass of the bubbling French beverage off the tray. *Should she give voice to her concern?* Luckily, Charlotte chose that moment to spy a new friend.

"I met her at Amity's ball. I shall say hello and return shortly." Then she stopped. "Mr. Carson, will you please escort me to my friend?"

He looked startled, and Beatrice cocked her head in question.

Charlotte shrugged. "I'm trying to be on my best behavior. The etiquette book says I am not to wander around alone, and that men are to do any reasonable favor a lady asks."

"Of course," he said, taking her arm.

"Don't talk about treacle toffee," Beatrice warned, too late as her sister was already steps away. Mr. Carson looked over his shoulder making a funny face at her for this rather silly nod to etiquette. After all, he had but to take Charlotte a few yards to reach the other group of young ladies.

Beatrice watched him greet each of them in turn with Charlotte doing the introductions. It was for the best, Beatrice supposed, as he could now ask any of them to dance.

"Don't worry," Mr. Carson said, as soon as he returned to her. "I'm sure she will comport herself well."

Beatrice could only hope. But now they were alone, she could voice her question.

"You won't get yourself a wife for her title alone, will you?"

Clearly, he was taken aback. Then he smiled, and her heart seemed to skip a beat at the sight of it.

"You didn't think I was serious about the dowager, did you?"

"No," she snapped, "of course not. You ninny!" *So, what was troubling her?* "I wouldn't want you to . . . to settle for less than what my sister and her husband have, merely for the sake of a title." *How personal that sounded.* "Not that it's any of my business," she added quickly.

"Why, Miss Rare-Foure, are you worrying for my future?"

He was teasing her again, but she simply couldn't find it in her to make a jest in return. Admitting to herself she had very strong feelings for the man was hard and humbling enough. However, if he was determined to be with a lady who might not appreciate him as she did, then he had better at least love that woman like the devil loved sinners.

Of course, she couldn't say any of that, but she could stick up for the future bride.

"I don't think it would be chivalrous of you to take a lady for your wife unless you love her. She deserves that, don't you think?"

Hearing her earnest tone, he stopped smiling. "I hope you know me well enough to believe I will not play with a lady's affections, nor would I bind any female to a loveless marriage, both for her sake and my own. Every one of us deserves to find passionate love," he added, his gaze locked with hers. "Moreover, I have already discovered one lady with whom I might find myself attached."

The room seemed to shrink down to the two of them, while becoming devoid of air at the same time. For a ridiculous instant, she thought he might mean her.

"I've danced with her at two balls," he added.

Disappointment crashed through her. After a moment, she managed to catch her breath and offer him a serviceable nod. *The American had found someone!*

In the background, she heard the light, airy sound of a flageolet letting them know the first dance was about to begin.

She swallowed, feeling warm. "I'm glad we've cleared that up then."

For some reason, her utterance put the merriment back into his gaze. "The nicest part about this ball so far is I don't have to rush off in search of partners. I'm free to ask you to dance. Right now, in fact."

Beatrice let Mr. Carson take her hand even though she still felt stunned. As if they were in a formal situation, he bowed, and she returned it somewhat woodenly, and they took up their positions.

The musicians played a few notes, then stopped, giving the guests time to realize what type of dance it was, and if they didn't, the Dowager Duchess of Eastley announced in a loud voice, "A quadrille to begin." The elderly lady intended to enjoy her own ball and had a younger man at the ready.

Everyone with a partner approached the dance floor, and a floor manager made sure there were the correct number of couples in each group. There was a brief pause, filled with the anticipation of the evening's first dance, while hopeful dancers prayed not to make a single misstep. Last-minute partners were secured, until squares of four couples each were arranged up and down the ballroom.

Beatrice exchanged a glance with Mr. Carson, and then they began. She couldn't believe how far they'd come in a month and a half, but she felt confident in her steps and particularly comfortable as his partner. Recovering from the shock of his announcement, now that they were dancing, she began to relax. Moreover, to her delight, she saw Charlotte had her own handsome partner in the formation next to hers.

Beatrice wished she'd had time to ask Mr. Carson whether the lady he was interested in was in attendance. Since she hadn't, she couldn't help glancing around her, imagining which of the titled misses might have caught his eye.

And then, when she took a turn in the middle with Mr. Carson, another lady and her partner, Beatrice's foot slipped out from under her.

"Whoa!" she exclaimed before she could stop herself, sounding as if she were reining in a horse while throwing her hand out to steady her step. Something had sent her right slipper askew. Glancing down while regaining her position, she noticed one of the dowager's extraordinarily flaxen curls. With a swift swipe of her toe, Beatrice sent it flying as far as she could, watching it disappear between the feet of a couple in the outer ring.

Looking up, she caught Mr. Carson's gaze. He'd seen the entire thing. What's more, it had tickled his funny bone. Seeing him bite back a grin and fight to keep from laughing caused a bubble of mirth to rise in her unexpectedly. If she couldn't get ahold of herself, she was going to laugh. Sinking her teeth into her lower lip, she focused on the dance.

Looking away from him, her cheeks bulging with good humor, Beatrice heard the American's deep chuckle, and she was lost. A laugh escaped her like a dog's bark, and then another. The other couple dancing with them in the middle faltered and stared.

"I'm sorry," she said, her voice barely more than a whisper. Putting her hand up to her mouth, she bowed her head and coughed violently, as if she hadn't laughed at all but simply had a dry throat. However, this didn't help, as their steps were all off from the music and from the other dancers.

As their entire formation ground to a humiliating halt, Mr. Carson took her hand and escorted her from the floor. The other unfortunate couples in their group also had to cease dancing.

Back at their spot by the window where Charlotte could find them, Beatrice sat on one of the many chairs lining the wall and moaned. She wanted to put her hands over her red-cheeked face but didn't dare make such a public display.

"Don't worry, Miss Rare-Foure. I doubt anyone noticed."

"Are you insane? I am utterly mortified. From that blasted book Charlotte is always on about, one rule plainly stated how one must never draw attention to an error, not even one's own. Not only did I stumble across our hostess's fallen locks, I laughed and ruined a dance for six other guests."

"It wasn't your fault," Mr. Carson said. "It was mine."

"True," she agreed peevishly.

This made him chuckle again, with no one able to hear over the sound of the music and the many dancers.

"I might as well go home. No one will partner with me for the rest of the evening."

"Not true," he assured her. "Most won't know what happened, and only the formations near us even knew we broke ranks and left."

"Hush," she ordered. "You cannot make this better. Go find yourself a wife if you haven't already and leave me in peace."

"Come now, Miss Rare-Foure."

"Come now," she mimicked unkindly, which did nothing to wipe the smile from his face. "At least find us some champagne," she hissed, wishing she could go into the garden behind the townhouse and scream to the heavens.

She scanned the dancers for Charlotte and found her, looking happy and stepping merrily. The knot in her stomach eased. Even if Beatrice had ruined her own chances for finding a match at this pleasant ball, it seemed her sister had not been tarnished. People hadn't booted her off the floor as being related to the ridiculous toffee heiress.

"What are you thinking?" Mr. Carson asked when he returned and sat beside her. "Your usually lovely face looks like a thundercloud." He handed her a glass.

"Thank you for your kind words. How much better I feel knowing I look like a bit of bad weather. What a thing to say!"

He was completely unfazed by her shrewish tongue, which made her want to lambast him further.

"At least you are good for fetching a drink," Beatrice added tartly, taking a hasty sip. At once, she began to cough violently. Mr. Carson arose again and, after a brief hesitation, began to thump upon her back, making it nearly impossible to catch her breath.

Finally, she lifted a hand, and he stopped.

"What in blue blazes are you doing?" she demanded, hoping he hadn't torn the back of her gown or left her with bruises.

"Assisting you," Mr. Carson said uncertainly.

"Take your seat at once." Beatrice was about to say something more when Lord Melton from the Clarendon House ball approached. *Had he seen either her disastrous first dance or how she could hardly sip champagne without nearly choking herself?*

By the knowing look in his eyes, he had. However, with utmost propriety, he remained at a proper distance, bowed slightly, made some formal flourish with his right hand that had her momentarily captivated, and then finally spoke.

"If you wish, Miss Rare-Foure, may I have the honor of dancing with you when the next dance begins?"

He remained slightly bowed until she responded. She knew she was supposed to say something flowery about how pleased she was.

"Yes," she blurted at once, trying to keep from glancing

at Mr. Carson. It would be a good idea to get away from the man who affected her so much, both for good and for bad. "With pleasure," she added.

Unlike previous balls, after securing her agreement, Lord Melton did not immediately leave. He just stood there amiably. She knew it was up to her as the female to start a light and pleasant conversation, another tip from Charlotte's book.

"You did not dance the opening quadrille?" Beatrice turned it into a question and then hoped it was not inappropriate to ask. *What if he'd been unable to secure a partner?* In which case, her question might be unforgivably rude.

The viscount shook his head. "I arrived a little too late."

But not so late as to have missed her humiliation. She smiled at him, sipped her champagne more slowly, and felt as if she wanted the floor to swallow her. *What did one say to a man one hardly knew?* She glanced at Mr. Carson wondering if he might help to strike up a conversation. He raised a sardonic eyebrow.

"Now that you have an escort, Miss Rare-Foure, I will take my leave to find my next partner." Mr. Carson rose to his feet. "Thank you for the . . . ," he stopped abruptly, unable to thank her for the dance that had been so terribly abandoned.

His gaze caught hers with some unspoken message, perhaps an apology.

She pursed her lips at his making mention of their dance at all and looked away.

"Thank you," he repeated, bowed slightly, and walked away.

"Americans," quipped Lord Melton. "One never knows where one is with them."

On the contrary, Beatrice thought. Mr. Carson's frankness was unusually refreshing, especially in this upper-class arena of overwrought civility, controlled by so many restrictions and rules. Any event involving the nobility proved far more complicated than what she would have to deal with at a dinner dance thrown by her parents for their middle-class friends.

However, the American's ability to irk her and the way he incited her emotions to the surface in full view of everyone when she was better served if they remained buried, those were traits she could do without—particularly at a dowager duchess's ball. She sighed.

"May I sit?" he asked.

"Please, do," she responded, and yet, when he took the chair on the other side of her, it felt odd indeed to have a strange man so close his sleeve was brushing her shoulder.

It never felt odd with Mr. Carson, and she immediately felt the loss of him. Beatrice had to stop herself from craning her neck to see which way he had gone and to discover with whom he was speaking. Instead, smiling politely at the viscount, she wracked her brain for some of the inane conversation in which she knew she was supposed to engage.

"A fine evening, isn't it?" she asked. As there had been no rain, that seemed the perfect topic

"You look very pretty," he said, surprising her since that did not seem in keeping with the light, banal discourse she had come to expect.

"Thank you, my lord." She knew she must steer the conversation back to neutral topics. "This is my first time at a dance without cards. Is there generally an order to the types of dances, similar to the other balls?" While nearly yawning with boredom at her own question, for the life of her, Beatrice could think of nothing better.

"Not really," he said. "It is entirely up to the hostess. If she wishes, we may dance quadrilles all night. If we are lucky, we shall get to waltz next. I would very much like to waltz with you."

She nodded in agreement, then realized perhaps he was being too forward again. Waltzes were more intimate than quadrilles, to be sure.

Turning slightly in her chair, she observed the other

dancers, giving him more of her shoulder and profile. He ought now to say something politely banal about the beauty of the music or the fineness of the other dancers.

"I am glad I have a moment to speak alone with you," Lord Melton added. "I must offer my sincere apology."

Her gaze snapped back to his. He had her full attention. "Whatever for?"

"Why, for saying I would call upon you and then not following through. I feared you might be annoyed with me, but when you agreed to a dance tonight, I can hope you have forgiven my infraction."

Beatrice could hardly credit any of that long-winded claptrap, mostly because she'd forgotten his existence as soon as the last ball had ended. However, she could hardly say that. She formed her thoughts.

"I dare say I wondered at your"—*impudence* seemed too strong a word, as did *rudeness*—"at your inattentiveness, my lord. I was concerned some misfortune had befallen you." She had to stop herself from laughing at her own nonsense!

Incredibly, he nodded as if she'd said precisely the right thing. "I was called out of London on business, or I would not have left you waiting and wondering. Not for the world."

She smiled at him, for he seemed earnest and, as Charlotte had pointed out, he had good hair. "Then there is nothing for me to forgive. Let us start anew, shall we?" Beatrice thought she was getting quite good at this polite conversation, and prayed she didn't sound like an eighteenth-century lady-in-waiting.

Again, Lord Melton seemed perfectly happy at her words. A minute later, the long quadrille with its six parts ended, and Charlotte's partner escorted her over.

"This is Lord Feymor," she said, introducing him to Beatrice.

"Enchanted," the man said, bowing slightly, and Beatrice nodded in reply, not feeling particularly enchanting.

"How did you get here so quickly?" her sister asked.

"The dance just ended and you already have champagne."

Sighing, Beatrice had hoped not to have the debacle brought up.

"Your sister had a tickle in her throat that sadly forced her to vacate the dance floor early."

Lord Melton's diplomatic response surprised Beatrice, and she looked more warmly at him. Then back to Charlotte.

"I'm surprised you didn't see me leave, but glad it didn't disrupt those outside of my formation."

"No, I was so intent on dancing, I didn't notice. Lord Feymor is a very fine dancer," she added, sending the young man her winsome smile.

"As are you, Miss Rare-Foure," he responded. "May I return later in the evening for another?"

"Certainly," Charlotte agreed.

The gentleman made a fashionable bow and turned away.

"You are new this Season," Lord Melton suddenly spoke. "Two affluent sisters, both fair of face, unknown to any of us and unknowing of us, in return."

Beatrice glanced quickly at Charlotte, wondering how to process the viscount's classification of everyone else in the room as "us" and most assuredly not including *them*. And once more, she wondered if she should clear up the notion their family had a fortune to bestow upon her and Charlotte.

Lord Melton continued, "You ladies must be cautious during the Season. Sadly, there are the despicable among us pretending to be who they are not. Nevertheless, I am not providing a warning, as I would never cast aspersions on Feymor or anyone else, merely an observation of fact— something I know as well as most of the ladies here, but that you," he addressed Charlotte exclusively now, "probably do not. Feymor has been engaged to two ladies last year in rather quick succession, yet here he is, unmarried."

Beatrice watched her sister take in that bit of information. And then, not looking in any way dismayed or doubtful, Charlotte smiled, appearing as cheerful as ever she did.

"Thank you for the information, my lord. I am not looking to be fiancée number three for Lord Feymor, nor even number one for anyone else. We are mostly here for—"

Beatrice coughed loudly, not knowing if her sister were going to speak about Mr. Carson's hunt for a titled lady or for Beatrice's own task of finding a spouse. In the case of the former, his lordship might be offended at the notion of a wealthy American coming over to poach a fairer member of the nobility. As for the latter, she didn't particularly care for the viscount knowing she was husband-hunting.

Despite everyone knowing the Season was basically a marriage market, it was not something one wanted openly acknowledged or discussed. And then there was the awful realization that she and Charlotte were precisely the *despicable people* whom he'd mentioned.

"Sorry," Beatrice said into the abrupt silence. "The tickle returned momentarily. Perhaps we should all have more champagne." Realizing she still had some in her glass, she drank it down quickly and gave Lord Melton her best beseeching stare.

"We were going to dance," he pointed out.

"The next dance has already started. By the time we have some champagne, we shall be in perfect time for the following one."

"Very well." It didn't take long for him to snag a servant and procure three more glasses.

"It is chilled perfectly," Charlotte said. "The dowager is a wonderful hostess."

Except for her pesky hair coils, Beatrice thought.

# CHAPTER FIFTEEN

Lady Emily arrived late to the dowager duchess's ball. By keeping an eye out, Greer was able to be among the first to greet her and ask for the favor of the next dance. As he whirled her around the floor, he noticed Beatrice with Lord Melton. That fellow seemed to be the only one he'd seen her with more than once. He hoped the man was a good sort.

As Greer steered Lady Emily into a turn, he nearly tripped over his own feet, making his heart race. The last thing he wanted was to embarrass the lady and ruin his chances with her.

Perhaps he should keep his nose out of Beatrice's business. Moreover, he ought to keep his focus on his dance partner.

As Lady Emily suggested at the previous ball, Greer had called upon her earlier in the week, resulting in a most baffling encounter. As promised, she was in the parlor receiving visitors, but so was her mother. Thus, he couldn't talk privately with her, nor did they speak about much of anything beyond the weather and what concerts and plays were currently in London's theatres. And her mother did as much talking as Lady Emily. Then another visitor showed up—a rival, Greer realized—but he hadn't worked up much worry over that. If the next gentleman had to curb his conversation similarly, then this business of visiting brought no one any closer to forming an attachment than dancing a quadrille.

After about fifteen minutes, without making it too obvious, the lady's mother made him understand he should take his leave. He hadn't even been offered tea.

The next step, Greer supposed, was to send her a formal invitation asking to escort her to a ball or even to one of the plays her mother had discussed. If to a dance, then Lady Emily and her chaperone would be under his protection for the night. They would ride in his carriage, and in between dances, she would come back to stand by him for the evening, even while she would be expected to dance with others.

The whole process was making his head spin. In New York City, he'd heard of matchmakers who handled all this for a goodly sum. He hadn't thought to ask Beatrice if such a thing existed in London although he couldn't imagine nobility signing up for such a forthright method. They seemed to like to send messages with their silly fans— another lesson from the Duchess of Pelham that had been mostly lost on him. If a lady put her fan to her cheek or her ear, he assumed she was scratching an itch.

How was he to know if she were showing him some special attention?

And they had visiting hours in order to sit staunchly staring at one another and discuss the constant rainy skies. Why couldn't they simply throw bags of toffee at one another? Whomever they hit would become their chosen mate.

As the dance ended, Greer looked around for Beatrice and saw her returning to the chairs by the curtains.

Naturally, she was holding Lord Melton's arm. Quickly, Greer escorted Lady Emily back to her mother, bowed low, and hurried to claim a dance with his toffee-maker.

"Shall we try this again?" he asked after the viscount had walked away.

Beatrice offered him her sassy smile. "I suppose. I hope it's not another wretched quadrille."

"Why? We've mastered the steps, don't you think?"

"But with a waltz or a polka, if we make a mess of it, we don't affect anyone else. Far less stressful to my way of thinking."

"True, but there's no reason to think we will mess up again, unless the dowager is shedding."

Laughter burst out of her, and she clamped a hand over her mouth. "Don't do that!" she scolded. "Do *not* make me laugh."

"I like it when you laugh." The flageolet blew its pretty tune.

She sighed as he took her hand. "I am the only female here who is braying like a donkey. You must stop being so charming."

She found him charming! He liked that immensely, particularly as he wasn't even trying. It was easy with Beatrice. Too easy.

"You have your wish," he said as they got into position. "Not a quadrille but a waltz, the fast Viennese one, at that."

Greer swept her effortlessly around the dance floor, the sole partner with whom he felt completely at ease. The natural turn, the reverse turn, the change step in between— they moved as one, their bodies never losing contact. On the other hand, with a close dance like this, she was also the one female who made him well aware of his palm pressed to her back, her soft hand grasped in his other hand.

Despite being surrounded by others, they moved as if in a bubble of their own making, the two of them and the music, and her lovely dress swishing around his legs nearly tripping him.

If he told her that, she'd laugh, so he didn't.

"I could dance like this all night," he said, the exuberance of the waltz uplifting his spirit, the beauty of this woman touching his heart.

"We're not supposed to speak," she said, "but I agree."

Was that another rule, not speaking while dancing? He couldn't recall it.

"Are we not allowed to speak or is that a suggestion so we don't lose concentration? Because I for one—"

"Hush, Mr. Carson." She gave him another smile to soften the admonishment, and they finished the dance in silence with him able to feel her heart beating against him as her vanilla fragrance surrounded him. *How magnificent!*

When the dance ended, he didn't want to relinquish her. Seeing another man already lingering by their spot next to the curtains, obviously awaiting his turn, Greer did the unthinkable. He led Beatrice to the other side of the floor as if they were just about to partner for a dance rather than finishing.

"What are you doing?" she hissed, sounding alarmed that they were breaking some rule.

"I'm dancing with you again."

She frowned slightly, then relaxed. "I suppose that's all right since we don't have any prior commitments. You don't do you?"

"None." He didn't mention the man he'd seen who would now be sorely disappointed. While others paired up for a polka, Greer explained, "I have danced already with Lady Emily St. George, someone I'm considering as a potential wife. And I don't know if she would deem it uncivilized or possibly the downfall of polite society were I to ask her for another dance tonight."

"I see," was all Beatrice said, and then the music began.

BEATRICE FELT AS IF she'd been punched in the stomach. *Lady Emily St. George!* Now she had a name for the female he was interested in. It was happening so quickly. The Season had been going but a couple weeks. Sadness washed over her at the notion of losing her friend, as would most assuredly happen. And while he was eager to dance with her a second time in a row, when it came to his lady friend, Mr. Carson wouldn't risk staining her reputation with a second dance all evening.

Vaguely, she knew she ought to be insulted. On the other hand, no one cared about an unknown toffee heiress and an American, while a rumor about an earl's daughter could spread like fire through dry kindling. And she knew Lady Emily to be such, for Lord St. George had been in the newspapers over the years for his vociferous support of the '76 Medical Act and the Prison Act over the past summer. Besides, she didn't feel the least bit wronged, not while she was to remain in Mr. Carson's strong arms for another dance.

She might as well enjoy the best dance partner she had experienced so far. The others gripped her hand either too tightly, as Lord Melton had done, or disinterestedly. Some moved her around the floor as one might expect a general to direct his soldiers, while others seemed wholly disconnected. Some partners seemed to spend their time looking over her head and hardly seeming to notice whom they were leading.

With Mr. Carson, dancing was lively and warm. And although she knew she shouldn't have such feelings, it was also romantic. Increasingly, she found those emotions difficult to keep at bay. Where his hand landed in the middle of her back, she felt his warmth searing her through the thin layers of her ballgown. And where their hands clasped together, it was like a link forged from affection.

With their bodies in a constant state of motion and touching, brushing across one another over and over, Beatrice thought she might melt from the sizzling sensations coursing through her before they finished the polka.

It was nothing at all like dancing with Lord Melton, nor any of the other men at previous balls. Nevertheless, when the dance ended, she thanked him coolly and let him escort her back to the side of the room, where another man quickly asked her for the upcoming mazurka.

A few dances later, when the end of the evening was in sight, Mr. Carson returned again, this time with a sheepish, hopeful expression on his handsome face. Beatrice found she neither wanted nor tried to say no. If this was to be her only Season, and if Mr. Carson was soon to be courting a lady in earnest—maybe becoming engaged—then Beatrice would enjoy him while she still could.

When the final dance came and she was asked by Lord Longden, whom she'd met weeks earlier at Amity's ball, she watched Mr. Carson approach Lady Emily. Apparently he had decided he could risk her reputation after all.

And if it pained her more than it should, Beatrice at least had the memory of having been his friend and confidant. It would have to be enough.

BEATRICE WAS HUMMING AS she wandered into the confectionery nearly at closing time the next day. She'd done something she almost never did—slept the day away, knowing her sisters could handle the shop. Often Charlotte opened, then Amity came to make chocolates, while Beatrice showed up midday, going directly to the back room. Later, she would close up by herself or with Amity, if she stayed the whole day. All three of them were hardly ever there at the same time for more than an hour or two unless it was a holiday, with Easter and Christmas being their busiest times.

Thus, when Charlotte asked Amity to make tea despite it being almost time for her to leave, and Amity agreed to drink the brew rather than hot chocolate, Beatrice knew something was up.

"You spent most of the evening dancing with Mr. Carson," Charlotte said, once they had their mugs of steaming tea in hand.

So, her sisters were worried about her becoming attached to the one man at the ball she wasn't supposed to and whom she could never have.

Truthfully, during the excitement of the event, she'd worried about that herself. At home in the wee hours, she'd wrestled with her thoughts and feelings, finally concluding she'd mistaken friendship for something more. And while it had been easier to talk and dance with Greer, as she'd come to think of him, than with any other man, she must attribute such to their familiarity with one another. That didn't mean she was developing deep and lasting affection for him.

Nevertheless, when she laid her head upon her pillow and drew the American's ascot out from underneath, giving it a hearty sniff, tears had pricked her eyes.

"Did I?" she asked, keeping her face placid.

"You know you did," Charlotte said, then turned to Amity. "She did."

"We didn't have cards," Beatrice pointed out, "so I really couldn't keep track. I also danced with a viscount by the name of . . . ." Her mind emptied, and all she could think of was Greer, with his slightly tussled hair as he whirled her around the dance floor.

"Lord Melton," Charlotte supplied, while Amity pierced her with those rich brown eyes, both wise and warm.

"Yes, of course. Lord Melton," Beatrice agreed. "He was nice, too. I danced with him nearly as much as I did with Mr. Carson, I believe."

"She didn't," Charlotte said to Amity.

"Stop doing that," Beatrice scolded. "I didn't realize you were spying on me." She glared at her younger sibling.

"I wasn't," Charlotte protested hotly. "We were supposed to be looking out for one another, weren't we? In any case, all I did was search for you occasionally, and I always seemed to see you with Mr. Carson."

"At the next dance, I shall endeavor not to dance with him at all, if that will make you happy."

"I don't think Charlotte is worrying about her own happiness," Amity said softly, and Beatrice felt suitably chastised.

"I know." She glanced at her younger sister, who looked uncharacteristically glum. "I apologize." Brushing a stray curl from behind Charlotte's ear, she added, "But you needn't worry, at least not as to me and Mr. Carson. He told me he is pursuing Lady Emily St. George."

"How exciting!" Charlotte said, returning to her usual enthusiasm with alacrity. "To think your plan might succeed."

"Yes, to think." Beatrice sipped her tea and avoided Amity's questioning gaze until her eldest sister shrugged and let go of whatever thoughts were swirling in her inquisitive brain.

"Mother said you have quite a treat coming up later in the Season. In fact, we all do, for Henry and I shall attend as well. It's a fancy-dress ball."

"How exciting!" Charlotte exclaimed again, this time with a clap of her hands, and then, unable to contain her happiness another instant, she whistled her happiest note.

"Good God!" Beatrice said with a shake of her head. "Did you hear dogs barking in response?"

They all laughed and immediately, their interest turned to who would wear what costume.

Meanwhile, there were more events to get through, and increasingly, that was the feeling Beatrice had—that she must persevere, endure, and get through each one. Greer often had Lady Emily on his arm, and Beatrice found Lord Melton to be persistent in his pursuit of her, although she was careful not to lead him on since her regard for the viscount had not grown. She didn't even want to try out a kiss with him.

In truth, she felt more dispirited as the Season progressed, longing for the end of it. Charlotte, however, seemed to be feeling the opposite, growing ever more comfortable and happier.

Naturally, Greer still escorted them, but spoke no differently to her than he did to Charlotte. And when they did dance, as if by unspoken agreement, he remained politely distant, with no outbreaks of laughter between them, and never more than one dance. At the end of an event, when he took them home, he dropped them off with the briefest of parting words.

As soon as the sun was strong enough and no rain threatened, they attended a boating event. With lilacs in bloom and violets peeping from under every bush in Syon Park on the banks of the Duke of Northumberland's home, they were helped into long row boats, powered by strong men from the London Rowing Club.

Beatrice sat on a cushioned bench seat with Charlotte behind her, each of them partnered with a single gentleman of good repute. Lord Melton was nowhere to be seen, which bothered Beatrice not at all. As usual, her attention was on Greer in another boat, seated as he inevitably was with Lady Emily.

Down river they traveled toward Kew Bridge and under it, and then they were rowed back up to the duke's home. Although they were not welcomed inside Syon House, their medium-sized group of debutantes and eligible men were allowed to tour the neo-classical Great Conservatory, designed, as they all knew, by Charles Fowler, who'd also given Londoners the grandiose Piazza at Covent Garden.

Holding Charlotte's arm, Beatrice exited the glass-domed conservatory for the exploratory stroll of the gardens. Somewhere close, they were to find an idyllic picnic already set out for them by their hostess, a friend of the sixth Duke of Northumberland and his kind duchess.

Sure enough, around a copse of trees, Lady Anne Gravens, their hostess, stood with those intrepid souls who'd made it already to the luncheon site, including Lady Emily and Greer. Five long tables with white cloths and wooden folding chairs, with a brilliant white canopy overhead, that was Lady Gravens' idea of a rustic picnic.

"Let's hope it's not a four-hour affair," Beatrice grumbled, seeing Greer take a seat at the end of one table and making sure to point Charlotte toward a table as far away from him as possible. Naturally, the men with whom they'd boated now sought them out to pile on the agony by sitting with them for the picnic.

"But we came by train," Charlotte reminded her. "It will take us practically no time to get home. We can stay here all day."

It seemed to Beatrice as if she already had been there all day, and as rolls and roast chicken, cold ham, and meat pies were set out along with every type of vegetable, she longed to climb back into a carriage for the quick jaunt to Kew Bridge railway station, then board a train and go home.

"Isn't this fun?" asked the man who'd sat beside Charlotte on the rowboat.

"Is it?" Beatrice snapped, setting down her glass of lemonade with a thump. "The threat of rain seems to be growing, and the longer this food sits out, the more apt we are to find flies feasting on it. Everyone ought to eat quickly so we can go home at a reasonable hour. I'm sure none of the ladies here want to be trudging out of Charing Cross station in the pitch black."

Charlotte sighed and shook her head, making Beatrice feel childish and dramatic. She would try to do better. To that end, she offered her silent companions the slightest of smiles, which was all she could muster.

"The repast does look delicious. Decidedly tasty," she conceded. "Lady Gravens' caterer has done very well."

However, a few minutes later, seeing Greer and Lady Emily laughing over some private joke made her nearly lose her lunch and ruined any enjoyment of the cream sponge-cake she was about to eat. She set down her fork.

"What's next?" she asked Charlotte.

"I believe they're serving tea," Charlotte said, pointing to servants striding across the lawn from an outbuilding where they were handling all the lunch preparations.

"Drat it all!" Beatrice exclaimed, unable to maintain her pleasant demeanor when the harpy inside of her was feeling wounded and envious. The tea service could extend the outing by an hour.

"If you will excuse me," she said, encompassing both her sister and their tag-alongs, "I'm going to take a walk."

Striding off through Syon Park, Beatrice wondered if she would be tossed out on her bustle should she attempt to gain entrance to the duke's magnificent home. Perhaps she could explain how she had a duke in her family, so they were all as one.

Amused by her own thoughts, Beatrice soon reached the water's edge where they had launched the rowboats hours earlier, and then she made her way to a gazebo overlooking the Thames.

It was surprisingly peaceful, rather like the back room at Rare Confectionery when everyone else had left and no pesky customers had entered. Despite the river rushing by five yards away, filled with boats of every shape and size, and despite knowing there was a group of eager single people over the knoll drinking tea and gorging on sponge-cake, Beatrice felt alone. At the same time, she wasn't lonely, only contemplative.

Sitting on the built-in bench that ringed the gazebo's interior, she leaned her head back and looked up at the cooing sounds. Pigeons roosted in the rafters overhead. At that moment, one decided to let loose a nasty, whitish-grey mess that plopped beside her.

"Bugger it," she muttered, wondering whether to risk sitting beneath them or try to make them vacate the structure. "Shoo," she called out, but, except for them jostling around and more of the nasty droppings, none of them paid her any mind.

Perhaps if she chucked something at them, but she could see nothing at hand, and she wasn't about to break limbs off the duke's shrubberies, even if she could.

All at once, she had the answer. One of her ankle boots would get them to shift so she could sit without fear of them ruining the tidy, fitted blue jacket and skirt she wore. With that intent, she unlaced one of her boots, stood on the bench she'd just vacated, and hurled it at the bustling birds.

Two things happened at once—all the pigeons took flight, heading directly toward her, and as she screamed in alarm, she heard Greer Carson's voice, "What on earth are you playing at?"

Waving her hands over her head, eyes closed, she was sure she felt a beak or a claw graze her gloved hands and snag at the pretty ribbons on her hat, and then abruptly, they were gone. When Beatrice opened her eyes at the silence, the American stood in front of her and a few feathers floated in the air.

"I simply wanted to scare them off," she said, her heart racing both at the birds and at Greer looking up at her.

After staring at her a long moment, he offered his hand so he could help her down, but she looked over his shoulder. "Where is Lady Emily?"

"Drinking tea, as you should be, as every English lass should."

His smile made her stomach flip.

"Take my hand, Miss Rare-Foure, and step down."

She let him grasp her fingers in his, but as she went to jump down, he moved closer and caught her by the waist, letting her slide down the front of him. Her feet landed on top of his leather boots, and the toes of her right foot could feel the hard leather through her stockings.

Looking up at him, she knew they were much too close for civility's sake. If someone found them like this—anyone who gave a tinker's damn—he or she might get the wrong impression. Beatrice could see deep silvery flecks in his gray-blue eyes and smell his fresh, cedar-soap scent. What's more, his penetrating gaze locked on hers before dropping to her mouth. She licked her suddenly dry lips, and his pupils dilated.

Oh dear!

CHAPTER SIXTEEN

Greer could not have imagined when he went off in search of his toffee-maker, whom he'd noticed wandering alone toward the river, that a minute later he would have her in his arms, looking up at him with those vivid blue eyes.

But he reminded himself he was a gentleman, and the lady he was trying to woo to be his wife was not far away.

After giving Beatrice's tempting lips a good long look, nearly groaning when she licked them, he stepped back.

Or he tried to, but she came with him, her dainty feet—*small*, he thought, *for a woman of her height*—were resting on top of his boots.

"My boot," she said inexplicably. "Please back me up toward the bench." He did so, with the absurdity of her feet still atop his until she took a seat.

"Your boot?" he asked, still mesmerized by her eyes and her mouth and how hard he'd had to fight to keep from kissing her.

She raised her right leg and drew up her skirt, causing his

skin to get prickly hot until he realized she was showing him her stocking foot.

"I tossed my boot up to get rid of the birds, and it didn't come back."

They both looked up. Sure enough, there was her ankle boot, high in the rafters, resting on a cross beam.

He wanted to laugh but wasn't sure if she found the situation funny.

"You probably couldn't have done that if you had tried hard and wanted to."

"I'm sure I couldn't. Shall I try with my other one?"

He was glad to learn she *did* find it amusing.

"And I succeeded in scaring off the pigeons, although they gave me quite a fright in the process."

"I heard you shriek," he said.

"Did I? I hadn't realized it. What a ninny-pated woman, I am!"

"Never mind. I think you were quite resourceful. But let's get your boot down."

He could send his hat flying but doubted it had enough weight to it. On the other hand, if he sent his coat up there and it got hung up, then nothing he had short of tossing Beatrice into the air would bring it down.

"My hat or my coat?" he pondered aloud, taking his hat off and considering it.

"I doubt your hat will make it up there," she said, coming to the same conclusion as he had.

Agreeing, he set it down on the bench beside her and shrugged out of his coat and began to scrunch it into a round shape.

"But your coat might get soiled with pigeon droppings," she said. "There must be dung all over the rafters. You had best use your footwear as I did."

Greer sat down next to her and removed his new square-toed half-boots.

"Those are nice," she remarked.

"Thank you. I'm quite fond of them."

She laughed. "I don't think it will get damaged."

He sighed. "You couldn't simply stay at the picnic and have a cup of tea with everyone else."

Feeling odd to be standing out in public with one stockinged foot, he aimed at her boot and let his own fly. It knocked hers off the wooden beam to drop perfectly at his feet, while his own went sailing out the opening between the roof and the beams. He watched his boot hit the grass outside and roll heel-over-toe toward the river.

"Oh!" Beatrice exclaimed. "I think you threw it with a bit too much enthusiasm, Mr. Carson."

He glanced at her, seeing an expression of mirth upon her pretty face. Bending, he picked up her boot and placed it on the floor in front of her.

"I'll be right back." He dashed out of the gazebo, thinking it felt strange indeed to feel grass under his stocking.

Luckily, his boot had stopped short of entering the Thames, lying on its side at the water's edge. Picking it up, Greer turned back to the gazebo, raising it in triumph. Then he saw Lady Emily and their hostess, as well as Miss Charlotte and two strangers. They'd approached from the other side and now watched as he strolled back up the bank on one boot, hatless, and in his shirtsleeves.

Miss Charlotte's eyes were wide. "Were you going to take a swim, Mr. Carson?"

"No, I had to retrieve my boot," he said.

Lady Emily's expression was guarded. "Without your coat and hat, sir?"

Beatrice appeared at the gazebo's railing. "He kindly retrieved my boot," she explained, and Greer knew she'd made the situation even more opaque.

"Because of the pigeons," she added, gesturing behind her to where there were obviously no birds at all. Even more damning, she held his jacket and his hat. To his way of thinking, it appeared as though he'd stripped off in her presence, which he had.

Hurrying the rest of the way, he reclaimed his belongings.

"Thank you, Mr. Carson," she said, after handing them to him. With that, she took hold of Charlotte's arm and walked away, their two male companions in tow.

"Will you be all right, Lady Emily, if I leave you and get back to the other guests?" Lady Gravens asked, eyeing him warily as he doffed his hat and began slipping his arms into his coat sleeves.

Greer watched the earl's daughter hesitate. "Yes, I believe I will," she said at last.

Of course she would! Greer wanted to laugh at their silly dramatics, but he dared not. Strangely, he never felt any compunction to behave inappropriately with the earl's daughter the way he did with Beatrice.

In any case, he bowed to Lady Gravens as she took her leave. If his toffee-maker had still been standing there, he might have made mention of a certain dried fruit, specifically a prune, but with Lady Emily, he remained serious.

"You came to find me?" he asked. He should feel flattered. *Why didn't he?*

"Naturally. I didn't expect to see you in that state of undress. However, I'm sure there is a reasonable explanation."

Did he owe her one? "I was helping Miss Rare-Foure to get her boot out of the gazebo's rafters. But the story is so inconsequential, I think we should leave it at that."

He hadn't been caught with Beatrice's skirts up and his trousers down, for goodness sake. Recalling how he'd held her close and nearly kissed her, however, he thought he'd best add something.

"I was undecided as to whether to use my own boot, hat, or coat as a projectile."

"That makes perfect sense," Lady Emily said. "I appreciate your gentlemanly manner in assisting her."

With relief, he smiled and took her arm.

Then she added, "The only nonsensical thing is how her boot got up in the rafters in the first place. Was she using it to lure a man to help her? If so, it worked."

Greer froze mid-step. "I assure you, my lady, Miss Rare-Foure had no way of knowing anyone would come after her, particularly a man."

"Hm," she said. "If you say so. In any case, she should not have wandered off alone away from a group picnic. That's simply ill-mannered and not done in polite society."

He started walking again with no rejoinder. In truth, it wasn't the smartest thing Beatrice had ever done, although he couldn't understand why it was bad manners for her to want a little time alone with her thoughts. No one would mind if he went for a walk by himself.

They returned to the picnic area, and he realized people were starting to leave. Carriages had pulled up on the road across the other side of the lawn, waiting to take them to the train station.

"It was a very pleasant day," Lady Emily said.

"I hope you didn't miss out on your tea in order to come find me."

"That's fine. I'm glad I came and saw with my own two eyes. If a rumor comes out about you being half-clothed on the banks of the Thames with a woman nearby, at least I shall know the truth."

"A rumor," he echoed. "Do you think there might be? Will that harm Miss Rare-Foure's reputation?"

He felt Lady Emily stiffen where their arms touched. "I should not worry," she said, but he was unconvinced. He should never have removed his coat. *What a bungler!*

"Do you think Lady Gravens will say something?"

Lady Emily made a tut-tutting sound. "Doubtful. It would reflect badly on her hostessing duties, particularly as there are debutantes attending."

"Then that's all right. Her sister won't say anything, nor the gentleman with whom she partnered all day. A gentleman would never start vile gossip, would he? And I certainly won't say anything since it was all my fault in the first place. I should have taken my boot off at once or found a rock."

That left Lady Emily, and he couldn't believe she would say anything.

"I CANNOT BELIEVE THAT snout-nosed lady has made a mountain out of a mole's hill!" Beatrice fumed at breakfast the following day. "She must have gone home by racehorse to get her nasty story into the right ears before the printers went to bed."

"We don't know for certain," Charlotte began, seated across from her at breakfast.

However, Beatrice was convinced. The papers had mentioned a Miss R-F caught far from her group with a Mr. A undressing nearby.

"Why would she say anything?" Charlotte mused, putting strawberry jam on her toast.

"It wasn't you, nor I. It wasn't Mr. Carson, and I doubt it was our hostess, since I was supposed to be under her watchful eye. And I doubt our two partners for the day cared a hoot or even knew who Mr. Carson was."

"But why would anyone call him Mr. A?" Charlotte asked.

Beatrice took a bite of her rasher of bacon. "I think it was Lady Emily. She is forming an attachment to him so she concealed his real name, not wanting to sully him and therefore herself by connection. Yet she knows him to be an American, hence the A. Ultimately, I think it was a message to me."

Charlotte frowned. "Do tell."

"She has seen us together at more than one ball, so she is warning me off."

Her sister nodded. "That's possible."

"What's possible?" their mother asked, entering in a cloud of rose-scented toilet water, a comforting, familiar scent.

"That Mr. Carson's love interest is jealous of Beatrice," Charlotte volunteered.

Beatrice poured her mother a cup of tea and wished her sister would occasionally think before she spoke.

"Does Mr. Carson have a potential wife in mind so quickly?" Felicity Rare-Foure asked.

"Yes, Mother," Beatrice told her. "That was his goal, and he has pursued it admirably. He has danced with many women, and then, when he found one who was titled, attractive, and didn't mind him being American, he closed in on her."

Charlotte giggled. "Like a spaniel at a pheasant hunt."

"Someone from a family I know?" Felicity asked.

"Lady Emily St. George," Beatrice told her mother. "Do you know her or her parents?"

"No. I don't think they've ever placed an order at our shop. Do you like her?"

What a strange question for her mother to ask. "It is of no concern to me except in wishing Mr. Carson the best of luck."

"I see," her mother said, giving her a long look. "In that case, give the lady no reason to feel jealous. If he has made a match, I suppose you and Mr. Carson should part ways. I shall escort you and Charlotte for the rest of the Season."

"Are you saying I can no longer be friends with him?" Beatrice knew it was for the best, but it gave her a shock all the same.

Her mother looked thoughtful. "Married men do not have single female friends. That is simply a known truth, a fact as irrefutable as grass being green. Besides, it is irresponsible, ill-advised, and looks sordid even when it isn't. While Mr. Carson is still unengaged, you may call him your friend, but as soon as he has offered for Lady Emily, it would be wise to withdraw from any association with him."

Beatrice felt morose, and her expression must have shown it.

"Mother's right," Charlotte chimed in. "You don't see Amity taking tea with her old beau, Mr. Cole, since marrying the duke."

"That's because the duke wouldn't approve, and Amity wouldn't want to hurt her husband's feelings even if he did."

"Exactly," their mother said. "Lady Emily deserves the same respect afforded the duke. Moreover, Mr. Carson wouldn't want to be put in a position wherein he must choose between you. If he truly intends to wed the lady, then you, dear daughter, will be in the way, and I don't want to see you hurt."

"Very well," Beatrice said. "I shall keep my distance. After all, I don't wish to be hurt either."

"It's a pity," Charlotte said, then she sighed. "He is good company in the carriage and at the events."

"He is," Beatrice said, trying not to sound wistful.

For the next three weeks, despite having a very busy social schedule, she hardly saw the American. All the fun went out of the Season. Lord Melton seemed to always be buzzing around like a bee to a flower. He was usually witty and sometimes made an amusing remark, although it was often cutting or sarcastic, a different kind of humor from Greer Carson's lighthearted silliness.

And Greer didn't ask her to dance once. He kept his distance, as her mother predicted he should. Nor did he return to the shop for toffee or to chat. It was as if after the incident at the gazebo, they left the blossoming friendship on the banks of the Thames.

Beatrice had to keep reminding herself it was for the best. After all, she had grown so terribly fond of him, it had been hard to see him with another woman. Now that she'd grown used to that, it didn't sting quite so much to see him waltz with Lady Emily. If she were pressed, however, Beatrice would swear Greer and she danced more smoothly than he did with the earl's daughter.

Regardless, she expected an announcement in the newspaper any day. She hoped he didn't feel cheated, having paid for all her gowns and her tickets so she could invite him as the guest of the Duchess of Pelham's sister to the Season's best balls. As it turned out, once he got his foot in the door of the *haut ton*, he had been well able to keep his foot and the rest of his person on the inside without her help.

But there was still the costume ball at Marlborough House, hosted by the queen's son and his wife, and none of them would be going without the particular benefaction of Amity's husband.

"I have something to tell you girls," her mother said upon entering Rare Confectionery one afternoon. Beatrice poked her head out from the back room at such a serious utterance.

The day before, they'd been at Lord's Cricket Ground at St. John's Wood. Beatrice and Lord Melton and Charlotte and Lord Someone-or-Other—she couldn't recall whom exactly—had been partnered to watch the match. She'd spotted Greer and Lady Emily eating flavored ices under a nearby umbrella. At one point, the American had looked over and noticed her.

Mortified at being caught spying, Beatrice nodded and quickly looked past them, pointing at something in the distance that didn't exist and nudging Charlotte to look, too. Hopefully, Greer believed her silly pretense that he and his lady-love had not been the object of her scrutiny.

Having thought of little else except the happy pair all day, Beatrice now waited to hear news of her former friend's engagement.

"Your father and I are going to France to see his family," her mother said unexpectedly. "If you need anything, Amity and the duke will expect you to turn to them. And if you wish to stay at St. James's Place, you will be welcome."

Beatrice glanced at Charlotte, already bright-eyed with anticipation at the notion of their being without supervision for . . .

"How long will you be gone?" Beatrice asked.

"The better part of two weeks, I expect." She looked around the shop. "I hope no longer, but one never knows. I suppose I ought to take my in-laws some of our best confectionery. Obviously, they have Debauve and Gallais at their disposal, but they don't have my clever girls, do they?"

Felicity beamed at them, and Beatrice's heart warmed. "Charlotte and I will make up some special tins for you to take. When do you leave?"

"You know how your father likes to take off on a whim. He received a letter from Grand-mère Foure, and off we go. He wanted to leave in the morning, but I insisted on a day to pack and prepare."

"Plenty of time for us to gather our best sweets for you," Charlotte said, a gleam in her eye.

Beatrice and her mother both saw it. "I am awfully glad you don't have a beau," Felicity said to her youngest. Then she hesitated. "You don't do you, my dear girl?"

"No," Charlotte said with an exaggerated roll of her pretty brown eyes.

"Good, or I fear I couldn't go away at all."

"Mother!" Charlotte said with exasperation. "Don't you trust me?"

"You are a beautiful young woman with men hoping to catch you off guard. It is not a mother's place to trust. It is my place to nurture and protect. Speaking of which, who will escort you to events while I'm away? There must be at least five in the coming weeks. Maybe I shouldn't go," she fretted.

Knowing how her parents enjoyed traveling together, Beatrice intervened. "We can ask Amity. I'm sure she won't mind, and if she's busy, we'll skip them."

"Skip them?" Charlotte exclaimed.

Beatrice could easily pass upon the entire rest of the Season. The fun had entirely gone out of it. However, for Charlotte's sake, she would rally.

"Surely Amity is now considered a suitable chaperone, as a married lady and a duchess."

"Yes, of course," her mother agreed. "Otherwise, I was going to suggest contacting Mr. Carson."

"Absolutely not, Mother. You were correct that I must keep my distance from him." Her vehemence sounded suspicious. "I mean for the sake of Lady Emily's feelings, of course."

"Of course."

Nonetheless, four days later, the American stood in Rare Confectionery, and he wasn't there to buy toffee.

CHAPTER SEVENTEEN

"Mr. Carson!" Beatrice heard Charlotte's cheery exclamation of delight after the bell tinkled, and her breath caught for a moment.

Rising abruptly from her favorite stool, her hands greasy from the butter she was using to coat the toffee pans, it took her a few minutes to clean herself up. She left her apron on, however. He already knew she was a confectioner. There was no point in putting on airs. Nevertheless, her heart was thumping when she finally stepped through the blue velvet curtain and saw him.

He stood with one of his broad hands leaning on the glass as he chatted with Charlotte.

I shall have to get out the vinegar and clean that, she thought.

"Yes," he was saying, mirth in his deep tone, "I thought the violinists were playing too fast. I nearly swung Lady Emily into a very large fern."

Their last ball had been at Clyethen House, in a large conservatory turned into a ballroom. It was some fanciful idea of their hostess that the participants could all pretend to be outside in a tropical climate while the last of the cool spring evenings gave way to summer.

Beatrice thought it had been a little warm inside the massive glass and iron structure, and as Greer just mentioned, the musicians had played every song too quickly. She'd found it amusing at the time, although Lord Melton had fussed and fumed.

Eventually, he'd spoken to the hostess, but the musicians had not slowed down. Perhaps they, too, had been warm and eager to get out of the pungent, moist, enclosed glasshouse.

Greer turned to her, his gray-blue eyes taking her measure, his expression so familiar it made her long for a month earlier when they'd laughed together and chatted about anything.

"Hello, Miss Rare-Foure," he greeted.

"Hello, Mr. Carson. Are you here for confectionery?" *What a priggish thing to ask!*

"Yes, and no. I mean, I will buy something while I'm here because the enticing aroma has my mouth watering already, but I came to speak to you two about the costume ball."

Charlotte clapped her hands. "I cannot wait. It will be so much fun, don't you think? Beatrice and I have already planned our costumes."

"Good, then you can tell me where to purchase mine and what's appropriate. Also, are we to be in disguise?"

Beatrice had been distracted, watching his mouth. But his question was directed at her.

"No," she told him. "It's not a masked ball."

Charlotte sighed. "I think that would have been very exciting, as well."

"Too exciting," Beatrice said. "Mother told me they stopped holding masked balls to which any debutantes were invited, as it was considered an invitation for mischief."

"Mischief?" her sister asked, looking perplexed.

Beatrice exchanged a look with Greer, who seemed to

understand precisely what type of mischief anonymous young people could get up to.

"Don't worry about it," Beatrice told her. "A fancy-dress ball will be thrilling anyway."

"True," Charlotte agreed, turning again to Greer. "I am going to be a Turkish lady. I have silken trousers to wear under a mid-length skirt. It's so colorful, and I shall wear my hair down."

Beatrice hid her smile at the way her sister said that, as if it were the most scandalous things she'd ever done. In fact, it probably was.

"And you, Miss Rare-Foure?" Greer asked.

For a moment, she thought he was asking about the most scandalous thing she'd ever done. Absolutely, that had been kissing him! But she realized a second later he was asking about her costume.

"I am planning on being Dresden china."

He shook his head. "You are going as a tea cup?"

She and Charlotte both started laughing, and Beatrice thought it felt very good to do so, especially when Greer joined in.

"Will you have to hold your arm like this all night for a handle?" And he rested his hand on his hip.

"I suppose if I stuck my other arm out, I could be a teapot," she said. "*Dresden china* means a pastoral character, like one of those figures you see in a bric-a-brac or curiosity shop. Such as a girl who tends sheep."

A confounded expression crossed his face. "You're dressing up like a shepherdess? No offense, Miss Rare-Foure, but don't the farm boys and gals wear something closer to rags than ballroom attire?"

"True, but my costume will be nobility's idealized image of a pastoral young woman, or at least the modiste's fanciful vision."

"Oh, yes, Mr. Carson," Charlotte chimed in. "She'll have a curly blonde wig and lots of white lace petticoats and a blue skirt that only reaches her ankles."

He raised his eyebrows and looked at her. "Will you have to carry a crook, too, and have a lamb by your side?"

"No, although you will see costumes for which people hold and carry all manner of things. Just wait. Personally, I hope to be comfortable and unencumbered," Beatrice insisted.

"Maybe you should at least have a straw basket on your arm," Charlotte considered.

"We'll see." Beatrice had no intention of having either a crook or a basket. "As for you, Mr. Carson, have you given it any thought?"

"A knight or Shakespeare," he offered.

"An armored knight's costume would be most uncomfortable, not to mention expensive, and you wouldn't be able to dance," Beatrice pointed out. Lady Emily couldn't get anywhere close to him. *Maybe it was the ideal costume!*

"Shakespeare might be fine," Charlotte said, "but boring. Some people go as things, like a magpie, or even abstract notions such as music or the night, but I think those are usually costumes for women."

"How does one embody music or nighttime?" he asked. He and Beatrice both looked to Charlotte for answers.

"I've seen it in the fashion magazines. Imagine a woman in a midnight blue gown with a panel of stars, and a moon, and a headdress of stars, too. And for music, the lady in the magazine wore a Grecian costume sewn with musical notes and holding a lyre."

Beatrice wrinkled her nose. "I would hate to hold that all night. Besides some ninny would ask me if I could play it, I'd warrant, and I would have to whack him over the head with my lyre." But their discussion wasn't helping Greer to make a good choice. "What have you seen in your fashion magazines for dashing men?"

"Yes," he chimed in, "I want to hear about fancy dress solely for dashing men."

Beatrice rolled her eyes at his tone. He loved to tease her.

Without speaking, Charlotte reached into the case and

grabbed out three chocolates and handed one to each of them. Beatrice didn't normally indulge, but welcomed the sweet deliciousness of one of Amity's treats.

"Creamy and . . . is that coffee I taste?" Greer asked with wonder.

"Yes," Charlotte said, "it's Amity's famed Pelham. The duke loves coffee. It gives one an afternoon pick-you-up, especially if we all eat another."

With that said, she handed them both another and then ate one herself. "As for dashing men," she mused, "the magazines have no end to what you can achieve. I've seen them dressed as crusaders, and every king or prince, and as brigands, and as knights but only with a breastplate. Of course, some go as a brightly clad Shakespearean fool or clown."

"Probably best to stay away from those last ones," Beatrice advised him, "seeing as you're already an American in our midst."

"Bea!" Charlotte admonished.

"It's quite all right, Miss Charlotte," Greer said, "I take your sister's point. I am seen by many as an uncouth outsider from across the ocean. Best not dress up as a fool."

"Exactly," Beatrice said. "That's all I meant. Anyway, the problem with dressing as a king or even a famous soldier is how will anyone know whom you are supposed to be? I think something befitting your heritage would be nice." She imagined him in a kilt as a Scottish warrior. Moreover, she would like to see his legs.

"A good idea," he agreed. "You ladies have given me a great deal to think about. I shall buy a pound of toffee, please. And two heart-shaped chocolates."

For his lady-love, Beatrice realized, and all her good humor vanished as swiftly as the London sun on any given afternoon.

"I must get back to work," she said curtly. "Good day," and turned on her heel. As she parted the curtain, she realized her heart ached.

Biting her lower lip to keep from crying, she cursed silently! She'd been doing so well, and now it was as if she'd just lost her friend all over again and would have to rally once more.

Hearing the bell tinkle when he left, she kicked her stool across the floor.

CHARLOTTE WAS ALREADY IN the dining room eating breakfast when Beatrice had entered. She was sketching, and Beatrice looked over her sister's shoulder when she passed behind her chair to see what her subject was—a woman in a Turkish costume.

"I vow every event now seems a pale shadow of the fancy-dress ball, and it's only a week away!" Charlotte crowed.

In the workroom of the shop later that day, Beatrice stood at the stove, hardly paying attention to what she did. She would almost give up the marvelous experience ahead of them at Marlborough House if she could retire from the Season, stay home, and tend her invisible wounds. No longer could she deny that she was heartbroken, a word she never thought to apply to herself. How else could she describe the ache in her chest or the distraught emotions and feeling of hopelessness? Moreover, a lump of sadness seemed firmly wedged in her throat, and tears made her eyes feel hot as she worked determinedly not to let them spill over. There was no point in crying, no point in wanting what she couldn't have.

Beatrice and the wonderfully likeable Greer Carson had entered into their arrangement with plain, honest speaking, knowing they were not going to end up together. However, as the days had turned into weeks and then into months, it seemed the one man she had any interest in getting to know better and in spending more time with was him.

Now the American had achieved his goal. He'd found his coveted titled lady.

As for Beatrice, well, she'd met a man or two who would suffice if all she wanted was a pleasant smile, commonplace conversation, and a regular husband. Probably they would beget her perfectly ordinary babies, too. Lord Melton topped the list since he was persistent and attentive.

Nonetheless, she wanted Greer and his crooked grin. She wanted his funny, accented way of speaking and the sense of humor they shared. She wanted an uncommon husband exactly like him and the unique babies they would create.

She'd been staring at her work area for ten minutes at least with unseeing eyes, and shook her head. Lately, her toffee had been off. She'd had a batch crystallize, becoming a grainy mess. One was too soft and had to be boiled again. Another one had curdled, and she'd experienced the fat separate from the rest of the mixture in a batch she had stirred too quickly. *Like a brand new confectioner!*

Picking up a pound of butter, she dropped it haphazardly into the large pot on the stove, belatedly realizing she hadn't turned on the flames. Doing so, she started to stir the butter until it softened and then added three cups of sugar, along with a healthy quantity of milk and vanilla. She stirred this mindlessly for a few minutes, never stopping her movements.

Keeping the sugar off the sides, she brought the entire mixture up to the right temperature. Using a long spoon, she lifted some of the blend up into the air to make sure it was the correct consistency. She knew when it was exactly right. Any longer and it would burn.

Strange thing about toffee—even when cooked too long, it wouldn't look burnt, although to her trained eye, it would appear a shade too dark, having gone past honey-colored to oaken. The toffee would still set up the same in her tray, but with the first taste, one would know it had cooked a minute too long.

From the outside, she mused, *one could never tell there was anything wrong with her heart, either.*

Working in silence, Beatrice didn't realize she'd been crying until, turning away from the heat of the stove with the heavy pot, she felt the cooler air on her tear-stained cheeks.

Ignoring her own sappy emotions, she poured the toffee into the two prepared trays. It smelled like heaven. It had better be heavenly, for this might be her task every day for the rest of her life.

When it came right down to it, she knew she would never settle for one of the other men she'd met that Season. If she couldn't have Greer, she would wait until another man touched her heart the way he had done, no matter how long it took, no matter if it never happened. And while she was waiting, she would continue making her toffee as best she could.

She retrieved the handkerchief tucked in her sleeve and wiped her cheeks. Then she blew her nose.

Suddenly, Charlotte came into the back and froze mid-step.

"Have you been crying?"

"Of course not," Beatrice snapped. "I stoked the stove and some coal dust got in my eyes. Made my nose run, that's all."

Charlotte nodded, looking unconvinced, then said, "Nearly closing time. I'm counting up now."

Often, after they'd closed and when Charlotte had left, Beatrice remained to make extra batches of toffee. She wasn't sure she was up for staying in the shop alone that night.

"I'll probably go with you," Beatrice said, being careful to restore her tone to the pleasant one her youngest sister deserved. None of this horrid, misplaced affection was her fault. Besides, the Season hadn't treated Charlotte any better—she hadn't made a love match, and yet she wasn't sobbing in her treacle.

Treacle! Good Lord! Beatrice had forgotten to add it. Turning, she saw the tin of it, still unopened, next to the cooktop.

"As it happens, I have to stay longer," she amended. "I'll be home for dinner though."

Unexpectedly, Charlotte took a step forward and hugged her. Beatrice stiffened, then after a moment, she returned the hug. The next instant, her younger sister snagged her cloak off the hook and disappeared through the blue velvet curtain to finish up her duties before leaving.

Beatrice retrieved two more pans from the shelves and coated them in butter. And then she started over. People liked tasting the distinctive treacle flavor, and she would have to sell the last two trays as a new milder toffee.

"I'll see you at home," Charlotte called out as she left.

Home. Beatrice might remain a spinster and her parents' home would always be hers as well. She put the pot on the stove with more butter. Then, she heard the familiar bell tinkle someone's arrival.

Drat! She should have followed Charlotte's departure by locking the shop door.

Turning off the stove, she parted the blue curtain and went out front.

"Miss Rare-Foure."

His familiar, welcome voice stabbed at her heart and made her breath catch in her chest. Nevertheless, she tried to give him a welcoming smile.

"Just like my first time coming into Rare Confectionery, when you were loitering in the back room like a dog by the butcher's door, and I thought no one was here."

"Mr. Carson," she said, smoothing down her apron, waiting for her heart to stop racing. "We are closed."

With that said, the door opened again, but Beatrice was not in the mood.

"I'm sorry, we're closed," she said hurrying forward between the two counters to block the woman's entrance.

"But I need some—"

"You should have come earlier," she said sharply. With a quick glance, she confirmed, and sure enough, Charlotte had already turned the closed sign around. "You'll have to come back tomorrow."

"I just got off work and hurried all the way here." The woman looked past her to take note of Greer, but wisely, she said nothing.

"The cash drawer has been counted already and put aside."

"Please, I want only a box of your toffee for my son," the woman said. "It's his birthday."

Beatrice took a step back. "Hold on, please." Reaching beside her to the top of the glass display, she snatched down one of their nicest tins with "Rare Confectionery" stamped on it in blue ink.

"There you go. A pound of plain toffee."

"Oh, dear," the woman said. "I can't afford a whole pound at once. A quarter's all I can manage."

"Take it," Beatrice insisted, shoving it into her hands. "Compliments of our resident toffee-maker. Enjoy! And please tell your son I hope he has many happy returns of the day."

"Why, thank you, that's so kind of—"

Beatrice managed to push her backward and close the door. Then she drew down the shade, turned, and faced the man who rattled her like seeds in a nutshell.

"You must have seen the closed sign," she said, gesturing behind her but instantly wishing she didn't sound cross with him.

"I did, but if the door opened, then I knew you would still be here. That was kind of you to give toffee to that woman."

Beatrice shrugged, pleased he'd thought her kind. "A boy's birthday," she muttered.

Then Greer shook his head, his smile breaking out over his face. "And yet, you managed to be kind *and* rude to her at the same time." He started to laugh.

About to take offense, she realized he spoke the truth. Besides, she didn't really mind him stating the obvious.

"She was lucky you handed her the tin and used it merely to push her onto the pavement. I was waiting for you to chuck it at her head. A pound tin might have killed her." He was laughing harder, bending double.

Beatrice frowned, fighting the bubble of mirth struggling to expand and set her to laughing.

"Killed by a toffee tin," he added. "Can you imagine?"

That did it! She started to laugh, too. And neither of them stopped for minutes. Good, refreshing, relaxing minutes that Beatrice greatly appreciated.

"I'll have you know I've never killed anyone, with a toffee tin or otherwise. What's more, you're the sole person at whom I've ever tossed any of our sweets."

He straightened, still smiling. "Then I'm honored."

"Of course, *you* would be, although I cannot imagine why."

"Because right from the start, you treated me like we were already friends. At least, you didn't pretend to rigid politeness or false congeniality."

"So, you're saying I was insolent and too familiar, right from when we first met?"

He nodded. "Something like that, yes."

Was it possible she'd seen something in him from the first moments? Greer had certainly got under her skin with his initial appearance in the store. That had been somewhat acceptable. It was when he'd worked his way into her heart that she'd realized the danger in growing close to him.

"I have another batch of toffee to make. What do you want?"

"Ah, there's my sassy girl."

She nearly gasped at the shard of pain slicing through her.

"I am nothing of the kind, neither sassy, nor your girl." With that, she went around him to stand on the other side of the counter, with the velvet curtain at her back.

"Tell me what you want and then you must go," she insisted.

"It's nearly time for the costume ball. Are the three of us going together?"

Her stomach twinged and regret washed over her. "Under the circumstances, I don't think that would be prudent, do you?"

His handsome face looked genuinely surprised. "Why not? We have gone together to everything else that was important."

Was he going to make her spell it out?

"That was before. In case you truly don't understand how these things work, you must send a note to your new lady love and ask to escort her to the fancy-dress ball. I would offer to help you with the missive, but since I know nothing about inviting a young woman, it would be best if you asked the duke. Or even my father. Or perhaps the concierge at your hotel," she finished tartly.

In fact, she'd never received an invitation, let alone written one. Lord Melton had come twice to her house, each time with unremarkable conversation, staying ten minutes and then leaving, as if doing some sort of duty. She'd hoped he would never stop by again.

"I see." He paused, crossing his arms. "Nonetheless, I thought we would still go together. Once at the ball, I can simply approach Lady Emily and ask her if I could pencil my name in her dance card three times. That would signal my desire to court her, wouldn't it?"

"Again, you probably should ask the duke." Beatrice felt the tears welling up again and, with her hands hidden in her skirts, she dug her fingernails into her palms until she had control of herself.

"I don't think your arriving with me is a good idea. Not any longer. It might damage your suit with her, and it will hinder my own matchmaking quest."

He uncrossed his arms, his expression solemn.

"Really? How so? What man has caught your eye? I

thought you and Charlotte indicated the Season had been a loss in that respect so far."

"I won't speak for my sister, and actually, I won't even speak for me. You Americans discuss everything and anything, no matter how personal, but I am not obligated to tell you which gentleman has captured my attention, nor should you ask, since you are not family." She released her palms. "In other words, it's none of your concern."

"The hell it isn't," he said a little gruffly, surprising her. Then he coughed and gave a shrug as if he wasn't really pressing her for information. "We started this with an agreement to work together to help each other find spouses."

"We've accomplished that. You have your titled lady."

"And you have whom? Tell me, for the sake of our pact. Is it that viscount?"

She merely stared at him. "Our pact! You are simply being a nose-poker, like an old biddy with a pot of truly hot gossip-water." *How could she tell him any man's name when they were all alike to her?* She didn't prefer one over the other.

"A nose-poker! I thought I was being a friend. Perhaps I've run into your beau outside of the civilized confines of the ballroom and know him to be a loud-mouthed churl, hiding his flaws from unsuspecting females."

"You make him sound deliciously devious. Even exciting."

"Who?" he pressed again.

"Whoever this 'him' is, of course!"

"So you won't tell me?"

Ridiculously, the conversation had gone from a discussion of what his actual lady-love might want to her fictional beau's nefarious hidden nature.

"You must leave now. Luckily, I turned the stove off when the bell rang, but I must get back to it if I hope to be home by dinnertime."

"I will escort you home. It could be dangerous for a woman alone."

Again, she gave him her long stare. "I've been doing it for a few years, and I most likely will do it for many more."

"Will your beau allow it? Will you continue to make toffee?"

His repeated questions irritated her no end. All she could think of was the Viscount Melton and the other one. *What was his name?* Donnelley, Longley, Dongley? *Blast!* They all spoke alike and dressed alike, and they all made her feel the same—frankly, nothing.

"I suppose his lordship might ask me to stop making treacle toffee, but I shall point out how my sister is a duchess, and if she can do it, then so can I."

"His lordship," he repeated, raising an eyebrow.

"Are you going to let me see you out and lock up so I can get back to work? Or are you going to delay my dinner further after my long day?"

"I was busy, too. I had to take care of Miss Sylvia."

Beatrice shook her head. "She takes care of herself."

"I made some inquiries at an estate agency about potential townhouses for sale. With your economy having been depressed as ours since '73, I shall be able to get a home at a fair price, maybe even a steal."

She could picture him and pretty Lady Emily St. George living on one of the elegant Mayfair squares with a central park, letting Miss Sylvia play outside in the greenery. Or maybe they would have a private back garden big enough for the cat to roam in.

Beatrice didn't know if it were the walks with his cat or something else that had given him a fine figure, muscular and trim. She swallowed, knowing she oughtn't to be thinking about his private person in any manner, and absolutely not his figure.

Throwing up her hands at his obstinacy and immovability, she returned to the back room and lit the stovetop. Out of the corner of her eye, she saw him enter.

It was on the tip of her tongue to tell him how inappropriate it was for him to be there with her alone, but she stopped herself. He knew that and wasn't bothered, so obviously he had no ill intentions.

Nevertheless, as she added the ingredients, including the treacle, when he poked around the room, moving behind her to reach the other end, her neck prickled with awareness as he passed.

She couldn't help recalling their first kiss. It had been spontaneous, outrageous, and wonderful. And had never been mentioned nor repeated, despite their having been alone together upon a few occasions since then.

It wasn't as if they couldn't keep their hands off one another when by themselves.

She stirred more vigorously as he opened the cold box against the far wall.

"Close it," she ordered just as her mother used to say when Beatrice would look inside as a little girl. He did so at once.

"That's a clever invention."

Beatrice said nothing to that, but realizing he was staring at her, flustered, she dropped the spoon into the toffee pot splattering the hot mixture onto her hand and apron.

"Ow!" she said, quickly brushing at the back of her hand to get the sticky substance off her skin.

"Did you get burned?" he asked, swiftly coming to her side. "Let me see."

"I'm fine," she said, turning off the stove. But it did sting, and she couldn't recall the last time she'd been so careless. Toffee was a dangerous substance, and she had only been allowed to create it after much training and many warnings.

Before she could stop him, Greer took hold of her hand and inspected it.

"Some cold water would help to ease your pain and cool your skin," he insisted.

Turning back to the cold storage, he drew out the pitcher of water Amity always kept inside. "Hold your hand over the sink."

She did as he instructed and let him pour the blissfully chilled water over her hand until her skin went numb. After he'd poured half the pitcher out, he stopped. Turning, he looked around and grabbed one of Amity's bowls, pouring the remainder into it.

"Come here and soak your hand for a while." He drew out her blue stool from under the marble counter, and she sat. Her hand was throbbing again already, so she plunged it into the water and hissed at the searing sensation.

Then she remembered her confection.

"The toffee!" she exclaimed, starting to stand.

CHAPTER EIGHTEEN

Greer knew she was going to pull her hand out of the water and try to finish her job.

"I'll handle it," he said. "Tell me what to do."

"Can you fish the spoon out without touching the toffee? It will be scalding hot for a long while yet."

"No, I can't."

"Here." Beatrice snatched another spoon from the counter beside her and handed it to him. "Use this as a lever to get the other one out. Don't worry how messy."

He did as she asked, using one spoon to carefully flip the other one out.

"Please turn the stove on again and start stirring. I'm sure we can salvage that batch. I can't possibly lose two in the same day."

Her tone, strangely despondent, made him want to make things right. Quickly, he got the flame lit under the toffee and began to stir.

"Make sure all the sugar has dissolved and there's none going up the sides," she instructed. "Elsewise, the cooler sides of the pot will crystallize it. If it becomes a grainy mess, I vow I shall toss it into the trash."

Stirring intently, he felt the strain of not wanting to let her down, even though it was simply a pot of candy. He stirred for ten minutes before she asked him to lift some into the air.

"That's fine," she said. "Pour into these two trays, easy does it."

Greer poured while she watched him with a critical eye, and then she sighed.

"At least my second batch of the afternoon was saved. Thank you. If you could set everything into the sink and run some water into the pot, I would appreciate it."

"Do you have hot water?" he asked.

She looked puzzled. "We heat the water on the stove to a good temperature and then wash the dishes with it in the sink."

"I ask because some of the homes in New York have added coils to the back of coal-burning cooking stoves like this one, to heat water. Works like a charm."

"If they do that in America, then I'm sure there are places in England that have the same. In any case, at least we have taps rather than a pump."

He smiled at her constant attempt to prove Britain superior.

"My father would like to exchange this," she added, pointing to the cast iron stove, "for a gas one as soon as possible, only because the coal makes such a mess when dumped."

They both looked at the coal shoot from the alleyway out back.

"Deliveries are made twice a week into the coal bin," she said, "and if we've left the bin open, as soon as it come down the chute, coal dust goes everywhere."

To him, the place looked clean as a whistle, and he couldn't imagine coal dust covering the white marble counter or polished floor.

"Anyway, you can't stick your hands into water that's even the least bit warm. It will hurt like the devil. I shall clean everything," he promised the pretty woman who was taking her pain in stride.

"Just heat water in the toffee pot to clean it. If it hardens, you'll have to use bathbrick to get it off," she advised.

He did as she suggested. While he scrubbed with a boar-bristle brush and wiped and dried the pots and spoons, he couldn't help chatting to her about his adventures on the railroad to make her laugh. Eventually, he asked, "How old were you when you started to make toffee?"

She frowned slightly, but it didn't mar her beauty. Her blue eyes gazed at him, unfathomable thoughts flickering in their depths.

"About eight or nine, I suppose."

"Seems a risky thing to do at such a young age."

She smiled then, and it was a glorious smile no matter it being quite small.

"That's a silly thing to say," she admonished.

"This from the woman with a burned hand," he pointed out.

She shrugged. "My mother watched us all carefully in the early years. Besides, after you are burned once, then you're very careful."

"Once, eh?" he couldn't help teasing her

Her cheeks pinkened. "I have hardly ever been so careless. It is your fault entirely."

"Mine?" Greer couldn't wait to hear how this was possible.

"For distracting me while I was at the hot stove."

"I see. I confess, I didn't realize I was such a tempting distraction."

Her cheeks blushed a deeper rose, spurring him to joke a little longer.

"I shall have to attempt to diminish my highly potent appeal."

"Oh," she exclaimed. "Potent appeal, indeed! You are

insufferable. I never said you were tempting. It was the way you were opening the ice box, letting all the cold out, and lurking behind me."

"Lurking?" He couldn't help laughing, but in truth, Greer liked being close to her. She made him feel . . . happy, even when she was crabby. "I don't think I've been accused of lurking before."

"Well, you were," she insisted. "In any case, I'm ready to go home."

She lifted her hand from the water. There were no blisters, which he took to be a good sign.

"When I used to ride the rails for my uncle, inspecting tracks and all that, I encountered a lot of folk with injuries, as you can imagine, and those who lived close to the land swore by the aloe plant for burns. They got the knowledge from the natives. I don't suppose you have any."

"No. I've never even heard of it." She got to her feet.

"It's a cactus," he explained.

Beatrice frowned at him again. "Mr. Carson, how can you imagine I would have a prickly cactus in the middle of England. In any case, I wouldn't put such a thing on my hand."

"You slice it open and . . . never mind," he said when faced with her glare. "What remedies do you use?"

"I don't know. My mother would, but she's away still, longer than expected."

"When folks don't have aloe, they use honey. Do you have that at least? And then we'll put a clean cloth around it."

"Yes, we have honey." She reached over the marble top to the shelf and grabbed a jar. "I can't imagine how it will do any good."

Opening the jar, he took hold of her hand and carefully poured some of the pale amber liquid on it. She shivered, and he looked into her sparkling eyes.

"You're not cold, are you?"

"No. It just felt strange. What is it supposed to do?"

Her voice had gone all quiet and raspy.

He had a strange feeling, himself. Something about holding her soft hand and standing close, gazing down at her. It was a heady sensation indeed. He could even smell her distinctly sweet, fresh fragrance.

"They say, whoever *they* are, that honey soothes a burn."

"Do they?" she asked, her gaze locked with his.

"Yes." He was hardly speaking now as his glance moved to her lips. So pretty, so kissable. *How could he resist this vanilla-scented angel?*

Still cradling her hand and holding the honey jar, he couldn't draw her to him with either of his hands, but he lowered his mouth to hers. She could step back easily if she wanted, but she didn't.

Greer kissed her, and, surprisingly, she kissed him back, her satin-smooth lips applying firm pressure. Slanting his head, he opened his mouth a little, making it easier to fully encircle hers. And then, wondrously, her lips parted slightly, and the kiss quickly escalated to a new level of excitement.

If only both his hands weren't occupied! He wanted to take hold of her waist, or at the very least her head, and hold her in place. He reached out with the sole appendage he could, his tongue, feeling her gasp against his mouth when he stroked her tongue with his. She stroked right back, not boldly but tentatively, with an exploring caress along its length.

At her startling retaliation, his blood pounded in his ears, but then Beatrice stepped back, as he'd expected her to do from the beginning.

Since he still held her hand, she didn't go far, looking up at him with a confused expression.

"Mr. Carson, are you dallying with me?"

Dallying? Was he?

"I . . . I . . . ," he couldn't finish. He had enjoyed female company before, but kissing a girl who wasn't paid for the pleasure or hadn't indicated herself ready for a romp in the hay of some mid-western barn to stave off the sheer loneliness of the plains—no, he'd never done the like before!

But she had kissed him back.

"Are *you* dallying with *me*, Miss Rare-Foure?"

She narrowed those beautiful eyes. "Absolutely not. I'm going home. And if our maid Delia says this honey was a mistake, I shall throttle you the next time I see you, even if it is at a ball and I am in my finest gown."

She was in high dander, for sure. He still intended to see her home, but he wished he could talk to her about the kiss, if he only knew what to say. Apologizing would be a lie, so he decided to pretend it never happened.

"You normally walk. Let me hail a hackney and get you home more quickly and in comfort."

"I like to walk," she insisted.

"Very well, I will accompany you. Is there anything else we need to do here to close up shop?"

"Yes," she bit out. "I must cover the toffee trays if they're cool enough, and bank the coals in the stove, but since my hand is now slathered in honey, I don't see how I can help. And how can I put my glove on without ruining it?"

"Keep the honey on until your maid tells you what else to do. And forget your glove. We should wrap your hand in a clean cloth."

She indicated the drawer beneath a cupboard, and he pulled out a white cloth.

"Are you sure?" she asked. "If the cloth sticks to the honey, won't it tear my skin when I unwrap it?"

"Let me think a moment." Greer glanced around then saw a butter pot. Lifting the lid, he dug his fingers into the creamy, pale grease, and before she could gainsay him, he coated the honey with the thick butter. She remained silent, probably with utter disbelief, as he wrapped her hand loosely with the cloth.

"Now, I'll cover the toffee and we'll be on our way. Four trays," he muttered. "You've been busy."

She said nothing to that, still looking at the wrapping on her hand.

He used flat sheets of tin to cover the trays, stacking one atop the other, and then banked the coals, feeling more useful than he had since he'd stepped off the boat.

"Ready?" he asked.

"Will you at least tug my glove onto my other hand? I shall feel exposed otherwise."

Greer took the white glove Beatrice held out. She raised her hand to him, and he slid the soft cotton over her fingertips and tugged it down. Unexpectedly, he felt a tightening in his loins at the intimate act, one he'd never done for any other female.

When he glanced up from the glove to her face, her intense blue gaze caught his and captured it, and more than anything, he wanted to kiss her again. If he did, he certainly could be accused of dallying with her, and a futile dalliance at that for they both knew she could not be his wife.

She licked her lip, and he groaned, causing her eyes to widen and her glance to drop to his mouth.

This was insanity, sheer madness, as they both knew they were destined for other people. He was compelled, all the same.

"I'm sorry you got burned," he said, his voice low, rough, unfamiliar to his own ears.

She nodded slightly, still looking at his mouth and then her lips parted.

Greer had to give in to whatever this was between them. Leaning forward, this time with his hands free to sink into her hair, which he did, he held her head steady and captured her soft mouth under his.

Beatrice didn't protest. She snaked her one good hand up his chest and behind his neck to clasp ahold of him. Their kiss lasted longer than the first, and even when it was over and their lips no longer touched, he rested his cheek on hers, reluctant to break the physical contact.

"This is wrong," he professed softly.

"Agreed," she said, her voice a breathy whisper that inflamed his desire.

He claimed her lips again, stroking the seam with his tongue until she opened for him. Expectantly this time, their tongues touched in a delicate dance. He cocked his head to the side and deepened the kiss.

It might have been only a minute or so, but it felt as if time had halted and they stood by the velvet curtain with their mouths melded for eternity. His body thrummed with pleasure, imagining taking Beatrice to bed, worshiping her as he wanted to, pleasuring her as she deserved. He knew their union would be glorious.

Her fingers slid from his hair, and she pulled away, but his own hands were still holding her head gently.

She looked confused, which was no surprise since this impossible longing was an utterly confusing matter.

"I believe that time I was dallying with you, Miss Rare-Foure."

"And I, you," she confessed. "but I know it was terribly wrong."

For so many reasons, she was absolutely correct.

"Undoubtedly wrong," he concluded. "It was probably our being alone in close quarters that did it. We were overcome with fervent magnetism."

"Yes," she agreed. "Magnetism. It need never happen again. I mean, it *should* not."

"Of course not," Greer said, releasing her, trying to disregard the feel of her silken hair, soft skin, and plump lips. But inside, some part of him was protesting the thought of never kissing her again. *And why wouldn't he want to?* She was everything he liked and wanted in a woman.

"Let me take you home," he insisted, in case she was about to start behaving all strangely with him.

She nodded. "My hat," she said. "Do you know how to pin one on?"

He had a frightful thought of jabbing her. "No, but I'll hold it in place and you can pin it with one hand, can't you?"

They managed, and he tried to keep from looking into her eyes or sniffing her delicious scent. She glanced in the mirror under the shelf containing more gloves and some stray hat pins.

"I'm not dreadfully untidy, am I?"

"No," he assured her, feeling a lump in his throat. She looked perfect as far as he was concerned, but it seemed inappropriate to voice such an opinion.

Finally, he draped her cloak around her shoulders and took hold of a leather satchel, which she'd started to remove from a hook.

"I'll carry it," Greer said.

Outside the door, after turning the key in the lock, she handed it to him to put in the bag, and they started to walk north along New Bond Street.

"What do you keep in here?" he asked, wondering if he dared take her arm and thread it under his and deciding against it. "It's quite a bit larger than those tiny bags you and your sister take to dances."

"Bits and bobs," she said. "Sometimes I have a book or a newspaper with me if I think I'm going to finish work early while having to stay until closing time for pesky customers."

He smiled at her little joke. "How about a penny-dreadful?" he teased.

She gave him a sidelong glance, and he hoped he hadn't insulted her.

After a second, Beatrice admitted, "Occasionally."

He liked the fact she would confess to such a sinfully frivolous indulgence. He couldn't imagine Lady Emily saying she'd read a penny-dreadful, even if she had.

He also couldn't imagine Lady Emily allowing him to take liberties with her person in the way he had with Beatrice, and that shamed him into silence.

CHAPTER NINETEEN

Beatrice knew she ought to be embarrassed or even ashamed at letting herself be kissed, not once but twice. And yet, she wasn't. She had thoroughly enjoyed both kisses. Moreover, they'd harmed no one in the process although if they'd been caught, it would have been an entirely different story.

She could well imagine her mother might demand Greer marry her and ruin all his plans! Beatrice wouldn't have cooperated, but it would have irrevocably ended their friendship. It was a good thing Felicity Rare-Foure was in France.

In any case, Beatrice didn't feel as though he were playing with her. He seemed as compelled to kiss her as she'd been to accept his inappropriate attentions. If he had tried to do more while they were secluded, she would have known him for a rogue, but he had hardly touched her except for his warm hands on her head.

The touch of his hands alone had caused her stomach to twinge with excitement. And the feel of his mouth upon hers! That had made her insides heat up and become like melted butter.

She hoped her hair wasn't in disarray. On the pretense of glancing in the next store window, Beatrice took in her reflection. Her hat was a little crooked, but her cloak hid any crumpled clothing. *Would the maid notice? Or Charlotte?*

"It's merely a fifteen-minute stroll," she said suddenly, hoping he didn't think her odd for walking when everyone was mad for cabs. "Not too far from Madame Tussaud's Wax Museum. Have you visited it?"

"No. I've certainly heard of it. It has a gruesome room, I understand."

"Indeed, a Chamber of Horrors," she explained. "It's not for the faint of heart, unless you keep reminding yourself the people are wax, after all. On the other hand, since the so-called dungeon represents actual events, when you look at such realistic figures enduring the French 'reign of terror,' it's hard not to be alarmed. It gives me gooseflesh. There are also wonderful likenesses upstairs, like George IV, in his magnificent coronation robes, and the queen herself, bless her, along with the late prince consort."

"I would like to see it," he said. "Will you go with me? My treat."

She hesitated, not because it was a shilling and sixpence for entrance into the whole museum, but because it seemed the type of thing he should do with his new lady friend.

"What are you thinking?" he asked.

"That you should take Lady Emily."

He went quiet for a few moments. At last, he asked, "Do you think it a particularly romantic place?"

Beatrice laughed. "Hardly that."

"Then I see no reason we could not go as friends. Lady Emily might not find it to her liking, and I would prefer to go with you."

"Why?" She wasn't fishing for a compliment, but knowing Greer to be forthright, she was curious to hear his answer.

"Because you are fun. I'm sure we would laugh a lot even in the dungeon."

"The museum displays the 'celebrated' murderers as well as their victims. Do you know Madame Tussaud herself nearly went to the guillotine? If not for an influential friend, such a great artist would be long dead," Beatrice told him with a shake of her head, "and we wouldn't have wax dummies in the perfect likeness of Louis XVI and Marie Antoinette."

"I look forward to it," he said.

"It is definitely worth seeing," she admitted, still not committing. She recalled her mother had told her to stay clear of Greer Carson so as not to annoy Lady Emily.

"We can go tomorrow or the next day," Greer proposed, "or whenever it suits you."

He was certainly being accommodating. "We'll see. Meanwhile, tell me, what else you have seen."

"Westminster Abbey, naturally, St. Paul's Cathedral, the Houses of Parliament, and The Tower."

She nodded. "All worthy sights. And so many more to see. Parks and museums, palaces and London Bridge. And we have some lovely theatres."

Then she considered his new station as a beau. "I think most of those you will find to be romantic and perfect for escorting your new lady."

"We'll see," he said, as noncommittally as she had.

"Perhaps Lady Emily would enjoy the crypt at Gerard's Hall," she said, teasingly.

He coughed. "Perhaps."

"Or the crypt at Guildhall or St. John's."

He started to laugh. "I cannot imagine the reaction if I showed up to escort her and told her and her chaperone we were going to tour crypts."

She chuckled, glad he found it amusing.

"I've heard the Elgin marbles are worth a look," he added.

"Definitely. As well as the Townley marbles. I don't

know why everyone focuses on Lord Elgin's clever bit of thievery from the Greeks."

"Precisely because it was so clever, I suspect. But I would like to see what Townley brought back from Italy, too."

She spoke carefully, measuring her words. "I believe museums, except for Madame Tussaud's, are considered to have an aura of romance. At least, I think they do. The paintings and sculptures can bring one to quite a passionate sentiment, best experienced with one for whom you have deep emotions."

Greer stopped dead in his tracks. "Why, Miss Rare-Foure, that is the most surprising thing you've said to me yet."

"Really?" Beatrice couldn't imagine why. "Do you not have a great appreciation for the arts?"

"I do, in fact. Although I've felt that *passionate sentiment* you mention when looking at the spacious sky over the plains of America on a sunny day, as blue as your eyes and about as deep."

Funny he should mention her eyes, which she'd thought to be almost a failing in her family of richly warm, brown-eyed siblings and parents.

"Or the mountains in Colorado, or even the ocean waves. I suppose one can never guess where or what may cause passion to spring up in one. However, I suppose you believe I should go to museums solely with Lady Emily, in case I am overcome."

She chuckled at how ridiculous he made that sound.

"I might swoon into her arms in front of a Dutch masterpiece," he continued. "Or collapse at her feet at the sight of a bust of some long-dead king."

"One never knows, Mr. Carson. Best to be with the right person at the time."

"Nevertheless, I would risk going to see the Elgin marbles with you, Miss Rare-Foure, because you are good company."

She felt warm all over. "Let's go to Tussaud's and see how we do. Naturally, we will need a chaperone. Charlotte, at the very least."

He shook his head. "Yet we are walking alone at present."

"Hardly alone," she pointed out, as they fought the tide of pedestrians. "Surrounded by well-heeled Londoners on a street of luxury shops. We might not even be associated with one another, but simply allowing happenstance to push our feet along the same path."

"I wondered if it were appropriate to take your arm," he offered.

"No, thank you. That would imply an arrangement between us, an understanding of the kind you seek with Lady Emily."

The kind she had hoped to have with some eligible bachelor, but could no longer imagine with anyone other than Greer Carson. It was downright irritating! He was an uncouth American, and she had danced with London's finest. And she had found them all lacking, or at least not as appealing in comparison to the man she'd come to know. She supposed Lord Melton was the least objectionable of the lot.

"I think the more time you devote to Lady Emily, or I spend with some viscount or other"—*it didn't matter which one!*—"the better it will be. Truthfully, I think you should reserve all museum-going and other sightseeing for someone you are trying to woo and win."

"Except for Madame Tussaud's," he persisted, and she glanced at him. Greer was smiling down at her.

"Except for that, yes," she agreed.

And then, he ran headlong into a couple coming in the other direction, knocking down the woman, while the man who'd been holding her arm nearly fell as well.

"My word!" the man exclaimed, as his hat went flying. Immediately, he turned to assist the woman off the pavement.

Greer dove forward, grabbed hold of her other hand, and yanked her to her feet. Beatrice put a hand to her mouth, gasping. He should not have touched the lady so informally without even a by-your-leave. What's more, she watched as the man's hat rolled a few feet and disappeared into the sea of pant legs and gowns.

Dashing forward, she tried to retrieve it only to spy it at the exact moment a man trod upon it unaware. Looking down, he kicked it to the side and continued on.

"Bugger it!" Beatrice muttered under her breath. A second later, a familiar face bent down and retrieved the hat.

Hurrying toward him, Beatrice said, "Lord Melton, so good of you to pick up the hat."

When he hesitated, she feared he had no idea who she was outside of the ballroom and a gorgeous gown. She saw the instant he realized it was her, clad in a simple day dress. Smiling, he bowed, and she nodded in return.

"Miss Rare-Foure. How unexpected, and most fortunate in this case. We were both doing a little shopping apparently."

She didn't correct his assumption, which was perfectly sensible when seeing someone on New Bond Street, except she didn't have a package or bag as evidence of such an idle pastime.

Keeping her wrapped hand under her cloak in case he asked questions, she gestured with her other one to the flattened felt bowler.

Lord Melton examined the squashed hat in his hands, turning it over to look inside. "A shame. It was a good one from Lock's," he proclaimed. Then he gave her a quizzical look. "This ruined hat cannot possibly be yours."

"Thankfully, no. But I saw it come off the head of a gentleman over there," she pointed behind her, "and was hoping to recover it for him."

"I dare say the man will not care for its return in such a condition, but let us try."

Walking beside her, they returned to the scene where the

lady was turning in circles so her husband, as Beatrice assumed him to be, could determine if she had ripped or soiled her skirts. Alas, she had done both. Greer was uttering words of apology, which were being ignored.

"My hat!" the man exclaimed, sadly eyeing the damaged item that Lord Melton handed him.

"It was trod upon before I could rescue it," Beatrice explained.

"This lady is correct," Lord Melton said. "It seems you need to take better care of your headwear and your companion."

While Lord Melton said the insulting words, he didn't so much as crack a smile. Greer, however, made the dreadful error of chuckling. Beatrice cringed inwardly. The American apparently thought they were all going to have a good and friendly laugh over the couple's mishap.

He was wrong.

The man with the ruined hat began to splutter. The lady whose dress was torn, with her petticoats on display, began to cry, and Beatrice wished she could back away from the mess, but Greer still held her satchel.

Lord Melton, on the other hand, was able to leave. Leaning close to the affronted couple, the viscount said conspiratorially yet so all could hear, "You must forgive him. He is an American."

With that, he turned to Beatrice. "I shall see you at the fancy-dress ball, I hope." Then he nodded and strode off. *Lucky nobleman*, she thought.

"My friend will make restitutions for any damage," she offered.

"Yes, yes, of course," Greer said cheerfully. To her horror, he started digging in his pocket. Quick as a lightning flash, she set her hand on his arm and stilled his movements.

"If you will give us your card," she said to the man, "my friend will—"

"Don't *you* have a card?" the affronted woman asked, her nose high.

Greer didn't take offense. "I do, but it will do you no good as my last fixed abode was in New York City. My name is Carson, and I'm staying at the Langham, if you wish to send me a bill there."

"The Langham!" repeated the man. Then he glanced at his wife, looking more respectful as Beatrice noticed the hint of money often caused people to be. "Very well. I'll send you an account of my purchase of a new hat, and whatever my wife needs."

"Well, not *whatever* your wife needs," Greer joked.

Beatrice nearly slapped a hand over his mouth. He truly was beyond the pale. "He's joking," she said. "He's from—"

"America," the wife repeated. "Yes, we heard. I'm sure I'll need a new skirt and maybe a petticoat. Good day." She grabbed her husband's arm, and they marched off.

"You'll probably end up buying them both a new wardrobe," she said. "You really mustn't joke with the wrong people."

"Everyone around here seems to be the wrong people, except you. And they can try, but I'm no dupe. I'll pay for her skirt and his hat, and that's all."

She sighed.

"I CANNOT BELIEVE MOTHER is missing all this," Charlotte said as she stood with her two sisters in costume at Marlborough House, "including seeing us." She twirled happily where she stood.

Since they were neighbors with the Prince and Princess of Wales, Amity and the duke had eschewed their carriage and walked to the fancy-dress ball dressed as King Louis and Marie Antoinette.

"I don't know how you can hold your head up with that powdered monstrosity on your head," Beatrice said to her older sister, whose rose-and-gold silk gown consisted of a rigid, eighteenth-century-style front panel encrusted with seed pearls, a low décolletage, and miles of silk looped up over her hips to show her fine matching petticoats.

"You could be at one of Queen Victoria's famed *bal poudré* we read about from when she was a young bride," Charlotte agreed.

"It's not so bad," Amity said, lifting a bejeweled hand to touch the tall wig from which swags of pearls were draped. "But I can hardly breathe in this stomacher."

Beatrice's own wig of blond ringlets was much simpler and manageable. Seeing herself in the mirror at home as Charlotte helped her apply pink to her cheeks and perfectly painted her lips, she'd allowed herself a satisfied smile. Then Delia had set a pastoral bonnet atop the wig and offered her a basket. She'd refused it, flowers and all.

"Don't forget to take cloaks," their maid reminded them, although they'd decided not to wear them until after the ball. "Keep them over your arms for now," Delia said, "but wear them home, or you'll catch your death of cold."

Beatrice had sighed. Her brother-in-law's coach was heated with bricks for evening rides, and he had sent it to fetch them.

"We are not coming home tonight," she had reminded Delia. "We'll be at Amity's house after the ball, so please don't worry or wait up."

Finally meeting up with Amity and the duke at Marlborough House, Beatrice thought it breathtaking, scarcely believing she and Charlotte were a part of this extravagant event. *The Rare-Foure sisters! A shopkeeper's daughters!*

The pretense was not merely in their costumes, it was in their even being at such a place with the highest echelon of British society, not to mention some of Europe's heads of state. They were interlopers, except for Amity who legitimately belonged.

"How do I look?" Charlotte asked for the umpteenth

time. "It will be so much fun to dance dressed like this." And she did a few steps and curtsied before them.

"I wish I could move that easily," Amity said, remaining rigidly upright as Lord Pelham returned to their little group followed by a servant carrying glasses of champagne. "But dance I shall," she added, looking at her beloved husband.

"My wife never misses a moment to be in my arms," he said, his kingly costume every bit as impressive as Amity's, right down to his full-skirted knee-length coat, knee breeches, and long waistcoat, all in pale pink silk to complement his queen's gown.

"Matching wigs, how adorable," Beatrice quipped, even though the duke's was down to his shoulders and partly covered by a gigantic tricorne hat. This was the one event in which men wore hats of every shape and size and didn't remove them, not even to dance.

"How do *I* look?" Charlotte repeated.

"Like a true Turkish peasant," Amity assured her, even though Beatrice doubted very much whether any of them looked authentic. Surely Charlotte's scarlet bodice was too finely made, not to mention low-cut, to have been worn on a daily basis, and her sister's short, midnight-blue skirt showed a bit too much of her brightly colored silk pantaloons. A small blue turban and scarlet slippers with toes that curled up, purchased specially for the occasion, completed her costume.

Beatrice's own white cotton pantaloons were also on display with her blue brushed-cotton overskirt looped up to reveal her shortened petticoats consisting of many layers of voluminous Belgian lace. With puffy, white cotton sleeves, and her simple blue bodice laced up the front, she was their modiste's idea of a shepherdess.

"I can only hope I don't look a fool," she mused. "I think most of the costumes here were made to fatten the tailors' and seamstresses' bank accounts more than to make any of us look good."

"I look good," Charlotte insisted.

"You do," the duke said. "Nevertheless, your sister is correct. This single ball has boosted London's economy as well as that of Paris and Brussels."

They looked out over the sea of partygoers, the upper classes decked out in the finest costumes, none of which would probably ever be worn again.

Suddenly, they were surrounded by nobility. The Duke of Pelham's friends, Lords Waverly and Jeffcoat, who hadn't been at any of the events all Season, had turned out for this one. Lord Waverly was a Viking, with a horned helmet, leather straps going up and down his sleeves, and a floor-length fur mantle. And Lord Jeffcoat was dressed in knee-high boots, green hose, and a thigh-length tunic. The small cocky cap on his head with a feather in it, the quiver slung over one shoulder, and the bow made evident his identity.

"Robin Hood," Charlotte exclaimed, and he stuck his pointed boot out, bowing to her with an exaggerated salute of his hat brushed low across his outstretched ankle.

Looking the two men up and down, the duke laughed.

"You cannot possibly find our costumes amusing," Waverly remarked, "not when you are dressed like a man who couldn't keep his head."

"If I had to wear that ridiculous horned thing, I wouldn't *want* to keep my head," the duke returned. "Nor Jeffcoat's green stockings, either."

After the ladies had all been complimented, the three men began to converse about the recent Water Act, glad it had passed. With Amity and Charlotte discussing the dances that would be performed by members of the royal family and their friends before the rest of the guests took to the floor, Beatrice's gaze wandered out over the growing throng.

Luckily, with the duke having been inside Marlborough House on prior occasions, he'd been able to give her a landmark as to where they would stand—in the Blenheim Saloon, as it was called, because of the painting of the Battle of Blenheim. Many called it the "handsomest room in London." The black-and-white marble floor reminded Beatrice of a chess board, but she remained to the left of the great fireplace, as this was the location she'd given to Greer. Otherwise, considering how the palace, elegantly designed by the famed Sir Christopher Wren, had grown to something on the order of two hundred rooms, Beatrice knew it would be highly probable she and the American wouldn't even encounter one another that night. And that would make the entire event seem almost like a waste of time.

She reminded herself she had also promised a dance to Lord Melton, who had increased his pursuit of her recently, calling upon her at home again the day after the hat incident, luckily before she'd had to leave for the shop. Strangely, he'd assumed she played the pianoforte, sang like a bird, or both, and he'd been perplexed by her parents' poor preparation for their daughter's future as wife and hostess when she told him she could do neither.

"How will you entertain dinner guests?" he had asked, looking perplexed, tilting his good head of hair to the side.

She paused for a moment. "I don't suppose you approve of a round of Happy Families?"

He'd frowned and repeated, "Happy Families?"

"It's a card game," Beatrice had told him. His eyebrows shot together in consternation.

What did Amity do to amuse her guests? Beatrice assumed she and the duke hired musicians since her sister couldn't play or sing either.

"I could take guests into the kitchen and show them how to make toffee," she offered, only half-joking, hoping to discover if he still thought her an heiress.

"Truly?" Lord Melton had looked interested in toffee-making as if he assumed it was quite a difficult skill, almost magical, rather than something any half-decent cook could do, in her opinion. Not as well as she could, naturally, but passably.

"Or I could recite a passage," Beatrice had offered. "I have a good memory and am well-read."

"While I think recitation is a good exercise, I fear your feminine literature might not be enjoyed by all our guests."

"You mean by the men?" she'd asked, a little distracted by his use of "our." *Did he assume they had an understanding?* "I didn't realize gentlemen wouldn't enjoy hearing the adventures of Odysseus, perhaps in the original Greek, or a passage from Shakespeare's *Hamlet*."

He'd coughed, firmly put in his place. *Feminine literature indeed!* She'd shown him the door soon after, as she'd had to get to work.

As if thinking of the viscount conjured the man, Lord Melton appeared in their midst. He greeted everyone in turn.

"Good evening, Dresden china miss."

She looked him up and down. "Good evening, Ali Baba." He appeared exotic in his turban and silks, and even somewhat appealing.

"You look quite the part," he commented. "The blonde hair suits you very well." She'd grown used to him and his ways over the past weeks. He was attentive when they danced and, during conversation, was apt to toss in a compliment regarding her looks, as if he assumed that would please her beyond anything else.

On the other hand, he was often aristocratically cool, and Beatrice realized she couldn't tell if he was becoming attached to her. *Was he even truly interested?*

She promised him a dance after the opening royal quadrilles, and he said he would return in due time, plainly unbothered whether they conversed or not in the meanwhile. As she watched his retreating figure, the notion Lord Melton would ever try to kiss her or that she would feel sizzling passion emanating from him seemed laughable.

After he left, she waited for the three lords to take a breath before interrupting.

"Tell me, Your Grace, do members of the ton behave in

a cool and disinterested manner right up until the time they ask a woman for her hand?"

Along with Waverly and Jeffcoat, Amity's husband was taken aback, his mouth opening and then closing, while the duchess waited for his answer along with Beatrice and Charlotte.

"Did I hear the flageolet?" the duke asked cocking his head, his eyes looking slightly wild.

"No," Lord Waverly said, his mouth working into a wicked smile. "You didn't. When the first dancers come out, believe me, it will be as if the Red Sea has parted, and we shall be flattened like shirts in a valet's mangle. Answer the lady, Pelham."

His Grace frowned, and Amity put her hand on his shoulder. "I'm sure my sister is trying to figure out the strange ways of noblemen, just as I am still doing."

The duke shrugged while Lords Waverly and Jeffcoat laughed. "Strange ways of noblemen, indeed," the latter said.

However, since all three Rare-Foure sisters, including his wife, were still gazing at him, the duke shrugged. "I suppose we are counseled to remain impassive until we have an inkling that a lady returns our affection."

"Agreed," Jeffcoat said. "It's prudent to do so and avoid embarrassment on all sides." Lord Waverly nodded in agreement.

"So, a lord might actually be interested in our Beatrice," Charlotte asked, "even if he has all the warmth of a dead fish?"

The men all laughed even harder.

"Inappropriate," Beatrice reprimanded her, then looked at the duke. "Might he?"

His eyes widened. "I assure you I have no idea. Which gentleman are we talking about?"

Realizing His Grace hadn't apparently noticed Lord Melton's arrival and quick departure, Beatrice opened her mouth to tell him when Charlotte sighed loudly.

"I hope your viscount is interested. How exciting for you and in only one Season!"

"Perhaps. Perhaps not," Beatrice said, thinking it unlikely Lord Melton would unexpectedly spark her interest or declare himself. "But we can still appreciate Mr. Carson's success."

She glanced around and those around her did, too. "I don't mean at present, for I have no idea where he is. What I mean to say is, he seems to have found himself a suitable wife."

The words came out sounding displeased, causing Amity to send her a sharp glance.

"A nice lady, I understand," Beatrice amended in a kinder tone. "Do you know Lady Emily St. George, Duke?"

"I do not, although I know of the St. George family. Nothing scandalous nor particularly interesting comes to mind."

He looked to his friends who shrugged in agreement. "I think I danced with her once," Waverly added.

"I think you've danced with everyone once," Jeffcoat quipped.

"At any rate," the duke continued, "the earl is active in Parliament, and I agree with many of his views."

"Good," Beatrice said softly, as if that concerned her. It didn't. She wasn't sure if she were jealous enough to have hoped for a hot cup of gossip-water, which she could relate to Greer, perhaps to end his pursuit of Lady Emily, or whether she was simply looking out for her friend. Moreover, she didn't want to examine her motives too closely.

"Shouldn't we mingle before the dancing?" Charlotte asked. "I want to see the Prince and Princess of Wales up close if possible, and as many costumes as I can."

"Yes, let's," Amity agreed, and the six of them began the rounds of the large rooms opened for the ball, filled with merrymakers dressed for every period and place on earth, or so it seemed.

"They say there will be fourteen hundred people here tonight," Lord Jeffcoat remarked.

"It wouldn't surprise me," Lord Waverly replied. "The royals always have to do it better than anyone else."

Beatrice trailed behind, reluctant to leave the prearranged meeting spot. Despite the vast number of guests, there was really only one she wanted to see.

When Amity dropped back with her and Charlotte, they let the three men walk ahead.

"Henry's friends are pleasant," Amity said.

Beatrice frowned. Neither man interested her. "Are they?" she asked crabbily.

Although glancing sideways, she noticed Charlotte had blushed at their sister's comment. Perhaps she *was* interested in one of the lords.

Before she could pry further, Beatrice felt a tap upon her shoulder. Spinning around, there at last was Greer Carson.

CHAPTER TWENTY

"Good evening." Greer Carson bowed. "I'm glad I caught up with you, china doll, clearly the best-dressed shepherdess who ever attempted to herd sheep."

Beatrice took in the welcome sight of him, with her heart immediately beating faster and her happiness level spiking.

"A savage!" she exclaimed.

"A native of my country," he confirmed.

"Well done!" She'd never seen anything quite like it except in a book. He wore a headdress that was as tall as Amity's wig but made of feathers, and a leather vest over—*an entirely bare chest!*—and soft leather pants. Even his feet were clad in strange shoes with beaded tassels, more like women's dancing slippers than anything she'd ever seen on a man.

"Moccasins," he said, lifting a foot. "Very comfortable."

They smiled at each other, but she couldn't help her glance returning to his chest. From what she could see, it was a nice one, not that she was any judge. She wanted to reach out and brush the sprinkling of hair visible where his buckskin vest didn't close, and she clenched her hands at her sides. *Imagine the scandal if she gave in to her impulse!*

Dragging her gaze back to his, Beatrice recalled their discussion of costumes weeks earlier. "I thought you didn't want to bring too much attention to yourself not being from here," she challenged.

"I changed my mind," he said. "My accent gives me away anyway, and most people have been welcoming."

Beatrice thought of Lord Melton, who'd said something slightly disparaging on more than one occasion regarding the habits of Americans. However, as long as Lady Emily didn't mind Greer's foreignness, she supposed that was all he cared about.

Looking her up and down with a glimmer in his eye, he asked, "So no crook or lamb? What a disappointment."

She shrugged. "And you don't have a buffalo. Another disappointment."

"I suppose I could have put a costume on Miss Sylvia and brought her as my companion."

They grinned at each other at the notion.

As usual, he then asked about her hand, which had healed nicely due to his ministrations—followed by Delia soaking Beatrice's hand in milk before gently cleaning off the butter and honey, and then applying a poultice of tea leaves held in place with a clean linen bandage, which she'd kept on overnight.

"Perfectly fine, thanks to you," Beatrice responded as she did whenever he asked.

Greer nodded his satisfaction. "Are you heading for the dance floor?" he asked.

"No, we were going to make the rounds." Looking behind her, she realized the rest of her group had kept walking and were now lost to her sight. "Would you care to accompany me?"

"I would be honored." He took her arm, and she could feel the warmth emanating from him, particularly aware of his bare chest so close to her.

"You managed to find a very authentic costume," she managed.

"Not really. If I'd had the brazenness of an Indian warrior, I would not be wearing this vest. The tailor I went to suggested I might not be allowed in without it, or if I was, the focus would be wholly on me rather than on the Prince and Princess of Wales."

The man had been right about that. As it was, Beatrice could hardly credit she was walking through one of the most opulent homes in London, if not all of England, with a scantily clad, shirtless man.

Out loud, she mused, "I wonder what Lady Emily will have to say."

He chuckled. "The odds I shall even see her tonight are very slim. I can hardly believe I found you for that matter. Another moment of your walking away from that mammoth fireplace, and I wouldn't have."

"When the flageolet sounds, or whatever they're using here tonight, perhaps a trumpet—"

"Or twenty," he joked.

"Indeed! I shall have to return to the Blenheim Saloon if I am ever to find my sisters again. That's where they will go looking, perhaps after the dancing." She tightened her grip upon his arm and pointed. "Look at that costume."

"The wasp woman? Very clever." They watched the lady stroll past with a black-and-yellow, sharply pointed front panel to her gown, and small wings protruding from her shoulders.

Greer pointed out the next stunning one, a woman dressed as a snowflake. "Now I can truly say that I have seen the elephant."

"Where?" she demanded, craning her neck. Someone dressed as an elephant would be far more impressive than a wasp.

He chuckled. "Just a saying. I guess it's an American one if you don't know it."

She frowned, shaking her head slightly.

"Have you ever seen one?" he asked.

"An elephant? Of course. This is London. There is almost nothing you cannot find here. Ten years ago, our Zoological Society traded a rhinoceros to the French for an elephant. Don't you think that was silly of the French? I mean, an elephant! It's the most amazing creature."

"And that's what the phrase means. I can't imagine seeing a ball or even a group of people more spectacular than this one."

"Very good, Mr. Carson. I like that. *To see the elephant.* I shall use it in the future."

They continued their promenade. Beatrice couldn't help noticing more than one lady gave her escort a second glance, and a third. It was not every day one saw so much of a man's upper body. In fact, never.

There were so many daring and inventive costumes, Beatrice felt almost dowdy. "That lady is a rainbow," Greer directed her gaze. "And that man can only be Henry the VIII. And you said I wouldn't know one king from another."

"I should have thought of something more exciting," Beatrice fretted.

"You look absolutely perfect," he told her, stopping their forward progress and gazing down at her. "Your dressmaker captured the color of your eyes exactly right in your gown, and the whole effect makes me feel as if you've brought a summer's day, complete with green fields and sheep, right here into this palace, even without a crook in your hand."

Her cheeks warmed. "That's very kind of you. Certainly more thoughtful than what Lord Melton said." She bit her tongue for even mentioning the man. She was not trying to make Greer jealous. *Was she?*

He frowned. "I'm surprised the man was able to find you. What did the churl say?"

She giggled. "He's not a churl, for goodness sake. Simply reserved and a little—"

"Lifeless." His forearm tightened and bulged under her fingers, causing her attention to be completely captivated for a moment. Never would she have guessed Greer had been concealing such a muscular physique under his clothing.

"You deserve someone more invigorating," he continued.

And more fun, she thought. *Like the man whose arm she was holding.*

Suddenly, a loud trumpet sounded signifying the start of the evening's entertainment, and a surge of guests bore down upon them, racing in the direction of the horn.

Greer tightened his hold on her arm, and Beatrice was grateful not to be swept away from him on a tide of wigs, massive hoop skirts, and sea captains' sabers.

"I think we should go back to where my sisters can discover us."

Greer led the way, and she held onto him with a firm grip, fearing if she lost hold of his arm, she would never see anyone she knew for the rest of the evening. A lost Dresden china, without her flock.

"As long as we can see something from that vantage point," he said. "Let's keep a little away from the wall."

All at once, the music began, and crowds surged again to give space to the dancers getting into formation.

Beatrice and Greer were both tall enough to see what was happening, but she feared Amity and Charlotte would miss the royals dancing unless they were on the very front edge of the enraptured audience. With all the participants of the first dance dressed as Venetian characters, including the Princess of Wales in a ruby-colored satin dress, with a blue paneled front and sleeves of satin puffings edged with gold and pearls, the first quadrille was underway.

Out of the corner of her eye, Beatrice saw a small group approaching. Assuming it was her sisters and the duke, she turned with a welcoming smile.

Lord Melton, wearing a furious expression, came to a

halt, putting hands to his hips. Of all people, Lady Emily accompanied him. She was dressed as Faust's Marguerite with the telltale square neckline and sleeves with horizontal puffs, looking far more sophisticated than Beatrice, she noted with dismay. With them was the St. George cousin with whom Charlotte had once danced, dressed as a gondolier with long striped pants and a cap.

The one who'd asked questions, as Beatrice recalled with a start. She caught her breath, knowing by the countenances of Lord Melton and the two St. Georges that the jig was up.

"You are an imposter!" Lord Melton said with evident virulence while still two yards away, in a voice loud enough to rival the musicians in the distance and causing a circle of onlookers to back up and make room for this latest entertainment. "I have been deceived all Season by this woman." He raised a hand and pointed toward her, as if there was any doubt as to whom he referred.

Beatrice felt the blood drain from her head. Finally, the icy viscount showed a little mettle. Unluckily, it was directed at her. She wished he'd retained his cool, aristocratic head rather than demonstrating he had a depth of emotion after all.

Glancing around himself, perhaps gauging the attention he was drawing, he appeared satisfied that he'd enticed at least a few to listen to his diatribe.

"She is a deceiver, an avaricious husband-hunter. A common *shopgirl*!" he bit out with absolute derision.

Beatrice swallowed, thinking she heard a collective gasp. She'd half-convinced herself the viscount had known all along. Apparently she had been mistaken, for he was genuinely irate. Moreover, by the smug look upon the face of Lady Emily's cousin, standing watching with amusement and crossed arms, he had been the arbiter of the news leading to her denouncement.

"A shopgirl as a guest at Marlborough House," Lord Melton continued in a rage. "Can anyone else imagine such impudence?"

What could she say? She certainly couldn't defend herself, for everything he said was blatantly true. Lady Emily, to her credit, was not enjoying the scene at all. She looked as shocked as Beatrice felt, her face white and pinched.

"You are out of line," Greer said, stepping forward to place his leather-clad self between her silly pastoral persona and the outraged viscount.

Beatrice had forgotten he was there as all eyes were upon her. Ladies dressed as the subjects of famous paintings stared and gestured with their fans, and men as court jesters and long-dead soldiers scowled. Someone dressed as Zenobia turned and gave her the cut direct, a bold Cleopatra sneered at her, and a cavalier stared as if she were a farm animal someone had let inside to run amuck at the ball.

If only the floor tiles would open up and let her slide beneath them!

"You are behaving badly, sir," the American said heatedly. "This is neither the time nor the place for your vicious accusations."

Lady Emily, with her glance slicing between Beatrice and Greer, took a step toward him, perhaps wondering if he also was not who he claimed to be.

"She is *not* a toffee heiress," Lord Melton proclaimed, causing a murmur to go up around them. Some people were plainly confused. A few snickered.

Beatrice knew she ought to be as ashamed as she had been mortified a moment earlier. Yet, the viscount's ridiculous statement made her shake her head while holding back a laugh. That Charlotte had managed to make anyone believe such a thing, even for a second, was a wondrous achievement.

"Not as such, no, I am not," she told him, feeling crabby. "But then, who is?"

A few more people laughed. "A toffee heiress!" someone exclaimed.

Lord Melton's face reddened. "You work at Rare Confectionery. That's why you were on New Bond Street."

"I never claimed otherwise," Beatrice told him.

"You said you were shopping that day I rescued the hat," he persisted.

"Rescued the hat?" someone repeated, and loud guffaws ensued.

"You made an assumption," she began, then stopped. They were bickering like children, and it was pointless. She sighed. "Regardless, I am sorry you felt deceived."

"You mean you are sorry you were caught," he said with vehemence that surprised her. "I want you thrown out of here at once." The viscount looked at his friend St. George and then at Greer, as if one of them would help toss her out.

Lady Emily appeared shocked at his words. Beatrice accepted she might find herself momentarily standing in the foggy night air of Pall Mall, walking back to Amity's house. However, Greer was not so easygoing.

"This is absurd. Miss Rare-Foure—"

"Of Rare Confectionery, a *sweet* shop," the viscount hissed, reminding everyone of her middle-class origins.

"Yes, and she is the most magnificent toffee-maker you can imagine," Greer said, which Beatrice didn't think really helped the situation, but he was not to be stopped now that he was in high dudgeon. "As I was saying, Miss Rare-Foure has every right to be here—"

"Who says she hasn't?" asked the Duke of Pelham, unexpectedly in their midst, with Amity and Charlotte. He took in everything, pausing and raising a single eyebrow as his glance landed on Greer's costume. Then he demanded, "What's going on here?"

The viscount, as well as Lord St. George, Lady Emily, and everyone else in the vicinity gave a low bow or curtsey. It wasn't every day someone was in close company with a duke and duchess.

"This woman is impersonating an heiress," Lord Melton said after he'd straightened.

Lord St. George grabbed his friend's elbow to stop him saying more. Beatrice wondered at the viscount's ignorance of the marital connection between herself and the duke.

However, as Greer had said once, hardly anyone knew of the Duchess of Pelham's origins. Nor did they care, not once she had become one of them.

"You are plainly an ass impersonating a man," Greer said, taking a step toward the viscount, but her brother-in-law put up his hand. The duke was made even more impressive by being clad in his King Louis XVI costume. Instantly, silence fell around them.

"No one gives a fig for your righteous indignation, Melton," His Grace said. "Everyone knows your estate has fallen on hard times and you are barely keeping your head above water. My *sister-in-law* is here as my guest, and she certainly doesn't need to deal with the likes of you, a sordid fortune hunter!"

Lord Melton's face was scarlet, but he didn't gainsay a word the duke had uttered, so Beatrice assumed he had been paying her suit while thinking her wealthy. With a great show of turning on his heel, his Persian silks swirling, the viscount walked away with St. George trailing along. The rest of the onlookers dispersed shortly after to watch the real entertainment, the quadrilles.

"To think," Beatrice said with mock indignation, "he was after me for my money!"

Charlotte and Amity began to laugh, but Greer still looked offended. "What a buffoon, causing a scene. If only I had a tomahawk on me."

Beatrice was simply glad no longer to be the focus of any attention. "I guess I will spend the rest of the Season as the Duke of Pelham's penniless sister-in-law rather than as a toffee heiress."

"A *treacle* toffee heiress," Charlotte murmured.

Beatrice glanced at Greer, expecting him to laugh, but he was distracted. Lady Emily hadn't walked away with the viscount and her cousin. Instead, she remained standing uncertainly, staring at the American.

If the ugly scene that had just transpired didn't scare off the lady, and if she still fancied Greer despite him standing up for a false toffee heiress, then she must truly care for him. Beatrice felt more disturbed by that fact than anything else which had happened.

"Did you get to see any of the cards' quadrille?" Charlotte asked.

"What does that mean?" Beatrice asked, preoccupied as Greer approached Lady Emily, put his head close to hers to say something, and then placed her hand on his arm. As the claws of jealousy encircled Beatrice's heart, Greer walked away with Lady Emily now the one next to his half-bare, muscular chest.

Drat! She keenly felt the loss of him already. She loved the way he'd stood up for her, loved the way he made her happy and made her laugh. Plainly, she loved *him!*

The realization had crept upon her over the course of days and weeks, and now it hit her with such force, she wanted to sit before she fell.

"Henry!" Amity exclaimed as Beatrice closed her eyes and started to sway. She felt lightheaded, probably from lack of nourishment during the day, and the way Delia had laced her corset too tightly.

The duke grabbed her arm to support her, and Beatrice was glad Greer was too far away to notice her weakness.

"You don't want to go home, do you?" Charlotte asked, plainly dreading such a circumstance when the evening had barely begun.

Taking a fortifying breath, Beatrice shook her head. "Of course not. I missed dancing cards. I don't intend to miss another moment."

Relieved, Charlotte nearly whistled, and Beatrice saw the instant she caught herself. Then her sister explained, "The dining room doors opened and the royal procession of dancers appeared. A polonaise was played, did you hear it?"

"Yes," Beatrice said. "I saw the Venetians dance."

"There was a grand marshal," Charlotte continued as if Beatrice hadn't spoken, "a man with a white wand dressed like an Elizabethan chamberlain."

"That was Lord Colville," the duke informed them.

"And he was followed by six guardsmen in laced coats with powdered wigs like Amity and His Grace," Charlotte added. "They were followed by the young princes, and—"

Amity interrupted Charlotte, "And there was another group in Van Dyke costumes, so clever."

"Oh, yes, the Duchess of Sutherland was in a Henrietta Maria dress of white satin. Most becoming," Charlotte continued.

"What does any of this have to do with cards?" Beatrice asked the duke, since her sisters were overcome with describing the costumes.

"Another quadrille set," he told her. "More royals. Princess Christian dressed as the Queen of Clubs and the Duke of Athole as the King of Spades and whatnot."

"Why weren't you with the other dukes?" she asked, feeling better the more distance she had between her and Greer and the disturbing sight of him walking away with Lady Emily.

"I'm not one of the royal dukes," he said, with a shrug, clearly not bothered. "Merely a regular duke."

That made her laugh, as if being a duke of any kind could be regular.

"Come along," Charlotte urged them, "the fairy tales are going to dance next, Cinderella, Puss in Boots, and Little Boy Blue. And the Prince of Wales is the fairy prince in a ruby tunic with grey satin tights and a leopard's head! I want Beatrice to see them."

Letting her younger sister grab hold of her, Beatrice released the duke's arm, and they all moved forward to watch the next royal quadrille.

AT HALF PAST TWELVE, their Royal Highnesses led their guests through the ballroom, down a few steps, and into the gardens. Two supper tents, finely decorated, had been set up. A smaller one with a massive buffet was festooned with crimson velvet Indian carpets and scarlet geraniums displayed throughout, both hanging from the roof and set upon the tables. A longer tent held tables stretching out for three hundred people to sit and eat..

Naturally, the royals and their guests would sit and be served. And just as naturally, the Duke of Pelham and his family went with them.

Beatrice kept an eye out for Greer, but if he was not with them upon entering, he would undoubtedly end up at the buffet in the other tent. With Lady Emily.

Charlotte had lost none of her excitement as the evening progressed and they took seats among life-sized, decorative armored figures and rich tapestries, making it seem like a medieval feast.

However, her sister quietened after they sat. "Are you terribly disappointed?"

Beatrice froze as she'd been thinking of Greer. "What do you mean? I knew all along Mr. Carson . . . ," then she trailed off at her sister's expression.

"I meant with Lord Melton's odious behavior. You have danced quite a bit with him over the past few weeks, and Delia told me he came to the house."

Beatrice was pleased to be able to put her sister's mind at ease. "I could not possibly be less affected by the behavior of the Viscount Melton. Do not worry for me, dear sister. He is of no consequence whatsoever."

"That's good. The duke said he never did invite him to St. James's Place. Lord Melton wasn't at our first ball. He lied."

Beatrice nodded and sipped her wine. *More deception, but who was she to raise an eyebrow at a blatant lie?*

Nonetheless, she decided this would be her last event. She could no longer pretend an interest in any of the men she'd met. It was impossible while her bolder-than-life American strode around the ballrooms and dining rooms of

London, vastly more appealing to her than anyone else.

Moreover, she loved him, and he was going to marry Lady Emily.

Despite her decision to end her foray into high society, the evening was not yet over. After they ate, they danced until daylight in three rooms facing the garden—the ballroom where the quadrilles had been, and the library and the dining room on either side of it. Beatrice couldn't imagine a grander event. It was a perfect time to retreat, as all the rest of the Season would pale in comparison and seem practically shabby. Hopefully, Amity would go with Charlotte in her place.

And then, when Beatrice had danced with so many strangers, made stranger still by their costumes, and when she couldn't imagine taking another step, Greer appeared before her.

"I've been looking for you for ages, Dresden china," he said. "Dinner was grand, wasn't it?"

She wanted to say she would have enjoyed it more with him seated beside her, but she didn't. "It was. I think definitely the best we've had all Season, but don't tell Amity I said so."

He smiled. "Will you dance with me? I was worried I wouldn't find you before you left, and that would be a shame. I have grabbed hold of the arm of two other Dresden chinas and been sorely disappointed. Not only that, they seemed ready to scream for help at my familiar manner."

She chuckled. "I am sure the papers will discuss the opening quadrilles, the tent suppers, and the dangerous Indian chief accosting pastoral young ladies."

The musicians played the first few notes of a waltz, then stopped to let everyone find a partner and, more importantly, to find room on the dance floor.

"Come along, my toffee heiress, let us dance."

A thrill went through her at his possessive words until she recalled he'd spent hours dancing with Lady Emily.

Swallowing her ridiculous jealousy, Beatrice put her hand on his shoulder, felt his arm around her, his warm fingers resting on her back. Their other hands were perfectly aligned, grasping hold, and then the music began.

A few minutes earlier, she'd been near exhaustion. Now, Beatrice didn't want the waltz to end.

CHAPTER TWENTY-ONE

Greer wandered back to his hotel from the Marlborough House ball, unable to get a hackney that morning. Maybe it was his savage costume. In any case, the Langham wasn't too far, perhaps half an hour's stroll. He planned to take care of Miss Sylvia and then sleep the day away.

It had been a revelatory event, and his heart had finally shouted at him what he could no longer deny. He had to have Beatrice.

Lady Emily was a nice enough sort of girl, but nothing about her called to him, demanding he be with her. He'd walked away from the scene of scandal and name-calling to have a moment alone and explain how he would no longer be paying her suit and wished her well. Briefly, he felt guilty, especially since she'd seemed willing to continue their tepid courtship, and maybe would have said yes to being his wife.

How well his plans would have worked out if he had loved her. But he didn't. He loved Beatrice with all his heart. And Carsonbank House in Scotland be damned!

He knew his blue-eyed toffee-maker wasn't immune to him, either. The exquisite simplicity of a kiss with her—easy to fall into and soul-shattering at the same time—had awakened in him an ardent longing for more. He was confident she felt the same. Even if she didn't, if she had no more thought for him than for that wretched Melton, he would spend the rest of his days wooing her until she fell head-over-heels for him.

The following day, after he'd rested and hoped she'd done the same, he went to Rare Confectionery to find her.

BEATRICE HEARD THE BELL tinkle and by Charlotte's greeting knew who it was. She'd been waiting for Greer to drop by so they could share thoughts on the fancy-dress ball. On the other hand, she'd been half-dreading it, so strong now were her feelings for him. Soon, he would be able to see it plainly upon her face. *What if he pitied her?*

She went out front. There he was, dressed normally again. How sad to think she'd seen her last glimpse of the American's impressive chest. Probably many women from the night before felt the same way.

Without preamble, he asked her, "Will you come tour a townhouse with me tomorrow? I need a woman's opinion."

His question brought her out of her futile ponderings. She focused on his earnest face and intelligent eyes, avidly wishing she didn't love him so much. The very notion of him purchasing a home to which he could take Lady Emily caused Beatrice's irritation to bubble up and over.

"Shouldn't that woman be your future wife?" she snapped. "Everyone has their own likes and dislikes. I might prefer the drawing room on the upper floor, like at Amity's house, while others prefer it on the ground floor so guests don't have to go upstairs."

"A room is a room, surely," Greer said, "and you can furnish it for whatever use you like."

"Not every room is such," she protested, desperately wanting to make him leave her out of his plans.

"Come along, I entreat you. Come as my dear friend Beatrice, and tell me whether to choose the townhouse recently left empty by the death of a bachelor baronet, age 84, sadly not found for five days after passing, or the one which a couple fled due to an overpopulation of mice."

Charlotte made a noise of dismay. *Was he joking?*

"Neither of those," Beatrice said, crossing her arms stubbornly. "They both sound horrid."

"They do," her sister agreed.

"There's another one that a family lately vacated after buying a larger house toward Richmond."

"Richmond," she repeated, recalling their day at Syon Park. "It is lovely there."

"Too many pigeons as I recall," he teased. "Besides, I want to live in London. Will you help me?"

"Lady Emily should be the one," she insisted, and it hurt even to say the words. *Lady Emily Carson!* Beatrice had asked Amity who had asked the duke—apparently, the lady would keep her rank and title but take Greer's last name. He would have his fondest wish, a lady wife.

"I cannot ask her to traipse all over Mayfair looking at houses. We don't have that kind of easy friendship you and I share. If you and I do it, I don't think we'll need a chaperone, will we? We'll have the Chestertons' estate agent to keep us company in the house."

Beatrice shook her head. "Oh, Mr. Carson. Have you learned nothing? Of course we need a chaperone. We cannot be in a carriage together, especially not a hired hackney."

"I'll buy my own soon, when I have a place to keep it. Anyway, what if we take your maid, the one who is always chasing after you and Miss Charlotte with cloaks and extra slippers?"

"Delia." Beatrice considered it.

"Yes, can she perform the duties of a chaperone?"

"I suppose." Then she shook her head. "I didn't say I would go."

"Please, Miss Rare-Foure. We shall have fun as only the two of us do together."

She stared at him. *Was he blind to how he affected her?* And yet, she heard herself acquiesce with bad grace. "Very well, if I'm the one friend you have in London."

He grinned, neither confirming nor denying that to be the case. "Can you go tomorrow?"

"Yes," she said, feeling mulish anyway. "I shall speak to Delia tonight, as long as Charlotte doesn't mind my coming in late tomorrow."

"I don't," her sister said, proving she'd been listening the whole time.

"I shall collect you at eleven from your home."

He looked far too pleased with himself as he strode out the door.

GREER FELT AS IF the weight of the world had lifted from his shoulders. And that feeling continued even after he picked up Beatrice, looking supremely annoyed—*bless her!*—along with her maid.

"First stop, Brook Street and a townhouse with three floors."

"Is this the one that the bachelor baronet died in?"

"What?" exclaimed the maid.

"No, I crossed that from my list," he assured them. "This is the one the large family moved out of."

"So, no mice either?" Beatrice asked, with her saucebox mouth. "You might consider that one since you have Miss Sylvia to keep them at bay."

"I'm sure she can do an adept job," he said. "But I prefer we not start with an unwieldy population of rodents."

"We?" Beatrice repeated, looking even more sourly irritated, if that were possible.

"Never mind," he said quickly. "I hope this first one suits. It sounded perfect, but I suppose it's the agent's job to make any property sound ideal."

"Even one with a plethora of mice," Beatrice added.

"If it doesn't suit, there are other homes for sale."

"I say," Delia put forth, "I'm looking forward to poking about in someone else's house."

Greer caught Beatrice's eyes. "Truth be told," he said, "I am too. It's fun."

With her expression lightening, perhaps enjoying herself against her will, Beatrice confessed, "Me, too."

When the carriage drew up in front of the first townhouse, he doubted they needed to look further. It was on a square with a park out front, not a corner unit, but there was a back garden and a mews for his new carriage. He hoped Beatrice liked it.

"It's grand," said the forthright Delia as they assembled on the doorstep and rang the bell. The estate agent let them in and talked unceasingly for twenty minutes about every detail in every room for three floors. Greer was ready to muzzle the man for his prattle, mostly because it had kept Beatrice from expressing her opinions, and he wanted to know her thoughts.

Finally, when the man was spouting forth on the quality of the handrailing belonging to the main staircase, Greer snapped. "Mr. Spellman, would you be so kind as to let us have a few moments alone to wander the home. Perhaps you can tell Mrs. Delia about the quality of the plumbing in the laundry room."

"Well, I don't know," Mr. Spellman protested.

"Mrs. Delia has final say as to whether Mr. Carson purchases the house," Beatrice said. "If the servants' quarters aren't up to her standards, then he cannot possibly take the place. You know what they say, Mr. Spellman, about a happy servant."

He frowned. "No, what?"

Beatrice shrugged. "I'm sure I don't know." With that confounding statement, she walked down the hallway to the back of the house.

"She's right of course," Greer told the estate agent, who nodded in agreement. "The laundry *and* the servants' quarters, if you please." Then he wandered out of the room and along the corridor, keeping an ear cocked until he heard Mr. Spellman and Beatrice's maid go downstairs.

Dashing from one doorway to the next, he finally found Beatrice staring out the window to the back of the house.

"Thank you for your assistance," he said, coming to a halt close beside her.

"You're more than welcome. The man spoke as if he'd never had a chance to say a word in his life and had stored them all up for us."

Greer laughed. "What do you think of it?"

Even seeing her only in profile, he could tell her expression tightened, and he feared she would say she didn't like it. Personally, he thought it splendid.

"Anyone would be lucky to live in such a nice house," she said finally. "I'm sure you and Lady Emily will be happy here."

Before he could speak, she turned to face him. "I mean, I'm not confident of that at all. You might not be suited to one another, and the lady might be a stick who doesn't enjoy a bit of fun. No offense to your future wife."

"The woman I want for my wife knows how to enjoy more than a bit of fun," he assured her, taking a step forward.

She backed up, her cheeks paling. "I just realized, you shouldn't be here alone with me, especially not while speaking of her. And she doesn't look the sort to have fun, if I may say so."

"You may. However, I am not with you while speaking

of her. I'm with you while speaking of *you*. For quite plainly, it's you I love, and you whom I wish to marry. Will you marry me, Miss Rare-Foure, and live in this house? Or would you prefer to see the one with the mice?"

He watched the play of emotions cross her face, a beloved face he'd come to depend upon seeing often, a face he wanted to wake up to every morning and go to sleep beside every night. A small frown creased her forehead, then her eyes widened, her lips opening in surprise, and then she gasped and clamped a hand to her mouth.

"Is that a yes?" he asked, for he was never entirely sure where he stood with his toffee-maker.

"How can it be?" she asked.

"How can it be what?" he returned.

"How can I answer yes, knowing you will lose your inheritance?"

He shook his head at her words. "You are worth more than any manor house or piece of land. Beatrice, you are worth a lifetime of love."

She backed up another step, looking alarmed. "You mustn't say that, nor change your perfect plan. It was the entire purpose of your coming to London and finding a titled lady. You said yourself that your estate turns a profit but needs you in charge to restore it. More importantly, you said you loved it. I cannot let you throw that away when you are about to achieve your goal."

He was starting to worry she didn't feel the same way about him. In the next moment, he would find out.

"My goal has changed," he said. "Quite simply, I want you."

Her eyes were glistening, but infuriatingly, she was shaking her head.

"No?" he asked, feeling a shard of fear slice through him. *Did this beautiful, smart, saucy, ornery, funny, wonderful woman really not want him?*

"Scotland," she protested feebly.

"What?" he demanded.

"If I am truly your friend, then I must counsel you," she paused, gulped a lungful of air, then continued, "to stay the course and claim your land. Everyone wants to own land. Even my parents have a small country house. It would be patently selfish on my part not to remind you of this, and I can't be selfish where you are concerned, you who have given me and my family so much."

"Selfish? Beatrice, dammit, for once be like an American and speak plainly. Do you want to be my wife? Yes or no. No more nonsense about my ridiculous goal or counseling me." He stepped closer and took her by the upper arms.

"I no longer give a damn about being a Scottish landowner, and I don't need you to guide my future. But I do want you to be in it."

Silence. Only those large blue eyes staring into his. And then he saw it, the moment her thoughts went from doubtful and even fearful to accepting and agreeable. The instant Beatrice made her decision.

"Yes! I want to be your wife." And she slid her arms up and around his neck, drew his head down, and kissed him.

He could have sworn the air around them sizzled when their lips touched. It was a long and satisfying kiss.

When he pulled back, he realized he had slid his hands behind her and was holding onto her tightly.

"I take it you aren't interested in any of the snout-noses you've met."

She smiled. "They all lacked a certain humor I've found with you."

"You like me for my ability to amuse you?"

"No, Mr. Carson. I *love* you for the way you make me feel when we're together. With you, I have seen the elephant!"

He lowered his mouth to hers again, breathing in her vanilla scent and teasing her with his lips.

"OH NO," CAME A familiar wailing voice. Not overly concerned, Beatrice turned her head at the same time as Greer to see Delia in the hallway, wearing an expression of dismay, with the Chestertons' estate agent beside her.

However, she didn't step back with guilt at being caught kissing. Instead, Beatrice slowly lowered her arms, and then her American—*the man who had asked her to marry him!*—took her hand in his as they faced their onlookers.

"I was shirking my duties," Delia moaned. "I never should have left you alone. But the servants' quarters were very nice," she added, glancing at the man beside her. "And the plumbing is all new." Then she frowned. "That's beside the point, though, isn't it? Miss Beatrice, you have behaved very badly."

"It's all right, Delia. Mr. Carson has asked me to marry him, and I said yes."

With an incoherent sound, the Rare-Foure maid rushed forward to hug her. "Your mother said it would turn out this way all along."

"Did she?" Beatrice asked. Then she recalled how Felicity had predicted they would marry the first time she'd found her and Greer alone together in the back room of the confectionery.

"She did, didn't she?" he remarked, clearly recalling that day, too. "Your mother is a perceptive woman."

"I can't wait for her to return so I can tell her she was right," Beatrice said. "That will make her day. On the other hand, I suppose it will be like every other day, for I don't think anyone's ever told my mother she was wrong."

"What about this property, Mr. Carson?"

The three of them had completely forgotten the estate agent. Greer looked at her, a questioning expression on his handsome face. She nodded.

"I'll buy it," he said.

GREER DROPPED OFF HIS English bride-to-be at Rare Confectionery where undoubtedly Miss Charlotte would shortly hear the good news. Beatrice had assured him her father would not be angry at his violation of polite custom by asking her to marry him before securing Mr. Foure's permission regarding his middle daughter's hand.

"He's not old fashioned," she'd said during the carriage ride.

"He's not," Delia had chimed in, as if the three of them were in it together, and they'd both looked at her and laughed. "Well, he's not," the maid had insisted. "Mr. Foure will come back from France and be ever so pleased for you both."

"Perhaps we can go to dinner at Amity's home tomorrow," Beatrice had mused.

"You feel like celebrating, do you?" he'd asked her.

"Yes." Her eyes were sparkling like sun on the water. "It would be nice to share our news and to do so at St. James's Place."

He had kissed her hand before leaving her and Delia at the shop door. Back at his hotel, Greer entered through the front vestibule because it was a treat each time he did. Nodding to the porters who congregated, ever ready to help, Greer traversed the main entrance hall. Taking a left, he eschewed the lifts for the staircase. As he passed the reception office, a porter stopped him.

"You have a letter from America," the man said and held out a silver tray.

Greer read the return address, seeing it was from his uncle. The hotel had its own postal office and a telegraph, which he'd used to let his mother's brother know where he was when he'd first settled in. He couldn't help wondering why his uncle hadn't responded in kind, rather than using the slow route of mail by sea.

Noting with glee there was also a single Rare Confectionery chocolate on the tray, perched on top of one of their familiar white-and-blue cards, he stuffed the envelope in his pocket before taking both the chocolate and the business card.

Thanking the man, he pulled a coin out of his pocket and gave it to him.

"The lift has arrived, sir," the porter said. With a shrug, Greer decided not to be rude but to take the hydraulic elevator the hotel was so proud of.

In the lift, he popped the sweet into his mouth. A burst of deliciousness exploded on his tongue, and he sighed, thinking of his toffee-maker. *Beatrice was going to be his!*

He didn't feel an ounce of regret for letting the Scottish estate go. And he hoped his distant cousin would somehow overcome the legalities and take it on, renovations and all. For his part, Greer would have a modern townhouse in London with his beautiful bride. Hopefully, they would be blessed with a large brood, and if they wanted, they would buy a modest country home for the months they wished to escape the city, as he heard the nobility liked to do.

Upon entering his suite of rooms, he was greeted by Miss Sylvia and one of her long feline sentences of meows. When he walked over to the writing desk, she jumped up onto it, scattering the newspaper he'd left there. He supposed she was ready for a walk.

"Wait until you see your new home," he told her, having become quite used to chatting to his fluffy companion as if she understood him. In truth, their closeness began on the ship when he realized he was leaving behind everything else from his old life, and that Miss Sylvia was the sole connection. He rubbed her head the way she liked.

"Three stories for you to rule and a walled-in garden to keep you safe. And the loveliest woman to fuss over you. Over both of us, in fact."

He slit open the letter with the silver opener provided by the hotel and scanned it in the light streaming in the window.

His mother's brother wished him well, and apologized for the bad news he was about to impart. And then Greer felt his world tilt as the words *ruined, tragedy*, and *worthless stocks* leaped out at him.

"You already know how '73 rippled through the banks, with the collapse of Cooke & Company and the Northern Pacific Railway debacle. Last year's railroad strike damaged the company more than I imagined," his uncle wrote, filling Greer in on the hit to their stocks, their labor force, and even how passenger use had fallen off.

"Grant left the country rudderless, and while Hayes is working on all fronts, he has a hundred fires to put out. The war your father died in is still being fought, with the South wanting all troops out and an end to reconstruction. Cotton prices have been cut in half. The president is still dealing with the silver coinage issue, and the clamoring to retire greenbacks grows ever stronger. While steel production is increasing, prices are not. In short, we are in a mess."

Greer took a breath. Even with his railroad stocks being all but worthless, he surely must have a large balance in his bank account. He would head to Barclay's Bank on Lombard Street immediately and have them wire his New York City bank.

"Meow," said Miss Sylvia.

His uncle concluded with an apology for not sending word via telegraph, but the exorbitant expense had seemed untenable at a hundred dollars for ten words. "Besides," his uncle wrote, "how could I have told you so much in ten words? I am sorry. I hope you make a life for yourself there in Great Britain."

"Meow," said Miss Sylvia again.

Even with all his dreams suddenly seeming precarious, and while his mind started to mull over the ramifications, Greer wouldn't shirk his obligations to his mother's precious cat. Dropping the letter onto the desk, he was at least thankful his uncle's missive had arrived before he'd attempted to buy the townhouse.

Hooking the cat's leash onto her collar, he picked her up and carried her from the hotel.

CHAPTER TWENTY-TWO

"I cannot imagine why he hasn't stopped by or sent a note. Amity has invited us to dinner," Beatrice told Charlotte the following morning. "You, too, of course. And I haven't even told him or made sure he will go." Although she had no doubt he would.

"You didn't keep her guessing, did you?"

Beatrice smiled. "No, I couldn't. I told her the minute she walked in here after you left yesterday."

Charlotte clapped her hands. "I'm so thrilled for you. And you didn't need to pretend to be a toffee heiress after all to get a husband."

"I never did pretend," she protested. "That was all you."

"Perhaps it was," her sister agreed. "In any case, now you will be a real one. A railroad heiress."

Beatrice wrinkled up her nose. "It seems hard to believe. I cannot wait for Mother and Father to return."

The shop door tinkled, and Greer entered. Feeling her love bubble up, she ran toward him, thinking to embrace him even though they weren't alone. However, the expression on his face halted her a step away as if she'd come upon a brick wall.

"Whatever is the matter?"

He didn't deny something was wrong. After glancing at Charlotte, for whom he spared a grimace of a smile, he asked, "May we speak privately?"

"I won't tattle if you go in the back room to be alone," Charlotte said. "And I'll stay over by the door to keep from overhearing anything."

Beatrice could tell something very serious had occurred. With her heart beating an erratic tattoo, she said, "Come along." Turning, she led the way into the back of the shop.

"What's wrong?" she asked at once, even as Greer was closing the heavy velvet drape behind him. He strolled toward the far end of the work room, then spun about and faced her, his hands on his hips, pushing his coat back, looking like a man with a difficult task to do.

She swallowed down her anxiety. After all, she loved him and he loved her. Nothing else mattered.

"Plainly, and without keeping anything from you," he said, "I have experienced a terrible downturn in my financial situation."

She blinked. Beatrice hadn't expected such a thing, but she also didn't know what it meant exactly. Moreover, for some reason, it didn't seem to be the most disastrous of announcements. It wasn't life or death, after all. Nor, as she feared, had he been called back to the United States. *Or had he?*

"Do you have to go back to America?" She wished her voice didn't sound so scared.

He frowned. "Honestly, I hadn't thought of that. I intended to speak with local railroad owners to see if I could find employment here. It seems folly to go back to America when I know they are in pandemonium already."

"You know we had our own railroad downturn, as you call it, but that was before I was born. We took a wonderful train trip to Edinburgh once, and my father told us about railway mania in the forties causing everyone and anyone to invest in them. Some of the planned railroads were fraudulent investments. More and more money was poured in and seemingly disappeared, like sugar into melted butter. The whole thing collapsed eventually, but not until after such vast expansion that we're still using all those rails today. I suppose that doesn't help the men who lost everything in the process."

He nodded. "My uncle kept our company's troubles from me for too long. When I left his employ, I thought he had everything under control. Instead, it turns out my fortune in stocks has disappeared, and they are now worthless. What's more, a telegram has confirmed my New York bank account is nearly empty since it is no longer being fed by dividends."

"Oh, Greer." Her heart ached for him. Yet surprisingly, he half-smiled.

"I think that's the first time you've used my given name."

"Out loud," she said. "In my head, you are Greer or . . . ," she trailed off, feeling her cheeks heat up.

"Or what?" he asked.

"Or *the American*."

"Ah," he nodded. "Iconic, am I?"

"Yes." To her he was the embodiment of all things she'd learned about America, rugged and frank and independent. "So we are not going to America after we marry, but will continue to live here. I will remain a confectioner, and you will find employment . . . doing something with railways."

She'd wrapped up the plan in her mind and put a bow on it, all the while seeing by his face that it was not to be.

"We cannot marry," he said, his voice strangely gruff.

She shook her head in protest. Her happiness had lasted barely twenty-four hours, and she wasn't going to let it go without a fight.

"I cannot ask you for your hand," he continued, "not while my situation is so precarious. I must move out of the Langham at once. Today."

"You have already asked me for my hand," she reminded him. "It would be extremely rude of you to withdraw your offer when I have said yes."

"I know. Believe me, I know." He closed his eyes for a second, presumably to gather his thoughts. "Miss Rare-Foure . . . Beatrice, I cannot go to your father in such a state. No father should give his daughter to me at present, and no respectable man would expect him to."

"I don't care about respectable men," she snapped. "I want you."

They stared at one another, then the oddity of her statement caused them both to smile.

"You know I didn't mean that," Beatrice told him.

"I know, but I can't buy the townhouse. I can't support a wife, let alone children we might have."

And that would probably happen sooner rather than later, she thought, having spent the better part of the previous evening fantasizing about the pleasures of the wedding night and their marital bed.

"Perhaps we could live with my parents," she began. "Amity moved out and there is more room. My mother would love Miss Sylvia."

"No," he said, his face closing over. "I'm not starting married life by living off of charity."

"You would prefer to break your word to me and not start our married life at all than live with my family?"

He sighed. "I cannot argue the point. It would make me feel—" He looked away, then down at the floor at her feet before finishing, "—emasculated."

She walked up to him until he had to look her in the eye. "Pride. Are you saying you choose your pride over me?"

"I'm saying I cannot drag you down when everything about our association was intended to lift you up. You could have chosen a nobleman—"

"Like Lord Melton!" she said with disdain.

"No, not like him. One with honor. Any number of whom you danced with this Season. But I have no intention of letting you chain yourself to a pauper, which I will surely be soon. I may not even be able to keep Miss Sylvia in whitefish and sardines."

He smiled again, trying to make light of it, but she was in no mood. "Everything about our association was for *you* to find a titled miss. I could not have cared less about finding a nobleman."

"Please, don't be angry." He yanked off his hat and tucked it under his arm. "You know I want more than anything to marry you."

She crossed her arms to prevent herself from grabbing hold of him as she wanted to do. "Then you shouldn't let a little thing like money stand in the way."

He shook his head. "It's not a little thing, and you know it. It's our future. I vow I will figure this out and when I do, I will ask you again. What's more, I will do it properly next time and ask your father first."

She softened when he said he would ask her again. He wasn't going to walk out of her life. He wasn't going to break her heart.

"You can find employment while we remain together. We can still become engaged as planned and—"

"I will not let you pledge yourself to me if I cannot support us. That's final."

Whoever said Americans were easygoing? She wanted to lash out at him for his stubbornness and his talk of emasculation. He seemed no less masculine to her today without his fortune than he had the day before. Her temper flared.

"I suppose you should go back to your original goal and woo the wealthy Lady Emily. With her money, you will be able to buy the townhouse, get your Scottish estate, and start your family. And I'm sure she can afford all the sardines Miss Sylvia could wish."

"I am not going to woo Lady Emily." He put a hand to her chin and held it. "For one thing, she wouldn't want me now that I have no money. And for another, I don't know if she likes cats."

He was mocking her. Beatrice tried to pull her head away, but he held her still.

"Please, Beatrice, I didn't want this to happen. I want only you."

She heard the anguish in his voice and relented. "Very well. I release you from the engagement, and I will tell Charlotte not to mention that it ever happened. What about the Season?"

He gave a mirthless laugh. "What about it?"

She shrugged. "It's already paid for and there is no getting that money back, nor the cost of the gowns or your suits. After the Marlborough House ball, I was finished with all of it, but then when we . . . when I thought we were to marry, I was looking forward to finishing the Season with you." She finally gave him a smile. "Perhaps we can still enjoy dancing together."

"I would feel like an imposter being with those people."

This time she laughed. "We already were. However, now you won't be pursuing any titled lady nor I any nobleman, we shall be more truthful than ever before. Let's finish out the Season, Greer."

He considered it. "What if some Lord Snit-Snot asks you for your hand?"

"Even if a king asked me, I would not give it to him."

Taking her face between his palms, he looked into her eyes. "Lord Snit-Snot could give you a life like that of your sister."

"I wouldn't want that life," she promised. Then smiled. "Not with Snit-Snot."

And then Greer kissed her, slowly, thoroughly, with a bittersweet tenderness that squeezed her heart. She wanted to hold onto him forever, but when he lifted his head, there was nothing more to say.

Ramming his hat back upon his head, he walked out.

GREER WAS WORRIED ABOUT Miss Sylvia. She most certainly did not like their new hotel. It was a single room on the ground floor and felt like a hovel in comparison to the Langham. That was because it *was* a hovel compared to just about anywhere else except a garden shed. But it also cost the same for three weeks as the previous hotel suite cost for a night.

Whenever he returned, the cat swished her tail angrily and tried to dart past him. Since there was no safe park across the street, he had to secure her and take her farther to find green grass. Walking on the pavement was a nightmare, as the pedestrian traffic was too dense and he risked her being kicked or trod upon.

He couldn't imagine how he was going to find an acceptable place to live and a good job. Moreover, despite what he'd said to Beatrice about not returning to America, he now considered whether it would be for the best. Perhaps he could help his uncle get the business back to its pinnacle, although his mother's brother had curiously not asked for his return or his assistance.

In point of fact, Greer felt decidedly cut off.

After walking and feeding Miss Sylvia, he went to The Cock Tavern on Fleet Street, as he had been doing every week unless there was an event on that Wednesday night. And even then, sometimes he would go from a hearty steak dinner to the ballroom, since the food at a dance was usually sparse and not provided until midnight.

That Wednesday, he found only two of his new friends, including John Delorey, the weaver, drinking stout, and Randall Molino, the antiquarian, drinking porter.

"Your gathering is smaller tonight," Greer said as he sat down.

Calling over the server, a comely waitress as all the servers were to keep the mostly male customers happy, he ordered ale and a steak. All at once, he realized he might have to cut out even this simple pleasure soon.

"George is dealing with a strike among his factory

workers," Delorey said. "And Jeremiah lost his job, so he's at home brooding with his wife."

At least the man had a wife. But seeing how everyone had troubles, Greer decided to focus on theirs more than his own.

"What type of work does Jeremiah do?" Greer didn't think he'd ever asked before.

"Coal-whipper at the Victoria Docks."

"Truly? I thought such a job would be assured."

"Too many can do it, and he was caught with gin for his lunch. But don't worry about Jeremiah. He'll find work again. He always does," Delorey said. "Probably at St. Katherine or Millwall docks."

Greer nodded, relieved when a pint of ale was placed before him. He'd downed half of it before he realized the others had stopped talking and were staring at him.

"You don't seem yourself, Mr. Carson," the quiet, watchful Molino observed. "A little morose this evening?"

Greer considered how much to say. He'd met with these men about six times. They were more than acquaintances, but perhaps not friends. Then he thought how little it mattered. He didn't have a reputation to uphold. They weren't nobility who would judge him, either.

"I find myself having swung from the top of the heap to the bottom in the course of a day. I had a woman who agreed to be my wife, and I thought I had a fat bank account to support her. Now I have neither, nor a job. Like Jeremiah, I am brooding."

Delorey gave him his usual slap on the back. "Then you're looking for work, are you?"

"I am, and a permanent place to live as hotels are expensive. Strangely, I have a family estate in Scotland that I cannot have, nor if I could, would I be able to pay for its upkeep. I have a woman who loves me, but I cannot pay for her upkeep, either."

The men laughed as if he'd spoken in jest, and Greer wished he could join in their merriment, but his heart had shattered in his chest, if he were to put a poetic twist upon the ache he was feeling.

"What type of work did you do in America?" Delorey asked. "I thought you were born to wealth."

"We all thought you rich as Croesus," Molino added.

"So did I," Greer said, draining the rest of his ale and gesturing to the server for another. "I've been spending like him, too, and now find my family's company has gone bankrupt. My railroad stocks are worthless."

"Railroads," Delorey repeated. "Can you work them or do you only know how to make money off of others working on them?"

"A fair question," Greer said. "I've done every job on the line, from switch man to boiler header, and I've argued with more than one tonnage hound over the safety of too long and heavy a train. I've also eaten my share of meals at the beanery."

"Fair enough. I'll ask around. There are certainly railroad jobs for the experienced."

Greer shrugged. "Who is striking on George's watch?"

"George has a team of lamplighters."

"Gas lamps?" Greer asked. "That sounds easier than working the railway."

His new friends laughed. "Maybe easier, but the pay is crap and with electric lights coming in, they're getting nervous."

"Hence the strike, I suppose," Greer said. In truth, he felt cheered talking jobs with these men. Ordering a third ale as his steak came, he mentioned what else had been bothering him. "If I could have got a hold of the land in Scotland, it has an income."

"Why can't you?" Delorey asked, his interest piqued.

Greer considered what to say, but the ale had loosened his tongue, and he told the truth. "Without money of my own, I can't offer for a titled lady, and without one, I can't meet the stipulations of my great-grandfather's will that would allow me to inherit."

"The woman who agreed to be your wife is a titled lady?"

He grinned. "No, I fell in love with a shopkeeper's daughter. I decided to give up my inheritance for her."

Delorey shook his head pityingly. "And now she won't marry you because you lost your wealth."

"Strangely, she will, but I won't marry her until I can support her."

Molino nodded in agreement. "A shame you can't get your estate, if, as you say, it runs at a profit. Must be good land to do that without a master at its head."

Greer recalled the conviction he'd felt when visiting the main house, to fix it up and bring a family of his own there. "If my father were alive, he'd no doubt fight for it and probably have a plan, too. There's a painting in one room that looks as I remember him, although I know it's not my father but his, as a young man."

In the portrait, his grandfather, filled with vim and vigor, stared out at the viewer, ramrod straight back, with one hand resting against the pommel of his sheathed sword— the very same one his father had taken and lost in the war— and a brightly colored necklace clutched in the other. Greer had thought it strange at the time, but while he'd wondered about the necklace, having never seen it on his mother, there'd been no one there to ask, except a skittish maid and some farm hands outside.

"Your thoughts are more than a furlong away," observed Delorey. "Like a man in love."

Greer started in on his steak, thinking of the portrait and Beatrice and the necklace . . . *and Miss Sylvia?* He stopped chewing unable to credit what his brain was thinking. The necklace in the portrait had been odd because it was not a strand of pearls or even diamonds or any single precious jewel. It was an ugly mish-mash of stones. Just like the cat's collar.

"Do you appraise jewelry?" he asked Molino, the antique dealer.

His eyes lit with interest. "I do. I specialize in the Tudor period, but I can look at anything. If I don't know about it, I can send you to someone who does."

"Have you suddenly remembered some hidden treasure?" Delorey asked with a chuckle.

Greer shook his head with wonder. "Maybe I have." He probably should keep it to himself until he was in the safety of Molino's shop, but with uncharacteristic good cheer, the man bought them all another round. With his tongue lubricated, Greer told them about Miss Sylvia's collar, describing the stones, and told them of the painting.

"It's possible when my grandfather set off for America, he took not that sword alone but also the jewels. I'll come by your shop tomorrow. I don't need to know a value precisely, just whether something is real or glass."

"I can do that," Molino agreed, "and with pleasure. But not tomorrow. I won't be in my shop. Come by on Friday morning, and we'll see what you've got."

GREER WAS ONLY HALF-CONVINCED the jewels on Miss Sylvia's collar resembled what he'd seen in the painting. But it was worth a try.

When he entered his new room, as usual, the cat tried to dash past him, and as usual, he was ready for her.

Grabbing her up by her scruff, he kicked the door closed and sat on the bed with her. There was no sofa, but an old chair and a small writing table.

"Yes, we shall go out but not until the morning. It's late, and you've had your walk," he said, soothing her with a rub behind her ears while he looked at her collar.

Never once had he considered the jewels could be real. Metal prong holders set in the wide leather strap clamped down over each stone, and now, while Miss Sylvia stayed relatively still, he thought it odd that every one was a different shape and size. If they were made of glass or even colored marbles, he imagined they would all be alike.

Turning the collar on her neck, he counted, fifteen jewels in all. If they were real . . .

Releasing her, he lay back, putting his hands behind his head. He mustn't get ahead of himself, or the disappointment would be too great. He must not even start imagining what it would mean if they were precious stones, but he couldn't help himself. *Beatrice!* He would be able to ask her again to be his wife.

With the proceeds from the jewels' sale, he could buy the townhouse outright and have enough for them to live on comfortably for a few years although not forever. But in the meanwhile, he would find a good job, perhaps even invest in the British market.

Miss Sylvia took that moment to step onto his stomach.

"Oof," he said, as her paws seemed to drive down into his organs, but he didn't care. If he weren't so tired and full of ale, he would do a happy jig around the tiny room.

"I shouldn't let myself get too excited," he said to her without raising his head. But for the first time in a week, he ignored the loud sounds of people fighting along the hall and slept soundly.

The next day, after tending to Miss Sylvia, he dashed out of the room, intent on going directly to Baker Street. He got a few feet down the street, hailed a hackney, and jumped in. Beatrice wouldn't be in the confectionery until nearly noon, as was her habit, but he would find her at home.

A street away, Greer yelled for the driver to stop and take him back. Two thoughts had crossed his mind, the first was how he'd already played with Beatrice's emotions once, even though it had been unintentional. He should say nothing until he knew for certain if the jewels in the collar were worth a fortune. *Maybe two fortunes!*

His second thought was, if he did go anywhere, he ought to take the collar so he could keep an eye on it.

Unsure which choice he would make, whether to see Beatrice or not, Greer paid the driver and let him go.

Another hackney would be around in a minute if he decided to go. By the time he let himself into the drab and dingy hotel, he had decided he would not selfishly raise his toffee-maker's hopes.

Strolling down the dark hallway, he encountered Miss Sylvia, unexpectedly running toward him along the threadbare carpet. It took him but a second to realize someone must have opened his door, someone who had not been ready for the cat's determined intent to escape.

Reaching down as he had many times, he scooped her up as she tried to race by him. Cautiously, with Miss Sylvia tucked under his arm, he continued along the hall but before he reached his own room, a man appeared. A stranger with his hat tugged down low over his face. He caught sight of Greer and ran in the opposite direction out the back to the alleyway, wrenching the door nearly off its hinges in his attempt to escape.

Greer didn't give chase. With Miss Sylvia in his arms, it was pointless. He wouldn't dare set her down, nor would he leave her alone in his room. The lock had been easily picked, and he couldn't trust it wouldn't happen again.

His things had been tossed around in disarray. Oddly, his silk ascots were still there, in a tumbled heap, his good shoes, too, and his suits had been pulled from the interior of the wardrobe, but nothing taken. He had not much else of value, as he wore his father's pocket watch and carried his wallet. He had some papers from America, including the letter from his uncle recently arrived to upend his life.

Luckily, he'd surprised the robber. Although, in reconsidering, he hadn't done anything. The man had come out, perhaps spooked when Miss Sylvia escaped. In any case, it wasn't safe for the cat there, and Greer supposed he was lucky in a week's time someone hadn't tried to rob him before.

With only one place he could think of to go, he turned his key in the lock, glad the man hadn't broken it or, worse, kicked the door in and splintered it, leaving everything

Greer owned laid open for the taking. Back outside, he hailed another hackney.

"To Baker Street," he said.

CHAPTER TWENTY-THREE

"Mr. Carson is here, and he's brought a friend," their man servant said with a long-suffering sigh. Frankly, Beatrice was surprised Mr. Finley had taken the time to find her and tell her. "They're in the parlor, miss."

"Thank you." Curious as to whom Greer had brought, she went to the closed parlor door and tried to push it open. It didn't budge, as if someone were leaning against it.

"Mr. Carson?" she called through the door.

"Yes, hang on a moment."

She waited, her anticipation growing.

"All right, come in."

This time, the door opened at her touch, and she spied Greer holding a skittish-looking Miss Sylvia.

Beatrice couldn't help smiling. "How nice of you both to come calling."

"Please close the door," he urged. "She's been trying to escape my room for days and today, she did. I think she's a little out of sorts after I caught her running down the hotel hallway."

Beatrice's smile vanished as she shut the door firmly behind her. "How awful! You could have lost her. How did she escape?"

"I was robbed!"

She gasped, and he rubbed his cat's head absently.

"In point of fact, I wasn't. My room was broken into, but nothing was taken. Perhaps the thief didn't like my taste in clothing. Maybe the fellow hoped I had something valuable, but he ran out after Miss Sylvia did. I saw him leave."

"I'm so sorry. This would never have happened if you were still at the Langham."

"True enough. May I put her down?"

"Of course." She watched him set her carefully on the floor, and the cat immediately slunk under the large sofa.

"She's had a lot of travel and upheaval in her life for a cat."

"For anyone," Beatrice agreed.

"I've brought her with the hopes you will keep her safe until I . . . until I find a better situation."

"You hesitated. What aren't you telling me?" she demanded.

He looked thunderstruck, and then he grinned. "We do know each other very well, do we not? I don't believe I can keep anything from you, nor should I try."

"No," she told him, "you shouldn't. If you're going to start hedging and not being my frank American friend, then you can leave and take Miss Sylvia with you."

"Right you are." He came closer and took hold of her hands. "I simply didn't want to raise false hopes."

Beatrice cocked her head at him, her heart thumping at his closeness. "Meaning?"

His gray-blue eyes crinkled at the corners. "I love the way you make demands."

"Explain yourself," she insisted.

Instead of doing any such thing, he kissed her. He didn't take his time, but simply planted his mouth upon hers, making her gasp again, and as she did, he swept his tongue between her lips and touched hers.

And while she was still processing this extraordinary turn of events to her otherwise humdrum morning, he lifted his head and rested his forehead upon hers.

"I apologize. I know kissing you here, in your parents' home is probably even worse than in Rare Confectionery—"

"Is it?" she asked.

"Most disrespectful," he added, "especially with their being away. They are away still, aren't they?"

She nodded, feeling giddy at how his tongue had stroked hers and the way he still clasped her hands so tightly.

"But as soon as I'm near you . . . ," he trailed off.

"I know. I feel the same."

"I don't want to lead you on," he said with a groan and released her. "Where has that cat got to?"

"She's . . . ," Beatrice scanned the room. "Miss Sylvia is now under the sideboard. Why?"

"Her collar," he said simply. "I think you hit the nail upon its head, and I was too stupid to realize it."

"Frankness, Greer," she admonished him.

"I believe her collar, the one my devoted, loving mother bestowed upon her, is encrusted with real gemstones after all."

"Dear God!" Beatrice approached the long walnut cabinet, crouching low so she could peer under it.

Miss Sylvia hissed and turned her back.

"She is definitely out of sorts." Beatrice stood up and turned to him. "What makes you think so?"

"The painting. Did I mention there is one hanging at Carsonbank, in the study?"

"You did. You said it was the spit and image of your own father."

"My grandfather is holding a strange, clunky chain with jewels upon it."

"We call that a necklace," Beatrice quipped.

"I know. I know. But it was, at least to my eyes, ugly. I mean look at the collar. Would you wear all those stones at once around your neck, even if they were on a gold chain rather than a leather strap?"

Beatrice tried to imagine such a gaudy display. "No, I suppose I wouldn't."

"In any case, I remembered seeing the necklace and thinking it odd. Then something distracted me, one of the rats racing about the place, perhaps—"

"Rats?" She shivered. The very notion of them scurrying about made her skin crawl.

"I told you, it's derelict in places. There was a hole where the fieldstone wall had caved in and no one had done more than stuff straw there and hang a blanket. It's not the bloody Langham." He gave a bark of laughter. "I thought about asking the caretaker if he knew about the painting, but he wasn't around, if there even is anyone besides the maid and the shepherds."

"Who is the executor of the trust?"

His eyes opened. "You are so sensible. I knew I came to the correct place to go over my own scattered thoughts. I'll write to the trustee in Edinburgh and ask about the jewels. Can I borrow a piece of stationery?" He ran a hand through his hair and walked around the room distractedly as if his mind were racing. "Meanwhile, I have a friend who offered to appraise it."

"You do? Who? Where?" Beatrice hadn't heard of such a person in his life.

"I have some men I meet with once a week," he said.

"Oh, yes, those at the chophouse."

"Exactly. One is an antiques dealer who knows about jewelry."

She shook her head. "Next door to Rare Confectionery is a world-class, fine jeweler. Haven't you noticed it? Asprey's?"

"Truthfully? No." He cocked his head and looked so appealing she almost sighed. "When I am anywhere near your shop, I'm usually in an almighty hurry to get inside and see you. I have my blinders on, my pace quickens, and I rush for the door."

"You should probably take the collar to Asprey's," she persisted.

"Maybe to sell it, yes. But I think I should let Mr. Molino take a look. I already said I would. Tomorrow."

"Are you taking Miss Sylvia with you?"

"No, I was hoping you would keep her safe here. Today. Right now, actually. If I had been a minute later going back to my room, she would have been gone."

Beatrice could hardly imagine his horror. "And with a potential fortune around her neck!"

"Exactly," he said again. "You understand the situation. May she stay with you? And I'd like to leave the collar here, too. I can't risk it at my fleabag hotel. I'll come pick up the collar tomorrow, about this time."

"Of course, but I have to go to work in an hour. We can lock Miss Sylvia in my room, once we catch her, and I'll tell the maid not to open my door. I'll go ask if we have some sardines in the pantry."

"Perfect. Thank you." He took hold of her hand. "May I escort you to the confectionery in an hour?"

"I would like that." She considered a moment. "But only if you'll let me go with you to see the antique dealer tomorrow."

Greer laughed at her suggestion.

"Why is that funny?" she demanded.

"You may come," he agreed. "After all, you're so good at charming people."

BEATRICE MIGHT NOT BE the most affable of people, nor get along with everyone as Charlotte and Amity did, but she considered herself a good judge of character. And from the moment she entered Mr. Molino's dimly lit antique store the next day, the back of her neck prickled.

Perhaps over a meal at a chophouse, the man seemed like a good sort of fellow, but the way he looked at her when Greer introduced them made her think he had something to hide. That and the layer of dust on many of his wares had her questioning his business sense. If she were running the shop, she would add more lamps, sweep the place, dust everything, and paint the walls a cheerful color.

Greer shook the man's hand. "As promised, I've brought my cat's collar for your appraisal."

When he drew it out of his pocket, Beatrice almost wished he would put it away at once. Mr. Molino's glance landed on the collar as quickly as Miss Sylvia had pounced on the sardines the day before, and his eyes flickered with interest. His face, however, remained impassive. From behind the counter, he brought out a black velvet pad and gestured for Greer to place the collar atop it. Then drawing out a magnifying glass, the man peered through it, his face inches from the stones.

When he raised his head, the evidence of several thoughts crossed his face. Beatrice wondered what they were.

"Well?" Greer asked, and she could hear the hopefulness in his tone.

After the briefest hesitation, Mr. Molino shook his head. "I'm sorry to say, I think they are imitation jewels. A few look like good quality paste."

"Paste?" Beatrice questioned. She imagined the pasty chocolate fondant Amity made or Charlotte's marzipan paste.

"That means hand-cut leaded glass, Miss Rare-Foure. Sometimes the glass is polished with colored metal or, alternately, it is set upon a foil base, colored to match whichever type of gem one seeks to imitate. Then it's polished until it resembles a ruby or an emerald."

She felt Greer's disappointment emanating from him.

"So they are worthless?" he asked.

"Not necessarily," Mr. Molino said. "I think these were made in the 1730s or thereabouts. Good quality fakes, I would say, over a century old. Someone will pay handsomely for them as each can be set in a ring or a pendant."

"How much?" Greer asked, sounding defeated. "I don't expect paste is worth what a true gemstone would be."

"No, certainly not. A fraction of the value, but not worthless, by any means."

'Thank you," Greer said, "for looking at them."

Mr. Molino set the collar back upon the velvet and gave Greer a long look. "I know this is important to you." His glance took in Beatrice, too. "There are many ladies who want to have fine but inexpensive jewelry that appears to be what it is not. Leave it with me, and I can fetch you the best price."

As he began to close his fingers around the collar once again, Beatrice reached out and snatched it from his grasp, holding it tightly in her own.

"Eh?" Mr. Molino exclaimed in surprise.

"Consider Miss Sylvia," Beatrice said to Greer, "and your mother. If it's not worth much, then—"

"Who is Miss Sylvia?" Mr. Molino interrupted, his glance darting to the collar in her hand and looking more animated than he had since they'd arrived.

She just knew in her gut if she hadn't taken it, he would never have given it back.

"My cat," Greer said, his tone amused. "Miss Rare-Foure, I doubt Miss Sylvia will care about her collar, and my mother is no longer of this world to have an opinion. Let's leave it with my friend and see what price he can get for it."

Mr. Molino put his hand out, palm up.

"Well, yes, we could certainly do that," Beatrice agreed, opening her satchel and dropping the collar inside so there would be no possible way either of the men could recover it. "And perhaps we will. However, you know what they say about decisions made in haste."

"What do they say?" Greer asked, looking surprised at her forcefulness in taking his cat's collar.

"Something about haste in every business brings failure—from Herodotus, I believe." She blinked at the antiquarian.

Mr. Molino folded his arms, looking displeased. "Perhaps you were thinking of Congreve's comedy *The Old Bachelor, a favorite of mine* in which he warns about marrying in haste and repenting at leisure." He nodded to Greer as if sending him a message, and Beatrice was sure she had been insulted.

"In any case," the man continued, "perhaps your lady friend is correct. Hold onto it until you decide. However, even paste gems should be kept safe. Your hotel is not the best, as I recall."

"You're right about that," Greer said. "My room has already been broken into once. Miss Rare-Foure will hold onto the collar for me."

Back outside, he turned to her. "What was all that about?"

"I didn't like him, nor trust him."

Greer smiled. "He's never given me any reason to distrust him, and he suggested we keep the collar safe."

"It sounded to me as if he wanted to know where you intended on keeping it."

This time he laughed. "Such devious thoughts. I will trust you to keep the paste stones safe, but I would still like to know how much I can sell them for."

HAVING BEEN DROPPED OFF directly at the confectionery after the dingy antique shop, Beatrice told Charlotte of the morning's events.

"Such a shame," Charlotte said. She'd said the same thing the night before when trying to make friends with their home's new resident. Naturally, Miss Sylvia had hissed and retreated under Beatrice's bed with an angry swish of her absurdly fluffy tail.

"It's not your fault," she'd assured Charlotte who'd looked disenchanted. "I think Miss Sylvia has experienced too much upheaval and is fair sick of it."

"The way you behaved the first night we were away in France last time," her sister had teased, recalling the family trip two years earlier.

"This is more than a mere *shame*," Beatrice said, removing her coat and hat, and tying on her apron. "This could be the ruination of my future happiness, and I don't intend to give in so easily."

"What can you do?" Charlotte asked.

"I'll get the toffee made first, and then I'm going next door to ask for a second opinion. I know Asprey's is not strictly a jewelry store, but if anyone will be honest, it is a company that holds a royal warrant."

"That's a grand idea," Charlotte agreed.

Two hours later, she entered the neighboring shop. It smelled like polish and leather, as well as the heady aroma from the sumptuous fresh flower arrangements in crystal vases dotted around Asprey's displays. She was greeted immediately by a shopgirl, dressed in a well-starched uniform.

Was she interested in a dressing case, the clerk wanted to know, or one of the leather travel cases that could withstand the rigors of the railway? Beatrice shook her head. Passing between the advertised "articles of exclusive design and high quality," as Asprey's proudly proclaimed in the papers and in their shop window, Beatrice reached the inobtrusive counter on one side of the store. Her mother had a long-standing, friendly relationship with the store manager, Mr. Russell, and Beatrice asked for him at once.

Whenever Asprey's held a special function, they served Rare Confectionery, and when Beatrice and her family had left London for their country home the year prior, Asprey's had taken the rest of their confectionery inventory, selling the sweets as a favor. Her father had been most impressed how Mr. Russell kept an account to the penny of what he owed them, not a piece of toffee or a chocolate unaccounted for.

While she waited for Mr. Russell to be summoned from his office in the back, Beatrice couldn't help admiring all the pretty things. Some were for the house, some for personal adornment, everything well-crafted, refined, and beautiful. So much so that Queen Victoria herself had recognized their achievement.

What if she were bringing them jewels made of paste?

"Miss Rare-Foure," came the booming voice of Mr. Russell. "To what do I owe this pleasure? Did you bring me something? Chocolate-covered toffee, perhaps?"

She smiled. She might be considered crabby, but she knew how to butter her bread. Setting a shiny silver Rare Confectionery tin on the counter, she said, "Toffee with chocolate for you, Mr. Russell."

"You are a sweet girl." Immediately opening the tin, he popped a piece in his mouth. "Help yourselves, girls," he called to the shopgirls on the floor, who came over like bees to pollen.

"But you didn't come by to bring me a gift, did you?" he asked, the toffee tucked into his cheek, which she politely ignored.

"No, sir. May I speak with you alone?"

He raised his eyebrows, then nodded. "Nancy, take the tin of sweets, make sure everyone gets a piece and save me some, will you?"

"Yes, sir," and the shopgirl moved away with three others around her.

"Now, how can I help you?"

"I have a cat collar with jewels. They may be merely paste, but I thought you might know, or one of your jewelers could take a look."

"Nothing wrong with paste," Mr. Russell said while she

set her bag on the counter and opened it. "Marie Antoinette wore paste jewels along with precious stones. Sometimes if something is pretty, it gives as much pleasure as something expensive."

"These are not particularly pretty, to tell you the truth."

She withdrew the collar and held it out to him on her palm. He swallowed loudly and then coughed. She hoped he wasn't going to choke on her sweet offering.

"A moment, if you will." Still coughing, he bent behind the counter and opened a drawer, extracting a jeweler's loupe fixed to a strap. He put this around his forehead before picking up the collar.

"*Hm,*" he said. "*Hm,* yes. As I thought. Yes." He turned it over and over, examining each jewel, and then looked at the leather itself. "For Greer, with all our love."

Her heart caught. *Was that message from his mother?* After all, she'd given him the cat.

"How did you come by this?" Mr. Russell asked.

"It belongs to my friend, Mr. Carson. He's from America."

"He may be, but the stones are European. And I was right, Marie Antoinette might have worn the like."

Her blossoming hope withered. "Then they are paste?"

"Oh no, Miss Rare-Foure. These are very fine stones that any queen would be pleased, even honored, to wear. It's not often I get to see and hold any such gems."

Her heart had sped up at his words and was threatening to burst from her chest.

"Are you saying they are actual gemstones? Real jewels?"

"Quite real," he said. "And worth a king's ransom."

"Dear God!" she exclaimed.

"Precisely, Miss Rare-Foure. If I were you, I would tell your friend not to put this back on his cat but in a safe at a bank."

"I believe he wishes to sell the jewels. Can you help?"

"Of course," Mr. Russell said, with a small nod. "But he should allow me to sell each separately. He will get more than if he sells it as a cat collar."

She felt almost light-headed. *A cat's collar worth a king's ransom!*

"I shall need to speak with him in person," Mr. Russell continued, "and have him sign a contract making Asprey's his broker, and he must agree to our commission. It's fair, I assure you. Any jewel we don't buy ourselves, I will find a jeweler or patron who will. In any case, your Mr. Carson will be a wealthy man."

Her Mr. Carson!

Mr. Russell reached into the drawer again and drew out a satin sack, dropping the collar inside. "There, that seems more fitting. I'll be here on Saturday morning if you want to—"

Suddenly, a commotion on the street interrupted him. Yelling and loud whistling, reminding her of Charlotte except it was plainly coming from a bobby's steel whistle, as she could see two of them in front. Taking the small sack from Mr. Russell, she returned it to her satchel.

"Let's see what's happening," he said, "shall we?"

Together, they walked to the spacious front of the shop with its wall of windows and double doors. He opened one and they stepped outside. And that's when she saw the hubbub was coming from Rare Confectionery next door.

"Charlotte!" she exclaimed, running as if her bustle were on fire toward the open front door of the shop, terrified at what she might find.

CHAPTER TWENTY-FOUR

Two policemen were inside with a scared-looking Charlotte, who had clearly been in a tussle. She held the cricket bat they kept for knocking the stuffing out of any ne'er do well. Her hair was half down from its usual tidy bun for work, with her curls dangling loosely over one shoulder and her apron askew. Worse than both was her shocked expression.

As soon as she saw Beatrice, she gave a cry, broke away from the bobbies, and launched herself into her sister's arms. Beatrice closed them around her and heard Charlotte begin to sniffle.

Instead of asking her questions, Beatrice gave her time to shed any tears she needed and then to gather her emotions. Meanwhile, the bobbies went into the back room and then returned.

With Charlotte still in her arms, Beatrice said, "This is my sister and this is our shop. Do you know what happened?"

"Your sister whistled—a cracking good loud one, too,"

one of the bobbies said, both looking at Charlotte with admiration. "That brought us in. I thought it was a fellow policeman in trouble. She was just telling us how a man entered, asked her if she was Miss Rare-Foure, knowing her by name apparently, and then demanded her purse."

"He went in the back room," Charlotte said, lifting her head but still clutching Beatrice around the waist. "I told him he had to leave, and then I pulled out the bat and tried to hit him."

"You shouldn't have engaged with the robber, miss," said one of the bobbies.

"Engage with him?" Charlotte sputtered. "I wanted to knock him out cold. Unfortunately, he turned as I lifted the bat."

Beatrice shivered with fear at the notion of Charlotte in there alone, trying to subdue a thief.

"He grabbed the bat and tossed it. And when he was trying to leave, I jumped on him."

"What?" Beatrice exclaimed, holding Charlotte away from her so she could look in her eyes. "He was leaving, for goodness' sake. Why on earth would you do that?"

Charlotte had recovered enough to shrug and even look composed. "He whirled around and dislodged me from his back, and I slid to the ground. I would have thought the number of hairpins I had in my hair would have kept it properly in place."

She started fiddling with the long locks at her shoulder.

"Did he look for the cash box?" Beatrice asked. Ever since Greer had got them the Langham account and suggested they mention Amity's newly aristocratic connections in their ads, business had been booming. The till was usually quite full by the end of the workday.

"No, he demanded my purse alone, and then he went into the back room and took it off the shelf." She stomped her foot. "My favorite green and silver bag, too!"

"What was in it, miss? Anything valuable?" asked one of the bobbies.

Charlotte sighed. "Not really. A comb my mother gave me, a mirror, and a few guineas." She shook her head. "My favorite bag."

Beatrice groaned. "Don't you dare ever fight for something like a bag or even the cash box. What if he'd turned violent? What if I'd come back to find he'd used the bat on you?"

They fell silent, staring at one another, and Beatrice's eyes teared up. For a moment, she wasn't sure what they should do next and wished her parents were not all the way across the English Channel. Felicity would know precisely what to do. Then she decided.

"Let's close up the shop and go home."

"One thing, miss," said the bobby, talking to Charlotte. "Can you describe the man who robbed you?"

"He had a knit hat pulled down over his brow, right to his eyes. He wasn't much taller than I am. I think he was a young man. He wore a tweed coat and brown pants."

"Any scars?" the bobby asked.

Charlotte looked down at her hands and arms. "No, I am unhurt, thank you."

The policeman smiled at her response, and Beatrice could see he was enchanted by her younger sister as most men were.

"Oh, well, that's very good, miss," he muttered. "What about on the intruder? Any visible markings?"

Charlotte shook her head. "None that I saw."

"Very well. We'll file a report. A detective may come and ask you to go to Whitehall station to give a statement, particularly if we find the culprit."

Charlotte glanced at Beatrice, who responded. "We'll cooperate however we can. Do you have a carriage?"

"No, miss. But we'll hail one and take you home."

GREER POUNDED UPON THE Rare-Foure's door on Baker Street, and then, knowing Mr. Finley was probably not going to answer in a timely fashion, he opened it and strode in. Seeing the parlor door was ajar and hearing female voices, he went in unannounced.

Beatrice and Charlotte were seated close together on the sofa, but Beatrice stood up at once and greeted him.

"Thank you for coming," she said.

"As soon as I got back to my room, your message was waiting for me. What happened?"

She filled him in on the robbery at the confectionery.

"Don't you think the thief behaved strangely by not wanting what was in the till, but only Charlotte's purse?"

Greer looked at Charlotte, whose deep brown eyes gazed back at him, making her seem particularly vulnerable. Anger boiled through him.

"You weren't hurt?" he asked.

The youngest sister shook her head. "I had the bat."

He cringed. "I cannot believe you ladies rely on a bat for protection."

"There is a store next door that sells the very finest of furnishings and jewelry," Beatrice pointed out. "A thief could go in there and snatch a lamp or a leather case, either one worth more than everything on our shelves. Thus, we've never worried about our confectionery being robbed. It seems absurd if you think about it."

"Besides," Charlotte chimed in, "the little man didn't want our sweets or even our cashbox. He wanted my purse."

"Was it lying on the counter?" Greer asked.

"Of course not," Charlotte scoffed. "It was in the back, but that's what he wanted, just the same."

"It is strange indeed," Greer mused. Then he considered her words. "A little man? Meaning he was below average height?"

"He was." Then Charlotte stood. "I think I shall go see if I can make friends with your cat. Perhaps I can lure her out from under Beatrice's bed. Then I need to change. I have my art class tonight."

"Wait, Miss Charlotte," Greer stopped her at the door. "Was he wearing a cap by chance?"

Her eyes widened. "He was. How did you know?"

"I believe I had the same nefarious visitor in my hotel room."

The two sisters looked at one another in alarm.

"Don't worry," Beatrice told her. "Mr. Carson will get it all sorted out."

Charlotte shrugged and left, apparently still intent on befriending Miss Sylvia.

As soon as the door closed behind her, Beatrice started to pace. "I know it's silly, but I don't want her to go out tonight to her art class. I wouldn't say that to her, however, as I don't want her to feel frightened or to worry. I can do that for both of us."

He nodded. "I wish I'd been there."

"As do I." She rubbed her hands up and down her arms.

Before he could ask what she meant, she added, "That's why I sent for you. I was next door at Asprey's. By the time I got back to the shop, the bobbies were already there. In any case, I have good news. Great news, in fact."

"Then why don't you look pleased?" he asked.

"Because of Charlotte's little man. The robber asked if she was Miss Rare-Foure and then demanded her purse. And the only Miss Rare-Foure with anything valuable in her purse—"

"Is you," he finished, knowing she referred to the collar she'd put into her bag.

"Precisely," she confirmed.

Greer stepped forward and took her in his arms. "I'm sorry I got you involved in this."

Then he realized what she'd said. "How valuable?"

She looked up at him and her excitement was now visible in her brilliant blue eyes. "You, sir, are a very rich man, one who can well afford to keep a wife."

A hundred thoughts raced through his head, but all he could say was, "The jewels are real?"

"It would seem so. Worth a king's ransom."

"My mother put real jewels on a cat!" Still holding her hand, he took Beatrice with him to the sofa and sat, pulling her down beside him. "And I almost lost Miss Sylvia yesterday."

She nodded. Then Greer realized the worst of it. "I told Molino *you* were going to keep hold of the collar."

"And he watched me drop it into my purse this morning. He took a chance that I was going straight to work. After all, since he told us the collar was studded with paste, why would I take the collar home or be careful with it?"

"Where is it now?" Greer asked, feeling a frisson of excitement blended with a healthy dose of raw tension. By now, Molino knew his thief had failed and Beatrice still had the collar.

"I have it here," she said, reaching for her bag on the table in front of them. "Frankly, I am reluctant to let it out of my sight." Withdrawing a silk sack from her satchel, she held it in her hands, the same way she held his heart and their future.

"Mr. Russell, Asprey's manager, gave me the little bag. I think he was shocked to see the jewels on a cat collar in the first place, and there I was, waving it about as if they were paste stones."

She giggled slightly, and he could tell it was from nervousness. "What if you hadn't brought Miss Sylvia to England?" she asked.

"Oh, there was little doubt I would. It wasn't solely my mother's will demanding I do so. Her last words were . . . ," he broke off, recalling his mother being adamant with her dying breath. Wheezing and barely able to open her eyes, she had repeatedly said, "Take Sylvia. Keep her safe."

"In any case, I promised her, and it eased her mind."

"Had you seen this?" she asked, withdrawing the collar and pointing to words etched into the leather.

He stared at his mother's message. *Our love? Both his parents?* He tried to think past the bitterness in his brain over losing his father when he was a lad of twelve. For most of his life, holding on to the irrational anger of a child, Greer had felt betrayed by him for going to war and dying.

Yet his mother had wrapped her fragile, cold hands around his and whispered, "From your father and me." Greer hadn't known what to make of it, thinking her words were muddled by her illness. But now, as if from the grave, his father and the Carson inheritance were saving him.

"I wonder why she didn't simply tell you about the jewels," Beatrice mused, recalling him to the present.

"From what's come to pass, I imagine she didn't want her brother to find out. They were close, but she said more than once to keep my purse strings closed when it came to my uncle. If I'd stayed in America and my uncle's railroad had started to fail, I probably would have sold off the jewels and sunk more money into his business."

"And your mother never needed to sell those jewels herself?" Beatrice asked.

"No, my mother had a wonderful life except for the loss of my father. She had money from her own parents. We didn't live like the Duke and Duchess of Pelham, but we didn't want for anything either."

He ran his thumb over the etched leather, then turned the collar over. "My grandfather must have brought the jewels from Scotland and given them to his bride, who must have given them to my father to give to his. Luckily, neither generation needed to sell them. And now the jewels will allow me to have you as my wife."

She rewarded him with her smile.

"And our townhouse," he added, finally letting his thoughts go farther into the future.

"You're counting your chickens before they've hatched," she warned. "You should find out what a 'king's ransom' is precisely before you spend it in your mind."

"A practical shopkeeper's daughter." Greer drew her

into his arms and kissed her. Slanting his mouth across hers, he nibbled on her lower lip, then, as she parted hers, he deepened his kiss. His body hummed with awareness of her.

"How long are engagements in Britain?" he asked when he broke away to breathe.

She smiled. "Long enough. Too long, if you're in the nobility, but luckily, we're not." Then she shook her head. "I just had the most galling thought. Your cat is more of a true heiress than I ever was, and not a toffee one, either!"

He blinked at her, and then he grinned. In a moment, they were both laughing at the absurdity of Miss Sylvia, the little feline heiress.

"I knew I liked that cat," he said.

Beatrice stroked the side of his cheek. "I feel so blessed by this turn of events. Mr. Russell wants you to sign a contract agreeing to let Asprey's be your jewelry broker, and then he'll proceed. I told him you might go in tomorrow."

"I will." Greer captured her hand under his, turned his face, and kissed her palm. A sizzle of desire shot through him, as he imagined loving her in every way. "I'm going to ask you to do me a favor."

"Anything," she whispered, blue eyes glossing over.

He grinned at her expression and her tone. "What *are* you thinking, saucy girl?"

When she blushed, he had to kiss her again, laying a trail of feather-light kisses along her jaw and down her neck. As she arched her head, he breathed in the warm scent of her skin. She smelled like home to him now.

"Mm," she murmured before threading her hands behind his neck and drawing his mouth back to hers. He claimed her lips again more urgently, tasting her sweetness. Finally, he leaned his forehead against hers and simply held her.

How had he ever thought he could walk away from her to marry a titled lady?

"I think you and Miss Charlotte should spend the night at your sister's home, and I hope you will let me take you there directly, and make sure Miss Charlotte goes there after her painting class."

"Because of the jewels?" she asked.

"I don't think it's safe for you to stay here, especially with your father away."

She barely hesitated. "I agree, but I don't want you in that mangy hotel room either, especially if it can be broken into so easily. Perhaps you would consider staying here with Miss Sylvia."

Her words made sense. "As you have proven time and again, you are a smart woman."

Her cheeks pinkened again, and she looked so delightful, he bent his head to kiss her once more, but she added, "I also think I should take the collar with me to Amity's."

The thought of her guarding the collar from robbers sent a chill down him. "I would hate to put your family in danger."

Beatrice burst out laughing. "No one would dare breach the sanctum of the Duke of Pelham's St. James's house. You've been there. You've seen the number of liveried footmen, practically in every room."

"Plus Nanny Beryl!" Greer teased. "Surely a fearsome woman with or without a cricket bat. You're correct. Any thief would be foolish to try. Very well. You shall take the collar with you. I imagine the duke has a safe in his study."

"That's settled then. Kiss me again, and I will go talk to Charlotte."

She'd said it so matter-of-factly, he almost missed her command.

"Whatever you ask, Miss Rare-Foure, I shall do."

And he did.

AT ONE IN THE morning, Greer heard the intruder. Determined not to be caught sleeping, he had stayed downstairs in the parlor, with the door open and his ears perked like a hunting dog.

A tinkling of glass from across the foyer meant someone was breaking in through Mr. Foure's small study. They had undoubtedly shattered the pane near the latch, reached in and raised the sash. *Would the thief begin to search the entire house?* It seemed a monumental task, looking for one small cat collar, but with such a fortune at stake, someone would be desperate enough to do exactly that.

In the darkness, Greer peered out into the hallway. So far, no one had exited the study. Probably, the easiest thing would be to contain the intruder inside there. Silently crossing the hall, he clasped the door handle when he heard a sound from the rear of the house.

Another robber? How many had Molino sent to search the Rare-Foure home? For there could be no doubt who was behind it. Greer had mentioned the collar on Wednesday night at The Cock Tavern and his hotel room had been vandalized on Thursday. When that had yielded nothing, the thief had gone to Rare Confectionery after he and Beatrice had visited the dealer. And now, their Baker Street townhouse.

Still, a second man didn't change Greer's plan. He would simply deal with one at a time. Even then, he could hear the first one crash into some piece of furniture. Then silence.

Pushing open the door, he confronted the thief. The open curtains and moonlight showed him it was same man he'd seen in his hotel passageway with his hat pulled down low. And he would guess Miss Charlotte might recognize him, too.

Upon being so quickly discovered, having undoubtedly believed everyone to be asleep upstairs, the robber's face was the very picture of surprise.

"Who do you answer to?" Greer demanded. He wanted to hear the name for certain. But the man, apparently not wanting to give up his boss, turned and ran back toward the broken window.

Grabbing him from behind and putting an arm around his neck, Greer wrestled the thief to the floor. Although small of stature, the man was a scrapper and didn't give up easily. They rolled around upon the rug, whacking against chair leg and table leg, but in short order, Greer put a knee in the intruder's back and his arms drawn behind him.

Hoping this would be the outcome, Greer had a length of rope in his pocket. After he secured the man's hands and feet, trussing him up like a prize calf, he stuffed a handkerchief in the robber's mouth to keep him from alerting his accomplice.

Rising to his feet, Greer caught his breath. Then, stepping cautiously out of the study and closing the door behind him, he started down the hall, hoping he could still surprise the second intruder.

To his dismay, from the dark passageway came not one but two shadowy figures. At first, Greer thought he was sunk and would end up knocked out and possibly tossed in the Thames. However, as they came closer, he recognized one of the figures as the Rare-Foure's oft-absent butler.

"Finley!" Greer exclaimed. "You've apprehended a burglar!"

"Have I, sir?" he asked with his usual indifference. "What shall I do with him?"

Sadly, the second thief was known to him. Jeremiah! His chophouse acquaintance.

"*Them*, Finley. I have another knocked out cold in the study."

At this news, that neither of them had succeeded, Jeremiah had the sense to look sheepish, being found where he didn't belong, detained by a butler holding the back of his collar in one hand and one of his arms behind his back.

"Look, Carson," he began, "I lost my job. I would take any work."

"This isn't work. This is thievery. I guess I have to tie you up, too, though it sorely irks me to see you up to this." He looked at the butler. "I only had one rope. Do you have something we can use?"

Finley nodded, released Jeremiah who didn't move, and

wandered down the hallway. Greer wasn't at all sure he would return.

"If you try to run, I will knock you out," he told Jeremiah, who had started to shift from one foot to the other.

"I won't leave my brother."

His brother! Both of them had been drawn into such an appalling deed. It was a shame.

"Will you bear witness against the man who hired you?" Greer demanded.

Jeremiah scowled. "I'm no prattler."

"If you do, you will assuredly get a lighter sentence than the man who engineered all this."

"No one got hurt," Jeremiah protested. "I wouldn't hurt no one, nor would my brother."

"True. Although your brother frightened a shopgirl today."

The man looked remorseful. "We was told to get her purse. That's all. And then tonight to get a cat collar. I'm starting to think he's a nutter and all," he added.

"Your boss thinks I have something very valuable, and he's willing to let you and your brother go to Newgate for it."

They still stood in the light of a single lamp that Finley had lit, but even so, Greer could see Jeremiah's face grow paler.

"Will you speak his name?"

"John Delorey."

CHAPTER TWENTY-FIVE

Rare Confectionery was bustling as usual on a Saturday mid-morning, filled with customers and smelling heavenly sweet. Amity and Charlotte were both assisting customers, and Beatrice was making toffee.

Her younger sister had already called out when Greer hurried by with a wave of his hand as he headed to Asprey's. And Beatrice had to cool her heels and wait. She had a new recipe to try and had decided it would be the perfect task to keep her mind occupied. Elsewise, she might go insane.

Thus, after mixing a cup of treacle, a pound of sugar, and a half pint of water, she let them boil and bubble until they were the color of straw. As soon as she removed the pot from the stove, setting it upon the marked and tarnished copper counter, she stirred in an ounce of bicarbonate of soda. As the recipe stated, it fizzed and frothed.

When it had finished expanding like a magician's trick, Beatrice turned the toffee out into a buttered pan—her first honeycomb toffee.

In a couple hours, after it had cooled, she would break it

with her little steel hammer and coat the pieces in Amity's melted chocolate. Her first new product in ages!

"He's here," Charlotte sang out, and Beatrice dashed through the curtain. She could hardly see him through the sizable crowd of customers, but when they locked eyes, she rushed forward, took his hand, and disregarding propriety and any witnesses, dragged him into the workroom.

She'd expected news from him. Nevertheless, when he told his tale of nighttime adventure, she was astonished.

"With Finley's help, I got the men to Whitehall. Honestly, I wish I could have let Jeremiah and his brother go, but seeing how I was such a terrible judge of character and all my so-called friends from the chophouse are dishonest, what could I do?"

She shook her head in wonder. "Then Mr. Molino was not behind it, but the other one, the one you said was a jolly sort."

"Delorey, who had a nice way of slapping me on the back and Jeremiah who recently lost his job. A detective will detain Delorey today, and I guess he'll tell the police whether Molino was part of it, as well. My suspicion is that he was involved. After all, a king's ransom is enough for a few men to share."

"And for them to do some despicable things," Beatrice added. But there was something else she was waiting for him to tell her.

"I know you probably are eager to know," he said.

"Yes!" Her heart beat fast. *How had his meeting with Mr. Russell gone?*

"I hired a glazer to fix the window in the study and the one by your servant's door in the back. By the time your parents return, they won't even notice there was damage."

She frowned. *Did he really think she gave a tinker's damn about a few broken windows when their future was at stake?*

"Greer, I . . . ," she trailed off at the way he was holding himself back from smiling. "Oh, you!" She smacked him on the shoulder. "Tell me how it went!"

"It went well. Very, very well. Miss Sylvia is an extremely wealthy cat."

Beatrice clamped a hand to her mouth as she gasped, feeling her eyes fill with tears. She'd been hopeful ever since speaking with Asprey's manager, but hopes could easily be dashed, as she knew. In this case, the opposite was true.

"I cannot believe it," she whispered.

"Nor can I. And if not for you, I would have given the entire fortune to Mr. Molino for the price of paste."

Unable to fight the warm feeling of love, she moved into the circle of his arms. "You know, you are simply back where you started," she said, with her cheek against his chest. "A rich American in search of a wife."

"Not exactly. I had money, but not anything like what Mr. Russell has just disclosed."

She shrugged. "Money or more money, that's all the same."

He laughed, perhaps at her nonchalance. She didn't mind.

"What I mean," Beatrice explained, "is that you're back to where you started, not being able to claim your ancestral home."

"I feel the same as I did before, when I thought I had a full bank account. I love you, Miss Rare-Foure, and I will not think twice about losing Carsonbank House if I gain you as my wife."

He loved her! And he'd finally said the words aloud.

"I love you, too," she said, feeling giddy with happiness. "But I've told you that already. I'm glad you didn't let me chase you away from our shop."

He laughed. "And I'm glad you make toffee, as it has become my favorite sweet in the whole world."

"Then I shall make you as much as you wish." She was standing in her family's confectionery, being held by the man who would become her husband, and she could not imagine ever feeling happier than she did at that moment. "What happens now?"

"Your parents are supposed to return any day, aren't they? And when they do, I will go with hat in hand to your frightening father—"

She laughed. "He is the least frightening of fathers."

"And then we will announce our engagement. That is, if you still want to marry a man who has to rely on his cat for his livelihood."

They both chuckled. She liked the feel of his laughter beneath her cheek.

"I stopped by Chestertons' agency this morning before even going to Asprey's and told the agent I wanted the townhouse after all."

"How wickedly daring of you, Mr. Carson," Beatrice said, drawing back. "You counted your chickens in advance."

"Luckily, Mr. Russell said they will all hatch quite nicely. In short, Miss Rare-Foure, things are looking rosy." He cocked his head to the constant noise in the front, the bell tinkling, Charlotte laughing, Amity explaining what was in the chocolates. "I know your shop is busy, but do you think your sisters would mind if you escape with me for a few hours?"

"When?" she asked.

"Now," he urged. "After all, they don't want you in the front with the customers, anyway. Not the glowering toffee-maker who lurks back here, stirring her bubbling potions."

"You make me sound like a witch." But she smiled.

"Say yes. The weather is fine," he added.

"It is," she agreed, feeling like the most agreeable woman in the world. *Why had she ever been short-tempered and crabby?* She doubted she would ever glower again.

"Will you take a walk with me?" he persisted.

"Somewhere in particular?" she asked.

"Perhaps.

In a few minutes, she had on her favorite blue cloak and was resting her gloved hand upon his arm. They walked south past Marlborough House and its walled gardens, still scarcely believing they'd been part of the event now declared "the fancy-dress ball of the decade." Crossing The Mall road, with Queen Victoria's Buckingham Palace down at the right end, they cut through St. James's Park and strolled east to the river.

"Do you know yet where we might be going?" he asked.

"Since we've passed Whitehall and Scotland Yard, I assume we're not visiting your chophouse chums."

"No, definitely not. After dealing with that shifty lot, I think I shall let you help me pick my friends in the future."

"In fairness, it sounds as though some of them were terribly desperate, and at least the brothers didn't harm anyone."

Greer stopped in his tracks and turned to her. "I cannot believe what I'm hearing. You are a changed woman, Miss Rare-Foure, from the one who seemed to have little patience even for nice old ladies trying to buy sweets."

She covered her mouth as she laughed. It had been the very thing she'd been thinking. But she protested anyway. "They are hardly ever *nice* old ladies. Usually snout-nosed younger ladies seemingly with sticks up the—"

"Beatrice!" he exclaimed looking right and left to see if any could overhear their discourse.

"What?" she asked, starting to walk again, pulling him with her. "Sticks up the back of their corsets was all I was going to say."

"*Hm.* In any case, we're nearly there."

She decided not to press the issue and ask. After all, they'd spent months trying to achieve goals that ultimately were for naught. Now she was happy simply to float idly along like a leaf on the wind and let things play out as they would.

However, as they approached the recently installed addition to the Embankment, there was no mistaking his destination.

"Cleopatra's Needle," she mused. "Of all the sights you want to see in London, this one seems an odd choice when there are so many old and magnificent structures."

"Older than Ancient Egypt?" he quipped.

"You have a point. But it's very new for London. Less than two weeks, isn't it, since they raised it? You must have noticed in the papers all the controversy." Then a memory flashed across her mind, stark and clear.

"Why, I believe I was reading about the officials arguing over its placement the very first day you entered Rare Confectionery. And now, here it is, and here we are!"

The grinned at one another.

"What do *you* think?" she asked him.

"As a visitor to your country, I think it impolitic for me to give my opinion first."

She poked him with her elbow. "You are no longer merely a visitor. You will move into a London townhouse in a week's time." *And have a wife and maybe children soon after that*, she added to herself.

"True, but still, you should tell me your thoughts first."

She nodded, but nevertheless, they walked the last few yards in silence, approaching the towering obelisk.

At its base, Greer said quietly, "Sixty-nine feet high and six men died to bring it here," and they craned their necks.

Together, they examined the Egyptian hieroglyphs going up the sides. "The deeds of Thutmose III and Ramses II," she remarked, having read about them, including the translations.

He nodded, and they walked to the other side of it, looking back toward the Houses of Parliament and Big Ben in the distance.

"It is the first time I've seen it close up. I like it, to tell you the truth. It's a little odd, but also awe-inspiring," she said. "Even the winches they used last month to set it in place were beyond impressive."

"I must say," Greer mused, "I think it looks completely out of place. The way I felt when I first got to your shores."

"You had a far easier time getting here than this monster. The obelisk and the ship it came over on nearly ended up at the bottom of the Bay of Biscay."

"Let's take a seat, shall we?" he asked. Taking her by the waist, he hoisted her onto the thick wall next to the obelisk. Behind her was the Thames, sparkling on the sunny late-September day.

"Did you read what they buried at its base?" he asked, sitting beside her.

"A time capsule, they called it," she said, arranging her skirts, happily still feeling the warmth where his hands had touched her and certain she was the luckiest woman alive, to be sitting there with Greer Carson.

"They made a terrible mistake," he said, sounding serious.

She stopped fidgeting and looked at him. "What do you mean?"

"Purportedly, they put in photographic images of twelve of the prettiest English women. But from where I'm sitting, they missed by far and away the best of the lot."

Beatrice felt her cheeks heat up. He stroked a finger across one of them, and she smiled.

"You are the only English beauty I care about, and your photograph ought to be in there," he added, then ruined the romantic nature of his comment by adding, "along with the box of cigars, the shilling razor, the baby's bottle, and the copy of Whitaker's *Almanack*."

She laughed. "Don't forget they included hairpins, a portrait of the queen, and the rupee."

"Yours should definitely be alongside Queen Victoria's." He took her hand in his, and she looked around to see if anyone was watching, but pedestrians who noticed didn't seem to think anything of a couple holding hands and enjoying the exotic, new monument.

"I have something for you," Greer said, "to commemorate this day."

"Really?" She'd never told anyone before that she quite enjoyed being surprised, as long as it was a nice surprise. And little gifts were the best type of surprise. "What is it?"

She nearly clapped her hands like a child.

From his pocket he pulled out a miniature bronze model of the obelisk and placed it on her palm. For some reason, the sight of it, a three-inch representation of something that weighed two-hundred tons tickled her. She laughed again.

"Thank you." She stared at the craftsmanship and minute detail of the small obelisk.

"Two shillings, six pence," he told her.

Beatrice shook her head. "Such an American! You're not supposed to tell me the cost of a gift, but I shall take very good care of it."

"The same price as lunch off the joint at The Grosvenor Gallery Restaurant, or a good joint dinner at the Criterion, a six o'clock meal at the Caledonian, or a half-past seven one at Provitali's."

She opened her mouth and blinked. "Oh my, you have learned a lot since the day you had no notion of what to pay for a small bag of toffee and even tried to give me a half-sovereign as a tip."

"I've been living in a hotel for so long without my own kitchen, I think I know every restaurant in London and what each meal costs."

"In any case, costly or not, I thank you for my miniature Cleopatra's Needle. I shall never forget this day."

Unexpectedly, he placed something else on her palm. "I also picked out this for you, my beautiful bride."

She looked down at an Asprey's ring box, and her heart skipped a beat.

Without opening it, she dropped it along with the bronze monument onto her lap, threaded her arms around Greer's neck, and kissed him.

Somewhere nearby, she heard a woman gasp, but Beatrice didn't give a fig for polite society.

EPILOGUE

They were seated in the Rare-Foure's small back patio behind Baker Street, surrounded by potted roses and ivy climbing up the fence, with Beatrice and Greer telling Charlotte about their trip to Madame Tussaud's.

"I shall tell you something. Amity and the duke really did look like King Louis and Queen Marie Antoinette," Beatrice mused. "I think their modiste and tailor went to the wax works for inspiration, rather than a painting."

She had enjoyed the outing as much for her fiancé's teasing and laughter, even in the wax museum's Chamber of Horrors, as for the fine artistry of the wax figures. Greer had frozen in place when another couple came down the staircase, causing them to examine him with the same scrutiny as they did Marat and Robespierre.

"Who is this supposed to be?" the woman had asked, peering closely, breathing on his cheek. Her companion had shrugged, about to check the guide booklet, when she'd added, "He doesn't look as realistic as some of the others."

At that statement, Greer's face had broken out into a

wide crooked grin, and even as the lady screamed, he and Beatrice had been unable to contain their laughter.

They had ended up at Gunter's eatery on Berkeley Square, known for its ices, and tasted three apiece before heading home to Baker Street.

"I still cannot believe how I was insulted. *Less* realistic than a wax dummy!" Greer remarked, making Charlotte laugh.

Suddenly, Armand and Felicity appeared in the patio doorway, finally returned from their holiday abroad.

Jumping up, the girls embraced their parents, and when the family stopped hugging, Greer shook their hands.

In short order, Beatrice let her sister fill in their parents on all they had missed.

"I wish you had seen our costumes," Charlotte said, after describing the wonders of the fancy-dress ball.

"You can model them for me later if you wish," Felicity said. "I would love to see them."

"We would have returned sooner if we could, but . . . ," their father paused and glanced at his wife. "We had to stay due to my brother's illness."

"Illness?" Beatrice exclaimed, looking from her mother to her father. "Why didn't you tell us?"

"Your uncle took ill, and your grandfather suggested we go, but we didn't think the whole family needed to go to France and sit at my brother's bedside. I had hoped he would recover. We thought we would be gone a fortnight, not a month. And no joy in it, either, I'll tell you." Her father sat down heavily in one of the vacated chairs.

Felicity turned to Greer. "My husband's older brother had a weak heart."

"I'm very sorry to hear that. My mother did, too," he offered. "It is painful to watch such a demise, but I am sure you're glad you were there."

"Oh, yes," Mr. Foure said. "My brother and I weren't close since I've lived in England all my life, while he chose to go back and live on our family estate outside of Paris."

"It's small but ever so pretty," Charlotte confirmed, and Beatrice nodded, staring hard at her father to see if he was terribly sad.

"Before he passed, he and I talked for hours, which was quite wonderful."

Felicity reached down and squeezed her husband's hand before taking a seat beside him. "We were able, at least, to comfort his parents, too."

"Oh, Mother," Charlotte said. "Poor Grand-mère and Grand-père." They all remained silent a moment, and then she added, "Shall I fetch some tea?"

"I would prefer chocolate," Felicity said, "but tea for the rest of you."

"I'll go ask Cook directly." She gave a smile. "It's so much faster than ringing the bell at Amity's and having to wait for someone to come and ask what you want. And I'll find some biscuits, too."

When she'd left, Beatrice and Greer sat opposite her parents.

"While we're alone," he began, and she wasn't sure whether to kick him under the table at his potentially bad timing as the specter of her dead uncle hung in the air, or let him carry on. Deciding her parents were not only forward-thinking enough but hopefully in need of some good news as a distraction, Beatrice held her tongue and her breath.

"I am in desperate love with your daughter."

Neither of her parents so much as raised an eyebrow. "Of course you are, dear boy," said her mother.

Her father beamed happily and nodded as if waiting for more news.

"Yes, well, Beatrice . . . ," Greer broke off, "I mean, Miss Rare-Foure professes to love me back."

"We know that, too," her mother said.

Beatrice rolled her eyes. They could at least seem the tiniest bit surprised.

"Your mother told me he was in the back room months

ago," her father said. "I thought this was all done and dusted."

Sighing, Beatrice sat back and crossed her arms, giving Greer an encouraging shrug.

"I have asked her to marry me. Twice actually. And while I realize I should have come to you first—"

"We don't stand upon ceremony," her father promised. "If we hadn't approved, you would have known about it long ago."

"Oh." Then Greer sat back, looking perplexed.

"For heaven's sake," Beatrice exclaimed, "my fiancé is trying to ask your permission to marry me *post factum*, and you two are making it seem like old news and a penny gaff."

"What?" her father said. "I don't understand half of what you young people are talking about."

"What did I miss?" Charlotte asked.

"Your sister is getting married to Mr. Carson," their mother said, mirth in her voice, "just as I predicted."

"Did you see the ring?" Charlotte asked. "It's from Asprey's."

Beatrice, with little grace since her parents were behaving like horse's asses, as far as she was concerned, uncrossed her arms and stuck her hand out unceremoniously.

Her mother leaned forward and examined the sapphire ring encircled with small diamonds. "Perfectly lovely."

"I don't know much about rings," her father said, "but I can see it matches your eyes, Bea, which is a very nice thing, indeed. It's certainly befitting a baron's daughter."

Beatrice drew her hand back slowly, glancing at Greer who wore a puzzled expression, undoubtedly matching her own.

"What do you mean? Since when am I a baron's daughter?"

"Since your uncle died," her mother said. "Your father went from heir presumptive to heir apparent, and is now the baron."

"What about Grandfather?" Beatrice asked.

Her father smiled. "We have what's known as a barony of the *ancient régime*, since the dawn of time, it seems. All the titles were stripped from the aristocratic class during the French revolution. *Vive l'égalité*, and all that. When they were restored in 1851—"

"1852, my love," interrupted Felicity.

"In 1852, my father asked my older brother to accept the barony in his stead, since he and your grandmother were moving away from the land to Paris."

"Everything is so much simpler in America," Greer said.

But Beatrice's thoughts were racing ahead. Reaching over, she took hold of her fiancé's hand. "So, as a baron's daughter, does this mean I'm a titled lady?"

She felt Greer jump under her touch.

"Well, in England, French aristocrats are considered a little less noble than our own, mainly because there are so many of them. You can't throw a stone without hitting a count or a baron in France." Her father had a laugh at his own wit.

"Yes," Beatrice persisted, "but might I be considered a lady in the eyes of the law?"

"Or at the very least, in the eyes of a dead Scottish great-grandfather?" Greer asked.

"I would say the rank of a Scottish baron is similar to that of a French baron," her father said. "You can now call yourself The Honorable Miss Rare-Foure, although only in writing. On an envelope or your calling card, for instance."

"In writing," Greer repeated, staring down at their entwined fingers, and then he looked at her, his gray-blue eyes dancing. "Do you know what this means?"

"Yes," Beatrice said, "I believe I do. You will be able to claim your inheritance."

"I've been engaged to a titled lady for a week!" Startlingly, he threw his arms around her, right there in front of her parents.

She buried her face in his neck, breathed in his familiar

Pears soap smell, and thought about what this development opened up for them.

Charlotte's whistle of happiness tore through the quietness of the back garden.

"Am I The Honorable Charlotte, as well?"

"Yes, dear girl," their mother said. "But there is nothing honorable about that infernal sound."

Releasing Beatrice, Greer stood up. "I must contact the chancery lawyer and write to the trustee at once. I can't wait for you all to see my home in Scotland . . . our home," he corrected looking down at her.

TWO MONTHS LATER, MR. Greer Carson and The Honorable Mrs. Carson stepped out of the carriage that had brought them from the train station. Despite the cold November weather, Carsonbank House was a hive of activity as Greer had already visited, fired the absentee manager, appointed a new one, and hired workers to start repairs.

Greer could see the improvements already. From the outside, the two story-building had been scrubbed to shows its gray and yellow fieldstone. Its missing windows had been replaced, and the rest re-glazed. He knew the mansard roof had been repaired, too, and the crumbling chimneys had been repointed by a master bricklayer. Although there were no gardens to speak of, their new home had a welcoming, even cheerful appearance.

Beatrice was silent as they approached the front. Then she laughed. "What on earth is *that?*"

He'd known she would remark upon the house's odd feature. "That, my honorable wife, is a square tower with castellated parapets."

"I can see it's something like that, but why is it stuck on the side of our house? It looks positively medieval."

He held his breath a moment, then she added, "I love it. I can't wait to see inside."

As they approached the front door, with workmen repairing the foundations on either side, Greer hesitated.

"I warn you. It's not quite as comfortable as our townhouse," he said, but he couldn't keep the glee from his voice. "Not yet anyway."

"Pish," she said. "A country estate is not meant to be like a townhouse, and I think it's marvelous. Miss Sylvia will adore it, too. Look, she already does."

They'd released her from the confines of the carriage, but kept her on the leash, which Beatrice now had around her wrist. Miss Sylvia strolled ahead of them, her new collar set with ostentatious colored glass glinting in the early winter sunlight. They'd seen it in a store window and bought it for fun, as without her gemstone collar, the cat had looked woefully unadorned.

The three of them entered to dark paneling and sparse furnishings, as well as a threadbare rug.

"I know it's not a ducal mansion," Greer said, feeling as if he ought to keep apologizing for bringing his new wife to such a rundown spot, "but I think we can give it a bit of spit and polish, as you British say."

Per his instructions, some of the house, such as the kitchen, one parlor, and the master bedroom, had already been thoroughly cleaned and prepared for their wedding stay. It wouldn't be long as they intended to be in London for the festive Christmas season. But while in Scotland, he and Beatrice would have a place to eat and sleep, and, of course, a bathroom for his bride who, he'd learned, enjoyed soaking in a tub of vanilla-scented hot water.

One of his favorite activities was enjoying the smell of her bare skin directly afterward and, with kisses and such, tasting her as well.

Just then, a maid greeted them. "Mr. Carson, you're back, and you've brought your bonnie bride. Welcome to Carsonbank. We're all so glad you're both here."

"Thank you. I'm sorry, I've forgotten your name," he said, assuming she was the one he'd met last time he'd been there.

"I'm Mrs. Dobbs. You promoted me to housekeeper," she said, with a glint in her eyes, "so I took it upon myself to hire maids and a cook. You also have a single footman and my brother's son would love to be your gardener."

"Very good, Mrs. Dobbs. Thank you."

Beatrice stuck out her hand, and the surprised housekeeper shook it. "I'm pleased to meet you. And this is Miss Sylvia."

The housekeeper looked down at the grey fluff straining at the leash. "And a good-looking cat, she is. There may be a few stray mice for her to catch, if she's willing." Then she fixed Greer with her gaze. "But I haven't seen a rat since you hired the catcher, and I'm most appreciative." She nodded her thanks. "Would you like to take tea now, or have me give you a tour?"

"Neither, thank you," Greer told her. "I'll show Mrs. Carson around."

BEATRICE LOVED BEING *MRS. Carson*. It still excited her every time she heard him say it.

"Very well," Mrs. Dobbs agreed. "If you don't need anything, I shall get back to my duties. I'll get some hearths to blazing including in your bedchamber and the cozy sitting room next to it. And I'll be pleased to introduce you to the rest of the staff at supper."

When she left, Beatrice confessed, "I think I am even more grateful you hired a rat catcher than she is. In truth, my husband, it was the one thing I was worried about." She had to refrain from shuddering at the thought of rats scurrying about the floor. "Now, if you please, I'm ready to see the painting."

Greer took her farther into the house. "There's an equally dark paneled parlor over there," he gestured to a gaping room on the right as they passed. The doors were missing. "I think some paint and lamps will help make it inviting. Not to mention a cheerful fire, a bottle of wine, and some rose-colored glasses," he added.

She squeezed his hand, still not bothered by the general shabbiness of the place. In the new year, when they returned, there would be plenty of time to set things right, to choose paint and wallpaper, and to air the whole house out.

"Back here, this must have been my great-grandfather's study. Naturally, he hung the portrait of his son. And I believe there had to have been one of his other son, too, the elder who died after my grandfather moved to America, but I didn't find it."

He led her into the study, releasing her hand and crossing the room to the windows. Hooking a thumb at the tattered remains of moth-eaten curtains, he quipped, "I can't even tell what color these once were." He drew them back to let in the afternoon light.

"That's where the large hole was." Greer pointed to the outside wall.

"The repairmen did a splendid job," Beatrice remarked. Even the paneling had been seamlessly replaced, except for it being lighter than the rest.

Greer grimaced. "Like all the rooms, this one needs a woman's touch."

Beatrice silently agreed. It was dark and cold, as no fire had been laid in the hearth, and the endless paneling was starting to make her feel as if she were inside a wine cask.

"Nothing we can't work on," she said encouragingly. *Spit and polish,* as her husband had said. *And lots of cheery redecorating!*

Releasing Miss Sylvia, who scampered around the room and then under a sheet-covered piece of furniture, Beatrice took up a spot in front of the painting. Someone had draped a sheet over it to protect it, probably while the wall was being repaired. Carefully, Greer removed it.

Gazing at her husband's grandfather's likeness, she studied it a minute, thinking of the man who'd headed off to the untamed America. Silently, she thanked him.

"I can see where you get your distinctive looks."

"Distinctive?" he repeated, looking at her. "Am I being insulted? Like the rhinoceros that was traded away?"

She smiled. "Distinctive as in appealing but uncommon. You are not like every pointy-nosed blue-blood. Like your grandfather, you're rugged and assured."

"That's all right then. I will accept being *distinctive*." He glanced back at the painting.

"You have his sandy-colored hair and gray-blue eyes, too," she added. "I wonder if your grandfather had your lopsided smile."

"A lucky devil if he did," Greer said, and flashed her a crooked grin. Then he gestured at the painting.

"In my memory, my father also looked very much like this man. I wish he hadn't gone to war, but I am proud of what he did. I'm sure he would have liked you." He paused, then added, "You haven't mentioned the jewels. What do you think of them?"

"In truth, it's peculiar to see them again in a painting. They seem far more impressive on that gold chain than they did on Miss Sylvia's collar." She shook her head. "Will we ever find out the whole story of where they came from and why your grandfather was given them to take to America?"

"To tell you the truth, a letter from the trustee is practically burning a hole in my coat pocket. I thought we could open it together over dinner to mark our first night in Carsonbank House."

Her mouth dropped open slightly. Her remarkable husband had surprised her again, and Beatrice realized she could put aside her curiosity, knowing there was an answer. "That sounds like a perfect idea. You *are* a clever American, aren't you?"

Shrugging off her words, Greer took hold of her hand, and a shiver of happiness coursed through her.

"I can't imagine any other outcome of my quest for a wife," he said. "Obviously, I was meant to go into Rare Confectionery that day, just as you were so plainly meant for me. Without you, none of my future would have turned out right."

"Thank goodness you came hunting for those blasted boiled balls!"

"Thank goodness." He took hold of her other hand, too, so they faced each other. "Do you realize you and I represent 'the Auld Alliance' between France and Scotland?"

"I suppose we do," she agreed. "That makes you King John Balliol and me, the French King Philip IV."

"I take it you and I were reading the same history book on the train."

"Of course." She smiled. "When you snoozed, I read. I was trying to figure out if the jewels were mentioned. All I discovered was that French wine made its way here early to Scotland, but strangely, haggis has made no influence on French cooking whatsoever."

They laughed. "Nor should it, in my opinion," Greer said. Then he drew her slowly closer, until he let go of her hands and wrapped his arms around her.

Her stomach fluttered wildly when he lowered his head and kissed her. He even nibbled on her lower lip the way she liked, sending waves of pleasure sizzling through her.

When he lifted his head, she sighed.

"Shall we continue the tour?" he offered, his hands still resting on the small of her back.

"Do we have a room with a bed for tonight? That's really all that I care about," Beatrice confessed, making his eyes widen slightly with happiness.

"Saucy wife! We do, and maybe, since we've had a long journey, we should take a nap *before* we tour the rest of our home."

Reaching up, she stroked his cheek, brushing the pad of her thumb across his mouth. "Agreed."

"Then let's get to napping." He took her by the hand and started for the door. "Did The Honorable Mrs. Carson bring some toffee with her by any chance?"

"Of course. What would a toffee heiress be without toffee on hand for every occasion? I brought a dozen tins to share with the staff, too."

Miss Sylvia took that moment to leave the safety of her hiding place and streak across the worn floor toward the doorway.

They glanced at one another, smiled, and took off after the ball of fluff before she disappeared from sight. After all, even though she no longer had a fortune around her neck, Miss Sylvia had captured both their hearts.

AUTHOR'S NOTE

In considering the landmarks and locales of Greer and Beatrice's story, I'm pleased to say some still exist. When you go to London, you can stroll along New Bond Street and even pop into Asprey's, which remains at your service, selling fine things to fine people. You can also see Marlborough House, St. James's Place, Cavendish Square, and Baker Street, made famous by Sir Arthur Conan Doyle who placed his fictional Sherlock Holmes in a townhouse not far from the Rare-Foure's home.

Sadly, you cannot go to Clarendon House, where I situated the Earl of Clarendon's ball, as it was sold out of the family long before this story took place and was torn down to become the site of Dover Street, Albemarle Street, and Old Bond Street (at the other end of which is New Bond Street and Rare Confectionery). The house was considered "the most useful, graceful and magnificent house in England" (John Evelyn, 1620 -1706), and many other homes, mostly country manors, were modeled after it. Belton House, in Lincolnshire, built around the same time, supposedly looks very similar, and you can see it on the internet.

The Marlborough House fancy-dress (costume) ball described in this book is based on an actual one held in 1874, considered one of the most magnificent events of the decade, perhaps not overshadowed until the Devonshire

House ball of 1897, also a fancy-dress ball. While the Marlborough ball was reported to have had 1,400 guests, some reports say the Devonshire one had 3,000 invitees. (Of course, some say the moon is made of green cheese, too!) In any case, a photographer was employed, and nearly three hundred photographs of the famous people in costume have been published and preserved. Amazing to see, and you can do so on the internet.

You can still go to Greer Carson's posh hotel, The Langham, nearly destroyed in 1980 to be replaced by an office building. (Perish the thought!) Instead, over the course of the next couple of decades, it was restored more than once and is a grand Victorian lady once again, naturally with all the modern conveniences and a very high nightly rate. Mr. Foure would be utterly stunned by the current cost of a room. Also, The Langham is considered one of the most haunted hotels in the world. (Tip: Ask to stay in room 333 if you are a ghost-hunter.)

Lastly, Cleopatra's Needle was erected on September 12, 1878, as mentioned in this story. The obelisk truly had nothing to do with the Queen of the Nile. The vessel it traveled upon, and which nearly sank on the journey, was named *The Cleopatra*. Many considered the monument an eyesore, but now, one cannot imagine the Victoria Embankment without it. Personally, I can't think of it without picturing Greer and Beatrice sitting on the stone wall beside the obelisk, holding hands, and pledging their troth.

As an aside, while writing this book, I tried to make toffee without a candy thermometer. Although I cooked it too long, giving it a distinctly scorched (*i.e.,* burned) flavor, I ate it anyway. I'm determined to try again.

Thank you for reading.

ABOUT THE AUTHOR

*U*SA *Today* bestselling author Sydney Jane Baily writes heartfelt historical romance with engaging characters and attention to period detail.

A first-generation American daughter of Brits from either end of London, Sydney resides in New England with her family—human, feline, and canine. The rest of her extended family live in the U.K. where she spent many happy childhood summers. She loves shandies, Maltesers, Cadbury chocolate, fish and chips, and anything from Harrod's food hall or in a Fortnum and Mason's basket.

You can learn more about her books, read her blog, sign up for her newsletter (and receive a free book), and contact her via her website at SydneyJaneBaily.com.